CLASH OF QUEENS

VEILBLOOD ACADEMY

BOOK THREE

CLARA WILS

Gryphon's Gate Publishing

Clash of Queens

Gryphon's Gate Publishing
550 King St. N.
PO Box 42088 Conestoga
Waterloo, ON
N2L 6K5

Print ISBN: 978-1-990587-75-7

IZZY

"WHAT? HOW...?" SALDREA'S EYES WENT WIDE, STUNNED.

I surged healing into myself and through the bond into Myel. I had no time to target our worst injuries and used too much anima but I didn't care. I needed to save Myel.

Vyns had been helping me, lending me strength through our bond in spirit, and I drew even more from him now, to ensure Myel was no longer in danger. But as my wounds closed and Myel gasped, returning from the brink of death, the spirit energy from Vyns... suddenly stopped.

I had no time to worry about what that meant. Saldrea would only be stunned for an instant. I had to act now.

Summoning an earthen wedge from the arena floor, I drove it up between Saldrea and Myel, pushing them apart. And once he was safely away from her, I launched myself at the false princess.

Saldrea recovered quickly, using her earth magic to throw up a stone wall between us.

Perhaps it was the incredible surge of spirit from Vyns, or the clarity of mind from Rook, or the primal energy which came from returning from death's door, but I was sharp as a razor's edge and nothing would stop me. I saw the stone wall begin to form and crushed it with my own earth magic, forcing another wall up *behind* Saldrea to block her escape.

She stumbled backward into my wall as terror painted her features. It was high time the false princess experienced the dread she so loved to inspire in others.

"No, please, no!" she cried out as I reached her. She tried to block my strike, but I was too fast, my fist connecting with her face.

I didn't consider myself a violent person, but it was hard to describe the satisfaction I got from that one hit. I'd dreamed of slapping the smug superiority off Saldrea's face for so long, and finally being able to do so, felt *so damned good*. It was like finishing a diet and finally allowing myself to have the cheesecake I'd put in the freezer as a reward. That level of sinful delight... yeah... *that's* what this felt like.

I hit Saldrea so hard her head bounced off the stone wall behind her with a hollow thud.

"Surrender and I'll be far kinder to you than you were to me," I hissed, because I was a good person. I'd give her a chance to stop this madness, no matter how much I wanted to hit her again.

With my mind clearer than it had ever been — thanks to Rook taking away my thoughts of doubt and uncertainty — I caught the quick flash of emotion in Saldrea's eyes: fear and defeat, then defiance and disgust. Even as her lip curled in a snarl and her mouth began to open for some snappy comeback, I hit her again.

Her head twisted to the side and bounced off the wall again. I clamped my other hand around her neck while she was stunned and lifted her, pinning her to the wall, restricting her air.

"Wrong choice!" I growled as I forced a binding on her. A few days ago, I'd had no clue how to do this, but thanks to Lhorine's training, I'd broken two binding collars and used several bindings to enhance Myel for his deathmatch. I'd come a long way in a short time, and since so much of my training had been on breaking bindings, I focused on making this one as resilient and hard to break as possible. I built a fortress of restrictions around the woman.

"Your punishment is to know your own pain!" I hissed as I carved the intricacies of the spell into her bones. Any time Saldrea thought about hurting someone else, she'd suffer the pain she planned to inflict back on herself. That hadn't been anything Lhorine had taught me. I hadn't known a binding could do such a thing, but that was what I wished upon her, and my will imprinted on her soul.

Saldrea slumped to the ground, a shocked look on her pristine features. Well, pristine except for the bruises forming on her cheek.

"How...?" she breathed, then twitched in pain. "Ah, fuck!" she hissed. I guessed she'd envisioned hurting me and felt the repercussions.

The once proud woman shrank in on herself as the finality of my victory sank in. Like all bullies, when put in their place, the pitiful coward beneath came out.

"Please..." she begged. "I—" Her eyes went wide and she began gasping. Even while begging, she'd thought about hurting me, probably strangling me, given how she was choking on nothing.

I shook my head, disgusted at this petty and vindictive woman, leaving her to her self-inflicted suffering as I went to tend to Myel.

Despite my initial healing, he was still in a bad way. I'd yanked him back from the brink of death, but he'd lost a lot of blood, not to mention vital organs. I'd stabilized him, but he was still unconscious. Sitting heavily beside him — so very done with today — I pulled him into my lap and used what little strength I had left to heal him fully.

His body went still, but in a good way, relaxed, no longer in pain, resting.

And with that I breathed a heavy sigh.

It was over.

I'd faced Saldrea and won, by some miracle.

Slowly I became aware of a roaring sound. My world had contracted down to two people: defeating Saldrea and healing Myel. Now that I'd done that, the rest of the world gradually returned, and I realized the crowd in the arena had gone wild. I looked around, a little stunned to remember I'd had an audience for everything which had just transpired.

I couldn't help a sour grimace as I wondered if they'd have cheered this loud for Saldrea. This had been a death-match after all. Had these people simply wished to see *someone* suffer? Did they care who?

Yet something about the cheering belied my bitter thoughts. As much as these people may have come for a gruesome spectacle, there seemed to be a note of... relief in their acclaim, a release of tension. I hadn't gone to many sporting events in my life, most of my experience with such things was through movies. This felt like one of those: "the underdog pulled out a win in the last seconds of the game" type of "oh my God, I can't believe we won" sort of cheers. They probably would have cheered if Saldrea had won, but only because they feared not doing so. Now they went wild because a tyrant had finally been defeated.

I recalled the statement I'd made to the authorities yesterday. *I will face her, knowing I'll find justice and peace. May my fate be an example to all those who might challenge the rule of the elves.*

And as I'd hoped, the words had been prophetic of *my* victory. The crowd seemed to realize the same thing. They couldn't stop cheering, if anything it got louder. Then a chant started. My name: "Izzy!" over and over.

And though the crowd was near to deafening, I heard my name shouted by a different voice over the tumult.

I turned. Koar rushed toward me. In the tunnel behind him, leading to the marshalling area off the arena floor, Saldrea's minions were being subdued by titans.

Titans?

Hadn't the titans been protecting the false princess and her crew?

I'd missed something.

Hell, I'd probably missed a lot of things.

That's when I remembered the strange disconnection from Vyns' spirit.

"Fuck," I whispered. Was he okay?

Koar practically threw himself at me, sliding on his knees through the sand and dust of the arena floor to wrap his arms around me.

This was new.

"I was an idiot to turn you down. I'm all in, if you'll have me," he whispered, his voice breaking with the emotion flowing through him. Was he crying? "I'm so sorry you had to go through that! I'm here now. What do you need?"

Wow... ah... okay...

I mean, yay for having a big, strong man wrap incredibly thick arms around me and profess his feelings, but it was a lot to process.

"Vyns," I murmured. "Is Vyns okay?"

"Is who...?" Koar released his bear hug to sit back and

look at me with a questioning expression, one brow raised. Then he gave a strange choking laugh. "You're a bloody mess, but you're worried about *Vyns* right now?"

Yup. It seemed so.

Vyns is okay, Rook spoke into my mind. He must have heard my concerned thoughts. *He's passed out, but he's still breathing, still alive.*

Oh, thank God! And thank you. I gave a long mental sigh.

I'm on the same level as a god, huh? I'll take it.

And... we still need to talk, don't we? I asked. He'd said as much — had it been only yesterday? — but we'd never had the chance. And when he'd linked to my thoughts to clear my head of all the fear and doubt and apprehension... he'd also said he loved me. That was... huge!

Yup. He sounded terrified. I took that as a good sign. I hoped he would finally explain why he'd ghosted me. I was still a little upset about that. Though the fact that he'd come through for me when it counted went a long way toward erasing that debt. It was a pattern with him: putting himself in my bad books, then dragging himself back out.

"I'll check on Vyns," Koar said, starting to leave. The big man had no clue I'd just talked to Rook.

I grabbed his iron-hard arm and pulled him back.

"No, stay. Vyns is okay."

Koar looked confused, but he settled back down, arms around me once again, holding me close, while I held Myel close to my chest.

"You'll pay for this!" Saldrea spat. "I'll—" She tried to rise, but her body shook violently. Nasty wounds opened up on her face and arms. She really needed to control those violent thoughts, or she was going to kill herself.

"What...?" Koar asked as he watched the false princess roll around screaming.

"I put a binding on her, so she'll suffer any harm she wishes on others."

His eyes went hard as he nodded. "She needs a taste of her own medicine."

The noise from the crowd started to die down, the cheering and chanting replaced with an excited hubbub. When I looked, everyone had their phones out, taking pictures. A tyrant had fallen, and they all wanted proof to share with others.

I should have been excited that Saldrea was no longer a threat, but all I felt was tired. A bone-weary exhaustion swept over me, and now that I was safe in Koar's arms, I let it run its course.

My eyes fluttered shut, but even as my awareness faded, I couldn't help but think: *if I wish to claim my throne and change this messed up world, this was only my first fight*. Things were going to get worse before they got better... probably a lot worse.

KOARTHANDRIS

IZZY NEVER LEFT MY ARMS. I CARRIED HER AND THE SHIFTER, one cradled in each arm, off the arena floor into the marshalling area, but I wasn't sure where to go after that. The training compound Lhorine had built was safe and secluded in the forest, but also low on amenities, and Izzy needed a soft place to rest, to recover. The dorm room that had once belonged to Rook also didn't seem right, nor the shifter barracks. I had my own room in the dracona atrium, where all the dragons stationed on campus were housed, but it too was lacking. Soon the entire world would know Izzy was the lost princess and hiding away in lack-luster dorms didn't seem fitting anymore.

Safir, the tiger shifter who always seemed at odds with Izzy, saw my confusion and hesitation as I moved through the inside of the arena complex.

"Don't know where to take her?" he asked. The man might be more astute than I gave him credit for. "Let me call someone." He made a quick call, I had no idea to whom, then smiled.

"There's a royal residence free, on the far side of campus.

I'm assuming it won't be an issue for you to carry her that far?"

I shook my head.

"And I'll arrange for some new clothes for Izzy — and perhaps some of yours as well — to be sent over." The man wrinkled his nose at my current state of dress. I'd shredded my clothes when I'd taken my dragon form, during our escape from the secret dungeons after rescuing the titan, Wensuria, Bayn's sister. So, I'd stolen some clothes from one of the now dead dragons who'd been protecting Saldrea. The clothes were torn up and covered in blood from the fight.

I was surprised when Rook joined me, carrying Vyns.

"Didn't think you two got along," I muttered.

"We don't... didn't... probably never will, but we both love the same woman so..." He shrugged.

I raised a brow at that. "An incubus in love?"

He sighed. "I'd say it was a slip of the tongue, but I'm done lying to myself. How I feel for Izzy is wrong on so many levels, but it's right... on the only level that counts."

I grunted.

Hadn't heard it put that way before, but the man seemed genuine. I wasn't sure what had brought him around. He'd avoided Izzy most of this past week. I was glad he'd come to his senses.

If Rook carrying Vyns had been a surprise, I was shocked and taken aback when Bayn, the big titan, joined us. His sister was with him, as were the three titans who'd survived the fight with Saldrea's minions. Two of them were badly hurt, but they limped along in our wake.

"You've got your sister, what do you want now?" I asked the stubborn titan.

The big man — I couldn't say that about most people,

but titans were even larger than us dragons — shrugged, face hard, refusing to answer.

His sister elbowed him in the ribs. "Just tell him, you big lug."

Bayn grunted. "Fine." He still took a moment, seemingly having a hard time finding the words, before he finally said, "Izzy's the true princess. She beat Saldrea, that pretty much proves it to the world. She can change things... but she'll have to fight first, and she'll need all the help she can get."

Fascinating.

"You want things to change?" I asked him.

He shrugged and gave a noncommittal nod. "Maybe. Nothing's been right in this world for a long time. We all know it. Maybe it's time for something different."

I wasn't sure I believed him, but he'd held up his end of our bargain. We'd freed his sister and he'd turned his titans on Saldrea's crew, though it had all come too late to save Izzy from fighting Saldrea. I still didn't trust the man any farther than I could throw him and given his weight — even with my strength — that wasn't far.

The trail of people following us only grew as we crossed the southern end of campus. The presence of the titans kept most at a respectable distance, but more and more people came to see the woman who'd beaten Saldrea. Some looked unimpressed, others disbelieving, but the majority looked hopeful, relieved. They could sense a change coming, even if they didn't yet know Izzy was a royal.

Safir, who also stayed close to me, took another short call before informing me that Lhorine and Olinara had taken care of Saldrea, who was now in a cell in the administration building. I hoped it was the one Izzy had stayed in last night, wrecked bed and all. Saldrea's crew had also been put in binding collars and imprisoned.

The insane false princess' reign of terror was finally at an end.

But given all of the pictures and messages being shared about her defeat, it wouldn't be long before word reached Saldrea's mother, Valnea, the queen regent. And she made Saldrea seem positively sane in comparison.

This was far from over.

But today, at least, we'd won the battle.

And it was as if nature itself knew it; the sun was out and a cool breeze off the ocean tempered the heat of the day. A perfect moment, and I had the perfect woman in my arms, even if she was out cold.

Safir led me to the free royal residence, not far from the lesser residence. Two mansions sat overlooking the stairs down to the beach — also known as The Tumble — and the ocean. Where the lesser and nobles' residences were meant to house many, these mansions housed only a single high ranked elf and their retinue. With so few actual royals left, most of the "royal residences" on campus had gone to the friends of the queen regent. But since the queen regent was notoriously insular and anti-social, only five of the six such residences were occupied.

The door was unlocked when we arrived, and waiting for us inside was Svokol, the dwarf who'd helped us in the past. Apparently, he wasn't afraid to hide his position anymore, coming out as a firm royalist.

"Everything's ready," he said to me as I entered. "Follow that hall to the end." He indicated a hall off the main entranceway and sitting area, and I took Izzy to the room in question, a grand master bedroom, worthy of her station. A wall of windows looked out over The Tumble and the ocean, a stunning view. The massive four-poster bed could easily fit Izzy six times over and only took up a small portion of the room. Several large wardrobes lined the wall behind me and before me was a sunken sitting area around an open fireplace. On the opposite side of the room from the bed was an office area with a grand desk and many bookshelves. And closer to the windows was a table and chairs, the perfect place to have a private breakfast or dinner while looking out at that spectacular view.

I laid Myel and Izzy on the bed. Her golden blond hair splayed out like a halo around her head, framing her pale features.

When I set her down, she stirred, sea-green eyes blinking open. Perfectly pink lips smiled.

"Where...?" she asked lazily.

"Don't worry, you're safe, rest for now." I don't know what came over me, but I kissed her brow softly.

She smiled.

"My big, strong dragon," she mumbled, eyes fluttering shut.

Had she liked that? I'd worried I'd gone too far, but... she didn't seem to mind.

I stood guard at the side of the bed, and now that the fight was over and Izzy was safe my thoughts slowly caught up to me.

I'd been so worried about losing Izzy and never having the chance to be with this perfect woman. But she *had* survived, and I *could* be with her... if she wanted me.

I'm all in, if you'll have me. My words still echoed in my mind.

She hadn't said yes, but she hadn't pushed me away either. And given her reaction when I'd kissed her, I assumed she was okay with me wanting to be with her, but I couldn't be sure. Perhaps she'd been half asleep and not known what she was saying. Although she had previously told me she wouldn't mind *exploring a new partner*.

There'd be plenty of time to confirm all of that later, and I'd make sure she was safe until then. Because it was still my duty to watch over her, protect her.

And somehow... I'd figure out how to protect her while also being with her.

My brain said it would be easy. I'd always be near her, always ready to leap into a fight. It wasn't like I needed armor or weapons. So even if I was naked in bed with her, I'd be able to protect her as well as any other time.

But still, questions plagued me.

Would this amazing woman be too much of a distraction?

Would I react fast enough when needed?

Would my feelings for her lead me to make the wrong choice in the heat of battle? I didn't even know what the wrong choice would be... only that I'd made it last time, leaving Mynrial to try to save her parents... or perhaps being with Mynrial in the first place?

What if I focused too much on Izzy and Myel got hurt again? I'd seen the torment she'd gone through when he'd been tortured. I'd need to protect both of them. But could I? Maybe, if they both stayed close to me, but I didn't see that being possible all the time.

Would I need more guards?

Did I trust anyone else to guard Izzy or those close to her?

Vyns maybe.

But even with his help, I couldn't protect everyone around Izzy all the time. Especially if Valnea was coming for us. With an all-out war brewing, and Izzy probably in a leadership position... it seemed impossible to protect her and those around her all the time.

But I couldn't fail her again.

I'd been so far away when she'd been tossed into that arena with Saldrea. Izzy had nearly died today and I'd not been there to protect her.

I couldn't reconcile these thoughts and was starting to spiral when the door to the room opened. I was instantly on high alert, but it was only Rook.

He staggered over and slumped into one of the soft chairs in the sitting area.

"I'm done." He laid his head back against the plump cushion and looked over at me. "Vyns is resting in another room. Thought you'd want to know."

"Thank you," I grunted. "How is he?"

Rook shrugged. "Other than still alive, I have no clue." The incubus grimaced. "He... gave a lot of himself. I was partially connected to him. He was infusing me with spirit so I could take Izzy's thoughts of doubt and pain. And he was giving his spirit to Izzy too... but I think he gave too much. Suddenly his infusion into me stopped and he slumped over."

That didn't sound good.

"I've never seen anyone give away all of their spirit before," Rook continued, "didn't think it was possible. If that's what he did, I have no clue what that means, other than, it's going to be a while before he wakes up."

I clenched my jaw.

Partly in concern for my friend, but mostly because Vyns had been able to help Izzy when she'd needed us the most, but I hadn't. I'd have happily given all of myself to free Izzy, but instead, Vyns had done it.

Everyone else was connected to Izzy in some way. Myel

was bonded to her, Vyns had a spirit link, and Rook had some sort of mental connection. I had nothing. The others could all help her in various ways when she was suffering. I could only protect her body. And I hadn't been there when she'd needed me today.

And the thought which plagued me was: what if I wasn't there when she needed me in the future?

IZZY

I WOKE WITH A CUT-OFF SCREAM AS THE NIGHTMARE OF Saldrea torturing Myel while I slowly died faded away.

Koar was at my side in an instant.

"It's over," he whispered. Then, as if sensing exactly what I needed, he poured some water from a pitcher on my night-stand into a glass and handed it to me. I slid up, reclining against a cushioned headboard, to drink. The chill water soothed my parched throat and cooled my sweat-slicked body.

As I did, I looked around. I had some vague memory, more like a dream, of Koar carrying me and laying me somewhere soft, but now that I got a good look...

Wow.

Wherever I was, it was swanky. This room was easily twice the size of my old apartment and didn't even have a kitchen.

"Thanks," I said to Koar, handing back the empty glass.

Koar refilled the glass, but I declined a second round. I was still thirsty, but if I drank the whole pitcher — which I probably could have — I'd have to pee in an hour, and all I wanted to do was stay in bed and rest.

"Anything else you need?" Koar asked, attentive. His golden eyes shone with dedication and a hint of concern. Long silver hair fell loose around his hard-featured face. I wasn't sure I'd completely noticed before how lustrous that silver hair was, how silky and soft. It seemed a bit discordant with that heavy brow and hard, square jaw. I wanted to run my hand through that hair but stopped myself. Now wasn't the time.

I smiled. "Just more rest," I said in response to Koar's question. Though as I looked around, spotting Myel on the bed not far away and Rook snoring, slumped in a chair in that lowered sitting area, I wondered...

"Where's Vyns?"

I tried to reach out through my spirit for his familiar humid feel, like a warm summers-rain... but I couldn't find him.

"He's in another room," Koar answered quickly. "He... he may have burned out his spirit helping you. We've summoned a spirit master to look at him."

"Oh."

He'd burned out his spirit?

That was possible?

I had so many questions, but I had a feeling the answers would only lead to even more questions, so I stopped myself from asking... for now.

Though one question I did ask was...

"Whose clothes are these?"

I was dressed in silk pajamas, a loose pale-pink top and matching long, billowy pants. They were hella comfortable, but definitely not mine. I didn't have much in this world. Most of what I'd been wearing lately had come from my grandmother's closet. This set definitely hadn't come from Olinara, far too conservative.

"The clothes you were wearing were dirty and shredded. Zora came and bathed you, then dressed you in these. I don't know where she got them."

I'd been bathed?

I certainly felt cleaner than I had after the fight with Saldrea, but I was surprised I'd been so out of it I hadn't noticed a bath.

"How long was I out?" I glanced at the massive bank of windows overlooking the ocean. Colors painted the sky. Evening. But was it the same day or...

"Twelve hours."

The same day. I still wasn't used to the strange thirty-hour days in this world, but then, I hadn't even been here two weeks. It felt more like two years with everything that had happened.

Wait...

"Have you slept?" I asked, concerned as I snuggled back down under the covers.

Koar gave a rumbling chuckle. "Dragons don't sleep like others. I'll sleep in a few hundred years for a century or two."

I blinked. Sometimes I forgot about the stupidly long lifespans of people around here. Casually throwing around "century" as a viable timeframe for *anything* broke my brain.

"Oh... good. Yeah. Okay."

"Rest," Koar whispered, leaning in to kiss my forehead. It felt familiar. He'd done that before... I think? It didn't matter. It felt good. What felt even better was his large hand smoothing down over my hair. I closed my eyes and let that soothing touch lull me back to sleep.

But sleep didn't come. I wasn't completely exhausted

anymore, just normally tired, and apparently that wasn't enough to stop thoughts trampling through my head like an army marching in every direction at once.

I sighed and sorted through my thoughts; maybe that would help me sleep.

First and foremost...

I rolled over and looked up at Koar.

"Saldrea?" I asked.

"In prison, along with her cronies."

I nodded against my pillow and rolled back over. Yet, knowing the false princess was out of the picture didn't really still my thoughts. As much as a part of me hoped things might settle and go back to normal — not that I'd known a *normal* day in this world — I had a feeling that wasn't going to happen. It might have been nice to be a student and go to classes for a while but given how many people had been there to witness Saldrea's fall, it wouldn't take long for word to reach her mother.

And what would the queen regent do?

I honestly had no clue. By all accounts, she was even more unstable than Saldrea, but I didn't really know what that meant. Would she fly off the handle and come down here to get her daughter... or would she do the last thing I expected, which by virtue of being the *last thing I expected*, I couldn't even imagine what it might look like?

All I could be certain of was, there'd be consequences for defeating Saldrea.

And without any more information, I put that rampaging train of thought aside and focused on other things.

Like... the increasing number of men in my life.

Koar had changed his tune. He'd gone from "duty before booty" to attentive caretaker who kissed my forehead and smoothed my hair. I had a feeling once I was back on my feet, he'd like to sweep me off them. And yet, despite him being *all in* — as he'd said at the arena — it wasn't like he was lying next to me in bed being my extra-large big spoon. He was still in guard position next to the bed.

Did that mean something?

Was he waiting for an invite... or was there still something holding him back? Because if that was the case, I wasn't sure I could handle any more emotional issues from the men in my life right now. Rook seemed to have come around from being a ghosting prick, but we still hadn't talked and I didn't know if that was going to be an emotionally draining conversation or not. And Myel... well the last time we'd talked — when I'd been transforming him, enhancing him for his fight with the troll, which felt like a lifetime ago — he'd been all uncertain and "I'm not worthy" and such. I couldn't handle another man giving me mixed messages. All of this "I want you, *but...*" was getting old fast. I hoped Koar wouldn't be like that, that he'd figured himself out, but I honestly didn't know.

Luckily, he was the only one awake right now, so if I wanted to talk to him and find out exactly how he felt, I could.

And I really should do that... but first I wanted to tackle some of the other thoughts swirling around in my head. Because if I was going to get all uppity about the guys being immature, then I should make sure I wasn't doing the same. I had my own issues with relationships, and perhaps I should figure out what I wanted before I talked to anyone.

So... what did I want?

With Myel, I wanted a bit more certainty and trust. I hadn't talked to him since before his fight with the troll, but I'd sensed his emotions, and there'd been a lot of self-doubt and pain and confusion and a general sense of being lost. To be fair, he'd been Saldrea's prisoner — and tortured to death, then revived — so all of those feelings were perfectly valid.

But still...

When we'd talked, he'd shared his fear that I would discard him once I was queen. And even when I'd told him I wanted him, he'd been concerned that my desires would change over time. He didn't trust me to keep being me and not turn into another oppressive elf. And given the thousands of years of ingrained indoctrination in this world, I really couldn't blame him.

We'd decided to take things one day at a time, to talk often and be open with each other, as terrifying a thought as that was for me.

And I guess that's what I was hung up on. I was trying so damned hard to be open and accepting of him and tell him everything he needed to hear, but I didn't always feel like I got that in return. Sure, he was *very* giving physically, and when I was near him the bond soothed me... but that was a passive thing. I wanted more active emotional support from him in the relationship.

I'd been forced to trust him, thrust into this world and our bond, but he didn't seem to trust me to be there for him.

And despite barely knowing each other — we had only met two weeks ago — he'd already professed his love for me... and I hadn't reciprocated. It sort of felt like he'd skipped to the end without doing the emotional work in between, while I was still stuck in the mire of overwhelming feelings.

Maybe if I committed fully, we could take a step back and actually get to know each other? It seemed backwards, but then, everything in this world was topsy-turvy, so that might just work.

Except, to do that, to commit, wouldn't I have to love him? I still wasn't sure I could say those words.

He'd done so much for me. He'd always been there for me. I *should* love him... right?

Yeah, that wasn't how love worked. Not that I was any expert, but if I had to ask myself that question, then I had a feeling something was missing.

And as I lay there, thinking through everything Myel and I had been through, I realized exactly what kept me from giving myself to him. Myel worshiped me, and that was nice and all, but it wasn't what I wanted in a partner. I wanted... *a partner*, someone who was my equal, who challenged me as much as I challenged them. I'd seen a lot of lopsided relationships in my time in foster care, and they never worked out.

But could Myel ever see me as an equal? He'd said it himself, I was an elf, a royal, and he was practically the lowest of the low in this world. I wanted him to step up, when this entire world had been keeping him down his entire life, and I honestly didn't know if he could do that.

I sighed.

He was doing his best, and perhaps now that I'd defeated Saldrea, he'd start to see things could change and he'd change with them.

Or so I hoped.

Okay, one complicated relationship down, who was next?

Rook.

Sigh.

Never had I known a man who could make me want him so damned much while also infuriating me to no end!

He'd said he loved me in the heat of the moment during my fight with Saldrea. But... what did that mean? Is that what he wanted to talk to me about? Did he want to apologize and make up? Or had that been an "I love you, but I can never be with you," and the talk was to break it off for good... *because* he loved me?

I'd never quite understood that, when I'd seen it in books and movies.

And the real question was: did I *want* him to love me?

I had no clue.

The last time we'd talked — in person, not in my head — he'd said he was afraid of me because I was an elf. Had that changed? Had that been another lie in a long series of lies he'd told me?

Thinking about Rook gave me a headache.

So, perhaps it required a different perspective.

Did I want him in my life?

As a fuckbuddy he was... sinfully good. Just thinking about our times together made my stomach bottom out, my toes curl, and heat bloom in my core. He consistently delivered top-tier orgasms and as a woman who had sexual needs, I did not want to give that up. Sure... I got stunningly great orgasms from Myel and Vyns, but Rook's were... indescribable. It must be a sex-demon thing.

As a friend, he'd been there for me when no one else was. He'd been kind and giving and a soft place to land... but then he'd gone cold for no reason, and I couldn't handle that drama.

He wasn't long-term relationship material. Friends with benefits, maybe, if he got his act together, but anything more?

Hell, it was men like him who'd put me off long-term relationships to begin with. I didn't get involved because the sex might be great, but then the guys turned... weird: clingy or distant or something.

So...

Maybe...

If he got his act together...

And stopped all the drama...

And was as consistent with his friendship as he was with his orgasms...

Then *maybe*, I could let him back in.

But then... what if he wanted to talk to tell me he was all in, that he'd meant it when he said he loved me?

Fuck.

It was too much of a change too quickly. I had no clue what to do with that. Maybe if we went back to fuckbuddies for a while he could worm his way into my heart? A few of his incredible orgasms and I might reconsider everything.

Let's hope that's what he wanted.

Then... there was Vyns...

He was the easy one, sort of. He'd started out all unsure and clingy, but all that had changed of late. He'd been a rock when I'd been imprisoned and I honestly didn't know if I'd have made it through that rough time without his support.

He gave me everything I wanted and everything I needed. Hell, he'd literally given me everything he had to help me win the fight with Saldrea. The man was a literal angel, why wouldn't I want him in my life?

And yet... could I give him what *he* needed?

He seemed to think so. But since the "L" word wasn't in my vocabulary, could I love him the way he deserved, with the same intensity he loved me?

I wasn't sure.

I appreciated the hell out of him and I couldn't imagine a life without him... but was that love?

Curiously... I wasn't really worried about things with Vyns. He had never put me off, never questioned our relationship. He'd always been a gentleman and a giving lover. I didn't feel any *pressure* from him. And I very much appreciated that.

I could let things with Vyns play out, and we'd be fine.

So... that seemed settled.

Right?

Right.

Which brought me back to Koar.

Actually no... before I had my conversation with the dragon... I needed to figure out what *I* really wanted, not in relation to the guys individually, but in general.

Did I want this strange conglomeration of men? All of them... together...?

It seemed a bit much. Greedy. Selfish.

And yet, it also felt really damned good. I liked being... part of a group. No, not just a group... a family. That's what this felt like. Sure, we were messed up, but most families were messed up, weren't they? I'd never had anything I could call a permanent family growing up. And it didn't matter that we weren't blood, this was a found family, we wanted to be close, which felt even more significant.

Though, it also felt weird to call them family. Thinking of them like brothers was kind of gross, even if I wanted that easy familiarity with them. With a brother, you could be close, but without any expectations. Was that asking too much?

Because... I wasn't sure I wanted four *husbands*?

The dreaded "H" word.

Could I even do that? Was polyandry a thing in this world? I'd have to ask someone, maybe Zora, or Lhorine, or... no, not my grandmother.

And if it *was* a thing, would the guys be okay with that? They… probably would be.

Okay… wow… what a thought: four sexy, giving husbands passing me around or… sharing me… at the same time…

I was suddenly way too hot under these blankets. Though I was cooled somewhat by the fact that several of my potential hubbies needed to figure their shit out before anything happened.

But still, a part of me wanted a close-knit little tribe so badly it hurt. I hadn't considered any of my foster homes "a family" because I'd known nothing was permanent. People got taken away, they left me or I left them. Nothing lasted.

And as much as I wanted these guys to be my family, I was terrified they'd get taken away from me. If I let them in, they'd become a weak spot, something for others to target if they wanted to hurt me. It had already happened with Myel. With *all* the guys, I'd just be making myself even more vulnerable, wouldn't I?

Because, if there was one lesson I'd learned on earth — that had been reinforced here in Seial — it was that nothing good ever stuck around for long.

IZZY

OKAY, NOW I REALLY NEEDED SOMEONE TO TALK TO.

I rolled back over.

Koar stood beside the bed, attentive, and looked down at me as I shifted.

"Can't sleep?"

I nodded.

"Can we... talk?"

He raised a brow as a secret little smile creased his hard features.

"Always."

I shimmied till I was sitting up in bed again, and he sat on the edge of the mattress, one leg hitched up to turn toward me.

"What's up?" he asked.

I blew out a long breath. Then I looked over at Myel's sleeping form and out at Rook dozing in the sitting area. I reached out to both of them. The bond with Myel was still, calm. That was... unusual. I'd have thought after everything we'd been through it would be desperate for us to be together. Not only had we been away from each other for a couple days now, but we'd both been through hell and back. My best guess as to why it wasn't acting up was that Myel was out cold and thus sex wasn't an option. If so, when he woke, we'd probably need to fuck like bunnies. Still, my connection to him was strong and I could tell he'd be resting for a while. I had time to talk… and he'd not hear it.

Then I reached out to Rook. I didn't really know how our mental connection worked, but I tried to think really hard at him, nothing specific, just wanting to connect with his thoughts. I didn't even know if it would be possible to sense his thoughts, or if all we could do was communicate. But I did catch a glimpse of something… a flash of an image: a small cozy cottage with a fire going in the hearth and a woman humming as she worked preparing a meal. That was it.

Huh…

I had no clue what I'd seen, but I hoped it meant Rook was in the middle of a pleasant dream and wouldn't wake any time soon.

Good.

I turned back to Koar.

"I need a sounding board. I need to figure myself out, but I'm also hoping to figure out… you… and all the guys."

He nodded, listening.

"And I was hoping we could talk, honestly, about… how we feel." I gave a little chuckle. "Not something I usually like to do, but I'm willing to be brave if you are."

The big man nodded.

"Go straight for the deep, intimate stuff?" He raised his brows and blew out a breath. "Sure, I can do that. Do you want to go first, or shall I?"

Wow… just like that? A man who was willing to talk feelings without balking. Koar always surprised me. I'd thought him a big lug of a man, until he'd been insightful and intelligent. Now he was all in about feelings after only just figuring out he wanted to be with me? What a guy.

I really wanted to hear what he had to say, but I had stuff to get off my chest first.

"I'll go," I whispered, then... didn't say anything for a while, searching for words. Koar waited patiently, not trying to prompt me or do anything other than sit there with a calm, supportive look on his rugged face.

I sighed. *Okay, here goes.*

"I like this little... family I've got going here," I whispered. "You, me, Vyns and Myel, maybe even Rook if he can get his head out of his ass long enough to tell me *why* he had his head up his ass."

Koar chuckled at that.

"But... I've never been one for deep relationships, and I feel like that's the way we're heading. I *like* you all, as friends and I find you all very sexy, in your own different ways."

"Good to hear," Koar muttered with a grin.

"But, if we were a family then... would you all be, like... my husbands? I don't know if I... love—" why was that word so hard to say, "—you all like that." Then, to distance myself from having said the "L" word, I quickly added, "And also, if I care for you all that much, then I feel like you'd all become weak points for me, people others could target to hurt me. It felt horrible when Saldrea did that with Myel and, with all of you..." I trailed off having rant-rambled through that last bit, not knowing where to go next.

Koar shifted a bit closer to lay a hand on my leg, which was still beneath the covers, his touch warm even through the many layers of cloth between us.

"That's... a lot," he said slowly. "Let me see if I have this straight. You like us all and find us sexy, but you aren't sure you love us like husbands, and if you did, you feel like we'd be a vulnerable spot for you?"

"Yup, that's pretty much it."

His brow furrowed as he looked away, seemingly contemplating this. "Well..." He drew out the word, as if speaking to break the silence, not quite ready to commit to a sentence yet.

He blew out a breath.

"I'm certainly no relationship expert," he began, gaze meeting mine again. "But from what I've seen over my long life, and all the relationships that worked or didn't work, it's not about loving someone like a husband."

I raised a brow, curious and surprised.

"The couples I've seen, who've worked, they were more like... best friends who also happened to find each other attractive and wanted a physical relationship. If I ever had to define love, that would be it. Wanting what's best for someone, giving to them in equal measure as they give to you, which may or may not include a healthy sex-life."

That was simple... but perhaps also profound? I didn't know yet. As I pondered, he continued.

"And as for being a weakness, sure, when you care for someone, others can hurt them to get to you, but I don't think that's a reason to avoid it. Your partner can also be a source of strength and resilience, helping you through tough times. So, they're a weakness and a strength."

Huh...

I shouldn't be so surprised that a centuries-old dragon was so wise.

Friends with benefits... could be love? Weaknesses could be strengths? It was a lot to take in, even if the big man hadn't said that much. I mulled it over.

And after I had, I realized... he was right, and it *was* rather profound, at least for me.

"I'd... never thought of it that way, thank you." I shook my head. "I'm so used to talking to people and not getting anything useful out of the conversation, but you've hit the nail right on the head... twice."

His hard features softened a little when that secret smile returned.

And yet something didn't sit quite right with me, and I decided to talk it through. "But... Rook and I, we were friends with benefits for a while, but that didn't feel like love. Not that I really know what love feels like, but it didn't feel like we were... close... if that makes sense."

Koar shrugged.

"There's a difference between friends who are close... and *best friends* who are close. The first is... probably more like affection. The second is love."

Yup, that hit the nail on the head once again.

I nodded.

"Yeah, you're right. We were close, but not *that* close." And also... "I'm not *that* close with any of you yet. I've only known you all for a few days. I've been forced to be close to Myel, but it's not the same. At least not for me." And that's when it hit me, Myel had gotten to *love* a lot quicker than I had, perhaps because he hadn't had any close friends and I'd instantly become his best friend, while I'd been keeping a bit more distance, not knowing where things were going. He hadn't had anyone and I'd been a light in the dark, something to hold onto for dear life. I hadn't had anyone, but I'd liked the darkness. I was still getting used to this new light.

This really was a revelation.

And since I needed time to assimilate this and figure out what it meant for me, I turned things back on Koar.

"And how do you feel? Where do you stand?"

That little smile grew, and it was such an out of place thing on his usually stoic face, he looked like a different person. Still big and hulking and handsome, but less hard and more ruggedly easy-going.

"I know we're not best friends yet, that'll take time." But his golden-eyed gaze intensified, making me feel quite warm in a delicious — if self-conscious— sort of way. "But I do find you very sexy."

Yup, okay, very warm now, edging toward hot. Lady bits swelling in all the right ways.

"I'm attracted, not just to your body, but to... everything that you are: kind, intelligent, and caring, soft at times but fierce at others. You have wit and grace and a blazingly determined spirit... but you're not hard, like everyone else in this world. You see things differently and want to help people, want to change, and that's sexy as hell to me."

If he kept going like this, we'd soon be pressing sexy bits together, conversation over.

But then he drew in a long breath, letting it out slowly and some of the heat faded from his gaze. I did the same, to temper my mounting lust.

"And... I should have told you that a long time ago, but I was afraid. Like you, I was afraid that getting too close would be a liability, that you'd distract me from my duty to protect you. Honestly, I still struggle with that, but when I thought you... might..." He clenched his jaw shut and blinked a few times.

Was there anything sexier than a big brute of a man on the verge of tears when talking about how much he couldn't bear the thought of losing you?

I didn't think so.

And the heat was back.

Keep going like this, big guy, and you'll be getting your dick wet real damned soon.

"I couldn't bear the thought of losing you and never having been with you or at least telling you how amazing you are."

"I'm *really* liking this big, strong, and vulnerable vibe you've got going," I warned him, my voice husky. And in case he didn't quite get my meaning I undid a button on my silk pajamas. Then another one. Then another. Someone had really buttoned me up tight and it took three before I was giving Koar a rather splendid view of my cleavage.

His eyes went wide, dilating, a low rumble radiating out of him.

But then... he seemed to clamp down on his arousal. He looked away, taking deep breaths through his mouth.

Huh... resisting me? Playing hard to get?

Damn, I really needed this man inside me now.

"I... would very much like to... tear you out of that silk," he mumbled.

And I very much wanted him to.

"But there was one more thing I wanted to say. Something I've never spoken aloud. The reason I've kept my distance." He dared to look back at me, his eyes instantly dilating again. "Before we move on to more pleasurable pursuits."

"Say it quickly," I said, undoing another button.

"Fuck," he growled, then looked away and quickly went on. "There was another woman once, one whom I should have protected and to whom I was attracted. She was a distraction too. I kept myself from her... until I didn't. But our one time together was the same night assassins attacked the palace. She died, as did all the royals. I couldn't save them. That still... tears at me."

Oh.

Given that, of course he'd have issues being attracted to the woman he was guarding!

"Okay..." I said, voice choked with a heady dose of lust for this hulking man with the heart of gold. "Hear me out."

He looked at me again, in time for me to finish unbuttoning my blouse. A pained grunt escaped him as the silk fell open, a delicious bulge growing in his pants.

"Why don't you take me to another room, so we don't disturb anyone here when you fuck my brains out... then we'll see if horrible things happen? If they do, it's a sign. If they don't, I guess that's a different sign. Either way, you're going to fulfill all my womanly desires right now, because we both really need it."

I threw the covers off.

An instant later, I was swept into Koar's massive arms and our lips met in a hard, needful kiss as he carried me toward a door at the side of the room.

Time to tempt fate.

IZZY

We entered a hella luxurious bathroom. It had a massive shower stall and a tub which could fit a small family under more windows overlooking the ocean. Beyond that, I didn't see much, preoccupied with the man holding me in his arms.

Koar set me down for the few seconds it took him to whip off his shirt and pants, and for me to slip out of my pajama bottoms and underwear.

Then he lifted me again, but this time, only to sit me on the vanity, back to a cold mirror. I didn't mind. I was burning up. I'd seen Koar's naked body before, several times, when he shifted into dragon form and back with no regard for clothing. He was... magnificent, with thick *everything*. Massive arms under bulging shoulders, next to a wide, heavy chest, looming over a stocky torso and legs like tree trunks.

I had, however, only seen his erect cock once, when he'd pleasured himself while watching me and Vyns together. At the time, I'd thought something to the effect of *so that's what extra-large looks like*. Seeing it again now, much closer, made me bite my lip and wonder if that delicious monstrosity would ever fit inside me.

I sure as hell wanted to find out!

My legs edged open of their own accord.

Koar chuckled in the sexiest, rumbling way as he gazed at me. That cock twitched and somehow got even bigger.

"You're not ready for me yet," he muttered as he stepped to the edge of the vanity and pulled me against him again. I wrapped my legs around him, grinding the slip'n'slide which was my core against his rigid erection as our lips met once more.

When we parted, I drew back enough to give him a sultry little stare.

"And what are you going to do about it?" I breathed.

He grinned.

"Two should do it."

"Two what?"

I couldn't help but imagine two of his thick fingers sliding inside me, tracing and touching and urging me to a screaming release.

"Orgasms, of course."

Oh...

Yup, that might do it.

His lips crashed back to mine, his arms pressing me against him so hard my breasts ached, on the verge where pleasure met pain. A whole-body shiver raced through me from head to toe from this incredible friction. Hell, I was on the verge of an orgasm just from his massive cock crushing my clit.

Then the big man eased off and I managed to take a breath. Had I been holding it before?

"I hope you don't mind," he rumbled, kissing my cheek,

breath hot on my ear. "But I'm going to take my time and savor every damned second of this.

Nope, didn't mind at all. Not that I could form words to say anything after that intense embrace.

Koar kissed my jaw, then lingered on my neck. I tilted my head to give him better access.

One of his large hands swept up and cupped a breast. Most men couldn't envelope my fullness with one hand, but Koar could. He gave a rough massage before gripping me, hard, once again finding that razor's edge between pleasure and pain.

I let out a little mewl, not sure whether it was to let him know that was enough... or to ask for more.

"I can be a bit rough," he gasped as he kissed over my collar bone.

"Yes, please!" I begged, not sure where that had come from. I'd never really been one to submit during sex, but with Koar, it seemed my only option. I wanted him to be rough. None of the other guys were. Myel and Vyns worshiped me with their bodies, Rook elevated me, but Koar... Koar could dominate me any time he wanted.

His hand crushed my breast a bit more, crossing the line. I yelped, but the word that came out when I did was, "Yes!" Somehow, a little pain added a lot of pleasure.

Okay, this was new, but I didn't mind.

"Fuck," Koar growled, and his cock twitched hard against my core, his entire body tensing for a second.

I couldn't help the giggle which escaped me.

"Am I too much for you, big boy?"

"Too much and more. Skies Above, you're perfect!"

Right answer.

He shifted, face buried in my cleavage before raking his

teeth along the side of a breast, the one he held. Never in my entire life, had a man made me feel like I was the forbidden fruit, so damned tempting and tasty he couldn't resist. But the way Koar pushed my breast into his mouth and bit down with a heady groan of pleasure... fuck yeah! That was sexy.

He didn't break skin, but he'd sure as hell leave a mark. He came away panting, whispering, "So damned good."

And suddenly he dropped to his knees his hands reaching around to grab my ass and keep me right where I was as he licked a hot stroke over my slit, lapping up my juices and once again groaning as if I were the tastiest treat in the whole damned world.

Something about that sound, coming from this big man, combined with the way his thick tongue flicked off my clit... was everything I needed.

My turn to be a bit rough. I grasped his head, forcing him against me as my hips shuddered and rocked with a soft-shivering orgasm. He chuckled, and the vibration against my core sent zings of heavenly satisfaction singing up my spine and shooting out to my toes and fingers. All my hair stood on end as he slowly licked and sucked and flicked and played, drawing out this divine peak.

But even when I eased off with my hands, stroking them softly through his long, luscious silvery hair — body untensing enough to lean back against that nice cool mirror again — Koar didn't let up.

Oh.

Then a thick finger slid inside me as he softly teased my clit with his tongue.

Oh!

That finger curled and gave a long, firm stroke against my G-Spot.

Ohhhhh!

My body levered itself up from the reclined position, at attention once more. Koar wasn't going to give me any down time to catch my breath or let things cool. Nope! He built on the first orgasm and was heading straight for the second. I was all in with this plan, despite my body being one giant, over-sensitive erogenous zone. Wherever he touched me, tingling fire lit up my skin. His one hand, clamped over my ass cheek to keep me close, burned an inferno over that delicate flesh. While the scruff of his face against the insides of my thighs was the sexiest sandpaper I'd ever felt, rubbed raw, but wanting more. I had the distinct feeling that between the abrasions on my thighs and the soreness in my core, I'd be walking funny tomorrow... and maybe the rest of this week. At least, I would if I hadn't been able to heal myself. Somehow, knowing I could make this pain go away at any time made it all the more stimulating.

My hands were back to raking over his scalp again.

And when he pulled his finger out and slid two back in... I nearly burst.

"Fuck, yes! God! More!"

He chuckled again, and I bent double at how good those vibrations felt, along with his two fingers stroking and stretching me. My hips began rocking, grinding, fucking his face, riding the edge of a tidal wave of bliss as it climbed higher and higher toward my second peak. God! I was going to explode, shatter when it finally hit.

Then he did something... something beyond the physical, something that felt like raw pleasure and life and ecstasy blasting into me. I would later realize he was infusing me with his life energy, like he'd done so many times. Only now, in the midst of such pleasure, it made me feel like he was pulsing and pushing pure thrilling rapture into my veins.

I screamed as I came, the tsunami of pleasure crushing me with how hard it hit.

Koar stood suddenly as I flopped and flailed. He caught both my arms in one of his and pinned them to the mirror. His other hand, still with two fingers inside me pulled out then added a third. Fucking with those digits, spreading me wider, as he watched me come, eyes hungry with a barely restrained desire.

I couldn't speak, other than to scream, but I spoke to him with my own gaze and told him how much I wanted him to break me open, till all the gooey pleasure spilled out.

He pulled his fingers out, grabbed his cock, and spread my wetness over himself before he pushed his dick down against my folds, then into me.

My world exploded for the second time in less than a minute.

KOARTHANDRIS

I COULDN'T HOLD MYSELF BACK ANY LONGER. I FORCED MY dick deeper, feeling how tight Izzy still was, despite my efforts. Yet also seeing the desperation in her gaze, the longing for exactly what I was giving her, despite the extreme stretch.

Her screams suddenly died out in a choked gasp and one of her hands slipped out of my grip, where I'd pinned her arms to the mirror, and pressed against my lower abdomen, stopping me.

Had I gone too early, pained her too much?

Her hips undulated, deliciously moving me around inside her. Then her eyes rolled back, tongue coming out a little as that same hand of hers slid over to grab my hips and pull me forward again.

She'd needed a moment to adjust.

Done.

I gave one hard thrust, crushing my loins to hers, and her head lolled back.

She gave the sexiest little gasps, and through those staccato breaths I caught one drawn out word.

"More!"

This was why Izzy was so damned perfect. All the brains and beauty and poise I wanted in a woman... who was also sturdy enough to take what I could give her physically. And not just take it but want *more* of it.

Which was good, because I was losing my shit at finally being with Izzy. Both hands slid down, tracing over her sides to her hips. I held her firm while I thrusted hard, my entire body shaking with the intensity of vigor and ecstasy pulsing through me. I'd not waste a single drop of passion with this woman, but I was getting to the end of my rope. I wanted to make this last, savor this encounter, but Izzy was too much for me and I could barely control myself. I moved with frenzied abandon, like nothing I'd ever felt before. No woman had ever made me lose myself the way Izzy did.

Izzy's back arched, her eyes going wide, entire body tensing as she came.

She found her voice and yelled, "Fuck, yes!" before she sat forward and threw her arms around me, her hips now moving in time with mine as her legs clamped around my body. It seemed this latest orgasm had revitalized her, and she was throwing herself into our encounter.

She pulled my face down to hers but shifted to the side so she could whisper in my ear with that sexy-as-hell hot, gasping, breathy voice.

"You made me feel so damned good, now it's your turn." And she redoubled her movements, bouncing on my cock, pressing that perfect body of hers against me.

Fuck.

I couldn't hold back any longer.

I clamped my hands on her hips to keep her in place as my final thrust hit home and I blasted my release inside her. A long, guttural grunt escaped my lips as Izzy leaned back, hands linked behind my neck, arms straight, to watch me come. It seemed only fair. I'd watched what I'd done to her... three times.

I hid nothing from her, showing her exactly how she made me feel, what she did to me. I'd never hide anything from her. Izzy was my life now. Not only as my calling, to protect her as the last royal, but also as my lover. I needed nothing but to keep her safe and love her.

I hoped I could do both of those things at the same time.

With her wrapped around me, it was easy enough to walk into the large shower as we both slowly came down from our respective highs. I had a feeling we were going to make a mess and given the sheen of sweat on Izzy, a bit of a wash off was probably in order.

And when I lifted her off me and set her down, she wobbled, steadying herself against the tiled wall.

"I'd say you've ruined me for all other guys," she breathed as she let the warm waters cascade over her perfect form. "But given the other guys in question are Vyns, who's no slouch, a sex demon, and my bonded, the playing field is pretty even." One of her hands slid down her slippery torso to cup her sex, giving a little shiver. "But... wow... that was intense!" She gave a sexy little laugh. "If I wasn't an elf, and didn't have healing powers, I'd be sore for a weak!"

I watched all this while soaping myself up, a broad smile on my face.

Skies! How long had it been since I'd smiled like this? Decades at least.

Izzy held out her hand, as if to shake. "Well, that was certainly one hell of an interview, I'd like to formally offer you the position of fourth man in my harem." Her playful grin made me smile even wider.

I took her hand, so small in mine, and shook it... while also passing her the soap.

"I hear the salary is shit, but the benefits are to die for," I responded.

Her eyes went wide and she laughed. "Did you...? Was that... a joke?" She lost herself to laughter and my spirits lifted at the sight of her mirth. "Who knew you had a sense of humor?" she added once she'd regained her composure then began soaping herself up as I rinsed.

"You... make me smile... and want to jest... which I haven't done in a long time," I admitted, voice quiet, somber.

Izzy turned to me and cocked her head. Then her expression turned hard. "This damned world," she muttered. "It takes so much from so many. It's time to change all of that."

I smiled again.

"If anyone can, it's you."

She stood a little taller.

"Hell yeah!" Her smile returned, and she leaned in to kiss my arm, her lips roughly level with where my biceps met my shoulder. "Thank you."

We finished our quick shower and toweled off, dressing again before making our way back into the bedroom. Myel was still out of it, but Rook was awake.

"I felt that," he accused both of us, but then he smiled and shook his head. Addressing Izzy, he added, "I'm glad you're feeling better." Then to me, "I'm glad you've loosened up a bit."

"And..." Izzy emphasized the word by raising a finger, "nothing bad happened." She turned to me with a grin. "Curse officially lifted!"

It hadn't really been a curse, but I appreciated the sentiment.

Then a knock sounded on the door, and before anyone could reply Safir entered looking grim.

"Good, you're up," he addressed Izzy, tone formal. "Get dressed, there's been word from the capital."

Fuck.

"Valnea forced a meeting of the crown council," Safir continued. "They've formally proclaimed her queen. She's coming, but she won't be alone. She doesn't just want her daughter back. She's declared all-out war on Veilblood Academy... on *you*."

And there it was.

"Lhorine and Svokol are gathering others from the campus for a meeting. You'll be required," the shifter finished.

"Well fuck, that didn't last long," Izzy said with a heavy sigh. Then she looked up at me and must have seen the scowl on my features. "Oh no you don't," she said slapping my arm. "Don't you dare go thinking that somehow sex with me caused this to happen, you know damned well it was going to happen anyway."

That was true, and I hadn't really been thinking I'd caused this, or that it had happened "while I'd been distracted." No, I was concerned because I knew what Valnea was capable of. In some ways, it would have been better if the woman had flown off the handle and come down here to face Izzy herself. Izzy could have defeated her, like she'd bested Saldrea. But Valnea, despite how mentally unstable she was, also wasn't stupid. She was taking her time with this, marshaling all her forces to crush Izzy and our little upstart rebellion. That's what worried me.

"Sex with the dragon caused this?" Rook asked, confused. "I missed something."

Safir shook his head and rolled his eyes.

"I'm fine, Perfection," I whispered to Izzy. "I know this wasn't me."

"Did you just call me *Perfection*?" she breathed, blushing.

I had, and I hadn't even realized it. Yet that was exactly how I thought of her.

"You big softy," she whispered, then leaned over to kiss my arm again. After that she straightened. "Time to get to work."

IZZY

When Safir had mentioned a meeting, I'd figured twenty people in a small boardroom, not an auditorium full of people with me as one of the primary figures on stage.

I was *not* ready for this.

"You'll be fine. You can do this," Rook whispered to me. I must have been yelling my insecurities into his mind. "You're a princess, a queen, the *real* queen, leadership is in your blood."

That was all nice and good, but I sure as hell didn't feel comfortable leading all these people — most likely — to their deaths.

I hoped some of the others on stage with me would handle most of this meeting. My grandmother, Olinara, was here, in an outfit which was mildly more conservative than usual, a short, tight, black pencil skirt to mid-thigh and a white blouse with only a couple buttons undone. I was in black slacks, which were somehow a perfect fit on me — thank you Zora — and a matching black blouse.

Lhorine was here, looking serene and serious, and next to her was Svokol, the dwarf, wearing a somber expression.

With Svokol was a woman who'd been introduced as Elnori, a dryad. With my limited knowledge of this world, I'd only just managed to recall that dryads were people of the forest and trees, linked to earth. The surprise member on the stage was Bayn, the titan, looming over all of us. God, he was big.

As we'd made our way from my new residence — which was huge and swanky as hell — to the auditorium, I'd been filled in on the deal the others had made with Bayn and how he'd helped to fight against Saldrea's forces in the end. Still, I got the feeling no one really trusted him. And looking at him now, I could see why. He wasn't the sort of man who exuded kindness and friendship. Even if he did have a baby-face — bald with full cheeks — his size and resting murder face screamed *danger*.

Safir and Zora were also up on stage with us, but standing behind some of the others, even if they'd been the ones who'd mostly organized this assembly.

Vyns and Myel were still not awake, so they'd not come. Tala, along with a contingent of guards Svokol trusted, were watching over them as they recovered.

The raked seating of the auditorium was filled with students and teachers and staff, including a group of shifters and another group of dragons. No one looked happy. Though, to be fair, I could only see the first few rows, the lights otherwise blinded me.

It reminded me of a school play when I'd been seven, where I'd stepped out into the light, taken one look at the gym full of people and frozen, unable to say the one line I'd had. I'd never wanted to be on stage since then.

As the ranking member of our group — the highest in status — Lhorine began the meeting, stepping forward to the narrow podium.

"I am El Siandalla Lhorine." The words echoed out

through the sound system and the crowd hushed their murmurings. "As most of you are aware, this woman—" she motioned toward me, "—defeated the false princess Saldrea earlier today. What you probably do not know, is that Sa Brown Izzy, as she has been known for most of her time here, is actually El Anadendyra Isolde, the lost princess." A rather significant murmur burbled through the crowd at that and suddenly *a lot* more attention was on me.

Great.

Hey there, world. I'm your new princess or queen or whatever... Nice to meet you?

Lhorine continued after the hubbub had died down. "Isolde... or Izzy, was born in the human realm to El Anadendyra Ysania, the banished princess, and her consort Sa Eofine Keomar. She is the rightful heir to the throne, hence the power and ability she displayed when fighting Saldrea, overcoming and *breaking* the binding collar she'd been wearing."

Sure, make me sound like some superhero. I really didn't feel like I could live up to this hype.

"She's a half-breed!" someone called from the audience. Others murmured agreement.

Yeah... *this* was the problem. Valnea had no direct claim to the throne. I did, but I wasn't pure elf, which mattered in this world, even if it shouldn't.

Lhorine turned hard. Voice booming through the speaker as she said, "Who would you rather have on the throne, a half-breed true royal, who's perhaps the strongest elf in generations, or Valnea, a power-hungry and vicious woman who — we have solid proof now — was party to the assassination of the royal family a hundred years ago?"

The silence which hung over the auditorium was complete. Lhorine had shut everyone up... until someone muttered what might have been a private, "shit," but was heard by everyone.

I guessed most people had been suspicious of Valnea, but having her treachery confirmed was something else entirely.

"And in case any of you *haven't* heard, Valnea is marshalling all of her forces to come here and deal with — what she sees as — the rebellion we've started by taking her daughter captive."

"Could we release Saldrea?" someone in the audience called out.

Lhorine shook her head. "The false princess is our one bargaining chip. If we send her to her mother, Valnea will simply wipe Veilblood off the map. With Saldrea here, Valnea must at least be somewhat tactical in her approach."

From the loud and furious reaction, that hadn't been what people had wanted to hear. Lhorine had to tap the mic to get everyone's attention once more.

"Now," she said, trying to get things back on track. "For some of you, this isn't your fight, and you're free to leave campus before things get... messy. But before you do, I urge you to listen to the words of Izzy, our true princess, as she has a rather radical view on this world and how *her* government would be run."

Fuck, fuck, fuck.

I had to speak?

I'd hoped I'd get away with being the sexy-as-fuck figurehead.

"You've got this," Rook whispered as Koar put a reassuring hand on my lower back... then slowly pushed me forward, in step behind me.

Whoa nelly, here we go!

Lhorine stepped aside, whispering, "Just tell them what

you want for this world, how you'd like to change things. It doesn't need to be eloquent, just heartfelt."

Easy for you to say, lady.

I stepped up to the podium, even more blinded by the lights here. Were those lights hot? I was sweltering. I'd sweat through my blouse in no time.

"I believe in you," Koar whispered.

And for some reason, his word, more than anyone else's, meant something. Perhaps it was because of the stunning sex we'd had, but I thought it more likely from the honest conversation beforehand. He hadn't held anything back, whether we'd been talking or fucking and I appreciated his honesty. If he believed in me, then I should be worthy of that belief.

"Ah... hey everyone, so... yeah, I'm your princess, isn't that crazy?"

Silence

Okay, so not the best start.

Tell them what you want... how you'd change things...

Since I didn't really have eloquence on my side, I decided for brute honestly.

"So... things in this world suck, am I right?"

There were a few laughs and snickers at that.

"Maybe it's because I was raised in the human realm — which I should say is fucked up in its own way — but this whole class system you have here is way more fucked up." More silence, but this time, I had the feeling it was because people were listening, waiting for more.

"When I first got here, I didn't know I was an elf. I had a binding which hid my power and my heritage." Wow, a coherent sentence with no curse words. *Way to go, me!*

"Everyone thought I was a nymph, so I was instantly *less* than others. Though, I was also surprised to find out there were even more people below me in status. But that didn't make me feel superior. I didn't want to boss those others around. It just felt... wrong. Honestly it was having people below me in this whole class structure which made me feel uneasy. Back in the human realm, I wasn't anyone important. Lots of people were above me in the grand scheme of things, but not many were below me, and those that were, they weren't people I could boss around, just people who had it worse off than I did."

I couldn't really see the audience, but I hoped I had their attention now.

"So... yeah. I quickly learned I didn't like the way things were here. I may be half elf, but I still feel like a common person. I want everyone in this realm, in *all* the fae realms, to be equal, to have a fair say in how things are done. I'm not sure democracy always works, but it has to be better than this crap. So... yeah. I want to tear down the system, make everyone equal, help those who have less, and make it so people are judged on the merit of what they do, not on their race or the station they were born to."

"She's nuts!" someone muttered.

"Yeah, probably," I responded without thinking. "But would you rather my form of crazy or Valnea's?"

Ha! Take that heckler!

"What about the elves?" someone else called out, probably an elf.

"What about them?" I asked back. "If you're asking if they'll retain power over everyone, control of everything, the answer is: nope. I won't be able to take away generational wealth, so it may take some time for change to really happen, but if everyone is equal, that means giving those who have nothing the same opportunities as those who have everything. And honestly, I have no clue how I'll do that, but that's my goal."

"Dreamer!" someone else shouted.

"And I say again, would you rather a dreamer like me, or a dictator — emphasis on dick — like Valnea?"

That got a laugh.

But once that died down someone else shouted, "You're going to get us all killed!" The words echoed in the hall.

I didn't have a snappy comeback for that.

"Look," I started, finding the words as I spoke them. "If I could face Valnea one on one and deal with her, I would. I'm *not* like other elves. I care about people. I don't want to start a war. I don't want people to fight for me, die for me! If I thought it would change anything to turn myself in, I'd do that."

I paused, partly for effect... mostly because I had no clue what I'd say next till it came to me.

"But turning myself over to that madwoman wouldn't change anything. You'd still be oppressed. Well, most of you. For the elves in the room, yeah, I'm sorry, but if you follow me, the best I can offer is that, if you're good people, then not much should change for you. If you're an asshat, then you're shit-outta-luck. Sorry. Actually, no, not sorry."

There was murmuring and shuffling. I got the feeling some people were leaving. Well, good riddance. If they didn't like that, they'd probably betray us to Valnea eventually.

"So yeah. If you choose me, if you choose to fight for a better life, then probably some of us are going to get hurt, some are going to die." I really hated saying that, but it needed to be said. "Most revolutions aren't pretty. We're all going to have to get our hands dirty to fight the power of this world, but that's what I'm all about."

Fuck, I really didn't want to be a general. I didn't want people following my orders and getting killed, but still.

"I'm going to fight," I shouted, raising my fist. "And I'll be on the front lines, if that helps. I wouldn't expect anyone to fight for a leader who isn't leading the charge, putting their own life on the line."

The crowd cheered.

Well shit, I'd done it now.

IZZY

As the cheers died down, I spoke again. "Now… I'm no tactician. And since I want us to survive this fight, I'm going to hand things over to someone who hopefully knows more than I do, so we can figure out how we're going to win this." I turned to Lhorine and mouthed the word: "help!"

She smiled and took over. I didn't return to the line of others on the stage, keeping myself apart. This was my place now, a figurehead if nothing else.

Lhorine looked out over the crowd. She must have done this sort of thing before, because I actually thought she was looking at them despite the fact that the lights were blinding and I'd not been able to see anyone out there.

"Valnea is going to marshal all her forces against us. She won't take any chances. She'll want this to be an overwhelming victory. And I'll be honest, it just might be. We have a slim chance of winning this with the right strategy, but also… we're going to need help."

Lhorine looked back at Svokol.

"Master Gurand," she addressed him formally, using his

last name. "What are the chances the dwarves will join us in this fight?"

He must have done some trick with stone, because even though he had no mic, his voice boomed through the hall when he spoke.

"I will talk to the clan leaders, but... dwarves are not a hasty bunch. I estimate the chances of them joining us at... ten percent."

Yikes!

"A more likely outcome and perhaps the best for us, would be that they stay out of the fight entirely, withdrawing to their caverns."

At least they wouldn't be fighting for Valnea, but still, that didn't sound good.

Svokol's dark-skinned features turned grim. "We were once elves but shunned for our lack of creation magic. We have long memories, and despite our otherwise vaunted place in society... we have no great love for the elves who pushed us away so long ago. I will speak with all the passion I have to convince them to join our cause, but... I do not think it likely."

Lhorine addressed the dwarf once more, asking, "Which I presume means it is unlikely that the dwarves would lend us the aid of their forces in Urval? The Salmaeri and concubi could be a boon in this fight."

Svokol shrugged. "Again, I deem it unlikely, but I'll do what I can."

"Thank you," Lhorine said, then looked out to the crowd. "Is Dean Estralla present to speak on behalf of the undines?"

Someone near the front rose, I could only see them because they were close and the lights weren't currently focused on me. The woman who made her way onto the stage was a stately and poised undine of middle years, which could mean fifty or five hundred, for all I knew. Nearly imperceptible scales highlighted her blue-pale skin, bringing out the sharp lines of her face: cheeks, chin, ears, and a strong brow. Raven hair was pulled back into a tight bun, and navy eyes studied me as she passed by. I got the feeling she hadn't made up her mind about me yet, but so far... I was getting a failing grade.

She approached the mic as Lhorine stepped aside.

"Knowing little of this new... *princess*." She gave me a rather savage side-eye glare. Her tone suggesting I was no princess to her. "I would probably council the undines to stay out of this fight, like Master Svokol has suggested."

Huh... Svokol hadn't suggested anything of the sort. He'd simply thought it *probable* the dwarves would stay out of the fight, not that he was advising them to.

"And once I'm home, I may not return," Dean Estralla continued. She then sighed, turning pensive. "If... however..." And it sounded like a very big *if*. "This princess can prove herself worthy, then it is *possible*, if unlikely, that the undines may come to her aid." Well, that was something. Not a resounding vote of confidence, but something.

"We undines and our triton attendants are quite happy beneath the waves and care little for affairs on land. But I will also admit to a certain... fear of Valnea and a hesitancy to see her rule over all of us."

I read the subtext of that as: *Valnea's a crazy-ass bitch and if this new princess can win this fight, we'd like that, but we probably won't help.*

The dean then nodded to Lhorine, ceding the mic. Yet she stopped as she passed me, giving me a closer once over.

In a hushed voice, she said, "If you wish to plead your case yourself to the undine council of elders, I will happily set that up. But we will not back a losing force and risk Valnea's ire. Prove your worth, and *maybe* we'll follow you."

I nodded, saying nothing.

She then returned to her seat.

Lhorine, seeming undaunted, continued.

"I have already spoken with a representative of the seraphim and they will happily join our cause, if only for equality in Elysial. However, the sylphim, as you might guess, hate this idea and already seem to be siding with Valnea. The seraphim outnumber the sylphim two to one, but it is uncertain how much of an advantage that might give us."

Wow, did we have any chance of winning at all?

Lhorine gave me a little side smile as she went on, saying, "the nymphs seemed to be mostly behind Izzy, and any who aren't will probably stay out of the fight if they can." Then she grew serious again, turning back to the audience. "The dryads, however, are evenly split, and those who oppose Valnea will likely stay out of the fight. Some few have sided with us, but not many."

Wow. Lhorine had been busy while I'd been resting today. She seemed to have met with everyone.

"Dragons, similarly, are split," she continued. Those on campus, who have seen what Izzy has done, have sided with her, but that is only about one fifth of the dragon's forces in Seial. The rest know little of Izzy and will probably side with Valnea. The dragons have always served the elves loyally, in particular the royals. Which means, if we can get the word out about Izzy's true nature, more might come to our side."

That last bit was good, but otherwise, only one fifth of the dragons being on our side... didn't sound great.

"Now, for the good news," Lhorine said, voice lifting.

"The pixies, hobgoblins, and shifters are flocking to our cause. They have the most to gain in this fight. Similarly, many trolls and ogres are siding with us, even though their dwarven masters haven't yet."

"Shifters? Really?" someone called from the audience. "And what can administrators and servants do for us?"

Lhorine kept her composure as she answered.

"I will remind you there are twice as many shifters than dragons, and you'll find they are rather savage fighters when they have something solid to fight for, like equality and a chance to live without the threat of death hanging over them every day. As for pixies and hobgoblins, well, let me say this... how many of you were aware of the massive underground spy network those races possessed?"

She waited as silence filled the hall.

"I didn't think so. Well, those administrators and servants are privy to all sorts of information, and they've been sharing it strategically for generations to benefit their cause. And you'll find they too will happily fight for their freedom." A mischievous gleam caught Lhorine's eye. "We all know how... *feisty* pixies can be. Imagine tens of thousands of them playing tricks on the enemy. Do not discount those who've been seen as lesser for so long. They have the most to fight for."

"Pixies rule!" someone shouted from the back.

"Exactly," Lhorine added. "And... there is one last force which... *may* come to our aid." She pursed her lips. I had a feeling I knew what she was going to say and that few here were going to like it.

Lhorine indicated Bayn, and I nodded to myself.

"Behind me is Baynaruk Dava, prince of the titans. He has joined our cause and has promised an army of titans to fight for us."

As the crowd erupted in shouts and jeers and rather furious sounding vitriol, I glanced over at Bayn. Maybe I was getting better at reading people because I had a feeling he was uncertain about... something. I didn't think it was helping me, he'd already done that, which meant... it might be his ability to bring other titans to the cause? I hoped Lhorine hadn't oversold things.

"Enough!" Lhorine shouted, and her voice boomed through the speakers mostly silencing the objections from the crowd.

"Yes," she said, voice moderated once things had calmed down, "I know the titans have been the enemies of the elves since the first age. And yes, I was... hesitant myself to accept a titan's help at first. But..." she held the pause, making sure she had the crowd's full attention, "Bayn has already proven his worth, fighting against Saldrea. And... we must ask ourselves *why* the titans have been shunned for so long. Who remembers the old tales?"

She didn't waste any time before continuing. "Let me remind you. After Titania had birthed her daughter, Anadendyra, and the three greater spirits: Dryada, Nymphyla, and Undira, there were only women in the world. From them, the races of Seial would flourish. The greater spirits brought forth both males and females of their species to procreate, but among the elves, there were only women, for elves do not require a male to bring forth life. Yet seeing the joy a male companion could bring, Titania brought forth Titanus to be her consort."

"Titania created Titanus to be proud and strong, a defender and protector. Yet perhaps he was too proud. After a few generations, as more and more males were born to elves, he saw how they were treated as secondary citizens, and he spoke up. He sought only... equality," she said that last word slowly, enunciating, making sure everyone understood.

"Titania saw the mere suggestion of men being equal to women as blasphemy. For his transgression, Titanus was punished, chained naked to a tree for a thousand years. She hoped his example would quell the rebellious talk amongst the men, but alas it only angered them. After a hundred years Titanus was freed by his supporters who fled into the wilds, thus creating the schism between elves and titans."

She let this story sit in an uncomfortable, drawn-out silence.

"*We* drove the titans away. *We* created our own enemy. An enemy who wishes only to be equal in standing to the rest of the elves. And since equality is exactly what Izzy is fighting for, then why shouldn't we accept the titans back into our fold?"

She hurried to add, "Yes, it's been tens of thousands of years, many generations, and the feud has only grown stronger, the divide between our races wider, but perhaps it is time for all of that to end. Think about it. And while you do... think about the power the titans could bring to our cause. A force of dauntless warriors, stronger than most of you, second only to elves."

She let that sit for a moment before finishing.

"We'll need all of you to win this fight, but our time is short. Myself and Sa Eofine Olinara — who was once a close confident of Queen Leastrine, her Inamora — will be organizing the forces. We'll be speaking to leaders of the various factions on campus to organize you. And as you heard, our true princess will be on the front lines, leading this fight. We can win this, if we learn to overcome our differences and work together. Any questions?"

There were *a lot*.

Luckily, I was spared that drawn-out debate as Bayn detached himself from the others and came to me.

"May I speak with you... privately?" the huge man asked, tone firm but respectful. His voice was deep and smooth like silk. He sounded like Barry White only somehow even sexier.

"Koar never leaves my side, but otherwise we'll be alone," I said, wanting the dragon there with me for this.

Bayn nodded and once we were off stage, a pixie functionary led us to a private room.

"What did you want?" I asked.

"It's time I told you the truth of why I'm here on campus and what Valnea is planning."

IZZY

This should be good.

"Hit me," I said. Then quickly realized that turn of phrase might not be a thing in this world as Bayn raised one bushy brow. "Tell me," I amended.

He nodded.

And not for the first time I marveled at how *huge* he was. Koar was big, almost seven feet tall and built, but Bayn was a full head taller and even *more* built. As tall as the tallest basketball player, and as filled out as a strongman, thick everywhere.

"First—" he looked at Koar, "—I want to thank you for freeing my sister. She has no part in any of this, a pawn used by my parents and Valnea."

His parents?

"You didn't give us much choice," Koar rumbled.

Bayn shrugged those massive shoulders. "Still, thank you." Then he turned to me. "I want you to know... I did not join your cause lightly. I strongly considered fleeing with my sister, finding some place safe to lay low and live out our lives."

"I wouldn't blame you," I said evenly. He raised a brow, perhaps not expecting me to agree with him. "If I didn't have to fight this fight, I wouldn't. I'm no warrior. I'd happily sit this out, but I can't. I'm hip deep in this and no matter how much I want to run away, I can't."

His lip twitched. Had that been the flash of a smile or a tick?

"I wish to join with you because you have proven your strength," he explained. "You defeated Saldrea, which is no small feat. What's more, you broke the binding collar you were wearing. I've... never seen anyone do that before."

Yeah, that was me, the breaker of chains. Call me Khaleesi... only not insane like she turned out to be. I really hated that they'd done that to her character. Can't a woman be strong and fierce without being a crazy bitch?

"I respect strength," Bayn continued, but his jaw tightened and twitched as he struggled to go on. "Almost as much as I hate elves."

Koar tensed, but I laid a hand on his chest, reminding myself how firm and sexy it was. I focused back on Bayn.

"He's not going to hurt me," I said to Koar, then to Bayn. "Are you?"

"No." He cocked his head, studying me. "You don't act like an elf. And you're a mixed breed so... somewhat more tolerable."

"I'm flattered," I deadpanned.

Another twitch of his mouth.

I wondered when he was going to get to the point, but didn't say anything, letting him continue.

"I was raised to hate elves... all titans are, and yet... my parents made a deal with Valnea. They've gone against everything we titans stand for, and what's worse... many titans agree with what they've done."

Okay that was weird.

"Why?" I asked.

"Because Valnea promised them the chance to destroy the elves."

Holy shitballs! That was one hell of a bombshell.

"You're going to have to explain that," I said, struggling to speak over my shock.

"Valnea hates her own kind," Bayn said. "She trusts no one, no elf. She's a backstabbing bitch and fears all elves are the same, so she sees enemies everywhere. She fears some elf will depose her — which is now happening, thanks to you — and wants to destroy her own kind, whittle down the numbers to something she can manage."

Fuck me.

I had so many questions, but I didn't know which to ask first. Bayn went on before I could settle on one.

"As a show of good faith, Valnea let titan assassins into the palace a hundred years ago to kill the royals. My parents were skeptical at first, but after that, they believed Valnea's claims."

Hadn't Lhorine mentioned we now had proof that Valnea was behind the death of the royals? It was Bayn, he was our proof.

"Valnea's plan is to slowly integrate titans back into society, starting with myself and my friends here on campus. It's meant to look like a show of peace. Then, once titans are more freely accepted and allowed nearly everywhere, she'll set them loose to attack from within and kill as many elves as they can."

"Holy fucking shit-balls!" I gasped.

Bayn's lip-twitch this time lasted a fraction of a second longer. Yeah, it was definitely a smile. I got the feeling smiling was not something the massive man did a lot.

"We need to tell everyone!" I said.

"They wouldn't believe you," Koar whispered. "Well, those following you would believe you, but everyone else would think you're spreading lies about your opponent. No matter how plausible it sounds, if you think this will turn other elves against Valnea, it won't. They have too much to lose if you come to power, while Valnea represents the status quo. Telling them Valnea wants to kill them all will sound too preposterous to believe, especially coming from someone trying to depose them."

Koar was right.

"Damned, fucking stupid elves!" I hissed.

This time Bayn did smile, a full-on grin, even if it didn't last long.

"See, you're not like them," he said.

"You got that right!" I barked.

But that's when the full implications of what Bayn had said hit me.

"Wait... you said most of the titans agree with your parents, and are following Valnea? Does that mean you can't give us an army?"

The large man's face twisted into a scowl.

"My hope is to sway them to my side. They'd still get to fight elves, just out in the open, which was always how we preferred things. But... I am only a prince and I fear my kind will not follow me... without a significant show of strength on my part."

And I had a feeling he had some idea what that would be.

"Which is?"

Bayn drew himself up. Yeah, whatever he'd been working toward, this was it, the main reason he'd pulled me aside. I didn't know what any of this had to do with me, but I had a feeling I was some integral part of his plan.

"Marry me," he said, stoic. "Make me your king, an equal sovereign. And everyone will see we titans taking our rightful place as rulers of this realm!"

What the fuck?

BAYN

IZZY SEEMED SHOCKED AT MY PROPOSAL. THIS WAS TO BE expected. As much as Izzy was a royal, she'd not been raised as one, having lived in the human realm. I didn't know if marriages of convenience or arranged marriages were a thing there, but here, especially among the elves, both were common practice.

"If you'll let me explain, I believe you'll see this is the right choice," I said.

"Yes, please explain, a lot... You want to marry me?" Her rather stunning sea-green eyes were a bit wild. "Where did this come from? I don't even know you!"

"You need not know me for this to work," I responded. "This would be a po—"

"Stop right there, Colossus. I think I do need to know you. Call me old-fashioned... well actually, old-fashioned people used to do this all the time, so I guess call me new-fashioned."

Ah, it seemed she *was* familiar with the idea of an arranged marriage. Good. This would require less of an explanation.

I spoke over her continued rant, raising my voice. "It would be a political marriage."

That silenced her.

"Political? How?" she asked, looking skeptical.

"You want to defeat Valnea?"

"Of course."

"Which means you need the titans, correct?" I waited for her agreement. She nodded slowly. "This is how you get them. If I can return home as king, ruler of elves, that will sway many of my people. Having power over the elves has been the driving force behind everything we titans have done for generations."

She regarded the dragon with a questioning look. He didn't seem happy about my proposal either, lending credence to my notion that he had feelings for her. Still, his answer was moderated.

"He's not wrong. From what I understand, that's exactly what drives the titans."

"Okay..." Izzy drew out the word, clearly still not convinced.

"And we have no time for a courtship, no time to get to know each other. This marriage need not be anything more than a political union, if that is what you wish." Though a part of me hoped for more. I found Izzy rather... fascinating.

She was strong and determined, a fierce warrior. I'd seen how she'd fought Saldrea every step of the way, even when imprisoned and with a binding collar on, she'd never relented, never given Saldrea the satisfaction of a scream while being tortured. She had grit and fire, and I admired that. She was also moderately attractive, if smaller than I usually liked my women.

"What I wish... is to marry for love... eventually... a long time from now," she replied. "Is there no other way to bring the titans around?"

I sighed.

"How much do you know about titans?" I asked.

"Next to nothing, other than you're big and you've been fighting the elves ever since some guy was chained to a tree for asking for equal rights."

A vast oversimplification.

"Let me give you some context."

She rolled her eyes and leaned heavily against a nearby wall, arms crossed over her chest.

"Mansplain away," she griped, not receptive.

I spoke slowly, picking the right words. "Titans... respect power and strength above all else. It's why we became titans. We pushed our physical magic to its limits, making ourselves stronger, larger, more powerful."

"This is not his normal form," the dragon interrupted. "Titans are normally thirty to forty feet tall. They can, however, reduce themselves to a more... palatable size."

That wasn't how I'd say it, but, "Yes."

"Forty feet tall?" Izzy gasped. She gave me a once over, mouth slightly gaping. "Jesus, you'd be huge!"

I nodded. "That is correct." I proceeded with my previous line of thought. "We titans focused so much on strength and power we changed our very nature to be giants. Our kings are chosen through a series of trials and combat. For the most part, it has passed through one line, my family's, the Davas. But as a prince, I would have to defeat my father — and any who sought to challenge me — to take the throne."

"That's barbaric!"

"Indeed. But it is our way." I met her gaze evenly. "We don't have time for all of the contests and fights a succession would produce," I explained. "But if you and I married, making me king of the elves and all the races of Seial, my kind would see that as a great accomplishment, for that is what we've always sought. It would elevate me *above* my father without the need for combat. I could sway many titans to our side."

She grimaced.

"That... makes sense," she ceded. "But is there no other way, other than marriage?"

I looked over at the dragon. What was his name again? If I was to marry Izzy, I should probably know her retainers. Koar...? Yes, that was it.

"Ask him," I advised.

The dragon squared his jaw as Izzy and I looked at him expectant.

"I don't like it, but he's probably right," Koar said, reluctant. "I've heard tell of the gruesome succession battles. And making Bayn your king—" he struggled to say those words, "—would put him in such a position of power that everyone, titans included, would have to acknowledge things were changing."

"Well fuck," Izzy grumbled, then pushed off from the wall and glared at me.

We stared at each other.

"So...?" I asked.

"I'm thinking!" she hissed.

"If it helps, marrying me would also give you a general for your armies. I know you said you'd fight, but you also made it clear you lack military experience, which I have. As king, I could fight by your side and lead *our* armies to victory." This had been one of my goals all along, but I'd added it into the conversation subtly, a secondary notion.

The dragon grumbled at this. "Non-titans wouldn't follow a titan general."

"What he said," Izzy agreed. "People around here have thousands of years of hating you to overcome. It might make things awkward. Being the general of the titan armies makes sense, but everyone else..." She grimaced and shook her head.

My ire rose. That wasn't good enough.

"No."

Izzy raised her brow. "No?"

"My people would not respect me if I was king in name only. If I don't command *all the armies*, rule over *all the people*, they'd see our marriage as a farce, with me ceding control to you. I need to be in control of everything." Fuck. I shouldn't have said that last part. I quickly amended my statement. "To get the titans on our side, they need to see me in command of all the races."

Perhaps that was an overstatement. It was possible the titans would follow me if I was simply king, and not commanding all the armies, but that wasn't what *I* wanted. The notion of taking orders from anyone rankled me. I would not let anyone control me. I was finally free from my parents and Saldrea and I'd not put on shackles for anyone else, ever again.

"Look buddy, we all have to make compromises," Izzy said. "And I'd be making a rather massive one by marrying you."

My anger flared.

"And I'd be making a rather massive one by letting you rule *beside* me, but that's as far as I'm willing to go," I growled. Because, as strong as she was, I wanted nothing more than to have Izzy submit to me. It was the only way I could trust her. If we were equals, I'd never know if she might betray me, like Osserime had.

"We can rule as equals, but since I'm the one with military experience, it only makes sense for me to command our armies, all of them!" That was my compromise. We'd both have a say in ruling the fae realms, but I'd control the military. That way I'd only have to worry about one person turning on me, betraying me... her.

The dragon bristled at my tone. Let him. I was not going to let this go. The calm that I'd tried so hard to maintain for this conversation finally broke, and words poured forth.

"My parents imprisoned me when I disagreed with them, then they gave my sister to Saldrea and I was forced to take orders from that psychopathic elf. I'm not going to take orders from you either, or *anyone else*!" Fuck. My fury had made me say too much.

"Who said I'd be giving the orders?" Izzy shouted back. "Wouldn't we be working together, *if* we did this? I don't even want to be giving orders, but I'm not so certain you should be the one doing it either. I don't think I want someone with an anger management problem in charge of our forces."

Anger management? If only she knew how well I was managing my anger and not giving in to my basest desires to tear this whole world apart for what it had done to me, and my sister.

Still, I took several deep breaths to rein myself in.

Izzy took advantage of that pause.

"Your parents imprisoned you? Why?"

This was why I shouldn't let my anger speak for me. Now I had to answer a question I didn't want to.

I gave the abridged version.

"I opposed working with Valnea. We should never have

listened to her. I thought it best to wage open war on the elves, not sneak around helping one elf gain power over another, with the promise of more elven deaths in the future. For that, I was imprisoned." That was the truth, if not all of it. It was the part Osserime had played in all of that which made my blood boil with resentment.

"That sucks, I'm sorry," Izzy said, shaking her head.

I didn't need her sympathy.

"But to be clear, you don't want to wage open war on the elves anymore, right?" she asked.

"I never said that," I admitted. "Why else do you think I want to lead our armies against Valnea? Her force will be primarily elves."

"So, you aren't fighting for freedom, just revenge." And I couldn't quite say why the look of reproach in her eyes stung me so much. "Typical."

"I am fighting for freedom: for my people... and all those who've suffered under the elves." That sounded reasonable, didn't it? But Izzy seemed to sense my evasion, eyeing me.

She sighed. "I need time to think about this. And yes, I know we don't have time, but you're going to give me some anyway. This is a *big* decision. *And...* you'll need to get over whatever hang-up you have about bossing everyone around and learn to work with me, work with all of us. That's the only way this is going to happen. I may be the next queen, but *I'm* not a dictator."

That stung too. I didn't want to be a dictator, I just didn't want others dictating how my life would be, and the only way I could think to do that, was to have utter control over every aspect of my life.

Izzy kept going. "And that means I'm going to consult with others and maybe put others in charge of things that I don't know anything about. And maybe that means you get to be general, but not unless everyone I trust agrees that's the best decision. Got it?"

I ground my teeth at her firm stance. I didn't like any of this. This is not how I'd hoped this conversation would go. Why couldn't she agree to marry me and be done with it?

Because she was no pushover.

And a part of me respected her for it. Hell, as infuriating as she was, a part of me really liked arguing with her. She felt like a good match for me, strength for strength, will for will.

"I could walk away, go and live a quiet life with my sister, then you'd have no titans at all," I said, testing her.

"But you won't." She stepped closer to me. Those sea-green eyes — so filled with her blazing spirit — were level with the bottom of my chest, so she had to crane her neck to meet my gaze. "Because you *want* this fight as much as I *don't* want to fight. And we'll need people who have your fire."

Fuck if she wasn't right.

"You have till morning," I said, mostly because I wanted to give a hard ultimatum.

Before she could argue, I stormed out. I needed to get away from her. She'd been so close, and for some reason I'd wanted nothing more than to grab her, lift her off her feet, and kiss her. And that infuriated me.

How could she affect me like that?

Where had those feelings come from?

She made me feel... vulnerable. Wanting her gave her power over me. I'd given that power to Osserime and she'd abused it. I wouldn't let another woman captivate my heart or mind.

And yet... I couldn't stop thinking about Izzy as I returned to my small residence. She was just *so different*!

She was an elf, she had their strength and pride, but none of the arrogance or haughty superiority. She had never once, while we'd talked, tried to dominate me or use force like Saldrea. She was powerful but didn't revel in her power. Hell, half the time it sounded like she didn't want to rule at all.

And that baffled me.

What sort of person didn't want to use their power to rule over others?

A good person...

So, what did that make me?

KOARTHANDRIS

"WHAT. THE. HELL!" IZZY HISSED, PACING. SHE LOOKED LIKE she needed to hit something. "Marry me," she muttered in a bad interpretation of Bayn's rather extreme bass voice. "Make me your king. Give me your armies. I'm a big, bad titan with serious control issues. Ugh!"

She reached one end of the small room and turned back to face me.

"Can you believe that?"

When I didn't answer right away, she stopped her pacing as she drew near.

"Koar... he was way out of line... right?"

I sighed.

"You agree with him?" she accused me.

"I didn't say that."

"You didn't say anything." She playfully slapped my arm and gave a heavy "harrumph." "Which makes me think you think Bayn's right. Do you really want me marrying him?"

"No," I said instantly. Then I winced a little even before I added, "But..."

"But? There's a *but*?"

I sighed. "Izzy, please." I grabbed her as she passed me again, pulling her against me. Skies Above! She felt so amazing, the warmth of her body hot against mine. "The thought of you and him together makes me want to level mountains and boil the ocean."

"Right answer," she mumbled against my chest.

"But..." and to minimize the word I gave her ass a playful slap. Her body stiffened... in a good way and had my body responding in turn, but I continued saying what I needed to say before we got distracted. "He's not wrong when he says we need the titans. If the dwarves and undines stay out of this, we won't have much of a chance without the titans."

Izzy deflated in my arms.

"Yeah... I know." She nuzzled into my chest, her arms encircling me, not quite reaching around me, but still giving me a tight squeeze. "I'd hoped to avoid the politics of being queen until *after* this whole war I've started. But... an arranged marriage!"

Her arms tightened around me.

I grunted as my ribs compressed. Izzy wasn't always aware of her elven strength.

"Oh... sorry," she mumbled. I barely heard her as she pressed her face harder into my chest. She sounded so... lost.

I held her tighter.

Sometimes we all forgot that — not so long ago — Izzy had been a normal person, and still probably wasn't used to being a super-strong, magic-wielding elf-nymph hybrid with all the pressure of an expectant throne weighing on her.

"Don't forget," I whispered. "You have people to help you. People you can lean on. People you trust. Bayn... sounds like he doesn't have anyone. And as much as I don't trust titans, he did help us against Saldrea's minions. I'm not saying you should marry him, just that... maybe we *all* need to rethink some of our preconceptions."

She turned her head to the side, still snuggled up against me. "When did you become the levelheaded one?"

"I've always been levelheaded," I said. "I just go a little nuts when you're in trouble and I can't help."

"You're helping now, thank you, Koar."

I smiled.

While Bayn had been talking, an idea had germinated in the back of my mind.

"Perhaps... there is a way to have Bayn prove himself, prove he's worthy of the position he so desperately wants."

"I'm listening," Izzy muttered. She didn't sound happy about it.

"Tell him you'll consider his proposal, if and only if he brings the titans to our side *first*. He can tell them whatever he wants, that you're married and he's king and general, whatever he has to. But you'll only entertain his request *after* the titans are on our side."

"So... he lies his ass off?" She sighed. "And... if he pulls it off, then... I marry him? Give him our armies?"

I gave a deep rumbling growl-sigh. I didn't like either of those propositions coming to fruition. But I also couldn't deny the truth that without the titans we'd most likely lose this war.

"We'd have to come up with some... controls. Perhaps some sort of ruling council which can overrule the king? It's not a bad idea, even for the future, to prevent tyrants." I'd just come up with that, but I liked the idea. "And that council could have a say over how our armies are utilized as well. Bayn would be king and commander, but he'd not have complete control."

Because an army of titans... a part of me was terrified they'd turn on us once this fight was over. But then... if they were following Bayn as their true leader, then it all came down to him, what he'd do.

And I had a sneaking suspicion he'd not turn on us. Something in how he'd looked at Izzy — and how he'd tensed when she'd gotten close — made me think... he wanted Izzy for more than just political reasons. Perhaps Izzy had affected him the same way she'd imprinted herself onto my life... and Vyns'... and the others.

Wouldn't that be wild?

But if anyone could sway a titan, it was Izzy. She was... Perfection.

"You're probably right," Izzy sighed and released me, looking up, an edge of darkness still dimming her brilliant sea-green eyes. "So logical and intelligent. Thank you, Koar."

My pride swelled.

I could be more than a protector and lover. I would be an adviser and confidante as well.

"We should probably get back," she said, blowing out a breath.

I put my arm around her, and she leaned on my shoulder as we left the auditorium.

Rook found us and joined us as we made our way back to Izzy's new residence. He caught us up on the discussion which had happened in the auditorium after we'd left. Mostly it had been Lhorine bringing people around to what needed to be done.

After a while I tuned the incubus out to focus on my own thoughts.

Izzy had praised me for my logic and level-headedness,

maybe I could use some of that to figure out my dilemma around how to protect her while being with her?

The fact that we'd been together and the world hadn't fallen apart around us — other than the declaration of a war we'd known was coming — gave me hope.

Izzy had joked about the curse being lifted... and maybe she was right? I'd given her my full attention, and no one had died. And... in the future, with all of the guys in Izzy's orbit... it wasn't like there wouldn't be others to keep watch when Izzy and I were together. And if they did, and something happened... it wasn't like I wouldn't be battle-ready at a moment's notice. I needed no weapon, no armor. I was as powerful naked as any other time.

So...

What was the problem?

The problem was... despite all of that, Talmarion and his family had still died on my watch. I hadn't been with Talmarion when the assassins came. Though... I had been with Mynrial... and perhaps she'd only died because I'd left her side to help her parents?

Huh.

Did that mean the problem wasn't me being distracted, but... distance? I wasn't close enough to Talmarion to save him, and Mynrial had died because I'd left? If that was the case, the answer was simple: never leave Izzy's side. As long as I was with her, near her, then I could protect her.

That felt too simple to be the answer, but... maybe...?

Either way, I vowed to stay by Izzy's side through whatever may come.

IZZY

As Koar, Rook, and I reached my new swanky residence, a large woman was coming out.

The reverence with which Koar bowed to her made me think she must be someone special.

"Spirit Master," Koar addressed the woman. "How is Vyns?"

Since I was finally starting to get a handle on how to tell the various peoples of this world apart — and from how Koar deferred to her — I assumed she was a dragon. She was a tall and statuesque woman, ears slightly tilted back under platinum hair, with eyes of steel blue.

"Your friend is recovering well. His spirit is still weak, but he's awake and was asking after—" her steely gaze turned to me, "—you, I presume." She gave me a quick once over, then a slow smile spread over her lips.

"If you could wield spirit, young one, you might give me a run for my money."

I took that as a compliment.

"Thank you, Spirit Master," Koar said with another bow of his head.

The stout woman stepped past me, and I felt... something. I assumed the strange wave of warmth was from her spirit, which was linked to fire.

If someone who didn't really know how to sense spirit could feel that... I had to assume she was quite powerful, hence her title.

As the three of us continued inside, I whispered to Koar, curious, "How old is she?"

"Over thirty millenniums."

Thirty-thousand-years?

"She's the last daughter of the dragons of the first age."

I had no clue what that meant, but it sounded extremely significant and important.

"See *that's* what baffles me," I said as we made our way across the large main sitting area. "With powerful women like that around, why do you need me? I'm only a couple decades old."

"Even so," Koar said with a knowing grin, "You're stronger than she is."

"How?" I asked, completely thrown by that. "Her spirit was—"

"Only slightly stronger than yours... and you're not even proficient with spirit," Rook finished for me. "Your powers with water would probably cancel out her fire easily enough and you'd be stronger in earth than she is."

Truly?

"Hey there, beautiful." Vyns' voice pulled me from this conversation. We'd been headed for his room, but he must have heard us coming. He was up and had just reached the doorway as we arrived. He leaned against the door frame, trying to act casual but looking rough.

"You don't look too bad yourself," Rook answered, preening himself, as if Vyns had been talking to him.

Vyns gave a weak laugh as I stepped over to him and embraced him carefully.

"Thank you so much for helping me against Saldrea," I breathed into his ear. "You gave so much... You scared me."

"I'd do it again, anytime, for you," he whispered.

"As long as you come back to me afterward, okay?" I said as I pulled back to look him in those stunning blue eyes. I swept some of his long golden hair back away from one eye. He closed his eyes, leaning into my soft touch. "Don't you dare die on me." I barely got the words out, my throat constricting, tears in my eyes.

He reached up and wiped a tear away.

"As long as you're alive, I have very strong incentive to stay alive myself. So, let's both live nice long lives, okay?"

I nodded, lips pursed, more tears on my cheeks.

With a war looming, who knew how long any of us would live? But I vowed to do everything I could to make sure myself, and these precious men... and everyone helping me lived. It might be impossible, but I'd do what I could to minimize casualties. I would not be the type of ruler who threw lives away.

Putting my hands on his cheeks, I kissed him, long and slow, savoring the wash of humidity from his spirit, our connection still strong.

"Come, we have to talk," I whispered when I pulled back, then I let him lean on me as we made our way to my room at the end of the hall.

And, as a nice surprise, Myel was awake when we arrived. He had recovered well, his own innate healing having mended what I couldn't after I'd saved his life. He came to me, smiling, giving me a peck on the cheek before helping Vyns down into the lowered sitting area. Vyns, Myel, and I all sat together on a long couch. Rook took a seat on his own, perhaps not ready to return to the cuddle pile, or thinking I wasn't ready for him.

Which reminded me, we *still* needed to talk.

But that would have to wait, yet again, till after what I had to say. All the guys deserved to know about Bayn's "offer."

Koar stood between the couch and the chair on which Rook sat, ever vigilant.

"So, something's come up, that you all need to know about," I began.

"Something to do with the titan, Bayn?" Rook asked. He'd seen Bayn and I leave the auditorium together.

"Yes. And since there's not a lot of time to sugarcoat it, I'll just say it. He's proposed an arranged marriage between him and me." That elicited several stunned and shocked reactions. I hurried on. "I haven't accepted, and Koar's come up with a bit of a work around, but the meat of the issue is that the titans probably won't go to war with us against Valnea unless Bayn is essentially in charge: king, general, what have you."

"A titan? We're at war?" Myel asked, even more dismayed.

Right... Vyns and Myel didn't even know how the fight with Saldrea had ended and Myel had no clue we'd teamed up with the titans against Saldrea.

I quickly caught them both up on Saldrea's defeat and Valnea's preparations to deal with me and everyone here on campus.

I ended with, "It seems we'll have some time to prepare. Valnea doesn't seem concerned about us amassing any great force to resist her. She'll take all the time she needs to make sure she crushes us, which I won't let happen, if I can help it."

"And having the titans on board would certainly help," Vyns finished. "Which means entertaining Bayn's offer. He looked at Koar. "What was your work around?" Vyns seemed to be handling this information well. I was glad he wasn't freaking out, like Myel was.

"Giving him what he wants only after he brings the titans to the table," the big man responded.

It occurred to me then, that if Bayn joined my growing harem, Koar would no longer be the biggest man. Could I still think of him as "the big man?" He was still objectively big, but Bayn was... massive. And that was in his shrunken form.

Never in my wildest dreams would I have imagined myself a queen, facing a political marriage with a forty-foot-tall giant.

"Yeah, that seems fair," Vyns responded. "I have no issues with this, as long as Izzy's okay with it."

Really?

"Just like that? A titan, my husband, and you have no qualms?"

"Well, I assume you made it clear that we'd all be your husbands as well, or at least prince consorts. None of us are going anywhere and if that's a deal-breaker for him, we should find that out as soon as possible."

Huh.

Vyns was right.

One of my deal-breaker conditions had to be that my men would stay in my life, no matter what relationship Bayn and I had.

"I... this is all... I don't know how I feel about this," Myel said, still shocked. He sank back into the cushions of the couch.

He didn't like it, that's how he felt. Our mate bond told

me as much. Myel, though tall and lean and far from "small," was still the smallest of my guys. And having a massive titan join the crew...? I already knew Myel had insecurities and self-doubt around me not needing him, especially once I was queen. He thought my desires would change, because I had changed, getting stronger, developing my elven abilities. But as much as I'd come into my power, who I was at my core was still the same, and Myel was still my bondmate. I could break the bond between us, but I had absolutely no inclination to do so. I wanted him in my life. But I could see how adding another extremely big, strong man to the harem might make him feel insecure.

"We should talk," I said reaching out to Myel, taking his hand in mine. The contact helped. Our bond was stirring rather heavily now that he was awake. We'd both been through a hell of a lot since the last time we'd been together and it needed some reassuring as well.

"First, I need to talk to Rook," I said, glancing over at the lithe, languid form of the relaxing incubus. A mane of flame red hair framed his sharp features. Two horns above his ears curved around his head before peeking up a little at the back. He gazed at me with eyes like smoldering embers and nodded, wordless. I turned back to Myel, "Then we can... have some alone time, okay?"

The shifter smiled tentatively. "Yeah, okay, thanks."

The smile was fake. I felt his uncertainty and a growing anger. Yeah, we really needed to talk.

God, handling all these relationships and emotions was practically a full-time job. When would I ever have time to lead an army or rule as queen?

I turned back to Rook. "Your thoughts on Bayn?"

He shrugged. "I'm not sure if I get an opinion... until we've had our talk and worked things out."

So, he did want to mend fences after having been a dick most of this past week.

Good.

"You do," I said, trying to reassure him. "What do you think?"

Another shrug. "If he can bring the titans, you'll probably need to entertain his proposal." He huffed out a long sigh. "I'm the only one who saw how things went in the auditorium after everyone was told about the war. It was chaos. Most of the elves and sylphim on campus are getting the fuck out. Everyone else seems split into two groups, those who are uncertain about fighting and want to stay out of it — mostly the dwarves and undines and dryads — and those who want to fight but already know we don't have a chance in hell. I don't care how many shifters and pixies and hobgoblins join us, our magic is barely a scratch compared to the full might of the elven forces, which includes dragons and sylphim and a good chunk of others who haven't heard about what's happened here on campus. We need those titans or..." Another rather fatalistic shrug.

Yikes.

That did not make me feel any better about winning this war.

I nodded. "Yeah, great, thanks," I muttered.

"We'll figure this out... somehow," Vyns said, squeezing my arm. I gave him the same fake smile Myel had given me. It was going to take more than empty reassurances to win this war.

There wasn't much to say after that, and a heavy silence hung over the room... until Myel's phone rang. It was across the room and rang several times before he sighed and moved to go get it.

"Myel."

He turned back to me, soulful eyes darker than usual. "Yeah?"

I honestly didn't know why I'd called after him. Mostly I wanted him to feel better but knew that wasn't going to happen with just a few words... so I repeated what I'd said earlier.

"After I talk to Rook, we'll spend some time together."

He nodded, looking tired and frustrated, then headed for his phone.

"I need some more rest," Vyns said, getting up gingerly.

"I'll help you back to your room," Koar said to him, then looked at me. "I'll be back."

I nodded and rose myself, as did Rook.

"Perhaps a walk outside?" Rook suggested.

I nodded.

We left the large new residence and strolled around the small field outside. It was a beautiful night, the stars twinkling above us, with a soft spray of salty sea air off the ocean below the cliffs.

"So..." I drew out the word.

"Yeah..." he said, blowing out a breath. "Give me a minute. I know I've had tons of time to think about this, but it's still... not really my thing, all this... talking and emotional shit."

"Me neither, we'll suffer through it together," I joked.

He laughed then sighed.

"I guess the best place to start is: I'm sorry for being a massive ass over the past week."

Yup, that was a good start.

"I said and did things I truly regret. I never should have said I was afraid of you because you were an elf. That wasn't true. I'm not afraid of you at all." I got the feeling there was more to that, that he *was* afraid of something. I didn't know where that supposition came from. Perhaps some faint whisper of his thoughts through our mental link? "I was confused, because... I wanted to be with you and only you, and for us incubi, wanting to be monogamous is considered a mental illness."

I laughed at that. It made sense, but it was still kind of silly to hear it said out loud.

"But... now that I've had time to think, I've realized I don't care about any of that. I want to be with you and only you, no other women... if you'll have me back."

As far as well thought out and sincere apologies went, that was a solid eight out of ten. It wasn't a ten, because I still felt like he was holding back. He still seemed on edge about something.

When I asked him about it, he replied, "It's the war. I've fought in wars before, in Urval. They're always nastier than you think they'll be, horrific. So yeah, I'm a little on edge."

I still wondered if there was more he wasn't telling me, but for now, I accepted that he was sincere in wanting to be back in my life and wasn't going to be a dick again.

"I've missed our friendship," I admitted. "And your orgasms."

"I've missed those two," he said with a soft chuckle. "The orgasms and the friendship, both... in case that wasn't clear."

"I'm probably going to need to refresh my bond with Myel," I said, playing coy. "Would you like to... join us?"

Rook let out a heady, long, shivering sigh. "You have no clue how much I want to join you."

I slipped my hand in his and pulled him back toward the residence.

Koar wasn't far off, watching us, giving us space while still being my dedicated protector.

Should I invite him as well? God! Rook, Myel, and Koar… together? The thought blew my mind.

"Want to join us?" I asked Koar as we reached him and headed inside. My other hand slipped naturally into his.

"Fuck," Rook breathed. "Yes please!"

I looked over at him with a smile and furrowed brow.

He answered my questioning look, "I felt the passion off you two earlier. That alone brought me back to being fully revitalized!"

Right… sometimes I forgot incubi fed off lust and sex, even when they weren't involved.

Koar accepted my offer, but one look at Myel once we were back in the bedroom and I knew something was wrong. I'd been ignoring our bond while talking to Rook, but it overflowed with anxiety, stress, resentment, vulnerability, despair, hurt, and a hefty dose of infuriated frustration.

"Ah… sorry guys," I said to Rook and Koar. "I need some time with Myel, *alone*."

"I'll be outside if you need me," Koar whispered. Then the big man leaned down to kiss me softly on the cheek.

"I'll… be with him," Rook added and the two left the room.

I went to Myel.

"What's wrong, what do you need?" I held out my hands and he came to me.

"You, Izzy, I need you!" he whispered, intent, flying into my arms.

What came next was rather intense. We had times when we could take it slow and truly enjoy being with each other. This was not one of those times.

IZZY

Clothes went flying, ripped off. Fast and dirty seemed all Myel and I could manage these days. It seemed like forever since the last time our bond had been settled enough for us to have some quality physical time together.

Once we were naked, our bodies mashed together, lips furiously seeking every aching inch of our partner's flesh.

We didn't even make it to the bed, or anywhere near the bed for that matter. We'd been closer to the couch and when I turned to lead him to that softness, Myel couldn't wait, bending me over the arm of the couch instead. His raging erection found the sodden mess of my core and plunged into me from behind.

I opened my mouth to protest, finding our times more intimate when we were facing each other, but once he was thrusting, I lost all capacity for speech or coherent thought and bucked back against him, using my arms on the couch for leverage. Who needed intimacy when you had raw, hot, steamy sex and a bond which demanded this physical connection?

Myel's hands slid up my sides and under, finding my breasts and clasping on as he bent over behind me, lips kissing my spine and up into my hair as his thrusts grew more and more erratic. A climax sang through me at the feel of his body curled around mine, his hardness so damned hot inside me, and the clutching need of his hands raking over my breasts.

During the times we were apart, I sometimes wondered if what we had was real, or if the bond was forcing us together. But at times like this, when that was exactly what the bond was doing, I didn't care. My bondmate was perfect, everything I needed and more, filling my body and soul with bliss as we came crashing together.

Myel let out a long, desperate grunt as he plunged himself deep and stayed there, his cock swelling then pulsing with his release. And feeling his heat explode inside me elevated my orgasm into the realm of heavenly ecstasy. We both tensed as the pleasure seized us, locked together in a tableau of rapture. My blood pounded so hard it drowned out everything else. All I heard was the beating of my heart. All I felt was the hammering of Myel's pulse, mostly through his cock, but also vibrating his entire body, which was curled around mine. He sank his teeth into my neck and drank hungrily.

Right. It had been a while since he'd fed, and he'd gone through a lot in that time. I'd almost forgotten how good it felt, the renewed sense of bliss it sent through both of us. I was about to tell him to leave a little blood for me, starting to feel lightheaded, when he stopped. His lips softly kissed over my back as we slowly came down from that skin-tingling, body-clenching high. And when our bodies finally did go slack, we fell onto the couch together, with him still holding me from behind, desperately.

"Maybe," I whispered through my still panting breaths, "we could take it slow now?" I offered.

But a whirlwind of emotions swirled to life in Myel again as he sighed heavily against my back.

"I can't. I have to go."

"Go? Where?"

"Safir needs spies. And I'm one of the better shifters for that assignment. I'm headed to the capital."

The capital?

"There has to be others Safir can send. I need you here, with me." It was selfish, but I didn't want Myel sent away, straining our bond yet again.

Myel sighed, heavier. "Safir and I haven't agreed on much lately, but on this, he's not wrong. It's night and I'm at home in the dark. If a dragon can get me close to the capital, I could make it into the palace with no one being the wiser. There are few with my ability to move and hide in shadows."

Well fuck.

"Just return to me... soon, safe," I whispered and grabbed one of his hands over my belly to hold and squeeze tightly in mine.

"I will," he said, kissing my back again.

But... that hadn't been all that had been bothering him. I still felt a heady dose of anger and resentment and uncertainty flowing through our bond. And I didn't want him leaving on such a dangerous mission distracted by such strong emotions.

"I'm... sorry about Bayn," I offered.

And yup... those same feelings flared.

This time he didn't so much sigh, as huff out a long, hot breath. "*Another* man," he hissed. "Rook was understandable, Vyns — I am sorry I blew up about him at the time —

but I've accepted him now. Yet... it seems you've developed something with the dragon? And now, this titan wants to drag you to his marriage bed?"

I didn't know if Bayn wanted to *drag me to his marriage bed* or just wanted the power that came from being king and general.

But yeah, Koar and I hadn't really been a thing before Myel had been stolen away by Saldrea. I could see why he might seem upset about more men wanting to be with me.

But I'd come to accept that this was my life now, a growing harem of men supporting me. It felt... nice.

Until one of them got jealous...

Though oddly, I didn't really feel much in the way of jealousy from Myel, more anger and frustration.

"You don't really mind the men," I whispered. "I feel what you do, remember? So, what's really bothering you?"

Myel let out a long grunt. Even after that he didn't speak. His emotions warred within him. He couldn't speak his true fears, so I took a guess.

"You're worried I won't need you," I said softly, gently. "You aren't jealous of the men in my life, but worried they'll edge you out of it? Am I right?"

"Yes," he growled, the word torn out of him. Then, suddenly he exploded, ranting, the floodgates opened by that one word.

"You changed me, made me stronger, better, tougher, but somehow, I'm still the weakest of those around you. I'll never be able to change the fact that I'm just a shifter. And you've got dragons and titans vying to be with you. I can't compete with that!"

"You don't need to compete—" I don't think he heard my words as he rushed over me.

"With all these others to give you what you need, you

don't *need* me anymore. You won't... want me... anymore." He slowed down for that last bit, his true feelings finally coming out.

I stilled my own mounting frustration at having to go over this again, reminding myself Myel was dealing with thousands of years of indoctrination and societal oppression, telling him his kind were worthless.

This time I spoke over him as he tried to continue.

"Myel! No! Stop! I have no desire to break our bond. I *want* you in my life, period. Why do you keep thinking I don't? I'm not getting rid of you. You're stuck with me, whether you want it or not! I *like* having you in my life. I crave being close to you. And sure, maybe that's the bond speaking, but so what if it is? The bond makes me feel so damned good when you're near and I don't want to give that up. Got it?"

He didn't. His emotions were still unsettled, his forlorn mistrust weighing on him.

Maybe it was time for a different tactic.

"Let me be perfectly clear." I wriggled out of his grip enough to turn around and face him, our noses so close they brushed each other. This needed to be said eye to eye. "There is only one reason I'd ever consider breaking our bond, and that is if *you* asked me to. If you wanted to be free to live your own life, then I'd respect and honor that and let you go."

"Is. That. What. You. Want?" I asked point blank, emphasizing every word.

"No, I—"

"Then you're good. I'm not going anywhere." And I kissed him to punctuate the point. "I like having you nearby. I like our hot, sweaty times together, and our slow and sensual times together, and our non-sexy, soothing times together. I want you in my life. End of discussion."

Still his emotions weren't settled.

Fuck this.

"Say it," I said with a heavy sigh. "I know what you're feeling, so say it, out loud!"

Myel flinched as if struck and the words spilled out. "I don't believe you!" he shouted. Well, as much as he could shout at me, since we were so close.

I pushed him away, fed up. I sat on the edge of the couch and shook my head.

"Sure, fine, but that's *on you, not me*," I said firmly. "I've told you how I feel, and you know I'm telling the truth because you can feel it through our bond. And yeah, sure, Maybe I'm not at 'love' yet, but that doesn't change the fact that I *want you* in my life. How many times do I have to say it?"

This is not how I'd hoped our time together would go.

Though, to be fair. Myel had been through hell lately. He'd died and been revived, then nearly killed again in a most gruesome way. I could understand him being upset about *that*, but not about *me*.

"I'm just..." Another sigh as he sat up next to me. "I don't know what I am. After everything I've been through, I feel weak and useless. And I don't know why you'd want me around."

There, had that been so hard to say?

Though, given how tense he'd been while saying it... perhaps it had been difficult. Once he'd said it, most of his emotions drained away, leaving only a faint despair and a lot of amorphous anxiety.

"Even though I'm upset," I whispered. "I still want you." I looked over at him. "You can be angry at someone you care for. In fact, the ones we care for make us the angriest at times."

He nodded.

"I hear you," he said. "The rest... is for me to work out."

It was really hard not to shout: *hell yeah!*

He leaned over and gave me a soft kiss on the cheek. "I should go. I'll... be careful."

And now a part of me worried that he wouldn't be careful, that he'd push himself to prove he was worthy of me, or something stupid like that, and get himself killed.

"Just... come back," I whispered as we both got up and went hunting for discarded clothes.

"I will." He dressed quickly, then left.

I felt like shit.

So much for our time together making me feel better.

"Be safe," I whispered to the air, even as my heart constricted at the thought of him lurking around the capital.

MYELAS

I REALLY SHOULDN'T BE THIS DISTRACTED IF I WANTED TO survive what was to come. I'd need to be at my best to spy on the elves in the capital.

Which meant figuring myself out.

Now.

Izzy's words kept ringing in my head: *that's on you, not me*. And she was right. She'd been doing everything she could to convince me she wanted me in her life, and I'd kept thinking she didn't. I hadn't believed her.

But... why?

Where was that coming from?

And thinking back to when Izzy had told us about the titan, Bayn, none of the other guys had seemed that thrown by it. Why not?

Because they were all secure in themselves. They were all big and strong and not part of the lower echelons of society. Not that seraphim and incubi were particularly high up, but they were on par with nymphs, at least.

But me... for some reason the addition of another big,

strong man made me feel more unworthy of Izzy, even though she insisted she still wanted me.

So... why was that?

I stopped in the middle of the wide stone path leading from the southwest end of campus to the shifter's barracks. It wasn't late, but it wasn't evening either, a few people were out. Those that were, ran past me on one errand or another. The campus was quiet, but with an undertone of frenetic tension.

I stood there for longer than I should have as a slow-creeping realization enveloped me.

It wasn't that I was unworthy of Izzy... it's that I'd *always been* unworthy... of anything. It was so ingrained in me that I couldn't shake it.

Shifters were the lowest of the low in elven society. Technically we were on par with hobgoblins and ogres, but in reality, we were even lower. Hobgoblins held a certain place of respect as servants. They were needed to help others, even if it was with the most mundane of tasks. Ogres were respected for their strength, the front-line warriors of dwarven society. They were basically cannon-fodder but still afforded more consideration than shifters. We beastfolk were despised by elves. We'd been taken from the titans thousands of years ago, the spoils of war, and since then we'd been made to fight each other till we died. Supposedly we were defenders of the realm, cannon-fodder, but in truth we'd never seen any battle except with our own kind. We'd been turned into a massive object lesson. Side against the elves and they won't just kill you, they'll have you exterminate yourselves.

We were nothing.

Hence, *I* was nothing.

And even as a shifter, I'd never been the smartest or

fastest or strongest. I'd stayed alive only by virtue of my shadow abilities. I was stronger now, but that sense of weakness had stuck with me.

And yet, some shifters defied the oppression of our station. Safir had been fighting back his whole life, even if it was in secret.

But he'd had a master who'd treated him with respect. He'd grown up in a place where he'd been worth something.

I hadn't.

And Safir himself, had — at least in part — contributed to my inferiority complex. To him, I'd always been a tool. Sure, most people were tools to him, but I was a blunt weapon with no real value.

Huh...

I really hated Safir for that. Why hadn't he shown me some of the respect he'd been shown? I knew why: because I wasn't as smart as he was. To Safir, value came from brains, cunning, wits. He respected people who could compete with his mind. And I couldn't compete with him in mind or body.

That's why I felt so damn unworthy of anything.

And despite Izzy repeatedly telling me I was worth something, I hadn't believed her, because I was still telling myself I wasn't worthy. That's what I believed, in my heart.

But if that's what I'd always believed, what I *still* believed, how in hell could I change that?

Someone else telling me I had worth hadn't worked. Hell, even Izzy making me stronger than any shifter out there hadn't made me feel any different on the inside. Because despite being — perhaps — the strongest shifter, and maybe even stronger than ogres or trolls, I was still pretty darned low on the power scale of this world. I had no chance against an elf in an open fight. Saldrea had... I shivered remembering what she'd done to me, my mind flinching away from those dark memories. I quickly moved on.

It was becoming clear that my physical capabilities had nothing to do with how I felt about myself.

Maybe that was the key?

Maybe I could be "weaker" than others but still feel I had worth as a person? It seemed simple enough to contemplate, but... how did I get rid of these ingrained thoughts and beliefs?

I had no clue.

I blew out a heavy breath. I should get going. I'd spent a little too long standing here, so I shadow-stepped to Safir's room, still wondering how one went about changing one's self-worth.

I was pretty sure it wasn't something I could do overnight.

And I had no more time to ponder it. I needed to put those thoughts from my mind if I was going to survive a covert trip to the capital.

Instead, I told myself that this mission finally showed I had skills Safir needed, that I could do useful things and wasn't just another shifter ground down and killed by his own kind.

Maybe this mission itself was the key to proving my worth, to myself and to others.

That gave me hope, which I carried with me into my meeting with Safir.

There were twelve others there when I arrived, a mix of races. I didn't know what the others could do, but I assumed they all had some form of stealth or listening or related abilities.

The briefing was simple, even if our task was not: We'd be flown close to the capital by dragons. Since they'd be detected flying in, they'd shift between realms quickly, to Urval or Elysial and back, drop us off, then vanish once again back to another realm.

Those of us being dropped off would then have to get as far from that location as we could as fast as we could, since other dragons and guards would have sensed the appearance of the dragon. We were to remain hidden, then head to specific locations to listen and gather information as Valnea began to mobilize her forces.

My destination was the palace. A high value target. I guessed it had something to do with my shadow-step ability. Teleportation like that was rare, so being able to get in and out unseen was a valuable asset.

We were also given extraction times and locations.

After the meeting Safir took me aside.

"I'm sending you on one of the most dangerous missions, only because I believe you have a good chance of success. Your power will let you get into the palace, find useful information, and get out alive. Izzy will flay me alive, if you die. So... don't. If I could send anyone else to do this, I would, but I need *you*."

This was new. Maybe I'd been wrong about Safir and what he'd thought of me?

Maybe I'd assumed he thought I was a tool... because that's how I saw myself?

Maybe I did have value?

I let that thought inspire me as I was handed over to my dragon and the two of us left the building. The big woman didn't talk as we made our way back outside, except to ask, "you ready?"

I nodded and she put a hand on my shoulder.

The world spun into darkness.

Time to prove my worth... to the world... and myself.

VYNSIEL

I SENSED HER COMING BEFORE SHE KNOCKED ON MY DOOR. Izzy's spirit washed through me, a dark tide, not her usual radiant waves of light and life and power.

"Come in," I said before the knock actually hit my door.

Izzy slid the door open and slunk to the side of my bed, sitting heavily.

"Myel?" I guessed. The shifter hadn't seemed thrilled about the addition of Bayn to Izzy's ever-growing circle of lovers.

She nodded. "I need..."

I sat up and wrapped her in my arms.

"Yeah... this," she whispered. "And now, he's off to the capital on some covert mission and I'm afraid..." She drew in a shuddering breath. "*I'm afraid.*"

I held her tighter.

War was a gruesome affair, and Izzy was right to be afraid. People were going to die. But that wasn't what she needed to hear right now.

"I've only just gotten to know all of you," she whispered. "I can't lose you now." Her voice grew harsh, an edge to it.

"This is why I never got close to anyone. They always left or died or..."

The tears came as heavy sobs wracked my soulmate.

Koar came over from his post at the door and knelt to add his arms around Izzy. That wasn't a surprise. I'd sensed the two of them had gotten closer while I'd been out of it. No... the real shock came when Rook followed the dragon in and held her as well.

I was glad he'd mended things with Izzy, but I'd never known an incubus to be so caring and giving when sex wasn't involved.

We all comforted Izzy till her sobs abated and her tears had washed out her despair.

"Thank you, all of you," she whispered.

"We're here for you, whatever you need," I replied.

"And... you're all sure it's okay... this thing with Bayn?"

"Is it what you want?" Koar asked.

She drew in a long breath, then let it out equally as slowly. "I... he's... I don't know." Her shoulders slumped beneath me.

"We need the titans," she went on. "And he's... not horrible to look at. If it's just a political thing, then I think I could live with it, as long as I still have all of you. I don't know if my wants have any say right now. If I'm going to be the next queen, I need to learn to do what's best for my people." She sighed. "With all of you... well, you sort of fell into my life. I don't think I trusted any of you right away, but you all did things to show me your hearts, how dedicated and wonderful you are."

"Except me, I was a dick," Rook said.

She laughed, the sort of gasping, awkward laugh of one who was deep in their emotions.

"Before that, you were nice, then you were a dick, now

you're back and you're here with me, and that's what counts." Her next breath was stronger, surer. "But Bayn, he's... he doesn't want *me*, he wants something from me."

"I wouldn't be so sure he doesn't want you," Koar muttered. "I can't be certain, but something in how he reacted to you makes me think he wouldn't mind sharing a marriage bed with you."

That was interesting.

"Ugh, gross, please don't ever say it that way again," Izzy said, but her tone was less disgusted and more playful. After a pause, she asked, "Do you... really think he likes me?"

"There is a strong possibility," Rook said.

Oh?

"Oh?" Izzy echoed my own thoughts.

"When you were up on stage, giving your impressive speech to sway the campus to our cause... I felt something from him," Rook said. "It wasn't quite lust, but it certainly had notes of admiration and potentially some desire."

Koar picked up from there. "I don't think he'd ever consider making this deal with anyone but you. You're an elf, but you aren't. You're strong and determined and beautiful, but you're also caring and kind. He hates elves, but for you... he has a much more... complex set of emotions."

"Don't we all," I added.

That made her laugh.

"So, I should seduce him to our side?" It was a joke, and I was glad she was feeling good enough to make it.

"No," Koar said evenly. "He'd trust you less if you did. Just be your wonderful, perfect self and he'll come around. He'll see you as we do. And, if you want him like you want us, then... things might work out. If you don't... then he's a king in name only, a figurehead with no part of your heart."

"He gets one room, with a small bed, and you get another, with a bed big enough for all of us," Rook added.

"I think I could get used to being a prince consort, or even just an inamorati in your harem," I said.

Izzy sighed, then squirmed her way out from under our three-fold embrace to look at each of us in turn.

"I'm never giving any of you up," she said softly. "Whether or not my marriage has any love in it, I want you all close to me. I can't do this without you."

"You could, you're strong enough to do anything, but you don't want to do it without us, and that's even better," Rook whispered.

"Agreed," Koar and I said at the same time.

Her spirit swelled, the light within her shining once more.

"I don't suppose... you three... want to show me just how much you love me? Together... at the same time... in my bed... naked. In case that wasn't clear."

I chuckled, then kissed her cheek. "Hell yes."

Koar bent and kissed the top of her head, while Rook kissed her shoulder.

"If that's what you want," Rook whispered.

"If that's what you need," Koar breathed.

"It is," she said.

Koar lifted her easily, while I got out of bed and followed behind with Rook.

"You sure you're okay sharing a bed with an angel?" I asked the incubus.

"You okay sharing one with a demon?"

"I see you less as a demon and more as a sentient sex toy for the woman I love," I said, teasing.

Rook laughed.

"And I see you less as an angel and more… a limp and lifeless body-pillow that same woman likes to sleep with."

Ouch.

But I laughed too.

"I see you both as sex toys and body pillows," Izzy called back from Koar's arms.

"And what am I?" the dragon asked.

"You're a combination of a giant dildo — the kind every sexually adventurous woman has on her shelf for when she really wants to test her limits — and a giant cuddly teddy-bear."

"He's got us both beat," Rook whispered to me.

"It's not a competition," I replied.

"But if it was, I win," Koar mumbled.

That made Izzy laugh and I felt better hearing that light and joyful sound. She laughed even more — after a yelp of surprise — when Koar tossed her onto the massive bed in her room.

"What would you like?" I asked as we three men stood arrayed before her.

"Surprise me," she breathed, eyes widening a little as she took us all in. "I can't believe I'm going to do this. A threesome was one thing, but I don't even know how a four-some would work!"

"You've got three holes, we have three dicks, it seems logical to me," Rook responded so casually it took a moment for his rather blunt words to sink in.

Izzy giggled, a manic little sound, eyes going wide as she seemed to contemplate that. Meanwhile I slapped Rook upside his head.

"Do you have to be so crude?"

"Hey! What? Fine!" He straightened and put on a posh accent. "Izzy, I would like to formally request that you allow us suitors access to your mouth, your vagina, and your anus, so that we might pleasure you as we see fit."

I glared at the incubus.

He gave a big smile back. "Refined enough for you?"

Izzy was rolling, laughing by this point. Though there was still a wild *I can't believe we're going to do this*, quality to her mirth.

"You two keep talking, I'm going to pleasure this perfect woman," Koar said, quickly stripping off his clothes.

"What he said!" Izzy gasped through her chuckles.

Rook must have used some incubus magic, because he was out of his clothes even before the dragon.

I couldn't help but show the other two up and let out a brief incandescent flash of light... which incinerated my clothes. They were the ones I'd been in for the past two days and I didn't mind losing them.

Izzy's eyes went round as saucers as we climbed onto the bed around her.

"I must be dreaming," she whispered.

"You are," Rook breathed as he lay down to one side of her, turning her head to take her lips. Koar laid on her other side his kisses ranging over her neck, shoulder, and chest. That left me between Izzy's legs. She opened them as I lowered myself, my hands sliding under her thighs and buttocks to lift her so I could press my mouth to her core.

She and I both sighed out a moan, though I doubt hers was because of her heavenly apples and cinnamon taste. I didn't know how that was possible, but I wasn't going to question it.

I ran my tongue up her slit once more and was rewarded as she opened for me. I dove in, tongue lashing, teeth raking, softly sucking on her clit. Her hips rocked against my face, her moans lost in Rook's mouth.

Sliding one of my hands out from under her perfect ass, I tested her opening and she practically sucked my finger inside her. She needed this. I stroked her G-Spot while rolling her clit around on my tongue and heard a desperate little cry, still muffled by Rook's attentions.

Her spirit roiled and heaved against mine, a heady heat-wave of sweltering need, pulsing in time with her heart, and pounding through her loins.

She squirmed beneath me, her body rose, back arching, a prolonged groan bubbling up from within her...

...and I instantly eased off, withdrawing my mouth and finger, simply blowing hot air over her soaked folds.

She tore her lips off Rook as I glanced up at her.

"Please!" she begged.

Rook chuckled. "Good job Body-Pillow, I think she's ready."

IZZY

Oh. My. God!

Never before in my life had I felt this… alive and alight with energy and passion. All my nerves were firing, my skin searing, my mind keenly aware of the three sexy-as-sin guys all around me.

Rook's kisses were to die for, a sinful release, which drew out all the tension and stress inside me and let it go, vanishing into sexy moans and soft sighs. Incubus kisses really were the solution to all of life's problems. And if it had just been that I'd have been pleasantly buzzed with bliss, but it wasn't.

The hard, insistent press of Koar's large hands stroking over my ever-so-sensitive flesh, cupping one breast while he kissed another, or bringing a peak to his lips to suck and play, was sensual heaven and filling me with a bubbling heat. And Vyns' rather aggressive oral assault on my core had turned molten desire into a near eruption of ecstasy. Then he'd eased off, while I teetered on the brink of a massive orgasm. So. Damn. Close!

Yet what really made this sexy as hell was the three of

them working together. No qualms, no fighting, no teasing, just a unified dedication to my pleasure which blew my mind wide open. Never would I have imagined anything like this to be possible and the fact that it was, elevated my ecstasy to a whole new level of heaven.

And the fact that Vyns held me at the ragged edge of an epic orgasm was both infuriating and miraculous.

Then Rook began tracing a single finger down from my neck, and where he touched a line of divine fire followed, blazing over my skin and sinking deep, seizing the expectant pleasure in my core, ratcheting up my ecstasy while still keeping me on this near peak. He slid his finger around one breast, then down over my stomach, before his hand cupped my sex and... wow. That hot all-encompassing touch was perfect, elevating me even further without the release of an orgasm.

Hello cloud nine!

"Lay back," Rook commanded, and it took me a moment of confusion — I was already laying back — before I realized he was speaking to Vyns.

All three of us shifted, as Rook subtly guided us, till Vyns lay on the bed, I was on my knees poised over him, with Rook behind me and Koar standing. Rook held me close in both arms, one hand languidly massaging a breast, the other slowly slipping each finger through my slick slit. Then the hand on my core withdrew, sliding behind me, one finger gently brushing my rear opening, coated in my wetness.

"Let me show you a neat trick we incubi can do," Rook breathed in my ear, the hot breath adding to my tantalized state.

Then his finger ever so softly pressed on that spot and I

felt a sinful surge of raw lust. I opened, ready, as my bliss bumped up a notch.

Was there a cloud beyond nine? If so, I was there.

Hello cloud ten!

Then Rook shifted and his cock brushed behind me, sliding perfectly into position. Knowing what would come next made me whimper. I had a feeling as soon as any guy was inside me, I'd explode.

Yet the sexual miracle that was Rook managed to lower me onto Vyns' waiting erection just as he slipped inside me, both cocks slowly filling me.

I lost my breath. It wasn't possible to breathe with this much euphoria blasting through me, still with no release!

I gave a pathetic little gasp-whimper.

"Hush, soon, My Flame," Rook whispered again. I'd forgotten his nickname for me, and right now, it was extremely apt. I might combust any second.

Then Rook and Vyns began moving together, rocking back and forth, Rook's hands keeping me upright, moving over my blazing hot flesh, grasping and kneading, massaging and fondling.

I would lose my mind if I didn't come soon.

Koar stepped close. I couldn't help myself with that thickness before me, I reached up and brought it to my lips, licking it like an ice cream cone. Only it wasn't cold, but sinfully hot.

"Perfect," Rook breathed, and one of his hands slid down to my clit just over where Vyns' dick was giving my insides one hell of a massage, and with a single casual flick of my ragingly sensitive bud… I shattered.

Breath returned as I screamed out my rapture. My body shook violently but was held firm by Rook as he and Vyns picked up their pace. I pulled Koar closer and wrapped my lips around his tip, humming and crying out around him as savage pleasure ripped through me.

"Fuck, yes!" Vyns cried out. His cock twitched. Every inch of his delicious length pressed perfectly against me, or rather, I was clamped down on him like a vise, the throb of my pleasure squeezing him in time with my own contractions of bliss.

"You're so damned... ugh... everything!" Rook hissed behind me, his dick also getting the same treatment.

Koar's hands softly glided through my hair as I bobbed my face over his rigid shaft.

"So perfect!" Koar whispered with desperation before his release filled my mouth. I drank him down, loving the feel of his trembling, twitching body at my command.

Then Vyns cried out and heat pulsed within me, sending my own endless orgasm into overdrive. And when Rook joined the other two, grunting as he came, a feeling of sublime perfection washed over me. I had three men at my whim, not just pleasuring me, but worshiping me. Never before had I felt so... powerful and commanding.

I wasn't sure what I'd expected from a foursome, but it was so much more than the sum of its parts, an exponentially euphoric experience. Though, to be fair, that could also be because an incubus was involved and they had a way of making sex a thousand times better.

Either way.

Best. Sex. Ever!

We all collapsed onto the bed, and I couldn't stop giggling between my panting breaths.

And I couldn't help but wonder — given how my bond with Myel elevated our intimacy — what it might feel like with all four men at the same time. Logistically, it seemed outrageous, impossible, but somehow, we'd make it work.

I had to wait for Myel to return from a dangerous mission — and probably win a war — before I'd get to try it, but that made me want to win, and make sure everyone survived all the more.

I could do this, I could face the future, I could take on the world, if it meant having more moments like this.

I'd known I'd had to fight before. I'd wanted to help the people of this world, and that necessitated a conflict. Helping these people was the reason I fought. However, until now, I hadn't had a reason *to win*. But ultimate sex with four nearly perfect guys… *that* was something worth winning for!

Silly? Maybe, but we all needed our own quiet motivations for the things we did, and no one ever had to know about this.

I FELT LIKE A MILLION BUCKS THE NEXT MORNING WHEN I sought out Bayn, well pleasured, then well rested. The guys had stayed with me, all piled together on that big bed, and I'd never had as peaceful and perfect a sleep.

Bayn, and the few other titans on campus, had taken possession of one of the other royal residences, recently vacated by elves who'd left campus. He wasn't going to ingratiate himself to any elves still remaining around by doing so, but then, I didn't think ingratiation was high on hist list of priorities.

I was directed to him by Zora, who I'd found in the large sitting room of my own residence. She'd taken it over and set it up as a base of operations, runners coming and going with information I needed to know. I'd told her I'd catch up with her when I got back.

Koar was with me, of course, my oversized shadow.

Bayn answered the door when I knocked.

"What have you decided," he asked, blunt, harsh, down to business. I could play that game.

"I told you yesterday, there would be conditions on your proposal, are you ready to hear them.

He grunted, his eyes hard. Though, as I gazed into those eyes, meeting him stare for stare, I noticed how they weren't as dark as I'd initially thought, more of a chocolate brown. And something about that delicious color and his round cheeks and youthful face softened his entire look enough that... he wasn't as brutish anymore. He still had a square face and the thick body of a powerlifter who just happened to be well over seven feet tall, which gave him quite the imposing look, but that bit of softness made him more handsome than I'd given him credit for initially.

Maybe he wouldn't be so bad as an addition to my harem? If what hung between his legs was as big as the rest of him, I couldn't quite imagine how sex would even work, but the dirty little part of my brain sure wanted to find out.

And... now I was staring at his crotch.

Fuck!

Back to the eyes.

He was saying something. I tuned in.

"... in and we can discuss your terms." Given how he was opening the door and making room for me, I assumed the first part of that sentence had been: *come in*.

I turned to Koar. "Wait out here." I wanted to do this alone. "If you hear anything that doesn't sound like me getting my way, feel free to break down the door and level this place."

He nodded.

I entered, head held high. I would not let Bayn take an

inch more than I was willing to give him. Though he could give me all of his inches anytime... *Stop it. Dirty little brain*!

I didn't sit, neither did he. A standoff in the foyer.

"I accept your proposal for a political marriage," I said, pinning him down with my gaze. "*With* the following terms and conditions."

He set himself. Though the hints of softness in his look meant he wasn't quite as daunting as he made himself out to be.

"Go on."

"First, I have other men, other lovers, and I will not give them up. No matter the... physical relationship we may have, my part will always include them. This is a deal-breaker, if you can't accept me *and* them, then we're done here."

"You can fuck whoever you like."

And... do you want to be in that group? I didn't ask. Now wasn't the time.

"Good, and no matter your title, I won't *hide* them either. They'll be my prince consorts or Inamorati. I want everyone to know I care for these men, part of how I'll show the world that all races are equal in my eyes."

He shrugged. "Yeah, sure, whatever. Anything else."

"Second, you will not have the complete control you seem to want."

He stiffened, muscles bunching and tensing under his shirt and pants. Wow... the fact that I could see it through the fabric only emphasized how damned huge he was.

"I will not let you rule over me," he growled.

"I heard you well enough, yesterday. We will rule together, as equals, neither dictating anything for the other. Fair?"

He gave a sharp nod, but his jaw was clenched so tight I feared he'd shatter his teeth.

"The control I'm referring to will be a third party. I do not plan to be a tyrant or a dictator. The government I wish to set up will be a conglomeration of voices from all races. You and I will only be a part of it, and if you are chosen as general of our armies, then you'll still have to answer to that council. Again, this is a deal-breaker. Take it or leave it."

"You're pushing your luck," he muttered.

I might be, but I wouldn't let him take control of this world. I was here to depose dictators, not set up new ones.

"Agreed?" I pressed.

"Fine!" he hissed. "That better be it."

"Nope, one more condition and I'm fairly certain you're not going to like it."

Oh... wow. His glower was intense. He stepped in, looming over me, very close. I didn't give an inch. It was a pain to crane my neck to look up at him, but I wouldn't give him any room.

In fact, I stepped in too, which brough my body so very close to his. My rather prominent chest brushed over his abdomen, roughly level with his bellybutton. Koar had said not to try to seduce Bayn last night, and I was fairly certain this stand-off was anything but a seduction, but I still couldn't help taking a *really deep* breath, pressing my breasts against him.

Something shifted, caressing the underside of my bust, and it was everything I could do not to break eye contact with Bayn as I realized exactly what was moving beneath his clothes.

Don't think about his dick. Don't think about his dick. Don't think about... God! It must be huge!

I took a hard, dry-throated swallow, then finally spoke

up, breaking the silence and the iron-corded tension between us.

"The marriage is on *only if* you can bring the titans to our side. You can tell them you'll be king, or even that you *are* king, but nothing official will happen on my end until the titans are here and ready to fight. Prove you can bring the army you say you can bring and the marriage is on. I will not give you anything until *after* you give it to me first."

And wow, that last sentence had come out a little huskier than I'd hoped.

"Oh, I'll give it to you," Bayn growled, shifting in a tad more. Now, his thick-as-a-wine-bottle cock was pressed to my stomach. I had my head all the way back, looking up over his mountainous chest to meet his gaze. Was there a huskiness in his voice as well?

Koar might have been right about Bayn's feelings. There was more than a little sexual tension mixed in with our normal *two-alphas-fighting-for-dominance* tension.

"And I'll take *everything* you've got," I sassed right back. Oh... wait... I probably shouldn't have said that, especially *how* I'd said it. I quickly added, "*After* you bring me the titans."

His cock twitched, pulsing against my stomach and tickling the undersides of my breasts.

Was it hot in here? Because I was hot and he was hot, and if one of us didn't break soon, I had a feeling we'd end up tearing each other's clothes off.

I didn't give.

Neither did he.

BAYN

I WANTED NOTHING MORE THAN TO TEAR THE CLOTHES OFF this infuriating woman and show her exactly what I could give her. Maybe then, once I'd stretched her beyond her limits and given her pleasure like no man ever had, she'd submit to me and let me have my way.

And I wasn't entirely sure she didn't want me to do just that.

She'd been the one to get close enough for our bodies to touch, her breasts pressed to my abdomen. I really shouldn't have gotten any closer than that, but I'd not been able to help myself. Feeling my cock touch the underside of her breasts had been the most deliciously sensual thing I'd felt in a *very* long time.

In the hundred years since Osserime's betrayal, I'd been with only a handful of women. But, since I couldn't trust they wouldn't take advantage of me while my defenses were down, like she had, I insisted they be restrained. Bondage — on their part — was the only way I felt comfortable being intimate.

And I didn't think Izzy would ever submit to me. I had a

strong suspicion she needed to be in charge, in control, dominating. And yet... maybe I was wrong. Maybe that was the face she showed to the world and in private she was all sighs and submission, with ropes tied around her limbs, stretching her taut, her legs pulled wide and her glistening pussy...

...was way off topic.

What were we talking about?

Oh right. Kingship and armies, who would break first and show weakness in this face-off.

Honestly, her terms weren't horrible. Having other prince consorts, or a harem or whatever wouldn't harm me in any way. I was man enough to know I could please her as well as any other, *if* she ever came to our marriage bed.

Which was something I hadn't thought I'd wanted initially, but now. By My Bones! I wanted her. I wanted to tie her down and test her limits, put a few bruises on that pristine pale skin of hers, make her pay for what she'd done to me.

Whoa!

Wait...

Izzy hadn't done anything to me.

It was Osserime I wanted to make pay. I didn't just want to bruise that betraying bitch, I wanted to make her bleed, rip out her heart, like she'd ripped out mine!

Izzy was demanding yes, but... she wasn't trying to control me. I blinked myself back to our argument and once again assured myself that her terms weren't horrible. Sure, I didn't like them. A ruling council having a say over what I could and couldn't do, was infuriating. But some logical part of my mind knew it was a reasonable request, even sensible, to stop tyrants from ever being a thing again. It grated that I wouldn't have the control I so desperately desired.

And Izzy's condition that the marriage be finalized only after I'd brought the titans to our side... also made sense. If I had to lie to my own kind to get them to see reason, I didn't mind that. I'd bring them to our side then Izzy would submit to me... I mean... marry me and I'd get what I wanted.

Everything she'd asked for made sense, even if I didn't like it. But I mostly didn't like it *because* she was challenging me, my authority, making this a test of wills from which I couldn't back down.

I also wasn't entirely certain I could bring the titans on board. How much had my parents poisoned my own kind against me? And Osserime was still out there. She'd have spread word of my humiliation at her hands. Would my people follow a prince who'd been dominated by his betrothed? Would they follow a humiliated outcast?

And if I couldn't do what I'd proposed, bringing the titans to Izzy's side, I'd have nothing. Izzy wouldn't respect me. I'd gain no power, not kingship, nor military might. I'd be...

Fuck I hated feeling so damned powerless!

I'd never allow myself to feel that way again.

I had to bring the titans to our side.

And I had to show Izzy who was boss.

I gripped her upper arms. She tensed but didn't cry out for her dragon bodyguard.

I couldn't quite get over how big my hands were on her. I could easily wrap my fingers around her biceps, hell, I could probably fit both hands around her waist. And, unbidden, my hands slid down her arms to grasp her above the hips. I'd been right, thumb to thumb and middle-finger to middle-finger, I encompassed her waist perfectly.

"Ah...?" she breathed. I had her off balance.

Good.

I lifted her and carried her to a nearby wall, pinning her so her eyes were more level with mine. Not perfectly at my height, I still wanted to look down at her, but so she didn't have to crane her neck to see me as I told her what for.

What I didn't expect was her legs wrapping around me, gripping me tight, pressing the tip of my ragingly hard cock right into her heated core. My move to show dominance hadn't gone as I'd intended. The tables had turned, and I was about to lose my shit.

"So... we're doing this?" she asked, voice silken with desire. Her hips rocked and massaged the tip of my cock. I tensed so hard my muscles protested. "Seal the deal, so to speak?" And the grin she gave me made all my insides boil.

Fuck it.

I crushed my lips to hers... only to find her so damned receptive, mouth opening, inviting me in. Once again, I'd made the first move, but she'd turned it on me, making me question everything...

...which I would do later, *after* I finished devouring the soft moans of this intense woman. My cock twitched, aching to be buried inside her, and the way her hips moved, I didn't think she'd mind. Though... Izzy wasn't a large woman like the titans I'd been with. I might break her. Although, she was an elf, sturdy and strong. Maybe she could take my rather aggressive and forceful thickness.

And once again, I couldn't help but picture her tied up, legs open, begging me to break her, stretch her, punish her for all her sinful ways!

Fucking hell!

I released her like she was on fire, stepping back.

She let go of me and dropped to the floor, landing on her

feet well enough. But she gave a surprised little, "Oh!" and the door burst open, the dragon barging in.

"We're fine!" Izzy hissed, blushing beet red.

Koar looked between the two of us, shrewd enough to understand what had happened, then shrugged and left.

Did he not care that I'd forced myself on his woman?

No... he'd seen how *she* felt, that she'd liked it, and it hadn't mattered to him what I'd done because he knew she'd always be in control.

"Fuck, fine, you have a deal, bewitching wench!" I held out my hand.

She took it, her hand tiny in mine, yet her strength was evident, meeting me force for force when we shook.

Bloody Bones! She was infuriating! Strong and commanding and sexy!

"Bring me those armies, as soon as you can!" she said, straightening her clothes and calming herself before she left.

I put my fist through a wall after she'd gone.

"Brother? What's wrong?" Wensuria came out from the long hall leading to the bedrooms. She hurried to me when she saw the damage to the wall. "Breathe!" she encouraged me.

Wensuria knew about my control issues, my anger. I'd told her what Osserime had done to me and, of all who knew, my sister was the only one who'd consoled me. She'd seen what that betrayal had done to me.

She guided me to a chair and I sat heavily. The furniture creaked under my weight. Elven furniture was strong and well built, but still not meant for titans, who on average weighed well over five hundred pounds. I was closer to seven hundred.

"I assume your talk with Izzy didn't go well?" My sister had known I'd been meeting with the half-elf this morning.

How could I explain that every time I'd tried to control the small woman, she'd turned the tables and made me feel out of control.

"No," is all I said, because talking about my feelings wasn't my strong suit. Still, I explained, "Her terms are fair, but I still feel like I lost. And I'll be king—" meaning we'd be safe, "—only *after* I bring the titans to her, which... I'm not entirely certain I can do."

Best to leave out the kiss, and the raging hard-on, and Izzy accepting all of it without batting an eyelash.

"You'll have to stay clear of father and mother when you're back," she said. "They'll not be happy you broke your agreement with Saldrea, let alone usurping their power."

She was right. If my parents found out what I was doing, I wouldn't be surprised if they sent assassins after me. I wasn't afraid, I could deal with any titans they sent. Still, it would endanger others.

"You need to practice fighting more," I warned Wensuria.

"I fight well enough. I may not like it, but I'm a titan as much as you are. My magic is even stronger than yours. I can take care of myself."

Yet another reminder that earth magic invariably ran stronger in the female line.

Damned elves.

"You can do this. Being king of all of Seial... the titans will eat that up. I know they will. Just be as confident with them as you were with Saldrea. You never backed down with her, and you can do the same with our own people. Be the brother I know you are, and the titans will follow you."

How strong could I be if I needed a pep talk from my sister to accomplish my goals.

But she was right.

"I'll go immediately. Tell everyone here to prepare for an influx of titans, thousands of them." I smiled as I rose.

If Izzy wanted to test me, I'd show her exactly what I could do. Then she'd be my queen, and I'd show her exactly what I could do… in bed. Yes. Let *her* anticipate our wedding night, let *her* dream about being with a man as powerful as myself.

And I'd not think of her at all…

…was the lie I told myself as I prepared to depart.

IZZY

Flustered didn't begin to describe how I felt after my meeting with Bayn.

"You got everything you wanted," Koar said. It wasn't a question and there was a hint of mischief in his voice. "And more... it seems."

"Shut up, you big lug," I said, slapping his arm. "If you tell the others about this, I'll—"

"They'll know," he said. When I looked up at him, I was fairly certain he was hiding a smile behind that stoic expression of his.

"Vyns will sense the disturbance in your spirit. Rook will know you've been... lusty, and if Myel was here, he'd smell the arousal on you."

"Oh God, can you?"

"I can."

"And... you're not...?"

"Upset? No. Bayn is an ass with control issues, but if you two are into each other, then the rest of us will have to learn to accept him. And if he agrees to your terms, then you'll be keeping all of us and there's no problem."

"Why...? How...?" she stammered. "Most human guys would be all indignant about *another man being all over me, having his dick inside me.*" I deepened my voice to try and do an impression of a macho man.

Koar raised a brow. "Did he go that far?" the dragon asked.

"Not this time, but we were damned close. A little more friction and our clothes might have burned away, then who knows what might have happened," I exaggerated... a little.

"It matters not," Koar said, sounding so damned enlightened and above it all. "I am not concerned. I know no other dick can compare with mine. His may be larger, but he's probably an awkward oaf, trusting to his size to do all the work, not knowing how to pleasure a woman as she deserves."

"Ah... so that's it. You're not jealous because you have a superiority complex."

"I call it self-confidence."

"I call bullshit, but whatever."

He chuckled softly and I huffed out a breath, trying to get myself under control after that... very unexpected encounter with Bayn. I couldn't quite understand our mutual reactions to each other. He was an ass. And I was fairly certain I annoyed the hell out of him too. So... why the fireworks?

True, I'd always been attracted to bad boys... but usually I was smart enough to stay away from them. Ah... so *that* was the problem, if this all worked out, I'd be *forced* to get close to him. Hell, I'd be married to the bastard!

I didn't get his need for dominance, though I suspected something had happened to him. Hell, Saldrea had happened to him and her treatment of his sister might have been enough to give him control issues. And he'd said something about his parents imprisoning him, just for disagreeing with them?

I completely understood controlling parents who were assholes. And to a degree, I could sympathize with being a fish out of water, a titan in a world of elves. All of that together meant I'd apparently given him enough leeway for sexy feelings to take over. And we'd certainly had chemistry, even if it was the dangerous explosive type of chemistry.

I didn't mind a guy taking control in the bedroom, nor did I mind being in control. I could go either way. Sometimes it was sexy to have a man be all manly, as long as he wasn't an arrogant ass about it.

Bayn seriously needed to learn to compromise and let go. Though... he had agreed to all my conditions... so maybe he was slowly coming around? I couldn't be sure, because he also hadn't seemed happy about accepting my terms.

I huffed out another breath.

Koar slipped his hand into mine. His hands were large, but not Bayn large. The way the titan had wrapped his hands around my waist, like I was some tiny, slender waif of a woman!

Stop. Thinking. About. Him!

I thought about Koar instead. "Thanks for trusting me back there," I said. "It couldn't have been easy for you, staying outside."

He grunted and nodded.

Typical Koar reaction.

"And... thanks for coming running, even if I wasn't actually in trouble."

"Any time."

He pulled me a little closer and removed his hand from mine to hug me around the shoulders. I leaned into him, head resting on his shoulder as we walked.

This was nice.

Vyns and Rook were waiting in the sitting area of my residence when we returned.

"Everything okay?" Vyns asked. "Your spirit was... agitated for a while."

"She was hot and bothered is what she was," Rook muttered to Vyns. Then to me, "I've tried to tell the angel that you and Bayn must have really hit it off, given the sexy thoughts you were thinking."

Heat rushed to my face.

Yup, they all knew.

"Sorry," I mumbled.

Rook shrugged. "If he's going to be one of us, then it's probably a good thing you find him sexy. Even if he's also... frustrating."

"How much of my thoughts did you get?" I asked, curious.

"Ever since the arena... I've been getting most of them."

Oh.

I may have blushed even deeper.

"But... everything's good, he agreed to your terms?" Vyns asked.

I nodded. "Yup, all settled. He's going to go get the titans on board and assuming he does, I guess I'm getting married... far sooner than I ever thought I would."

I gave a terrified smile.

"You'll be a beautiful bride," Zora said, looking up from her paperwork, which was scattered around the large sitting room. "Also, there's going to be another, bigger meeting today. You're going to be front and center, so if you want help figuring out what you're going to say, we should talk."

Thank you, Zora.

"Yes, please!" I hurried to her side so I didn't have to look any of my guys in the face after everything they knew happened with Bayn.

The guys all stayed close though. Vyns relaxed, still on the mend. Rook paced, full of agitated energy, then decided to help Zora and I write my speech. Koar stood close, a comforting and silent presence.

And my other guy… was far away. My bond with Myel strained with the distance between us. I also felt Myel's undulating emotions, a bit of fear — but not too much, he was okay for now — mixed with excitement and a growing eager confidence. Something had changed in him or had started to. He didn't seem as much like the dejected, uncertain man who'd left here last night. That helped me not to worry too much about him and focus on this speech.

Today's meeting would be a lot bigger than yesterday's. It would be in the Great Hall, also known as Anadendyra Hall. That wasn't intimidating at all, having to give a speech in a hall named after my family before *everyone* on campus. This was my chance to tell them what they were fighting for, to help them understand the new world I wanted to build, equal and free for all.

Again… no pressure.

We worked furiously for the rest of the morning and I was too nervous to eat any lunch so we worked through lunch as well, right up until the mid-afternoon meeting time.

Then we all headed over to the Great Hall. As we did, a growing group formed around us, following us. An excited — if also nervous — hubbub rose up from them as we paraded across campus.

I'd tried to comprehend the vastness of responsibility I'd have when I became queen. But it was only as I made my way into that massive hall, filled with *tens of thousands* of people, all focused on me, that I began to understand the overwhelming depth of my obligation and duty to these people.

A cold terror gripped me, and I stuttered to a stop, frozen in place.

I couldn't do this.

But I *had* to do this.

Hell, all I was doing was giving a speech. How much harder would things get when I was making decisions which would impact people's lives? For now, I wasn't much more than a figurehead, a focus, an ideal. Eventually I'd have to fight a war, then somehow make good on all the promises I was about to make. Maybe that's what scared me, the things I was saying. Could I make them happen? The words seemed easy to say but following through... suddenly that seemed nearly impossible.

"You can do this," Koar whispered to me.

"Don't think about how you're going to help them," Rook murmured from my other side. "Think about how much they need help. They *need* this Izzy. They *want* this desperately. Right now, all you have to be is a symbol of hope. Give them hope for a better future and you'll have won today."

That helped.

Okay, sometimes it wasn't so bad having someone reading all my thoughts.

"Thanks, guys."

I drew a steadying breath and continued across the floor of the great hall to the raised area in the middle. The Great Hall was laid out a lot like Clifftop Arena, only slightly smaller and fully enclosed, inside. Three levels of raked seating circled nearly all the way around the massive room, except for a slice of perhaps one eighth of the space. There, on a raised area, was the podium where I'd make my speech.

Behind that were special box seats below a massive magical screen, on which my face would be splashed.

I climbed the stairs up to the stage and tried not to freak out.

I'd heard someone once say most people feared public speaking more than death. I embodied that sentiment as I looked around at the filling stands. Fighting was easy. You didn't have to think too much, just focus on your opponent and your next move. I'd been scared going into the dominion match against Saldrea and even more worried going into my one-on-one fight with her, but it was nothing compared to the elephant sized butterflies bombarding my stomach as I approached that podium and gazed out over a sea of people.

It had been a lot easier yesterday, in a smaller room, with lights blinding me. Being able to see the tens of thousands of people filling the stands was... daunting to say the least.

You can do this. Rook sent to me.

Vyns' feeling of summer's heat gently buffeted my spirit and encouraged me.

When I looked over at Koar he gave me a wink and a nod. He trusted me.

Okay... sure... I could do this. Time to tell the world how I was going to turn it on its head and shake everything up.

No biggie.

IZZY

THIS TIME, SINCE WE WERE APPEALING TO ALL RACES, IT HAD been decided that Safir would introduce me, not Lhorine. The elf wasn't even on stage, we wanted to minimize elven presence for this speech.

I couldn't decide which was worse, having to speak, or waiting here, doing nothing while more and more people filled in. I really wished Myel was here, so his mere presence could soothe me, but Rook, Vyns, and Koar were doing a pretty good job of filling in. Small touches, whispered words, encouraging thoughts, bolstering spirit, it all went a long way toward helping me calm myself... a little.

Then, finally, the massive hall was filled and Safir spoke, the lights out over the thousands of spectators dimming.

"Assembled peoples of the three fae realms." Safir's voice boomed out through some sort of magical sound system. "Those of you here today have chosen to stay and fight or at least remain neutral in the fight to come. If you are in the latter group, thank you for coming. I don't know if our words today might sway you, but your willingness to listen is heartening."

I'd never heard or seen Safir like this. The tiger shifter was usually so... shifty. I couldn't help a tiny smile at my own pun. But this Safir wasn't the behind-the-scenes mastermind, but an orator of force and persuasion.

I had to admit, the man really was a boon, despite how much we'd butted heads in the beginning. Perhaps I hadn't given him enough credit. He had been an ass, but he was doing it all for the right reasons at least. He'd been fighting for my family when I'd been in diapers.

"For many thousands of years, so many of us have lived under some form of oppression or suppression. Whether you be dwarves, once elves but shunned by your own kind, or hobgoblins, created as servants, never knowing any other life. Perhaps you're dragons, proud and strong, fighting someone else's wars, or seraphim and salmaeri, forced into combat against forces in your realms. For all the nymphs and dryads, who lived in peace, but dreamed of more, and for all the pixies who've served, and the shifters who've died, it is time to take a stand, time to rise up and face our oppressors!"

A deafening cheer rose and persisted.

A shiver ran through me. Wow. Safir really knew how to inspire a crowd.

"And," Safir continued as the cheer began to die down, "here, to lead you into that new future, to stand with you and fight beside you, is a woman of two worlds, a half breed royal, someone who can, *and will*, finally change our fates and the fate of this very world!"

Another cheer as Safir motioned to me and I stepped forward.

Okay... I had no idea how I was going to compete with that, but Zora and I had spent hours on my speech and I had to hope it would speak to everyone here.

I laid the papers out before me on the lectern, taking several deep breaths and studying the first line as the cheer slowly died.

"My people," I began, voice cracking with nervousness. I cleared my throat and began again. "My people... and I can say that, because I have lived among you. I may be an elf, but I am not of their world."

Silence had fallen. The cheer faded. As I paused — yes even that pause was written into my speech — I looked out over the thousands arrayed before me.

"We have a chance, here and now, to change this world. I say we, because it will take all of us. I do not plan to rule alone. It has already been decided that when I become queen—" I'd really wanted to say "if" but Zora had insisted on "when," best to assume we'd win the fight to come, "—a ruling council shall be formed, composed of *all* people. Everyone shall have an equal voice. My own voice shall be one of many. I will be more of a figurehead, than a true ruling monarch."

I gave a nervous little laugh, feeling a teensy bit better as I worked through the speech. This next bit I'd insisted on putting in, even though Zora had thought it might minimize my potential.

"And that suits me just fine. I don't want that power. I'd rather it be in the hands of a democratic government. I will fight for you, with you, beside you. I will work to free you all, but once this war is finished, I will not seek to rule you. My goal is to have you rule yourselves."

A wave of applause, starting with a scattered few, then growing, washed over the crowd. As I waited for it to die down, a glint of light from deep in the audience caught my attention. Maybe someone was taking a picture?

I dismissed it.

"Let me be clear," I continued. "Everyone. Will. Be. Free." I punctuated those words with a soft pound of my fist on the lectern. "Dragons will no longer be protectors of the realm. They can choose to be whatever they wish. We already have an envoy speaking with the titans to stop the generations of bloodshed between us, and with peace in this realm, there will be no need for such protectors."

A bit of movement down one of the aisles caught my attention, someone getting up and moving forward slowly. I ignored them and kept going.

"Those who fight in Elysial and Urval will be given sanctuary here, and we shall endeavor to make peace with the ages-old enemies in those realms as well. No one will have to fight and die, no one will have to serve. Everyone shall be judged on their own merit and—"

I caught sight of the projectile, but too late. The crossbow bolt, fired by someone below, hit the lectern and deflected to one side, just missing me.

Men rushed the stage.

What the...!

Koar roared, racing to my side. Vyns blasted light. Rook threw fire. Even those in the seats below us fought, but the attackers seemed to be everywhere. Three men, clad in black, leaped — clearly enhanced in some way — hundreds of feet over the audience to land on the stage, engaging with Koar. They had weapons, but he didn't, using his own toughness to take their attacks, and his hands and feet to beat them back.

Other attackers soared down from above, wings on their backs. They'd go right over Koar and Vyns and Rook, who were engaged with those on the ground.

I summoned water from the air and slashed a thin wave

at them, cutting several of them down, but a handful still landed nearby.

The stage was made of wood, not stone, but I could still summon earth from farther below me. A wall shot up between me and the attackers, shattering the wooden stage. But I should have realized how silly that was... since they had wings.

Three quickly reached the top of the wall, clambering over, weapons ready.

A tiger-man-thing roared from nearby and leaped up to meet them... Safir in hybrid form. Wow, he was scary.

The fight closed in on me, my defenders blocking my view of the audience and everything else as more and more men rushed the stage, there had to be hundreds of them!

How naïve I'd been to assume this wouldn't happen, that Valnea wouldn't send assassins to take me out. Of course she would.

Safir leaped back off the wall, having dealt with the flyers, and landed beside me, bloody and wounded, but still going strong.

Another attacker pushed past Koar, who was taking on five others. I slashed water at the assassin and took him down.

But then two more rushed me from the other side.

I took one down with water while Safir engaged with the other, using tooth and claw.

Then... as suddenly as it had begun... it was over.

Koar spun to check on me.

"You okay?"

I nodded. "Yeah, you?" The big man didn't look okay, covered in wounds, some deep and bleeding. I went to heal him, but he stopped me.

"I'll be fine, dragons are immune to Kanali poison."

Poison?

"Help him." Koar pointed behind me and I turned to see Safir stagger and fall. He'd killed that last attacker but was clutching a dagger in his stomach.

I rushed to the shifter as his hybrid form faded and he returned to human, but that only exacerbated the wound, since this form was smaller, the knife cut him deeper when he shrank.

I laid my hands on his exposed chest, the suit he'd been wearing torn to ribbons. He pulled out the knife and tossed it far from me, smiling through his pain as I tried to heal him.

"Of all the ways—" Safir convulsed with a gurgling cough, "—I thought... I might die." He winced in pain, going limp, weakening. "This is... the least expected... and the most welcome."

"You're not dying!" I hissed at him, but something was wrong. His body was healing, his wounds closing, yet he still grew weaker. When I sensed into him, the grotesque taint of the poison was somehow everywhere in his system. It was too virulent, too strong. I couldn't heal it fast enough!

"I... fulfill... my oath." Safir struggled to say the words, then he gave a wan smile and went still.

"No!" I screamed, pushing everything I had into healing him, but even as my strength drained, the poison persisted. What the hell was this stuff?

And with my senses infused into Safir's body... I *felt* him die. His heart stopping, his life slipping away, the poison turning more and more of his tissue into necrotic filth.

"No, no, no, no, no!" I shouted. "You can't die!"

But my words did nothing.

Safir was gone.

AMARHUK (ROOK)

IZZY'S SPEECH DID NOT CONTINUE. THERE WAS TOO MUCH TO clean up, too many dead to continue with a speech about hope.

Looking at the devastation, the fire inside me burned with rage. Izzy had been the primary target of the assassins, that was clear, but it seemed sowing doubt and fear by killing any in their path and as many innocents as possible had also been an objective.

Koar got Izzy to safety, while Vyns and I stayed behind to help with the cleanup. And Safir... Fuck. His body had slowly disintegrated on stage, a blackened, festering husk.

Kanali poison was nasty stuff. One of the few toxins to which elves were vulnerable. It also wreaked havoc on any other natives of Seial, which had been most of those in attendance. Dwarves, dryads, nymphs, hobgoblins, and pixies were the most vulnerable with undines and tritons having a greater resistance. While those of us from Urval or Elysial were immune. And the assassins had unleashed several aerosol bombs of the poison into the crowd in addition to their weapons being coated in the stuff.

By the time evening had set in, we'd sorted through the bodies: one hundred attackers in total, all dead, and nearly seven hundred others killed in perhaps the worse way possible.

It was a gruesome scene.

The assassins themselves were mostly shifters, with a few pixies — known for their illusion magic and tricky ways — and a smattering of sylphim, dwarves, and elves, who'd probably been the leaders.

By that point the cleanup was well underway and handled by others, so Vyns and I could go, but I lingered, staring at the black stain on the stage where Safir had died. He'd probably saved Izzy's life. We'd all been fighting to protect her, but despite our best efforts some of the assassins had managed to get close and Safir had sacrificed himself to save her.

This was war. The horror we had ahead of us.

Valnea wouldn't play fair. Izzy would never do anything like this… but a part of me wondered if she didn't, would we still win?

"Come on, let's go," Vyns said, a hand on my shoulder, a boost of spirit helping to tear me away from my contemplation of Safir's sacrifice.

When Vyns and I returned to Izzy's residence, we told her what we'd discovered, and she was baffled.

"Shifters?" she breathed. "Why? Why would they still fight for Valnea, die for her, when I was promising a better life, where they didn't have to live every day in fear of death?"

"They probably had no clue who you were," Koar explained. "There are cabals of shifters who live their whole lives in seclusion, training as assassins for the crown, perfectly expendable and trained to be completely loyal."

"Ugh!" Izzy grunt-shouted. "I just... can't even!" She paced, distraught and frustrated and furious.

Vyns and I exchanged glances, both thinking the same thing. For all of Izzy's spirit and desire to change this world, she really had no clue how dark things got here.

"There's probably far worse than that going on in the depths below the capital," Vyns said, voicing what I'd been thinking. "This is the depravity you're fighting against."

Izzy stopped. "Could any of the audience be saved?" she asked, clearly concerned. I couldn't imagine the empathy it took to worry for so many others, who you didn't know at all. It blew my mind.

"About twenty," I said. "Though surviving Kanali poisoning is a life sentence of pain and chronic injury."

"Of course it is." Izzy threw her arms up and began pacing again. "Remind me to have the stuff banned when I'm queen. Oh... and to have a war-crimes tribunal for any who were involved in this, who survive the war." She stopped again, vibrating with rage. "I'm going to win this war, no matter what. I have to. This is just... intolerable!"

It was... and it was also what we'd all lived with our whole lives. To us, this was another day under the brutal regime of the elves. None of us said as much to Izzy, though.

And seeing Izzy so worked up and ready to fight made every instinct inside me want to pull her close and fly away with her, keep her safe. Now that I'd accepted my feelings for her — as much as it pained me to be monogamous — I was afraid all the time, worried something would happen to her and my heart would shatter.

I was terrified of losing Izzy. I don't think I'd ever fought as hard as I had today. I couldn't let anyone hurt Izzy, but also... I couldn't die knowing the pain she'd feel if I did. I'd been more motivated than ever, all because of a dread fear of loss.

I couldn't lose her. I didn't know what I'd do. I'd seen how Izzy had reacted when Myel had died, so lost and broken and even though Izzy and I didn't share a bond like that, I had a feeling I'd not be much better.

At the same time, I couldn't let her lose me either. If she cared for me as much as I did her... then how could I ever leave her and have her face that devastating pain.

But we were going to war for fuck's sake!

People were going to die.

I had to somehow make sure Izzy and I weren't among the dead, and that no longer seemed as easy as it had yesterday.

I tuned back in to the conversation as I sensed a change in Izzy's thoughts, moving from rage and ranting to cold determination and planning.

"The dwarves and undines have to come to our side now, right?" she asked. "Some of their kind were killed. Won't they see that as an act of war and retaliate?"

Again, Izzy didn't know this world.

"No," Koar said before I got there. "If anything, they'll further retreat into their cowardice. This attack was meant to show them they could be reached anywhere, anytime."

"Fucking hell, really?" Izzy shouted. She shook her head. "No, I won't accept that." She turned to me. "Get Svokol here, now. I need to talk to him."

Before I'd even gotten out my phone, she'd continued on. "And Rook?"

I paused in dialing. "Yeah?"

"You're part concubi and salmaeri, right? Do you think both races would listen to you if you went and talked with them?"

Me?

I shrugged. "They might. The dwarves are their masters, though. They probably wouldn't go to war unless the dwarves commanded them to."

"No more masters, no more commands," Izzy stated. "Tell them as much. Tell them if they come and fight for me, they'll be free to do whatever they wish after this."

"The dwarves—" I began to protest.

"Can suck balls for all I care," Izzy shouted over me.

I had to smile at that.

"If they don't like it, they should have been a part of this from the start. But if they're going to go and hide in their caves, and wait for the outcome, knowing that one of those outcomes is me winning and liberating everyone, then they have no recourse if I happen to liberate their forces a little early."

"That might turn the dwarves against you," Koar warned.

"Oh, don't worry, that's why I need Svokol. He's going to take me to see the leaders of the dwarves, and I'm going to tell them how it's going to be. Their choices are simple: fight for me, alongside those they've commanded for so long, or fight against me and I'll steal their followers out from under them to fight against them, because who wouldn't fight their oppressors for freedom. Or they can stay out of it, but I'm still taking their followers. Either way, they're going to lose their so-called minions. Hopefully they'll see that fighting *for* me means they'll be better off afterward."

I finished dialing Svokol. And while it rang, I marveled at how incredibly sexy it was to watch Izzy take control and tear down thousands of years of hierarchy.

"Rook?" Svokol answered.

"Get to Izzy's residence now." I hung up and felt a tad

guilty about not giving the man an explanation, but I also was getting caught up in Izzy's fervor. Svokol was a good man… but he'd also been my master. And all of that was going away. He didn't control me anymore, not that he'd ever been controlling, but still. I felt… liberated in Izzy's presence.

"Vyns." Izzy was on a roll. "You head to Elysial, offer the same thing to the seraphim. I don't think any sylphim will listen, but if any do, great. I'm not going to wait. I'm liberating folks now. If they're willing to fight for me, they can do it as free men and women."

Vyns nodded. "Will do."

This was happening.

Izzy was tearing down walls and freeing people who'd been beholden to others for thousands of years. Izzy had said in her speech that she didn't want to rule, didn't want power. I'd sensed her thoughts at the time, about how she wouldn't know what to do with power if she had it. But it seemed she knew exactly what to do.

She was taking control now, stealing it from the dwarves and the elves wherever she could. Izzy might not want to rule, but she'd be damned good at it, always fighting for the freedom of others.

The woman before me was a queen in truth, if not crowned yet.

And overcome by this realization. I fell to one knee, head bowed.

"It's damned sexy to watch you work, my queen," I said.

Izzy's thoughts stuttered.

"I'm not…" she stammered.

"Oh, but you are," Vyns said, and he knelt as well. "I will do as you ask, my queen."

"I will stand by your side, my queen." This from Koar as he knelt as well.

I looked up, seeing Izzy a bit dazed by this.

"This is... too much," she whispered.

"If you think so, then you haven't been listening to yourself, my queen," I said. "You've just vowed to take control of two armies and undermine thousands of years of authority... and... I'm pretty sure it'll work. That's the act of a queen."

She blinked. "Huh... I guess... so?"

I loved that she was so humble she couldn't see it.

Svokol burst through the door behind me. "What's wrong?" he panted. He must have sprinted here.

I craned my neck to look behind me and couldn't help my smile when Svokol, seeing we three men all kneeling... slowly sank to his knees.

"What... do you need of me?" he said, his tone turning submissive, compliant.

Izzy laughed. "I need you to stand up, then I need you to take me to see the dwarven leadership. I have a message for them I'd like to deliver in person."

Svokol stood. "Yes m'lady," he said without hesitation. "I'll make arrangements to leave first thing tomorrow." Then he rose and left.

Izzy sighed heavily. "Tomorrow," she echoed. "Which means... this is my last night with you three... together."

I caught the shift in her thoughts, she needed us, needed a distraction from everything.

"I don't suppose you'd consider helping your queen forget the shitstorm that is her life?" Her tone held a note of weariness. "I really could use a break from being the boss and thinking about the death and destruction at my doorstep."

The three of us rose and went to her, three pairs of arms wrapping around her.

"Just never forget the boss-bitch you just showed us," I whispered to her. "That's who you really are. We all know it. Hopefully you do too."

"Thanks for saying that. I'll try not to forget her, but that's not how I want to be with you." She looked around at the three of us.

"Out in the world, we serve you," Vyns whispered.

"But here, when we're alone, we're whatever you need us to be," Koar finished.

"So... what do you need?" I breathed playfully.

"I need to forget. I need to be naked and screaming. I'll leave the details to you," she replied.

I had a feeling we could make that happen.

IZZY

STANDING THERE, WITH THREE DELICIOUSLY SINFUL MEN pressed close around me, something clicked inside me. This was right. Having these men here with me was everything I wanted. As much as they'd helped me realize I was a "boss bitch" and could lead people, that still wasn't what I wanted out of life. But this, this warmth, this closeness, this intimacy with these men. *That's* what I wanted.

I wanted Vyns, my perfect angel. I wanted his spirit, proud and strong, mixing with mine. I wanted his pristine blue eyes and those feathery white-gold wings. I wanted his support and strength.

And Rook, I was so very thankful he was back to being a friend and lover. Despite feeling like he still held something back from me... I wanted his sinful and playful presence. I wanted his crude honesty and his banter. And let's not forget his devilishly delicious orgasms.

With Koar, his stalwart and trustworthy dedication was becoming a fixture in my life, and I hadn't realized how much I'd needed something like that, someone who was always there for me.

And I wanted Myel's comforting presence. Even the anticipation of it soothed me. There was something to be said for the soft and persistent devotion of my beautiful Goth hero.

I couldn't imagine any of them not being in my life. I needed all of them. We hadn't said any vows... but they'd all become my husbands in essence if not in truth. Although maybe we had said vows. Maybe every promise, every word of support and care, maybe those were our vows.

I wanted all these men in my life, but the little voice of doubt in the back of my mind kept wondering: *can I really have it all?*

Would we all survive this coming war?

...or Valnea's assassins?

God! Safir... I still couldn't believe he was gone. I'd never truly known or understood that man. How could he have been so... *happy* sacrificing himself for me? How many others would die in my name?

And, what about Bayn?

Those thoughts and questions melted away as soft kisses and roaming hands forced my attention back to my body and the heavenly sensations these three gorgeous men elicited.

We had all evening to be together, but there was a heavy undertone of urgency in our play that night. Once stoked, our fires all burned a little too bright. What began as leisurely and playful removal of clothes became a hurried and awkward thing by the end. The graceful union of three men working as one turned into fumbling and soft curses as they got in each other's way. Still, we managed to make it to the bed in the end.

Koar, who'd carried me, set me down right at the edge, then urged me to lay back as he knelt beside the bed. I lifted my legs onto his shoulders and hummed with contentment as his perma-stubble scraped the inside of my thighs, the perfect roughness to counter the pleasure he provided with his tongue and lips.

Rook and Vyns lay to either side of me, and I reached out to find two thick erections as they took their time kissing all over my face and shoulders and chest. My head lolled over to face Vyns, and his lips found mine in a deep kiss, his hand stroking over my side and belly and arms. Rook's heated kisses seemed to draw raw lust out of me, amplifying the work the others were doing. And I massaged their lengths with slow strokes... during the moments when pleasure wasn't overwhelming me and I remembered I had hands to work with.

And when Koar slid a thick finger inside me to press on my G-spot while Rook's sinful lips plucked at a nipple, a soft and soothing orgasm swept through me.

"Hmmm, yes, more!" I murmured through the low-rolling waves of pleasure. But where there'd been an unspoken unity in their movements last night, the guys all seemed to get in each other's way as they tried to shift around me. Vyns somehow kicked Koar in the side of the head while Rook elbowed Vyns in the solar plexus.

Sorry, My Flame, Rook apologized directly into my mind. *I should be the one coordinating this, but I'm too distracted by thoughts of being away from you... and convincing my kind to overthrow the dwarves and go to war.*

I understand, I don't want to be away from any of you either, I replied. I also sensed there was more going on in Rook's mind, but those thoughts weren't open to me.

And with the guys all getting in each other's way, it seemed I'd have to take control like I had earlier.

"If you can't work together, then you'll have to take

turns," I said, tone stern, a bit frustrated at this awkwardness. And when it looked like they were about to start arguing over what order to go in, I spoke up again. "Vyns first, then Koar. Rook last.

Best for last? Rook chuckled into my mind.

Don't tell the others that or you won't get a turn at all.

Fair.

Because as much as Vyns and Koar could send me over the moon, Rook's orgasms were on a whole other level. It was hard to compete with a sex demon.

So Koar and Rook slid to the sides of the massive bed while Vyns took his time with me. The angel put the "D" in devoted attention, first ensuring I was well worked up again, his tongue and teeth and massaging fingers making me a sodden mess before he entered me. And when he did, I wrapped my legs around him and he lifted me onto his kneeling lap. We moved together slowly, savoring this intimacy, his arms tight around me as mine were around him. His lips plucked gently at my breasts before he tilted his head back and I lowered my mouth to his as our merging culminated.

I moaned and shuddered as heated bliss took me. He grunted with his release. Our bodies were pressed so close I could feel the beat of his heart through his chest into mine. He flashed out his wings, so I could stroke the soft feathers behind him. Then he wrapped them around me, a cocoon of downy warmth. With me leaning over him, we hid behind the veil of my hair as our lips brushed lightly, foreheads pressed together. Then I pulled back, rocking softly on him, to draw out more from this peak. Our eyes locked onto each other's. I was the only thing in his world and he the only thing in mine.

That might be the most intimate encounter I'd ever had.

Wow.

"I'll miss you so much," he breathed.

"And I you," I replied.

I leaned in to kiss him again, long and lingering. And through that kiss we demonstrated how much we'd miss each other.

Then Vyns' wings brushed away and he slowly lowered me back to the bed.

Koar let me rest.

"What do you need?" he asked between light kisses all over my face.

"Just you, however you want me, however you need me," I mumbled dreamily, already feeling rather amazing. I'd forgotten all the awkwardness from earlier. It was astonishing what a good orgasm could do for you.

"Then relax," Koar whispered.

That I could do. I was pretty darned relaxed as it was. Though I was a bit curious exactly what the big man was going to do with me while I was relaxed.

He stayed where he was for a while, kissing me from his side, while his free hand roamed over my body, sometimes gently massaging my breasts to pleasant stimulation, sometimes sliding down to softly stroke my clit or test my folds. All of it kept me at a nice buzz... until his hand began to do a little more between my legs.

I hummed with rising pleasure as he slipped a thick finger inside me and curled it around as the base of his hand pressed over my clit. He rocked his hand back and forth, stimulating me inside and out. His lips drank down my moans as he got me all nice and wet and ready.

Then, finally, he shifted.

Still curious what he'd do, I watched as he straddled one leg and ever so slowly entered me. The delicious stretch of his thickness was like the best drug, sending tingling euphoria through me, all nice and relaxed and gooey.

My breath hitched with surprise when he slid my other leg in, now straddling both with his dick still inside me. And the way my legs squeezed around his thickness made him feel mind-breakingly massive as he gave gentle thrusts, deepening his contact.

My breath hitched again, when he shifted up my body, his legs now to either side of my torso as he leaned down to kiss me.

Oh! My! God!

The way his dick massaged my clit as he shifted in and out was *next level* good. It took all of three slow, delicious thrusts before I was coming hard, mewling and grunting and moaning against Koar's smiling lips.

"Thought you'd like this," he whispered.

I did.

A lot.

Very much.

Yes please!

He winced. "So. Tight!"

Yeah, I bet, given how colossal he felt. Even so, he took his time picking up speed, drawing out my orgasm over several mind-blurring minutes before he finally lost his cool and with a series of hard, vicious thrusts which put my perma-orgasm into overdrive, he finally grunted and heat pulsed with his release.

"Damn," he grunted. "You're too fucking sexy."

I was.

And so was he.

His lips played on mine as he finished. The other nice thing about this position was, he could put however much force on me he wanted, controlling the weight of his heavy body, not crushing me. He leaned over me, putting the right amount of pressure everywhere as we ebbed down from that stunning high.

When I'd initially told the guys to go one at a time, it was to sort them out and make it less awkward, but I realized now, there was another benefit. They'd each in turn give me an orgasm. And I had a feeling, as intimate as Vyns had been and as surprisingly powerful as Koar's had been... Rook was going to be an even more sinful delight.

"Can you stand... walk?" Rook asked as Koar rolled off me.

If I'd still been a human... huh, I'd never actually *been* a human, had I? If I'd still been a nymph, I probably wouldn't have been able to stand. I was a very satisfied puddle of goo. Yet, as an elf, I was stronger, sturdier. I slid off the bed and onto my feet. Yup, strong as ever.

But still.

"I thought you might like a shower after all that," Rook said.

Ooooh, shower sex? Yes please!

I held out my arms to him.

He cocked his head.

"Just because I *can* walk, doesn't mean I don't *want* you to carry me in there."

That devilish grin slid onto his lips and he stepped in to sweep me off my feet.

"Come on, you two, this involves you as well," Rook said to Vyns and Koar.

Curious, I wondered what he had planned.

Rook carried me into the spacious bathroom, and right into the massive walk-in shower. He set me down and turned on the water.

Vyns sat on the edge of the tub, Koar leaned on the vanity.

"Are we coming in?" the angel asked.

"Nope," Rook replied, that mischievous grin playing over his lips. "You get to watch as I teach our little nymph how to be an exhibitionist."

Vyns grinned, brow raised. Koar cocked his head but didn't seem upset by this.

Once the water was perfect, Rook and I stood under the wide spray, close and slippery, his lips finding mine in a long and sensuous kiss. I don't know why, but there was something a little extra sexy about doing it in the shower. All that water, the slippery skin, the wet heat all around us.

Then, suddenly Rook tore his lips off mine and I caught only a flash of his cocky grin before he spun me around.

Oh!

He pushed me up against the steamy glass of the side of the shower, then pressed himself against me.

Vyns and Koar, on the other side of the glass, both suddenly perked up, seeing my body pressed hard to the glass.

"They're going to see everything," Rook whispered, hot breath on my ear. "They're going to watch me make you come so hard that they can't stand it. They'll be stroking their dicks, ready again, because you're too damned sexy for them."

"But not for you?" I asked, liking where this was going.

Rook pressed his cock between my butt cheeks, so I could feel how hard he was. "Oh, you're too sexy for me too. It's been torture watching you come, feeling your passion, and not being inside you."

The heat coursing through me had nothing to do with

the hot water around us and everything to do with Rook's words and his searing arousal, hot body pressed to mine.

With a quick dip, his cock traced a scorching line between my legs and right up into my waiting folds, slipping inside me.

"Fuck, yeah, you feel so damned good," Rook purred behind me. I had a feeling he'd done something to me while we'd been kissing. He shouldn't feel this wonderfully large inside me after Koar, but as an incubus, he could refresh me, tighten me, make me ready again, and I was.

His hands came to my hips as he began to thrust, pushing me harder against the glass, my body shifting and squeaking as he pounded into me.

And yup, Vyns and Koar both had rising erections in their hands watching me. This felt... so wrong *and* so very right at the same time. I shouldn't be letting others see me this open and vulnerable and intimate... but it was two men I trusted and that changed everything.

Rook's hands slid up my sides till his fingers brushed the sides of my breasts, and there, he traced around where that soft flesh was pressed tight to the glass. And where he touched, searing lust zapped into me.

Having my aroused, sensitive chest pressed hard to the glass hadn't been comfortable, but now, with my nipples achingly hard as well, the whole area even more responsive... it verged on pain, extremely pleasurable pain.

I let out a very unladylike sound as Rook's cock slammed home, deep inside me, his body pressed hard to my back, with the glass pressed to my front like it was another lover.

"You like that?" Rook whispered. Then he did it again, one quick thrust to tap that secret, deep place inside me.

I mewled, so damn close to an orgasm.

"They like it too."

I'd had my eyes lidded, the agony of bliss pounding through me so hard I wanted nothing more than to find my release and let it all out. But I blinked my eyes open and focused on the other two.

They both stood, watching, hammering their cocks. Both seemed ready for another round, and I wasn't sure I'd be up for one after this. Was this night ever going to end?

I mean... not that I'd mind steamy sex all night.

"Do you want to feel their hot cum spraying all over you?" Rook whispered, as he jabbed his dick perfectly into me once more. "That's what they want, to watch you come, then blow their loads all over you. They can't control themselves. You make them lose control, My Flame."

I grunted. I couldn't talk.

Yes! I screamed into Rook's mind.

I thought so. Didn't I say best for last?

He had, and this was.

"You two, get in here," Rook called as he pulled me away from the glass, wrapping his arms around me to keep me close as he continued his hard, piercing thrusts from behind.

God! I was so damned close... In fact, I had a feeling Rook was doing something to delay my release, the pressure of pleasure building inside me, a massive crescendo.

Vyns and Koar joined us, replacing the glass, pressing close to me, their hands on my body. Well one hand on me, the other still wrapped around their dicks, pumping hard. Their lips found my hair, my face, my mouth, my... oh my oh my!

"Watch her come," Rook whispered, and with one final thrust the dam inside me burst and I came with screaming abandon.

"Keep your eyes open, watch them, watch what you do to them," Rook breathed into my ear.

I did. I watched as Vyns and Koar saw me shatter and shake and come so hard I seemed to lose control of my body.

The two powerful men grunted, jerking themselves harder, then both came in gushing waves, blasting their releases onto my body, even as the shower washed it away.

Fuck, that's perfect, Rook purred in my mind, then he lost control as well, pumping his release inside me, his body shuddering in time with mine.

If you'd asked me before this, if having two guys come on me in the shower was sexy — if I wanted that — I'd have said *hell no, gross, why?*

But Rook was right, there was something powerful about knowing I'd made these men lose control, all three of them. And it was sexy as fuck to watch and feel what I'd done to them.

And when we had all finished, we stayed under the water, the guys taking turns washing me and themselves. I was squeaky clean afterward, having been soaped up and rinsed down three times, because they each wanted a turn.

Then we all returned to the bed and collapsed.

Tomorrow we'd go our separate ways, but for tonight, we were together. All but Myel. I hoped my beautiful Goth hero was staying safe in the capital.

MYELAS

"We'll be ready to march in ten days," one of the elves below, a general, said to the false queen, Valnea.

I hid in the shadow of a column, on the second-floor balcony overlooking the massive round hall where the elves made their war plans. It had taken me a little over a day to shadow-step across the capital and get inside the palace. My ability to be next-to-invisible in shadows, jumping from one shaded place to another, was invaluable. No one knew I was here, and no alarms had been raised. There were sensors all over the palace to warn of someone using magic, but my ability was innate, not magical in nature.

I still took every precaution, hiding in little-used areas, keeping to the shadows the entire time, since my ability wasn't perfect. But it had gotten me this far, overlooking the queen and her advisors as they discussed their plans to assault Veilblood Academy.

"We'll have twelve wings of dragons, and four of sylphim for aerial assault," another general said.

That was eighty thousand warriors in the air alone!

The first man spoke again. "We'll have ten legions of

elves, assuming the seventh and ninth legions make it back from the wilds in time to march."

That was another fifty-thousand men, all elves, the strongest fighting force in all of the three realms.

The same man continued, "And we'll have five hundred dryads assigned to each legion to use tree-teleportation, moving each legion nearly instantaneously to the campus. We've picked five locations where we'll come out, hopefully surprising this upstart's forces."

That was extremely useful to know. Though where, exactly, would be better.

But then the general in question pointed to a map of the campus and mentioned the five locations in detail. Perfect. It looked like they planned to have three legions come out on the south end of campus, along the tree-lined cliff over the ocean. We wouldn't likely expect an attack from that side. Two legions each would come in from the east and west. A legion of "dummy" soldiers — cannon fodder shifters — would attack from the north as a distraction, engaging our forces while the others sneaked up behind us and slaughtered us. The last three legions would be stationed around the queen herself, also in the north.

It was a good plan; too bad I knew about it.

Now I just had to survive long enough to tell someone.

There was a little more talk of strategy after that, but it was mostly how they'd go about finding or luring out our commanders and Izzy, so they could be dealt with. They did not expect Izzy to be on the front lines.

The meeting broke up, and I instantly shadow-stepped away, to a shadowed corner of the royal suite. I'd already scouted the suite and had seven different shadows I could jump to if need be. When I hadn't found Valnea here previously, that's when I'd begun scouting the rest of the palace and overheard some servants talking about the meeting I'd just witnessed.

I waited for Valnea to return, masking myself in shadows, pulling them around me like a blanket. This would make it difficult to sense my life force or spirit. That was my one worry. Elves had power over creation, life itself. And the strongest elves could sense all living beings around them. Valnea certainly could do so... the question was: would she even think she needed to while safe within her own rooms?

While I waited, my thoughts slipped back to my last conversation with Izzy. Her words still haunted me.

There is only one reason I'd ever consider breaking our bond, and that is if you *asked me to.*

I want you in my life. Period.

How many times do I have to say it?

Apparently a few more. Some part of me still couldn't quite believe I was worthy of her. And she'd been right to say that was on me. I had a deeply ingrained belief that I wasn't worthy of anything or anyone.

And yet... here I was, unseen in the capital, in the palace, spying on the queen, doing perhaps the most important thing for Izzy and the rebellion. I had to be worthy of something to be here, doing this, didn't I?

Though, that niggling little voice of doubt whispered that I was only here because I was expendable, unimportant. If I was caught, no one would miss me.

Even though I had tangible proof that that wasn't the case — that Izzy would very much miss me if our bond was broken — the voice persisted.

In my head I was starting to see the value I had to Izzy, to Safir, to others. I was starting to truly *feel* my strength and capabilities. And yet, in my heart, I still felt like nothing. Not all the time, but enough to make me wonder what it would take to get past this persistent negative belief.

Footsteps approached and I pulled the shadows tighter around me.

Five dragons entered first. They spread out and did a visual inspection of the room. It seemed the false queen was paranoid. I leaped around from shadow to shadow, avoiding the five dragons as they searched every corner, never noticing me. Dragons were strong in spirit and if they hadn't noticed me, I had to assume my shadows kept even my spirit concealed.

They gave the all-clear, and Valnea entered.

She gave one cursory glance around — never even looking in my direction — then dismissed the dragons.

She was alone.

I didn't move, barely breathed. I didn't know what, if anything I might get from the queen while she was alone, but I hoped for something. And I was rewarded.

Valnea began muttering to herself, her ramblings slowly getting louder.

She let out a strange child-like giggle and spoke loud enough for me to hear as she paced frenetically around her suite.

"Yes, yes, yes, all coming together, all together. They'll pay. They'll all pay. They'll die and I'll live. Yes, perfect. Yes."

I'd known, in theory, that Valnea wasn't all there, but hearing her ramblings for myself was extremely disconcerting. How did everyone not know she was insane? She must have some awareness of it herself and have hidden it from others.

"First I crush this half-breed, yes, easy prey, squashed, like a bug." She pressed her foot down into the floor as if stepping on a particularly offensive insect. "Easy enough.

She has no chance. Not against my armies. No, no, no!" Another manic giggle.

She didn't think we'd put up much of a fight. She didn't know Izzy, and that ignorance, matched with her arrogance, might be her downfall. I hoped.

"Then, while the elves are recovering, the titans attack, crush them all, kill them all. One. By. One." She punctuated the last words with three vicious stabbing motions. "Then the dwarves and undines retaliate and kill the titans while they're still weak. Then the dragons and sylphim kill the dwarves. Yes, yes, yes! Undines can rot beneath the waves, they don't matter."

By the spirits!

She wasn't just insane, she truly believed she could play these races against each other like puppets. And the sad part was, it might work. All you needed was the right push at the right time.

If the dwarves and undines knew any of this...

And that's when it hit me. We had to tell them. I had to get this information back to Safir and the others. I didn't know if the dwarves would believe a secondhand report, but... they had to. They'd help us if they only knew the true depths of Valnea's plotting and treachery against those she should be protecting.

Another giggle interrupted my thoughts.

"Yes, yes, yes, all together. Slay the nymphs, squish the shifters." She made a shivering motion as if we shifters were disgusting bugs that she both feared and hated. "Then free Urval from the pyrkai and take all those pretty incubi as my pets. Yes, yes yes." She had a way of running those three "yesses" together, each pitched a little higher, making her sound truly unhinged.

"All will be mine. No rivals, only servants. All together."

I shook my head. The fact that she didn't even see the hobgoblins and pixies as a threat, as anything other than what they currently were, administrators and servants, was debasing.

I waited to see if there was more, and there was, but it was all some repetition of what she'd already said, rambled into one long diatribe of madness.

I couldn't wait any longer, I shadow-stepped away.

There might be more information I could glean here, but I already had their war plans and Valnea's true intentions. I needed to get back to the others. I jumped from shadow to shadow, out of the palace, out of the capital, to where I was to meet my dragon when she returned.

I still had more than a day to wait for my extraction time, but I hid well, keeping to the shadows of the forest outside the capital. I prayed I could get this information back to our forces. If everyone knew how insane Valnea was... they'd have to join us. Then we'd have a fighting chance against the elven armies.

AMARHUK (ROOK)

One on one, or in a small group, I could be very persuasive, especially when it came to sex. I was an incubus after all. But trying to convince the hundreds of men and women, concubi and salmaeri, arrayed before me to go against the dwarves and fight with Izzy... I'd never admit it, but I was scared shitless.

It was also strange being back in Urval after being away for so long. I'd gotten used to the blue skies and warm-temperate climate of Seial. Here, in Urval, it was ragingly hot all the time, the skies a twisting maelstrom of fiery reds and twisting ashen clouds.

I'd been transported to the main military camp outside the city of Baelzerus. I'd be able to reach the greatest number of salmaeri and concubi here. At least those of fighting age. The hope was, they'd spread the word to those in the nearby city and all over Urval.

"My fellow warriors!" I began, a magical microphone amplifying my voice. "I have stood where you stand now, listening to our leaders tell us victory was near, that we can end this ages-long war with one last push, one last battle."

There were grumbles through the crowd. They'd heard similar things and knew them to be lies. The pyrkai giants were strong and solidly entrenched in their strongholds. We might take down a few, but there were hundreds and their dark rituals of fire, brought forth more every year.

"We all know it's a lie. This war will not end, not any time soon, not without a massive force from another realm helping us. We all know it."

More grumbles and a few shouts and cheers.

I had to speak fast; I could already see people running to tell their leaders. I was undoing generations of programming and hindering their fighting force.

"I am not here to offer you false promises, only a choice." I paused after that word, looking out over the group below. "How often have we been able to choose our own fate? So very rarely, perhaps, in the heat of battle, but even then, it is often a choice of life or death."

I had them on the line now, listening intently.

"My choice, I'm afraid, is not much better. I wish I could offer you life, a way out, a way to live free, with no more fighting. I cannot."

There were some grumblings at that, probably wondering what I *was* offering.

"Instead, I offer you this..." *Okay here goes.* I drew in a deep breath and continued. "I offer you a chance to throw off the shackles of our masters. I offer you a chance to fight for your freedom instead of fighting some interminable war. I offer one last fight, but unlike any fight you've been in before. Not against the pyrkai, but against the elves in Seial!"

That got some gasps and a whole lot of wide eyes staring back at me.

"Stop him!" someone shouted, still far away.

No one nearby moved, I had a few more minutes.

"Come with me, leave this desolate place. I know it is your home, all you've ever known, but we all know that staying here is a death sentence. Come to Seial and fight in the rebellion against the elves. A new queen has emerged, an elf, who is not an elf, a queen who truly cares for her people, who wants equality and freedom for all races. If you don't believe me, then come and listen to her, hear her words. Then you'll believe."

People were moving at the fringes of the crowd. My time drew short.

"This queen will fight her own kind to free not only the races of Seial from oppression, but all races, you included. Her fight is just, and she needs your help. And if she wins, if we all win, then there will be a place for you in the lush lands of Seial, where you can live in peace and never have to worry about war again!"

I got a few cheers at that... but not as many as I'd hoped. When I looked into the crowd, what I saw instead was the exhaustion of having fought their whole lives and me only offering them yet another fight.

People were closing in, nearing the stage. I had one last chance to sway these folks.

"The dwarves, our liberators and masters are on side with Izzy, this new queen." That was mostly a lie. A few dwarves were, but most didn't seem interested in fighting. Still, many here respected the dwarves, saw them as liberators of our kind, helping us in our ages-old fight against the fire giants.

"Fight with them, but more importantly... fight *beside* them as equals. For if we win this fight, we will have no more masters. We will be truly free! Fight with me. Fight with this new queen who seeks equality for all. Fight with all the races striving for freedom, and we'll have a chance to claim that freedom once and for all!"

Yup, time to go, several generals and their toadies were about to take me into custody.

I nodded to the dragon who'd escorted me here and he grabbed me and shifted back to Seial.

My job was done. I'd sown the seeds of dissent, of freedom. By this time tomorrow one of two things would happen. Enough of the army would mutiny and overthrow the current generals... or all thoughts of freedom would be quashed.

Honestly, I wasn't hopeful. I figured we had a fifty-fifty chance.

"Go back?" the dragon asked, not one for many words.

I nodded and gave different coordinates for my return. I'd stay the night in Urval and sneak into the military camp tomorrow to see which way things had swayed. Until then... I was overdue to visit my mother.

A trip I was both looking forward to... and dreading.

The dragon returned me to Urval in a dark alley, deep in the warrens of Baelzerus. They left once again, agreeing to meet me back here tomorrow, and I slipped away through the shadows to the small house I'd grown up in.

As soon as I entered, I was assaulted with sights, sounds, and smells from my childhood. The scent hit me first, even before I'd opened the door, eleg stew with my mother's signature mix of herbs wafted out to greet me. Nothing said home like eleg stew. Elegs were a small deer-like beast here in Urval. Their meat was tough and stringy, but when boiled with the right herbs it became as tender as a lover's kiss.

And even as I took in the familiar front room of the house, the sound of my mother humming also took me back to my early years. She always hummed, well, she had before my father had passed. It had taken many years for the pain of that loss to dissipate enough for her to hum again. The sound drew my gaze to the left, the kitchen, where my mother swayed gently to the tune she hummed, stirring the pot on the stove. When she saw me, she smiled wide.

"Amar!" She was the only one who called me that. Another callback to my childhood. "You're home. It's so good to see you!"

As she bustled out to greet me, I took in the view. Nothing had changed. The front room remained a picture from days past. The kitchen to the left, then a small dining area, then a small sitting area to the right. Three doors in the far wall led to a bathroom and two small bedrooms. It wasn't much, but it was home.

Then she wrapped me in a warm hug and my tensions eased. Only a mother's embrace could release so much stress from me. I wrapped my arms around her and squeezed her right back.

"Hello, Mother."

"You're just in time for lunch! Come, sit, tell me everything, where you've been, what you've been... doing..." Her words trailed off as she stood back to look at me. She saw something in my eyes that stilled her tongue.

"Oh... my," she whispered.

Might as well get this over with. "I... I'm in love," I breathed.

My mother's lips went tight, tears coming to her eyes. "Oh, Amar, no... I'm so sorry! This is terrible."

There it was. For many races, finding one's true love was a reason to celebrate, but among concubi... not so much.

"Come sit," she said, ushering me to the table and helping me sit as if I were an invalid. "Tell me everything. Perhaps it's not too late to break it off."

I sighed as I sat, and she took a chair next to me, facing me, my hands in hers, her dark eyes filled with compassion and regret.

"I do not think it can be undone," I said. "I... don't know if I could. She's..." There were too many words, none of them doing Izzy justice.

My mother's lips compressed even more, the pain of her own loss radiating off her. She nodded. "Yes, I know." Then another, "I'm so sorry. I never wanted this for you."

Because the loss of my father had devastated her. I'd been a child, but I'd had enough awareness to notice the change, the light going out of her eyes, the heaviness to her step, the tears.

"It feels great," I said, voice soft.

"I know, I know it does, so wonderful... until..." A faint hope glimmered in her eyes. "But perhaps... your life is safe? You can live in peace now?"

Yeah... that wasn't going to happen.

"I'm about to go to war against all the elven armies... and the one I love is leading the charge."

Tears welled in my mother's eyes, and she shook her head, overcome.

Here in Urval, war was a way of life, a permanent thing. We'd always been at war with the pyrkai, and most thought... we always would be.

My mother blinked her tears away and hardened. "Then you have to end it, now." Her tone brokered no argument. "Walk away before fate takes her, or you. The loss is too great. End it now, Amar, you must!"

Yeah... that's what I'd expected from her, and it dragged up all my fears around myself and Izzy. I knew how likely it was that one of us would die in the coming war. When I'd served in the forces here, I'd seen so many of my friends and comrades fall. And being such empathetic creatures, I'd felt my mother's pain after my father's passing, the drowning depths of her loss. I feared the same would happen to me... or Izzy, but what could I do?

"I can't leave her," I said. "I've sworn to help her, to... stay with her."

My mother squeezed my hands hard, her head falling in regret and loss all over again. She shook her head and couldn't seem to stop.

"I'm sorry." My turn to say it. "I... I tried to stay away from her, but... I couldn't. I tried pushing her away and we were still drawn back together. I don't know what I'd do if I lost her. I know it's going to hurt like hell, but... what can I do?"

"Nothing," my mother said, voice faint. "If you're that far gone... you're lost." There was a note of disappointment in her voice, which tore at my heart.

And that was that.

I'd failed my mother, done the one thing she'd warned me against, the one thing she feared for me more than anything else.

Needless to say, it was a subdued visit after that. We ate dinner in sullen silence, then I returned to my old room and had a fitful sleep, my dreams plagued with images of Izzy in pain or dying.

I left early the next morning, having slept little, out the door before my mother woke. I sneaked across the city, then met with a few old friends outside the military compound, who let me in.

The generals had met, swayed by my words and those of their own men... and had agreed to lend us as much of a fighting force as they could. They'd withdraw all of their forces from the front and keep only what was needed to defend our settlements. The rest would come with me to Seial. Twelve thousand Salmaeri and three thousand concubi.

I'd done it. I'd brought the forces of Urval into the fight.

So why did I feel like I failed?

VYNSIEL

My meeting with the angels of Elysial had gone exactly as expected. The seraphim were all for fighting for freedom, while the sylphim — those that had even deigned to come and listen — were fervently against helping the rebellion.

The sylphim had prospered under the elves and even more under Valnea, who trusted them for some reason. And in return, the sylphim were fervently behind the false queen. They were also against the seraphim leaving Elysial to help us.

If anything, that was the upside to this little revolution in the realm of sky and light. If all the seraphim left, the sylphim would lose their fighting force against the nephilim. If they wanted to continue the war here, they'd have to fight it themselves. Moreover, they'd not be able to send as many troops to help Valnea, since they'd need warriors to defend the cities of Elysial, in case the nephilim attacked.

In many ways, it was nearly as good a result as if the sylphim had joined us.

And once preparations were underway to transport the

seraphim to Seial — coordinating with dragons and others for the mass teleportation — I had another task to attend to.

My family had come crawling back to me.

They'd lost their position of privilege when I'd turned on Saldrea and now had next to nothing. They'd be coming with me back to Seial, but my mother had asked to speak to me before that happened, all formal and apologetic.

I entered the room where they'd gathered.

"I have a lot to do, my time is limited. What do you have to say?" I asked, all brusque business.

All three of them rose from where they'd been sitting, only to collapse to the floor, heads bowed, prostrating themselves.

"We wish to apologize, dear son," my mother said, voice muffled by her face to the floor.

I'd expected something like this, but not quite to this degree. I took only a half-a-second to enjoy this show of supplication. I wasn't a petty man.

"Get up and say your peace. I'm listening."

All three picked themselves up and sat once again, still looking contrite, though... for my brother at least, I sensed more than a little resistance to this process.

"We have seen the error of our ways," my mother said, speaking for all of them. "We see now, your queen, Izzy, to be the one true royal and we wish to... serve her as you do."

I caught that slight hesitation, as well as the look of ambition behind my mother's blue eyes.

Time to set some expectations.

"I'm glad you've come around, but let's be clear: I will not do anything to elevate you in any way. If you want to serve Izzy, you'll do so like the rest of the seraphim, by helping with the war effort. I plan to fight, and if you aren't willing to do the same, there will be no place for you in this new world."

Their hopes were dashed. The only reason they'd gone through this farce of an apology had been to get back the positions of privilege they'd once held, using my connection to the queen to do so.

Before they could complain or push for more, I went on. "The new queen is all about equality and freedom. If you come, if you fight, you will be equal to every other person who does so, not above them in any way, but also not below them. And if you wish for more than that... this new regime will be based on merit. You'll have to show how you can help, what you can do, then do it well, to earn any place of authority. There is no easy route to power. Understood?"

"But you're her right hand, are you not?" my father blurted. My mother threw him a scathing look and he shut up.

My brother missed that look and kept pushing. "You have a position of power, and all you're doing is fucking her, from what I've heard. Maybe if I shared her bed, she'd see what a real man could do."

It was everything I could do not to throttle the man.

"I have done far more than share her bed," I whispered viciously. "I betrayed Saldrea and endured torment the likes of which you've never known, both physical and mental. I have stood at Izzy's side through all her trials. I've fought with her, bled for her, given her everything I have, sharing my spirit with her when she needed it most. *That's* what's earned me my place of power. If you wish to endure the harshest torture an elf can dish out, leaving you on the brink of death, then suffer at the hands of a psychotic sylph, your mind twisted against you over and over, all in service of our new queen, then by all means do so."

I took a breath and smiled as I finished with, "And by the way, Izzy would kick you out of her bed in an instant. You are no man. You're a leech, and she'd know that the instant she saw you."

My brother lurched to his feet ready for a fight.

"Kinlastriel Stop!" my mother shouted and my brother, seething, slowly sat once more.

"We will fight," my mother said stoically. The next bit she said directly to her husband and my brother. "After the war, we shall see how best we can help and make ourselves useful." Then back to me. "Shall that suffice?"

"It shall," I said, just as formal. "Prove yourselves in this fight, and I will rescind my disownment of you as my family."

That was as far as I was willing to go, for now.

"Thank you, Vyns, we shall do our best," my mother said.

I nodded then left.

They hadn't learned, not yet. A part of me still hated them for everything they'd put me through growing up, and not supporting me when I'd come to them initially. And yet... I had to give them a second chance. Everyone deserved one. Izzy had given me one, a chance to leave Saldrea — though the cost had been high — and serve her. I'd been through hell and back since, and perhaps, once my family had gone to those lengths for Izzy and this new world, I could begin to see them as family once more.

I truly hoped they could change, even if a part of me doubted it was possible... well for Kinlastriel at least.

I spared no thought for them after that. They were doing their part, like every other seraph, and all would be judged equally. But first I had to get all these angels to Seial, a mammoth task. I had a lot of work to do, and little time to do it.

IZZY

THE REALM OF DWARVES WAS NOTHING LIKE I'D EXPECTED. AN ex had once forced me to watch a Lord of the Rings marathon. I'd ditched him and the evening after the first four-hour slog of a movie. From that, I recalled something about dark caves of rough stone with a few massive halls held up by great pillars.

The caves of the dwarves here in Seial, were entirely different. I couldn't even tell I was deep underground most of the time. The dwarves had used their earth magic to carve and magically support massive caves, where the ground was level and the dome above was enchanted to look like blue sky. Great glowing stones traversed the domes: magical, make-shift sun, providing brilliant light. Each cave was its own city, with buildings of solid stone. Other stone formations had been summoned, looking like bushes and trees, enchanted to move and sway in a non-existent breeze. Each little leaf was intricately depicted and delicate, despite being made of rock.

Svokol, my guide, had explained that despite their banishment to this place, the dwarves still longed for the forests which had been their home before their kind had been shunned and gone into self-imposed exile. As we'd made our way to my meeting with the dwarves, I'd asked him to remind me why the dwarves had left the elves.

"Elves, *true elves,*" Svokol emphasized the words with a heavy dose of sarcasm, "Are those who can wield creation magic. The most potent and powerful of all magics. Over time, some elves lost that ability, still strong with earth and body, but not able to create in the way our kin could. We were looked down on, became second class citizens. Yet we still had our elven pride and after a while we could take no more of it, and left, seeking to create a new world of wonder for ourselves."

I nodded, drinking in this information. All of it would be useful in dealing with the dwarves. I'd need to know their grievance with the elves if I wanted to coax them into fighting for me *against* those who'd once been their own kind.

We'd even managed to swing it so some high-level representatives from the undines would be here as well.

"There is something else you should know," Svokol said as we approached a massive building. It reminded me of pictures of ancient Greek buildings before they'd been ruins, with thick white marble columns lining the front and a low-triangle-peaked stone roof.

"I'm all ears," I said, trying to listen intently while gawking at the strangeness of this luminous underground world.

"The reason the dwarves conquered and pacified the trolls and ogres... then took control of Urval and brought the demons under their sway... it was all for *fear* of the elves."

I cocked my head, one brow raised. This was interesting.

"Go on."

"Long ago, we dwarves realized the arrogant supremacy of the surface elves might lead them to... try to conquer us, instead of letting us live our own lives, here in the depths."

"So, you made your own army," I finished.

Svokol nodded. "We never told them that, always suggesting our forces were at their disposal if needed, but in secret we feared them. Perhaps... because we understood them better than most."

"So... the dwarves have always secretly been ready to fight the elves," I concluded.

"Yes and no. We wished to be ready, in case *they* decided to fight *us*. Do you see the difference?"

I did.

"You would never actively go against them."

He nodded.

"Because... you feared their armies, their strength, their creation magic, and so on?"

Another nod.

I sighed. I'd hoped Svokol had been giving me a way in, something to use to convince the dwarves to fight, but instead, it had been the opposite. The dwarves had been prepared to fight their cousins for thousands of years, but never had, dreading any conflict with the surface elves.

I had my work cut out for me.

We entered that massive, Greek-esque building after ascending three dozen marble stairs. The interior was cool and spacious. Columns lined either side of the long main hall, but they had some magic on them, so they could be seen through with only a slight distortion. Two side aisles were filled with steps, which acted like seats, all filled with dwarves who'd come to hear me speak.

I hoped they liked what I had to say.

Svokol and I — and my constant shadow, Koar — passed through more dwarves sitting in chairs in the central portion of the hall, eventually reaching a stage at the far end.

There, we had a quick private talk with a female dwarf named Kuatha, a friend of Svokol's. She was sympathetic to our cause and had helped set up this meeting. She introduced me... then I stood to address the dwarves.

It felt like this had been all I'd been doing of late: standing up before large groups to convince them to fight. I'd rather be doing the fighting. That at least was straightforward. This talking wasn't my forte.

Still, I'd been told to be blunt and frank with the dwarves, which helped.

"All your lives, you've feared the elves," I began, a solid punch to dwarven pride. There were many unhappy grumbles throughout the crowd below. "You've prepared for the day you must fight them. That day is coming." That quieted them down a bit.

I drew in a long breath. "Valnea is insane. If you can't see that, then you're blind. We have proof she conspired with the titans, allowing their assassins into the palace so she could eventually take control, which she has. She killed her own kind." I let that sink in.

"If she can do that, coming for the dwarves is more likely than ever. Do I have solid proof she will? No. But if you can't see the writing on the wall, and you stay out of this fight, and I lose... you will have no one to blame but yourselves when she comes for you."

More grumbling.

Time to appeal to that same dwarven pride.

"You have been shunned and pushed aside for generations, when in truth, elves should be your brothers!" That got a few angry-sounding shouts against the elves. Good. "You have made a life for yourself down here, but if you help me now, if you win this fight, you can return to the forests of Seial, a true sky above you, equal with the elves and all races. Is that not what you have always wished for?"

Several cheers rose up... but not as many as I'd hoped for.

"Are you not sick of being treated as less than those who are your equals?"

A few more cheers, but also still far too many stoic faces out there.

"Now is the time to fight, to rejoin your brethren and all races on the surface and reclaim that which you lost so long ago!"

That was my big finish... but it got only scant applause and a few cheers.

Yikes.

Tough crowd.

"What if we fight with you and lose?" someone called out. "Valnea *is* mad, and if we join you, she *will* definitely come for us, but if we stay out of this—"

"Then you're only delaying the inevitable!" I shouted back.

"More time to prepare, and perhaps the elves will be worn down by then!" another yelled.

As I tried to find a comeback for that, someone else bellowed, "And are you not working with titans? Foul scum!"

And... there it was. Thousands of years of prejudice rearing its ugly head.

I wanted to shout back that titans were their brethren too, but a hand on my shoulder stopped me.

"Quit while you're ahead," Svokol whispered. "You've

convinced some and given the rest something to think about. That is... the best we could have hoped for."

I clenched my jaw to keep myself from screaming that I could do more, the dwarves could do more. I nodded at him and we left through a back entrance, leaving the dwarves to their debates.

We were quickly joined by a representative from the undines, dressed in flowing silks, her blue-pale skin shimmering with tiny scales. She bowed to me.

"Your words were moving," she said, but as soon as she did, I sensed her hesitation, her careful compliment before she shot me down. "But the dwarves are a staunch people. They are safe for now and convincing them otherwise proves... difficult."

"And the undines?" I asked directly.

She gave a sad smile and shook her head. "I will convey your words, but we, even more so than the dwarves are safe beneath our waves. The elves have no desire to conquer us. I fear we have little to gain from this fight."

And I couldn't even argue with that. She was probably right.

I sighed and tried not to look like someone had kicked my puppy.

"Thank you for your honesty," I said.

The representative bowed and made her exit.

"Well, this was a bust." I crumpled into a seat, head in hands.

"It was... the best we could have hoped for," Koar rephrased it.

Svokol nodded his agreement.

"I sure hope Bayn can bring the titans to our side," I said with a huff. "If he can't... even if the angels and demons join us... I fear it won't be enough."

"Do not concede the fight in your mind before it is fought," Svokol advised. It sounded like some old proverb.

He was right, though. Time to return to campus and see how the others had done.

~

"The titans will not follow me," Bayn spat. "The fools!" He stomped around the residence he'd taken over in a rage.

I wasn't happy to hear this either, but Bayn's fury seemed to extend deeper than this refusal. I guessed it had something to do with his control issues. I remained silent, letting the man rant.

"They've sided with my parents, with Valnea. She offers them destruction of the elves and a place of power once they've destroyed their mortal enemies."

I hesitated to question him, but... isn't that what we'd offered as well?

He quickly went on. "They don't like the idea of *equality* with the elves, they seek only their destruction." Ah... yes, that had been a qualifier for me. "Can't they see the bigger picture? Valnea will betray them, but they seem blind to that fact!"

He paced to a wall, punched a hole in it — not the first — then turned and paced back.

"They're betraying themselves! They're betraying—" He cut himself off.

Ah... so *that's* why he was so upset. He felt betrayed. It made me wonder if his need for control stemmed from some betrayal.

"I need to convince them, need to save them from themselves, but... Argh!" He'd gone beyond curses to raw sounds of fury.

And I had to admit, when he got like this, the massive man was more than a little scary. Koar was nearby, and I had a feeling, as an elf, I could probably take Bayn, but... I didn't want to test that theory here and now.

"Did *any* of them listen to you?" I tried.

"If they did, they didn't come forward, bloody cowards!"

"Is there any other way?" I asked. I was pushing him when I probably shouldn't, but the truth was, without the dwarves and undines we needed the titans.

"Only to challenge my parents, but that will take too long!"

"Perhaps—?"

"No!" He spun and shouted in my face. "It won't work!"

I slapped him. I'd hoped the sting of pain might startle him back to reality and some sense of calm. It didn't.

Bayn snarled and moved in on me. One massive hand clamped around my waist and lifted me, pinning me to a wall. Only, unlike last time, there was no arousal mixed with his anger.

"Don't you dare touch me," he hissed.

I waved Koar away, the dragon ready to come to my defense. I wasn't that hurt yet. And if things were ever going to work out with Bayn, he and I needed to sort them out ourselves.

"Get a grip. We need to think, to plan. We can still bring the titans—"

"Weren't you listening!" he shouted in my face.

Yeah... I wasn't taking any more of this.

I grabbed his face in both hands, what looked like soft rounded cheeks weren't. Every part of him was hard.

I brought his face close, his wild eyes meeting mine.

"I am not your enemy," I snapped. "*Listen to me.* Calm. The fuck. Down!"

Magic flowed through me, and I knew it was wrong even as it happened, but the animal-brain part of my mind was terrified of this huge man and his fury. Even knowing I was probably stronger didn't seem to matter. Power surged through me into him, binding him to my will.

"What the—!" He immediately released me and staggered back.

Well, fuck.

This was going to complicate things.

BAYN

Oh hell, no!

She did NOT just put a binding on me.

The fuck?

I tried to slap her, like she'd done to me, but my arm only got so far, frozen in the air. I pushed harder, muscles bunching so hard they'd hurt tomorrow.

I roared my fury in her face… or I would have, but nothing came out. In fact, my rage was slowly draining out of me, despite that I should feel even *more* enraged at this violation.

"What… did… you… do?" I forced those words out, inwardly irate at how calm I sounded.

"Fuck," she hissed. "Sorry, I didn't mean to do that. It just happened. I'm not trying to control you, but you were a smidge terrifying there, so forgive me if I acted on instinct. Still, I was wrong to bind you, let me undo it."

No!

I wanted to recoil. I would not let her touch me again. But my body didn't get the message. My head nodded as I knelt to her level, tilting up my face for her to touch as she had before.

This binding forced me to obey her.

It galled me to no end, how easily she'd subdued me. I was nothing to her, a pawn, a toy. And that *should* have infuriated me, but it didn't, because she'd even somehow mastered my emotions.

I'd been more than a little distracted by my rage at the time, but I tried to recall what she'd said when I'd felt her power take me.

Listen to me. Calm. The fuck. Down!

The command implicit in both phrases had been imprinted on my soul. I would listen to her, do whatever she asked, and I would do it all like a passive little baby. She hadn't even left me my own feelings!

This was outrageous!

But also, acceptable.

No! It wasn't acceptable at all! But I couldn't stay mad at her for any length of time *because* of the binding!

She placed her hands on my face as she'd done before and closed her eyes.

Nothing happened. Her power flowed into me... but my fury didn't return.

She grimaced, face tightening. "Ah... I know how to break a binding," she mumbled. "And I should be able to break my own, but... nothing's happening."

Fucking hell!

Or rather, this was fine, I was sure she was trying really hard.

No! Fuck! Stop that!

"Izzy? You okay?" the dragon asked. "What's wrong?"

She released me with a huff.

"Sorry," she whispered intently at me, then turned to

him. "I don't know. I put a binding on him, but now I can't remove it, and I really should. No one should be forced to serve another like this. It's wrong."

Hell right, it is!

And since I agreed with her, some anger returned. I'd been allowed to feel that one.

"Please," I asked politely, which should have galled me. "I humbly ask you to remove this binding."

Both she and the dragon looked at me like I had two heads.

"Wow... is the binding making you... nice?" she asked. She didn't have to make it sound like such a foreign concept.

"Yes," I answered honestly. "My fury has been... quelled."

Her eyes went wide and she gave a nervous little laugh. "Huh, didn't know I could do that. Sorry. Ah... let me try and undo it again."

She touched me once more.

Without my fury, other emotions took its place. Her soft hands, cupping my face, drew forth a pleasant warmth, a soft arousal. I certainly couldn't deny her strength now, not after she'd subdued me like a meek little lamb. And her beauty was... rather awe-inspiring, now that I was calm enough to see it and bask in it.

The truly strange part was, when I questioned myself and these feelings, wondering if they were part of the binding, I discovered... they weren't. She was not making me desire her. That was all me.

Her power flowed again. This time, she added words.

"I release you," she whispered. "You can feel what you like and do as you like."

Nothing.

"Come on!" she hissed.

The words may have been an expression of her desire to free me, but no words were needed to make or break a binding, just intent.

More power flowed into me, and I was a little startled at the scale of her abilities. She was far stronger than me. I should have expected as much. I'd assumed I was roughly as strong as Saldrea, though I'd never had a chance to test myself against the false princess. And Izzy had easily defeated Saldrea, so of course her power would exceed mine.

Still.

This woman's power was...

...turning me on.

Fuck. No. I didn't want a strong woman. Well, I did, but I wanted a strong woman who willingly submitted to me and let me control her. It had to be that way, so I could be sure she'd never betray me.

"Come on!" Izzy grunted and even more power flowed into me.

Something snapped.

All my fury came rushing back in a flood so powerful it physically pushed me away from Izzy. I screamed in rage, not even having the words to convey how fucking pissed I was.

And as thankful as I was that Izzy had let me go, I was also going to teach her a lesson about controlling another.

"I'm going to..." I growled, but I couldn't finish that sentence. As blindingly enraged as I was, I couldn't focus that fury on her. I couldn't hurt her. Only part of the binding had been undone.

"Fuck, you only removed part of it!" I roared. "Let me go!"

"Well, your emotions are back. Yay?" she said, with a

tired smile. "Sorry, but I tried as hard as I could to remove the binding, the rest... seems stuck for some reason."

Stuck?

Stuck!

"You'd better find a way to unstick it, fast!" I screamed at her, then since looking at her was only inducing more fury — and giving me a headache because I couldn't act on it — I stormed out.

Most of the royal residences on campus were along the cliff overlooking the ocean. I headed for that drop off and leaped right off it. Hardening my body and strengthening my legs, I landed on my feet, throwing up a massive cloud of sand, creating a five-foot-deep crater. Then I turned and began punching the rock wall behind me.

I tried to imagine the rock was Izzy, but I couldn't. Hurting her, even in my own thoughts, wasn't possible. So, I hammered my fists into the rock until my power waned, my fists turned bloody, and I'd carved a cave thirty feet deep into the cliffside.

Even then, exhausted as I collapsed onto the rock, my anger still rode me.

How could she do this? Controlling me. It went against everything I stood for to have a woman control me... *again*!

There was no way I'd ever trust her. The thought of our political marriage sickened me. Though, that seemed unlikely now, since I'd failed to bring the titans to our side.

My rage turned into a vicious self-loathing, and I threw myself against the jagged rock in this cave over and over to punish myself.

I'd failed.

I'd failed myself.

I'd failed my sister.

I'd failed my own kind.

I'd failed the world!

Never in history had there been a more epic failure than me.

Izzy — treacherous bitch that she was — didn't deserve me.

Perhaps I'd walk into the ocean and die.

I didn't, but I stayed in the cave, bloody and broken, contemplating it for a long time.

IZZY

I SOUGHT OUT LHORINE.

I had a little time before Rook and Vyns returned from their realms — hopefully with better news than Bayn — and really wanted to get this situation with the titan sorted. I didn't like that I'd put a binding on him, it was just plain wrong, no matter how much of a dick he'd been.

Royal's Hall, once the hang-out for the elves on campus, had been turned into our HQ. Lhorine was busy, along with my grandmother and Zora, organizing everything and everyone. I probably shouldn't be pulling her away from this, but if Bayn was ever going to get his head on straight and figure out some way to bring the titans to our side, then I needed to free him of this binding.

"Can I borrow you, for a second?" I asked, gingerly.

She seemed about to refuse but must have seen something in my eyes and nodded, begging forgiveness from the others. We found a secluded spot.

"What's wrong?" she asked.

"Ah... well... I sort of put a binding on someone by accident... and now I can't remove it."

"On who?" she asked, shaking her head. "*By accident*? Really?"

I shrugged. "Yeah... on Bayn."

Her brows shot up. "You bound a titan... *by accident*?" This seemed like a big deal. "Binding anyone by accident really shouldn't be possible, but a titan? Their resistance would be quite high. That's... extremely impressive, if also incredibly reckless and stupid."

"Put that on my tombstone," I muttered. Because somehow: *extremely impressive, if also incredibly reckless and stupid*, seemed to fit me rather well.

Lhorine gave a little laugh as she let out a breath. "Wow... okay... and you tried to break the binding... but couldn't?" she verified.

"Yup." I nodded, lips tight. "I removed part of it, but not all."

"Okay." She seemed to have come up with something, nodding to herself. "It's not an issue of power, since you'd be able to remove your own just fine. Meaning... it's an issue of substance."

"Substance? I don't recall any lessons on that."

She laughed again. "If you recall, time was short, I only taught you the basics. Yes, substance. Essentially, there was something you were most likely feeling at the time, which was baked into the binding and you won't be able to remove it until that feeling, whatever it was... is resolved."

Oh.

That could be very bad.

I'd been feeling a lot of things when I'd put the binding on: threatened and scared, imperious and vengeful, maybe even... a little aroused. I didn't want to admit that last part, even to myself. Bayn had been flying off the handle, and I really shouldn't have been thinking that was sexy in any way, but it all came down to bad boys doing bad boy things. The way his massive hand had grabbed my waist and lifted me… one handed… pushing me against a wall — even though he'd had no sexy intent — may have turned me on… just a teensy, tiny bit.

Was it wrong?

Yes.

Was it messed up?

Sure.

Was it one hundred percent something I'd do?

Also, yes.

"Okay…" I drew the word out. "So… what does that mean… resolved?"

She cocked her head. "Why don't you tell me what you were feeling and we can walk through it."

I gave a tight smile. "Sure…" I elongated that word, not wanting to tell her everything, but knowing I should. "Just… don't tell my grandmother, okay? She'd never let me hear the end of it?"

"Wait… were you…" She cleared her throat, "…*with* Bayn… at the time?"

With him? Yes. The way she meant? Not really.

"No, nothing like that… well, something remotely like that." And I explained the whole scene and situation to Lhorine.

The elf wore a bemused and slightly confused expression when I finished.

"Yeah, Olinara would never let you live that down."

"I know, right?" I threw my hands out to the side. "So, what do I do? How do I resolve *that*?"

"Well…" The way *she* drew out the word and looked away.

"No, I'm not having sex with him."

"It might not require much... a little arousal, perhaps?"

"I'll take that under consideration," I groused. "Anything else?"

She sighed. "The fear is the harder part. Are you still afraid of him?"

Was I?

"Yes, a little. But... it's also sort of mixed up with the arousal I think, and the wanting to get back at him. It's... complicated."

"And that's your problem. You have complicated emotions for him, and until you sort them out and figure yourself out... you won't be able to undo the binding. The only other way is to find someone more powerful than you... and that's not likely."

Yeah, I'm a boss-bitch!

And in this case, it was causing problems.

Why couldn't I ever just be awesome with no issues?

That was another headstone for me: *Awesome, but with issues.*

"Okay, thanks, Lhorine. I'll figure something out."

She grimaced. "Sorry, I know it's not the easy answer you were looking for. So... think of that next time before you *accidentally* bind someone."

I gave her two thumbs up and a tight smile. "Will do."

Now... I had to figure myself out... while getting ready for a war... and do it all really quickly so Bayn and I could get back to figuring out how to convince the titans to help us.

No biggie.

It was a short walk back to Bayn's residence. I hadn't figured out anything by then. Luckily, it seemed he wasn't back from wherever he'd run off to. His sister met me at the door instead.

"I'm sorry my brother is... the way he is," Wensuria said as I turned away to go in search of the man. I turned back slowly. Perhaps she could help me?

"And... how is that... exactly?" I asked.

She invited me in, and we sat in what remained of the large sitting area. Bayn's previous tantrum had left the room in tatters. Koar stayed outside, so we could talk privately.

"It's not my place to say what happened to him, that's a story for him to tell you, if he ever gets his head out of his ass long enough to see you might be a good fit for him," Wensuria began.

I laughed at that.

I liked this woman. For one, she made me feel small, which wasn't something I felt around most women. I'd always been a bit taller and bigger than the girls around me. Luckily, my mother's binding had also kept me fairly svelte, and I'd never put on a lot of weight, but there had still been a lot of times when I'd felt damn awkward being taller than some guys and most girls. And, having been busty since the age of thirteen, that had added a whole other layer of awkwardness. Yet Wensuria was a full-figured woman, well over seven feet tall, and seemed to have absolutely no body issues. In my mind that made her a damned queen.

She was also understanding and open, which weren't words I associated with titans, given everything I'd heard about them... and the main example I'd been dealing with, namely Bayn. It gave me hope that maybe other titans weren't as dickish as I'd imagined.

She had dark hair and fair skin, brilliant golden eyes, and a kind smile.

"What I can say is this... he's... broken."

Oh yay, fixing a man, exactly what I wanted to be doing while getting ready for the fight of my life.

"And he has issues trusting... anyone." She pursed her lips, eyes a bit distant, perhaps trying to figure out what she could tell me. "Someone very close to him betrayed him... badly... in a humiliating way, and my parents were a part of it."

Yikes! That's messed up. Your parents helping someone humiliate you? No wonder he was broken and didn't trust people.

"He had differing views from my parents and spoke out against them, and after this... *thing*... happened, they imprisoned him for a while to keep him quiet. Then... they released him into Saldrea's custody, with me as the tool to keep him compliant."

Talk about shitty parents.

And that was saying something, since I'd been a child in the foster system.

I hesitated before asking, but I really wanted to know, "How do *you* feel about your parents, and what they did to him and you?"

She seemed to sense my hesitancy and waved it away with a grin. "Oh, they're fucking bastards, but I've always known that."

I had to laugh at that, and she joined me.

Which led me to another question. "Would you say more titans are reasonable, like you, or messed up, like Bayn and your parents?"

That got a roll of her eyes. "Yeah, sorry, I'm the aberrant one. Most titans are too twisted up with rage at the elves to be as charming as me."

Well fuck, so much for that.

Wensuria must have seen the question in my eyes and smiled again. "Why am I so different?"

I smiled and nodded with a shrug.

"I have no clue. Though... maybe..." She seemed lost in thought. "My parents were royals... and didn't have a lot of time for me, I was raised by nannies and servants. And one nanny in particular tried to teach me culture and art, kindness and generosity. Maybe she hoped I'd be a different sort of royal? Which does suggest there could be a faction of titans who really don't like or want our constant warring with the elves." She shrugged.

Fascinating. Maybe we could use that?

First, I had to find Bayn and help him get his head out of his ass.

"Any idea where your brother might have gone?"

"I know exactly where he is," she answered. What a relief. "He's almost directly below us, down on the beach." Again, she seemed to sense my curiosity at how she knew this and preempted my question. "After we found each other again, we decided we never wanted to lose each other, so we placed a mutual little binding on each other, so we'll always be able to locate the other."

Huh.

"He really cares for you, doesn't he?"

She smiled. "There's a decent man in there, buried beneath centuries of horrible treatment by our parents and a betrayal which utterly broke him. I hope you can find that part of him."

Yeah. Me too.

I got up. "Thank you, Wensuria," I said honestly. "If everything goes to plan, you'll be my sister-in-law and I couldn't think of a better sibling to have."

She smiled as she rose and came over to hug me, gently. It was kind of nice being enveloped by her massive form, comforting in a not-quite-smothered, sort of way.

"I look forward to having you as a sister," she said as she

drew back. "Now go, find my brother and kick some sense into him."

I laughed at that and left.

Koar followed me as I jogged along the main path through the residences, till I came to The Tumble, the stairs down to the beach which descended through a crevice in the rocky cliff, over some ancient rockslide.

Then I retraced my steps, heading back east, till I saw a cave which hadn't been there the last time I'd been down on the beach. It seemed like it was roughly under the residence where Bayn had been staying. Once again, I told Koar to stay back, out of sight, figuring his presence wouldn't help any while talking to Bayn. The dragon moved back down the beach as I checked inside the cave, finding a beaten and bloody Bayn laying inside it.

Fucking hell! What had happened to him?

I raced to him, looking around, wondering who'd done this to him... but with all the blood on the jagged stone of the cave, I realized he'd done this to himself.

Fuck me. If the man was willing to go to these lengths to deliver self-harm, then I had my work cut out for me, getting him to see reason.

IZZY

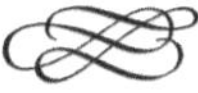

"FUCK, IT'S YOU," BAYN MUTTERED.

"Happy to see you too," I shot back.

"How...?" Bayn asked.

"Wensuria."

"She betrayed me?" he spat.

Yeah, this massive man really needed some sense kicked into him.

"No, she's trying to *help* you," I said, attempting to remain calm as I looked around the scene. He'd carved this new cavern by bashing it with his broken hands, then throwing himself bodily against the jagged stone. Wow. What level of rage and self-loathing did it take to do that?

"By sending you?" Bayn uttered, then gave a mirthless little laugh.

He certainly wasn't making it easy to help him.

Or like him.

Even if my traitorous body was slightly turned on by how this man had created this cave with his bare fists.

"Yes," I said, trying hard to keep my calm as I knelt next

to him. I really wanted to tell him to shut up and let me heal him, but I had to remember my binding would enforce those words and I didn't want to piss him off any more than I already had. I chose my words carefully.

"Would you like me to heal you?"

I reached for him and he swatted my hands away.

"I can heal myself just fine."

"Then why haven't you?" I asked, baffled.

It hit me: he *wanted* to be in pain. Fucking hell. I had a masochist on my hands. And I shouldn't have said it, but the words slipped out. "I can think of far more pleasurable ways to get beaten up. If that's what you're into?"

"Fuck you," Bayn bit out, lips curling. "I'd never let you dominate me!"

I didn't even want to dominate him, but this man brought out the sass in me.

"If you don't want to be my bitch, then don't act like one, and get yourself together!"

He snarled, even as he healed himself. He seemed to fight it the entire time, and I realized.... I'd told him to *get himself together* and the binding was making him do it.

Fuck! This was so damn complicated with that binding in place.

"Stop," I said and he did, breathing a little easier.

I sat back, though there was no comfortable place to sit nearby, all the rocks jagged and uneven.

"We need to talk. Work some shit out. Well, *I* need to work some shit out so I can release you from that binding. Now, will you help me? Will you talk to me? Or are you going to be a fucking asshat?"

"What do you need to work out?" he asked, clearly not wanting to speak to me at all.

"Feelings and shit."

"Fucking hell."

"Yeah, I don't want to either, but if you want to be free, then that's the price!"

"Can't you leave me in peace for a bit?" he grumbled.

"No! We don't have time for you to sulk. We need to get this shit sorted so we can figure out how to win over the titans."

"If I can't, you definitely won't!"

"Maybe *we* can!" I shouted back. Ugh! Why was this man so damned stubborn and infuriating?

"Go fuck yourself."

"Bite me!"

He lurched up and came to me. Lifting me off my precarious little seat, both hands around my waist. He seemed to like doing that. And a part of me liked it too, those massive hands easily encircling my not-so-little form.

"What...?" I squeaked, trying to figure out what had come over him.

Then he raked his teeth over my neck.

Oh fuck.

I'd told him to bite me!

"No! You don't—" My words were cut off, replaced with a grunting moan as Bane bit the base of my neck, not too hard but definitely breaking skin. And for some reason — probably from Myel feeding off me all those times during sex — that pierce of pain felt divine. Pleasure surged through my body, instantly hot, extremely bothered.

Not what I should be feeling right now!

"Fuck me," I moaned... then realized too late what I'd said.

One of Bayn's hands stayed gripping my waist as his other slid down and tore my pants and panties off with one vicious yank of cloth.

"No!" I cried out even as my body said *yes, yes, yes!* The brutal act of ripping my clothes away made every part of me light up with arousal. My core flooded, even as Bayn ripped open his own pants.

And there it was.

Oh God!

Oh, blessed lord above...

...and all the angels...

...and demons...

...and fucking hell that thing was HUGE!

When I'd felt his cock pressed to my belly previously, I recall thinking it felt like a wine bottle, that thick and hard. It wasn't *quite* that big, but it was damned close.

And I didn't have much time to react as he brought his hand back to my waist, then positioned me over that thick mass of man-flesh.

I probably had the time to shout *stop...* but I didn't. A part of me wanted this so damned bad. The big, rough, bad boy, taking me, making me his.

Hey, maybe this will resolve all that awkward sexual tension and allow me to break the binding?

However, since I didn't want him to break me open on that huge cock, I quickly used my nymph abilities to *adjust* myself, *down there.*

And even with that, when Bayn pushed me down onto him while thrusting up. The extreme stretch of my *should-have-been-looser* core instantly took my breath away. Then he pushed deeper, pressing me down on him, filling me. His cock slammed home, deep inside me, making my body sing with bliss.

I cried out, or I would have, no sound came out. My mouth gaped in a noiseless scream, my eyes crossed, my head lolled back, body going utterly limp... except for my legs, which instinctively wrapped around him.

I'd told Bayn to fuck me, not make soft passionate love to me, and he followed my instructions to the letter: hard, fast, raw fucking.

No man had ever been this rough with me. There was usually at least some tenderness in the act. And this brutal bashing of loins, along with the supreme stretch of my body around Bayn's massive cock, made this a rather shocking experience. Shocking but damned sexy and divinely delicious.

It was every dirty fantasy I'd ever had. I'd been coming since he'd crashed into my cervix that first time, and every repeated collision of his dick against me exploded pleasure through me.

Again.

And.

Again!

I hoped Bayn was getting something out of this, because I was riding a high I'd felt only a few rare times in my life. Myel and Rook together had given me this star-bursting level of bliss.

I lost time. I had no clue how long Bayn ravaged me, only that it was sinfully divine and I loved every sexy second of it.

I was brought back to myself when Bayn let out a savage roar and the impossibly large cock inside me swelled, then pulsed as he planted himself deep and caveman grunted his way through a *long* release.

Some distant — still functioning — part of my brain made a connection. Wensuria had said it had been someone close to Bayn who'd betrayed and humiliated him and given his rather vehement objection to being dominated, I guessed it had been a woman. I also guessed he hadn't had many women since, because he seemed to be draining all of his pent-up blue-balls into me.

And even after his dick had stopped throbbing and pulsing, it took both of us a while to come down, panting and huffing. I couldn't speak for him, but I felt the strangest mix of embarrassment and utter fulfilment. Neither of us had wanted this, and yet we'd also both desperately needed it. Yet another unfathomable paradox, which seemed to define our messed-up relationship.

"So... now... can we... talk... feelings?" I asked through heavy breaths.

Bayn grunted a laugh, but looked away from me, lifting me off his cock and setting me down. I couldn't stand, wobbling on my feet and finding part of the cave wall to uncomfortably lean against. I reached down and cupped my sex, groaning softly at both the ache and the extreme loss.

"Did I... hurt you?" Bayn asked as he turned away, heading deeper into the cave. He punched stone again, sending massive chunks flying.

"Best... pain... ever," I managed to say. "No regrets."

He looked back, confused, brow furrowed. Then he seemed to finally see me and he blinked. His cock, which had been slowly lowering, shrinking — even if it was still huge — twitched and rose again.

I gave a pathetic little sound. "I may need to wait a second before another round."

He gave a forced little laugh.

"But you...? I... Did you...?" He shook his head.

I too was a bit lost for words.

His remaining wounds closed, he finished healing himself. Maybe that meant he was ready to talk.

And all it had taken was sex, which we'd both not anticipated but perhaps we'd needed, to work some things out?

We'd see.

But first, I needed pants, my old ones were shredded.

I could send Koar running to get some, so I wouldn't have to walk through campus like this, but first...

...I'd have to explain it to Koar.

BAYN

I TRIED NOT TO LISTEN TO THE DISTANT, HEATED ARGUMENT Izzy had with the dragon, but I still caught snippets. Oddly, he didn't seem upset that we'd had sex. He'd been more concerned for her safety and physical condition, and once she'd assured him she was fine, he grumbled about it, but left, going to get clothes for both of us.

Not just her... both of us.

I didn't know why she was being kind to me. She could have left me here, mostly naked. My clothes hadn't been in great condition after my tantrum, throwing myself against these stone walls, my shirt mostly gone. Now my pants were entirely gone after I'd torn them off.

Bloody Bones!

Why hadn't Izzy stopped me from doing that? Because... she'd wanted it too? She'd liked it... a lot, it seemed. But I couldn't quite wrap my head around that. I'd been rough, with no foreplay other than a bite to her neck, which had apparently gotten her all worked up. Yet, she'd seemed to revel in it.

That seemed pretty messed up, but I wasn't one to talk

on that front. Perhaps we were *both* messed up? That made far too much sense. It might also explain why her binding on me was so hard to remove. The more complex the bindings, the harder they were to break. And given what the two of us had just done, I had a feeling our relationship — if you could call it that — was tangled and knotty as fuck.

Knotty.

Naughty.

I grinned.

Then I wiped that smile away. No. I couldn't let myself fall for this woman, even if we might someday be married. As soon as I gave her my heart, she'd stomp on it and laugh at my weakness. It's what women did. It's what Osserime had done.

Yet despite my wariness, Izzy burned in my veins. She'd been a curiosity before, but now, after having her, after seeing how much she'd liked it... I needed more of her. It didn't help that only a titan or an elf could have survived what I'd done with Izzy, but there were few titan women I'd ever let touch me, and certainly no elves.

Izzy was perfect. Not truly an elf, not a titan, but stronger than both. And for some reason, she wanted to be with me. She'd come looking for me, wanting to undo the binding, wanting to talk. I'd been the one to throw that out the window and fight instead. I'd seen how hard she'd tried to remain calm and be nice to me before I'd pissed her off, then we'd...

"Koar will be back in a bit. We have time to talk... if you're up for it," she said from behind me. I turned. She stood there, casually, even though she only wore a shirt, nothing more. And my lack of pants meant she could clearly see my cock respond to seeing her like that.

I looked away, otherwise we'd end up not talking.

She sighed. "Or... maybe we wait for pants to arrive before we talk?"

"No, say your piece," I said, sitting on the jagged stone and liking the bite of it, the pain. I kept my gaze averted.

"How can you sit on this stuff?" she asked.

"Pain is nothing new to me," I muttered.

"Ah, yeah... okay." She crouched down — I could just make her out in my periphery — but didn't sit. "It's nothing new to me either, but I still don't invite it."

I huffed a mirthless laugh at that.

"Maybe I'm a masochist."

"Oh, there's no question about that," she replied. "One look at this cave and I'd figured that much out."

I barked another laugh.

She sighed. "So... yeah. Turns out... I have complicated feelings for you, and that's hindering my ability to remove the binding."

"No shit," I mumbled.

"Yeah, well, I just figured that out." Her tone changed, more questioning. "Wait... do you have complicated feelings too?"

I didn't want to admit it, couldn't say the words. So, I flipped her a *what do you think* look before remembering why I wasn't looking at her and turned away again. Fuck she was sexy. She'd sweated a little from our exertions earlier, which made her blouse stick to her in all the right ways. And given that was all she was wearing, there was very little left to my imagination.

"Right... so we're both complicated and have feelings. It's like we're only human or something."

"Only titan," I corrected her.

She laughed. "Right, and I'm only half elf, half nymph, but that's a bit of a mouthful."

Her mention of *a mouthful* made me think of biting her and her reaction. My cock twitched again. Bones! She'd tasted so damned good. I wanted to press my lips to her in a very different way... but I quashed those feelings.

"Anyway," she drawled, continuing. "So yeah. I am a bit scared of you, but also a little turned on and I also seem to want to hit you all the time. That's a new combination for me and I need to figure that out before I can remove the binding."

I nodded. "What do you need from me?"

"It would be easier not to be scared of you or want to hit you, if you weren't so big of a dick sometimes." She gave the sexiest little groan.

Her own words were making her think of my big dick... or so I guessed.

"Sorry, my dick only comes in one size, extra-large," I joked.

"Don't I know it," she mumbled. "Can we stop talking about dicks?"

"You brought it up."

"I'm pretty sure you *brought it up* first." She gave another sexy groan. "Fuck! Why do I keep saying these things!"

I couldn't help the genuine laugh which escaped me. A smile broke over my lips.

No! Don't let her get to you.

She gave her own laughing sigh. "Where were we? Oh, right, complicated feelings and you're a... man who makes me want to hit you." Another sigh. "Look, I'm gonna take a wild stab in the dark and say someone close to you hurt you and you don't trust anyone anymore. You don't have to admit it, but if that's the case, what will it take for you to trust me? Maybe then, you won't want to fight me all the time and we can sort this out."

She'd hit the nail right on the head, but it only made me clam up. All I'd admit was, "I don't trust easily, you're right about that."

"But my friends helped you get your sister back, doesn't that count for something?"

"It does, it's why I'm talking to you at all."

"Ah."

I needed to give her something, though.

"I... I won't hurt you," I said slowly. "I... don't *want* to hurt you."

I didn't. She was different from any other woman I'd ever met, both powerful and caring. And that didn't make any sense to me, but I wanted to find out more. "But I also won't let you control me."

There. Maybe that would do it? It was as much as I would admit here and now.

"What makes you think I want to control you?" she asked, sounding confused.

I blinked.

Then I laughed.

"Sometimes I forget you didn't grow up in this world. Any elf who had... would want control."

"That's not true. The elf who taught me to use my powers, Lhorine, she's a good woman."

"Then she's the only one, perhaps... one in a million."

Izzy sighed heavily. "Given Saldrea and most of the others I've met... I can't say you're wrong." Another heavy breath. "But look, I *don't* want to control you. And I also don't want you to control me. I'm all about freedom, so everyone can live their lives in peace."

I'd heard her say it enough times, but it still hadn't sunk in for me.

"Could be the long con," I said, but my heart wasn't in it. I didn't think Izzy was that deceptive.

"Yes, make everyone free and equal so that I could what...? Take control and piss them all off so they'd rise up and dethrone me?"

Yeah, it didn't make much sense.

"It may... take me some time to get use to you then," I said.

She harrumphed. "That's the problem. We don't have time!"

She was right.

"I need you to trust me so we can go face the titans together and convince them to join us."

Face the titans... together?

"They'd never listen to you."

"Because I'm an elf, yes, I know, and yet they're *currently* listening to an elf, now, aren't they?"

Huh... she was right about that too.

"What would you tell them?" I asked, curious.

"I don't know. I haven't figured that out yet. I was hoping you'd help with that."

My shoulders slumped. I'd run out of arguments.

"I'll help you," I said, voice barely audible, but elves had good ears.

"Wow... ah... thanks," she said, surprised. Then she blew out a breath. Koar'll be here in a second. Why don't we pick this up later?"

I nodded to that. "Yeah sure."

The dragon arrived and threw some clothes at me, more than just pants. How thoughtful of him.

"Get dressed, both of you, Myel has returned from spying in the capital and has some important news. Actually... maybe take a dip in the ocean first, then get dressed. You two smell like... you don't want to know."

Izzy laughed at that. I turned in time to see her rip off her shirt and race naked into the water.

"Is she always this... carefree?" I asked Koar.

"When she feels safe," was his stoic reply.

"I don't know how anyone can feel safe in this world," I muttered.

Koar laughed. "That's Izzy for you, defying convention and expectation."

I grunted. That was true enough.

But could she spurn years of hatred and convince the titans to join her?

Maybe... just maybe... she could.

IZZY

Rook and Vyns had also returned, and the campus was now swarming with seraphim and demons. Thankfully, we'd planned for this and had them staying in different areas so they wouldn't clash... too much.

We all met up for a debriefing in the room where I'd found Lhorine earlier, along with other leaders from the campus. Several other spies had returned, in addition to Myel, and they reported on what they'd seen of the forces marshalling against us.

The sheer number of the enemy was staggering, though given the masses of people I'd seen on campus, we had a lot as well, I didn't know the exact numbers yet.

Then Myel spoke confirming those numbers from what he'd overheard in the palace, but more importantly...

"We have eight days before they march and they'll be on campus that same day." He outlined their plan to teleport the forces in, then he spoke of the queen. "She truly is insane. Her plan is... wild, and yet it just might work, given the animosities between the races and their tendency to follow elven orders no matter what."

Still, the scale of her betrayal, how she planned to keep turning forces against each other boggled my mind. Every ally turned into an enemy, fighting for her, then being destroyed while they recovered.

"Could we use this to win over the titans?" I whispered to Bayn.

The massive man shrugged those huge shoulders. "It *might* work." He didn't sound hopeful. Yeah, we didn't have any proof, just my word that Valnea was insane and would turn against them. Fuck.

The room was quiet after Myel finished.

It was Lhorine who took control. "Thank you, Myel." She turned to the rest of us. "How can we use this?"

"I'll return to the dwarves, try to convince them of the truth," Svokol said. "And I'll send word to the undines as well, but since Valnea doesn't intend to betray them, they may not do much."

"What are the exact numbers of our forces, now that the angels and demons have joined us?" someone asked.

Yeah, I was curious about that too.

"With the fifteen thousand demons and around forty thousand seraphim, that brings our total fighting force to over a hundred-and-twenty thousand," Zora replied. I loved how the hobgoblin was being given such a place of honor in this council and how so many listened to her and regarded her with respect. Maybe, just maybe, I could pull off this equality thing.

Also… a hundred and twenty thousand? Way to go us!

But it sounded like Valnea had as many men, and mostly elves and dragons, two of the fiercest and strongest forces in all the three realms.

"Which means the titans are truly the deciding factor," Bayn whispered, seemingly to himself. "Fuck."

Yeah, I had to agree.

"How large is the titan army?" I asked Bayn.

"Roughly eighty thousand," he whispered back.

Yeah... that many on Valnea's side would completely crush us, whereas that many on our side would definitely give us a strong advantage.

After that, there was a lot of talk about terrain and defenses. I paid attention as best I could, but I wasn't a tactician. I got the impression that despite us fighting on our "home turf," it wouldn't be a significant advantage. Especially with the forces against us coming in from all sides.

Then it came time for Bayn to speak. Everyone looked to him for an update on the titans and which side they'd be joining.

I stepped forward, saving the man from the shame of reporting his failure.

"Our initial foray into negotiations with the titans didn't go as planned." I figured that was the most diplomatic way to say: we failed to get the titans. "However, Bayn and I will be returning to their lands tomorrow to try again. Any and all suggestions for ways to sway them to our cause, are welcome."

There, now I'd thrown responsibility onto everyone else to help us brainstorm how to do this.

It was Grandma Oli, who spoke first. Even here and now, in a dead-serious war council, she couldn't be bothered to wear something modest. She was poured into skintight black leather pants and nearly bursting out of a cropped black halter top.

"Bayn, could you not challenge your father for the throne?" she asked.

He grumbled. "That... may be our only option now." He gave me a sidelong glance filled with... something, I couldn't say what, maybe *hope*? Though there seemed to be a fair amount of concern and resistance mixed in. "The problem with that is two-fold. First, in our culture those who are challenged set the time, and it can be up to a week away, which would be cutting things close. Second, winning... may not be enough. I would almost certainly receive other challenges the instant I take the throne. The only way I can think to stop that... would be to have a quick and overwhelming victory over my parents, which..." he shrugged, "...honestly isn't likely. They are as strong as I am."

Oh...

That look made a lot more sense now. He'd been wondering if I'd help him. He didn't know if he could trust me to fight beside him though.

Maybe it was time to show him I wasn't going to betray him.

"Could I fight with you... as your queen?"

It was so quick I nearly missed it, but the flash of a smile over those hard lips gave me my answer.

"Yes, that could work," he replied slowly, carefully. "Together we could take them, I'm certain. The only question would be, whether our victory would be overwhelming enough to quell any others from challenging me... us."

My turn to smile. That little word at the end, "us," meant a lot to me and I wanted him to see it.

Bayn nodded, acknowledging my smile, then turned back to the others. "This is probably our best chance. Even so, some titans still may not follow me if they've been poisoned by Valnea's lies."

Lhorine, who was clearly the one in charge of this meeting, nodded. "Proceed with that plan and... be careful. We need both of you back in one piece. Our strategy hinges on Izzy being alive and well for this fight."

Oh… did it?

"And what is our strategy, exactly?" I asked with a fake smile.

"Cut the head off the snake," Oli responded. "You and an elite team—" which I took to mean my guys, since they'd never let me fight on my own, "—will face Valnea directly. The hope being once she's dead, the rest of her force will see no reason to keep fighting."

There were nods all around.

I mean… okay, sure, I was probably the strongest one in this room, and hopefully stronger than Valnea, but still… sending me into the heart of the enemy camp?

"I may need more than my… elite team," I said, hopefully the guys didn't take any offence to that. "As I'm assuming Valnea will have a lot of guards around her."

Lhorine smiled. "Your team will be the ones facing the false queen directly, while a strike force will distract those around her."

Thank heavens.

"But," Olinara added, giving me a stern look, "the survival of that strike force depends on you, Izzy."

Sorry, what now?

My grandmother explained. "They will be keeping away many times their number in Valnea's forces, especially as word gets out that you're attacking their queen. The longer you take to defeat Valnea, the more of them will die."

Well shit-fuck-damn. There weren't enough curse words to express the heaviness falling on my shoulders.

This was what it meant to be queen. People would die serving me. In fact, more than that strike force would die. We'd lose others, from all our forces, the longer I took to win.

I swallowed hard.

"Understood."

There was a little more talk of strategy after that, but I barely heard any of it, too preoccupied with the burden of leadership sitting all too heavily on me.

Myel came to me, slipping his hand into mine and instantly I felt better, soothed. Comforting warmth seeped into my spirit as Vyns wrapped his arms around me from behind. Rook took my other hand and whispered a soft, *you can do this*, into my mind.

I breathed out my worries in a long sigh.

It was a lot easier to handle things when you had others to help you. Not so long ago, I wouldn't have wanted to believe that, but here and now, I accepted the truth.

As the meeting broke up, Myel whispered, "What do you need?" but through our bond, he was really saying: *we'll take care of you.*

"Let's *all* go back to my residence and figure that out," I whispered back, with a significant look at Bayn when I said "all."

The massive man seemed a bit taken aback by the invitation but followed us.

Grandma Oli called me over before I left, though.

"It seems your harem is growing," she whispered, pulling me away from prying ears.

"Is it that noticeable?"

"Only to me. I have a sixth sense about sex."

That didn't surprise me.

"Take it from someone who's lost more than a few friends and lovers: appreciate every second you have with them, all of them." There was a note of sadness in her voice. I recalled she'd been one of Queen Leastrine's lovers, the head of the inamorati, the queen's harem. Until now, I hadn't really registered what my grandmother had lost when the previous queen died: a friend, a lover, more?

I hugged her tightly and whispered a soft, "Thank you."

I hadn't had many tender moments with Oli, usually too put off by the fact that she looked like my younger sister and dressed in a rather immodest way most of the time.

I pulled back and held her at arm's length. "How are you doing?" I asked.

She smiled. "Oh, I'm well enough... just... remembering old times," she breathed. Then she drew a long breath and the slight gloom over her faded.

"Any advice on fighting Titans?" I asked her, since I had her here and I'd be heading off soon to do exactly that.

"They respect strength, and you're stronger than most. Don't hold back."

I nodded. That seemed wise.

"Thanks." I hugged her again. "Now, if you'll excuse me, I have lovers to appreciate before I leave tomorrow."

She laughed at that and waved me away.

I rejoined the guys, and we returned to my residence... going directly to the bedroom.

MYELAS

I WAS MORE THAN A LITTLE SURPRISED TO FIND THE TITAN, Bayn accompanying us all the way to Izzy's bedroom. Though I took some solace from the fact that the huge man seemed awkward, unsure what to do, staying a little back from all of us. It was like he didn't know why he'd been invited.

Izzy went to him, taking one of his hands — hers seemed tiny in his — and turned back to the rest of us.

"So... yeah, everyone, I'm sure you've met Bayn already, but in case anyone is unfamiliar... Bayn... this is Myel, Rook, Vyns, and Koar. There, now you all know each other and... Bayn will be joining us tonight." She looked up at him. "Right?"

He seemed surprised by this. "If that's what you want," he said.

Something strange was going on between them, I sensed it through their interactions, but I also felt it through my bond with Izzy. She was... connected to the man in some way. Curious.

"It is."

He looked from her to us.

"I… don't share well. I… might be…"

"A dick?" Rook finished. "Don't worry, we all know what to do with dicks."

I couldn't help a smile as Bayn tried to figure out what the incubus was implying.

"Sometimes none of us share well," Vyns conceded. I had a feeling something had happened while I'd been away which had caused him to say that. "Just remember, the main thing here is, we all want Izzy to be happy."

The titan bobbled his head at that, accepting the angel's advice.

Time for me to speak up. "Izzy… could I have a moment alone before we… get going?"

"Sure," she said easily, releasing the titan's hand and coming to me.

"I'm gonna go freshen up," Rook said, heading for the bathroom. "Make myself all washed and oiled for my lover, anyone wish to join me?"

Koar and Vyns caught on and began to leave. The dragon went over to the titan and pulled him out of the room as well, giving Izzy and I some privacy. Not that most of the guys didn't have exceptional hearing and would probably be able to listen in from the other room.

"What's up?" Izzy asked. "I know the bond's a little tight, since you were away for so long, but I get the feeling it's not that."

"It isn't," I said, taking her hands and drawing her to the couch, where we sat side by side. "I realized something while I was in the capital."

"Thanks for that, by the way. I didn't want you to go, but… your intel was amazing, it's changed everything." Her eyes suddenly widened. "Wait… you don't know yet do you?

Safir died. He fought off assassins trying to get to me, using some nasty poison and... I couldn't save him. I'm so sorry, I know you two were close."

I sighed heavily. I *had* heard. When I'd returned from my mission, Safir had been the man I'd sought out, but I'd been told what had happened and reported to Lhorine, Olinara, and Zora instead.

"I heard," I said heavily. My feelings for the man were complicated, to say the least. During the time I'd known him, I'd gone from loving him like a father, to hating his guts for how he treated me and my bond to Izzy. I'd also thought — for a while — that he was the reason for my inferiority issues. That wasn't the case. He may have taken advantage of my issues from time to time, being the leader I'd felt I needed in my life, but I was the one to blame for putting myself down.

"If we survive all this... I'll mourn him in my own time." I gave a sad smile. "But I know he would have been so damned happy to die protecting you."

Izzy's smile matched mine, bittersweet. "Yeah, he even said so at the end, something about fulfilling his oath."

"Sounds like him."

We sat in silent remembrance, before Izzy softly asked, "So, what did you want to talk about?"

"When I left... I said I had some things to work out... thank you for calling me out on that by the way. I had a lot of time alone to think in the capital and I've realized a few things."

She smiled and squeezed my hands, encouraging me.

"I haven't figured it all out yet," I began, prefacing everything. "But I've accepted that I have issues around feeling inferior, *less than* others. It's... how I've always felt, partly because I'm a shifter, but it goes even deeper than that. Even as a shifter, I wasn't the strongest and my own kind have been telling me that all my life."

"That can't have been easy," she sympathized.

I nodded. "It wasn't. And now, *in my head* at least, I can see that I've survived longer than so many others. I've gone through shit and I'm still here and *that* makes me strong. But *in my heart*, I'm still a terrified little shifter boy, cringing at all the loud noises around me. And I think the important part is that I take responsibility for that feeling. I acknowledge it and want to change... but I'm still figuring out how to do that."

Izzy leaned in and kissed my cheek. "I'm not particularly good with feelings stuff, but I'm fairly sure admitting what you just did, takes a whole lot of courage. Thank you for telling me."

I sat a little straighter. She was right.

Izzy lowered her voice to a conspiratorial whisper, "And, if it makes any difference, I can't tell you the specifics, but I'm pretty sure Bayn's issues make yours look like child's play."

Did that make a difference?

Not really... well okay, maybe a little.

Still, I felt good enough to joke about it. "Aw man, really? He's bigger and stronger and tougher and even his issues dwarf mine. I can't win!"

Izzy laughed... but only after I winked to let her know I wasn't serious.

"Thank you for listening," I said softly. "And for... pushing me to begin with. I'll figure myself out and become a man you... no... *I* can be proud of."

She kissed me again. "Yeah, because I'm already proud of you, you sexy, Goth, dreamboat."

She shifted, straddling me, crushing her core to my

hardening erection. "Think we have time for a quicky to satisfy the bond before the others get back?"

"I'd rather we take our time," I said, pulling her lips down to mine. Her arms went around my neck and we melted into each other.

"Don't know if that will be an option," she whispered between stolen kisses.

Yeah. She was right. The bond was straining, demanding passion.

We quickly stripped, not even getting off the couch. Then she was back on my lap, spearing herself on my waiting cock and sighing with the most delectable moan of pleasure as I filled her.

"I've been experimenting with letting go of my own control issues," she breathed as she rocked on me, quickly building her passion. "Want to help me with that?"

I could barely speak, her sensuous lust overwhelming me. I nodded.

"Good." She quickly shifted, though, not in the way I'd expected. She leaned back and to one side, pulling her leg up to drape it over my arm. Then she did the same with the other side. My hand slid down to her ass, it seemed natural in this position, cupping that lushness. And with her legs draped over my arms, I had all the control. She was at my mercy.

"I'm all yours," she breathed as I lifted her and set her back down, grinding on my cock. She bit her hip. "Yup, just like that." Her arousal spiked, climbing higher, billowing through our bond into me and driving me closer to a peak.

I sank my fingers into her ass and moved her, sometimes pressing her close and grinding against her clit, other times bouncing her on my cock, and all the while our lips meshed, her arms locked around me, our kiss so deep I felt it in my soul.

I drove her onto me harder and harder, then crushed her close, as her orgasm exploded through our bond. That incredible surge of ecstasy blasted into me and I came with her. We moaned and grunted together, drinking each other's lust like sweetest wine.

She pulled back a little from my lips, so she could gaze at me.

"No one can rock my world like you can," she whispered. "Bayn may be big and Rook's orgasms are divine, but with you... the bond... it's always special in a way I can't describe. I love you, Myel."

She blinked and I felt her confusion and surprise. But... she didn't take back the words. Then... slowly, like the sun rising, her face brightened, a wide smile on her lips.

"I *do* love you," she said again, leaning her forehead to mine, her hair draped around us. "You're the first man I've ever said that to. And it's not the bond speaking." This much I knew. If it had been the bond, she'd have said it long ago. "The bond brings us together, but you are... home to my heart." She kissed me softly, then added, "Just as you are."

And my own heart exploded with joy to hear this.

"I love you too, now and forever," I breathed.

She smiled wider.

"I know. I feel it."

Her love and adoration poured through the bond. It was the most glorious sensation. I felt a million times better than I had before we'd started. I may still have my issues, but she loved me, and if she could love me as I was...

...maybe I could too.

IZZY

I LET MYEL FEED FROM ME BEFORE WE WENT TO THE bathroom to clean up. The other four guys were all in and around the massive bathtub. Bayn sat on the side, his feet in the water, still looking like he felt out of place. Though as soon as he saw me, naked and proud, his entire demeanor changed from awkward to interested. His eyes dilated, he sat a little taller — which made him loom over the others — and something in his lap stood taller too. Vyns, Rook, and Koar all lounged in the tub, and even though none of them were small men, there was still lots of room. That tub really was huge. The water was nice and clear and gave me a very good view of all of them.

"Oooh! Candy!" I squealed, eyeing all that luscious man-meat.

"That's right," Myel whispered beside me. "I'm the main course, they're just dessert."

"Exactly," I whispered back, giving him a shoulder nudge and a secret smile. I hoped my emotions, through our bond, let him know how I felt. Myel was truly special. He was my first. Yes, Rook and I had hooked up in the human realm, but Myel was the first man I'd been with here in Seial, and the first who was really there for me in this strange place. And now, he was the first man... ever, whom I'd professed my love to.

That was... huge!

Love...

Like actual, big "L" love!

It was a rather overwhelming sensation, but an incredibly good one. I wasn't sure if I would've gotten to this point as quickly without the bond. That deep and intimate connection meant I knew Myel in a way I'd never known anyone else, and when he'd admitted his insecurities to me... I'd felt my heart open. Though it had been him taking responsibility for his feelings, being a mature adult, recognizing his weaknesses and working through them, which had really pushed me over the edge. My affection and respect and desire had all mingled and I'd felt so... light and joyous and wonderful.

I couldn't stop smiling.

And with the buffet of luscious men before me, I had even more reason to smile.

"Speaking of dessert," I said with a lick of my lips, "something tells me I'm going to be *very full* soon."

Myel and I sank into the tub with the others. Now, it was *starting* to feel full. If Bayn had actually joined us, we would have all fit, but it would have been tight.

"So, what's the plan?" I asked the guys. "You've had lots of time to discuss all the wonderful things you're going to do to me. Lay it on me."

Rook spoke up, because of course the sex demon had thoughts on this. "First, relax and let the water soothe you." As he said this, Vyns shifted one of my feet into his lap and began massaging it.

Heaven.

Ha! Angel... Heaven... I hadn't intended that, but it fit.

"We tried to convince Bayn to go first, since he's new, but he said he'd already... how did he put it?" Rook asked.

"Stretched her to her limits," Vyns replied with a wide-eyed, *are-you-okay*, look at me.

I laughed it off.

"Yes, that," Rook finished. "You've had some alone time already, it seems?"

"We have," I admitted.

"Then we thought, well, Myel's been a way for a while and with your bond, you'd need some time with him," Rook went on, "but from what I just felt, you've already taken care of that too."

"Yup," I said, popping the "p." Then, sensing this could be a teachable moment, I said, "He's worked through some pretty serious shit. Something some of you could learn from." I looked around, mostly at Bayn.

The massive man gave me a *you first* look, then leaned back on the wall behind him and casually stroked his huge erection.

Was my mouth watering?

I couldn't help it. That dick was too spectacular not to drool over.

"We'll worry about that when the time for orgasms has passed," Rook quipped.

"So... where does that leave us?" I asked.

"Well, I was going to say we three deserve another foursome," Rook suggested, indicating himself, Vyns, and Koar. "But given how you're eyeing Bayn's cock, maybe..." He chuckled. "I've got it."

I raised a brow in question.

"You look like you want to go over there and lick that

flesh-rod like a lollypop... so why don't you do that?" Rook said with a sinful grin. "And while you do, we three will take turns slipping in behind you."

Yup, sounded like a great idea to me.

I slid across the massive tub, right up between Bayn's legs, which he slid open to accommodate me. I shooed his hand away from his dick, then grabbed it myself, my fingers nowhere close to going all the way around. Then I licked a hot, wet line from his base all the way to his tip. And while I did that, I wiggled my ass behind me, waiting for one of the others to "slip in."

Hands gripped my hips, before one slid down and traced my seam, testing me. When it found me more than ready for one finger, two slid inside and began a rather delicious stroking while hot kisses landed on my back.

This was Vyns, from the sweltering heat billowing into my spirit. He was getting quite hot and bothered, and I was following suit.

I pushed my lips around Bayn's tip, but there was no way I was getting that monstrosity into my mouth.

I grumbled. "Can't you shrink it down a little?" I asked him.

He raised one brow in a *you-gotta-be-kidding* look.

I grimaced. "What? If you can make yourself this small from what... forty feet tall?"

"Forty-six feet actually."

Fuck me!

"Forty-six then, I'm sure you can make yourself a teensy bit smaller, *if* you want me to suck you off, that is."

He grunted, his dick twitching in my hand. Oh yeah, he wanted that.

He leaned down, curling around, rather flexible, till he was close to my head, and whispered. "Only for you, and only if you let me stretch your pussy at my full size again once these others are done with you."

"Deal!" I said.

He grinned as he sat back. Then all of him shrank down. I couldn't quite tell from my position, but I guessed he was roughly a foot shorter? But his dick.

Wow...

Even at this size, he was still so damned... *thick*!

I stretched my mouth and barely managed to fit around him. My teeth raked over him, top and bottom as I pushed him deeper.

"Bloody Bones!" he cursed, going super tense, one of his fists slamming down so hard it shattered the tiles beside him.

I would have said something about him liking a bit of pain, but I couldn't talk with this massive dick tickling my uvula. I swirled my tongue around him a little, then pulled back out, my teeth digging in again.

When I finally popped off, his dick twitched so hard it slapped him in the belly.

"Trying to eat me?" he asked, voice strained. "Your teeth..." He left that hanging, gasping. I'd left rough red scrape marks down the length of his erection.

I shrugged. "You like giving it rough, so it seems only fair."

Then Vyns shifted and move close behind me, his fingers leaving me and his shaft slowly filling me.

I grunted in delight, even as I licked Bayn's booboo's better. I added a touch of healing when I stroked my hand over his length, and the scrapes vanished. But I'd only done that... so I could take him in my mouth a second time and not hurt him more.

I pushed that massive dick between my lips and heard

a chuckle by my ear. "Vyns would never admit it," Rook whispered, his hot breath feeling sinfully good on the shell of my ear. "But by the look on his face, he likes seeing your lips stretched, swallowing a fat dick." Then Rook kissed behind my ear as one of his hands slid under me to cup my breast. He must have added some lust magic, because *wow!* That felt way too good. My nipples ached, so damned hard.

Vyns' pace quickened, as if adding credence to Rook's words. One of Vyns' hands slid around me, between my legs, finding my clit as he slammed into me.

I bucked.

Which shifted Bayn in my mouth and I may have bit down... a little.

"Fuck!" Bayn yelled, but he didn't pull out like I expected. Instead, his hands swept up, pushing Rook away, to clasp my head as his hips bucked hard into my mouth. My eyes went wide as he pushed deeper than I'd thought he could go.

"Again!" he demanded.

I didn't know exactly what he was asking for. Did he want me to bite him again?

In the end, I didn't have a choice. Vyns slammed into me, flicking my clit once more, his cock swelling, so close to his release. And that caused another full-body jerk from me, my teeth sinking into Bayn's dick again.

"Yes!" Bayn shouted, "Fuck yes!"

He... liked that?

To each their own, I guess. His cock throbbed hard in my mouth, then he pulled me off him and stroked himself vigorously. I'd drawn blood and he smeared it over his dick as he jerked himself hard.

"Lick it!" he demanded, and I did, slavering all over his

tip. His head tilted back and he seemed to lose it... but he didn't come.

Instead, he seemed to go through some extended orgasm without a release.

I didn't have time to ponder this, however, as a wave of wet heat slammed into my spirit when Vyns lost himself, his dick pulsing as his hands stroked my sides and back, his breath ragged.

Rook was back at my ear. "Oh yeah, he thought that was super-hot, dirty angel."

"Shut up, demon," Vyns hissed, but it was more playful than serious.

I didn't really care because I was hovering on the edge of an orgasm myself. And when Vyns' hand slid back between my legs to flick my clit, I joined him in his release, bucking back hard against him.

I was still super-buzzed when Vyns pulled out and I was shifted. Koar slid behind me as I was rotated a bit to find Rook in front. "Bayn needs a break," the incubus whispered. "That was a rather heady orgasm for him, and I'm impressed at his control. Show off. But that means it's my turn." He sat on the side of the tub, his dick thrust up before me.

Now this... this I could do.

AMARHUK(ROOK)

I WAS DROWNING IN LUST. CONCUBI LIVED FOR ORGIES, THE mass of roiling passion was a buffet from which to feed. I could still feel lingering ecstasy from Myel. But with Vyns, Bayn, and Izzy all brimming with orgasmic joy, I was in incubus heaven.

The lust of the other men empowered me, but Izzy's desire was like a drug, intoxicating me, making my head spin. She tested me every time I was with her. This time, empowered by the bliss of the others, I could withstand her tempting passion — barely — as she wrapped her lips around my cock and bobbed her head on me. That alone was sinfully thrilling, but the way she looked up at me, those sea-green eyes alive with desire, tested the limits of my control in the best possible way.

I slid my hands through her thick, soft hair and met her gaze for gaze, deepening the connection.

You like? Izzy's voice spoke into my mind.

I love, I whispered mentally. The word didn't come with the same hesitancy it had the first time. Perhaps because I wasn't adding in that last little three letter word which made the phrase so much more meaningful. Still, Izzy knew exactly what I meant. I saw it in her eyes.

And I hoped all she saw in my eyes was desire and affection, not the deep-seated fear of losing her.

The last thing I wanted to think about, while Izzy's lips were wrapped around my cock, was my mother and her pain and disappointment. Yet her words echoed in my mind.

Walk away before fate takes her...

The loss is too great...

If you're that far gone... you're lost...

And lost I was. Lost in passion, but I'd also lost my heart. I needed to keep this woman safe, to care for her, tend to her, see her smile and kiss away her tears.

I heard that, she said through our connection.

How much had she heard?

My heart skipped a beat.

And trust me, you're making me smile right now, no tears in sight.

Ah... just the last bit? Good.

You're doing so much more than making me smile, I replied, pushing all those other thoughts aside and refocusing on Izzy.

Oh? Don't tell me I'm too much for the incubus? Am I going to make you... oh God! Yes! Her thoughts were interrupted by Koar sliding his thickness into her and starting his thrusting in earnest.

Her eyes crossed.

Best... day... ever! she managed to stammer to me, then she seemed to lose herself to Koar's rather heated passion.

I felt the dragon's oppressive lust. His need was like the hammer of a bell, ringing through him with deafening power. There was something frenetic and immediate about the big man's desire.

Perhaps he felt it too, the fragility of our situation. War brewing. The fear of loss. Who knew how much time we had left with the ones we loved? With... a certain one in particular.

"Izzy! Yes!" he cried out and her crossed eyes went wide as the dragon pounded her harder and harder, each stroke pushed her deeper onto my cock, till her lips pressed around my base and I was deep in her throat. She didn't seem to mind, lost to desire.

I, however, was quickly losing my shit.

And I wasn't the only one. Myel looked positively pained as his erection grew once more. Vyns was stroking himself back to life. I couldn't quite get over the voyeuristic streak in the angel. He seemed to like to watch a lot more than I would have thought. His lust billowed as he watched Koar lose himself on Izzy. And Bayn... Well, he'd held his release through a heady orgasm and that meant he was still mostly ready to go.

I had a devilishly dirty idea.

"Everyone into the shower," I called out. Then to Izzy, "Don't worry, My Flame, you'll like this."

She popped off my cock with a single raised brow, then her face resumed its previous oh-my-god look as Koar gave one more thrust. I reached for the dragon, just in time, and with a touch delayed his release.

"You'll like this too," I said when his eyes went a bit wide.

"Trust me, everyone will like this."

Bayn grunted, unsure.

"Even you, Grumpy." That seemed a fitting name for the perpetually serious titan.

With little fuss we all hurried into the shower. It was a massive space with multiple heads, but even so, it was a tight fit with all six of us.

"You still want to wreck Izzy at your usual size?" I asked Bayn.

The titan gave a nod, a slow grin on his face.

"Then you go last," I said. Then I organized the rest of us. Koar lifted Izzy and quickly had her seated on his raging erection once more. Vyns slipped in behind her, and after I worked a little magic on Izzy's ass, he slipped inside her from behind and the two of them began rocking our shared lover between them.

"Gah... yes, fuck," Izzy hissed as her pleasure spiked back to where it had been before our little diversion. "What... ugh... about... yes... you?" she grunted.

I slid a finger up along Myel's rigid erection. "I've got things to play with, would you like to watch?"

Yes! came the mental reply since she was too busy moaning and groaning to talk.

"You didn't hear that, but she said yes," I said to Myel as I knelt and took his cock in my hand, bringing it to my lips. "You up?" I asked.

The shifter's eyes went wide at my offer.

I sensed his hesitation, but I knew how to bring him around. "Just keep your eyes on her," I said to him. "Let everything else go!"

Myel's gaze lifted from me up to Izzy, and when I slid my lips over him, his eyes closed, his body tense... in a good way. Oh yeah, he liked this.

"And I watch?" Bayn asked, pressed up against the side of the shower. He didn't seem happy.

I pulled off Myel to reply, "I have a feeling I know your kink. You'll like what's coming to you, if you can wait for it."

He grunted but didn't push back any more after that.

And I smiled as I looked up to see Izzy watching Myel and me, wide eyed. I made a show of swallowing the shifter's long dick and Izzy's eyes crossed as an orgasm swept through her.

It hit me hard, a wall of lust, and Myel must have felt it through their bond. But I strained my powers to keep us both from coming.

I had a surprise planned for Izzy, for us all, and like I'd said, I had a feeling everyone would like it.

IZZY

I COULDN'T SPEAK, COULD BARELY THINK, BREATHING WAS A challenge, and I might have gone temporarily blind. The sheer power of the orgasm, which seemed to bounce back and forth between Myel and me through our bond was savagely intense, but somehow it was growing even more potent with every second.

Before my momentary blackout, I'd seen the raw bliss painted on Myel's face, a similar look — matched by a devilish grin — on Rook's face as he worked Myel's dick like a master.

And all through this elevated ecstasy, Koar slammed himself into me like a madman, the dragon had lost control, and I loved it. I had my hands wrapped around his bull-like neck, while his hands on my hips kept me perfectly positioned for his frenzied thrusts, driving us both mad.

"Izzy!" he cried out, and his cock swelled inside me, testing my limits, even as I clamped down on him, tight as a vise and wet as a waterslide.

"Yes, yes!" Vyns echoed that cry behind me as he too

slammed himself home deep into my ass and his cock twitched with pounding power.

But, as much as the two men had clearly lost their shit, I felt no release.

There came a mischievous chuckle.

"I told you you'd like this," Rook said. "Now everyone is feeling what Izzy feels. My gift to you all." Ah, so that's what the incubus was doing. "As for your release, you're going to have to wait for a second."

Wait for what?

"Bayn, you're up," Rook said.

Oh.

My vision cleared enough to focus on Koar before me. "I love you, Perfection," he breathed, eyes locked on mine as restrained pleasure wracked his face.

"As do I, Angel," Vyns whispered from behind, his mouth so close to my left ear his hot breath warmed my cheek.

I couldn't quite process their words with the raging lust pounding through me.

Do you trust me? Rook asked into my mind. *Also... do you trust Bayn?*

What... do you have... in mind? I asked, even my mental voice was stuttering.

There's a position I think he'd like, but it puts you at his whim. You trust him enough for that?

I don't fucking care, let him do what he wants. I felt too damned good, and I didn't think Bayn was going to change that.

Then get yourself ready.

Koar and Vyns slipped back as I was handed over to the titan. Rook whispered something to the massive man, but I only heard the soft hissing of his voice, not the words.

Then Bayn grunted as he turned me in his arms so I was no longer facing him.

"You ready for me?" the massive man asked.

It took every ounce of concentration I had — which wasn't much, given this echoing orgasm stuck in my soul and wracking my body — to shift my core to accommodate him.

Luckily, I was so damned wet and sloppy, that when he pushed in, there was virtually no resistance, which for a man of his size was impressive, especially since he was back to his usual over-seven-foot-tall form.

He pulled my hips back till he was sheathed inside me, then stepped forward, so I was pressed hard to the glass of the shower.

"You're mine," he breathed on my ear and began pounding me from behind. And with every crash of his body, I was pressed harder to the glass, the cold surface somehow amplifying my bliss... as did the titan's rough loving.

Bayn hadn't come before. He'd held himself, but that meant this time it didn't take long before his pent-up lust overwhelmed him.

He came like a flood, and as he did, he peeled me off the glass, hands slipping under my arms to press my back to him as he turned.

And there were four seriously hot and desperate men, all ragingly hard, all paused at their peaks... before Rook with a wink... released them.

In most cases, a man pulling out to shoot his load on me... wasn't appealing. But here, in the shower with so much passion burning through all of us, it was hella hot to watch each of my beautiful men lose themselves, to watch the power of their arousal spraying over me... and everything else. The feel of their hot streams on my flesh fulfilled some dirty, erotic fantasy. I was powerless, but also somehow powerful, the object of their lust and desire, driving them mad and feeling every inch a lust-goddess as they emptied themselves.

"The incubus was right," Bayn whispered behind me. "This is damned hot." And a renewed pulse of his release blasted inside me.

I wasn't sure what the massive man was getting out of this, but then... I supposed for a control freak, this was heaven. I was his, impaled on his dick, and all the other men had to watch from a distance and couldn't have me as they lost themselves, desiring the one he had all to himself.

Rook really did understand people, at least when it came to sex.

It took a *very* long — and utterly euphoric — time for us to finish. Then Rook turned on the water and the shower sprayed over us, sluicing away the mess we'd made. I was passed around, each guy taking their turn to wash me down. Never before had I been so clean.

You like? Rook whispered into my mind after it was all done and we were drying off.

I love, I replied, and saw his smile grow.

We all piled onto my massive bed. Maybe these elven beds were made for harems? It seemed so. I hugged Myel close, his soothing presence helping me to drift off. Koar was close behind me. Rook lay on the other side of Myel and we made room for Vyns above us all, so he could cuddle close as well, even if it was a bit awkward.

Bayn would have fit as well, but the titan wasn't yet ready for this level of intimacy and pulled some cushions off the many couches and chairs to make a bed for himself on the floor.

I didn't know what would happen tomorrow — how I'd face the titans, if Bayn and I could win this challenge against his parents — but right now, none of that mattered. I was so damned blissed out from that epic sex and comforted by the presence of all these stunning men around me. Tomorrow would be what it would be.

I slept soundly, dreaming of baths and showers and five gorgeous men fawning over me.

WE PACKED FAR MORE THAN WE NEEDED INTO SPECIAL INFINITE storage packs. Vyns and Rook stayed behind, since too large of a party heading into titan lands might be seen as a raid. They would also help organize their own kind on campus. Bayn was insistent it should only be me and him going, but eventually we compromised, which I found both surprising and rewarding. Koar came, because he wouldn't let me out of his sight, and Myel and I had been separated far too often of late, so the shifter went as well. Part of Bayn letting them come, however, was that Myel had to take his bat form when we were in public. Either that or stick to shadows where he couldn't be seen. That way it only looked like there were three of us.

We left mid-morning and Bayn used some special earth-power — which I watched intently, curious to learn — where he made the miles fly by. It was called land-step and it shifted reality around our feet making each step stretch for miles.

As such, we reached the distant wasteland, home of the titans, by nightfall. Tomorrow would be six days till Valnea's attack. Time seemed so short, especially for the task of convincing an entire nation to switch sides and follow me... or rather me and Bayn.

We were shown directly into the great hall of the titan king.

It was *mind boggling* in scale. Here, the titans did not deign to shrink themselves. The king and queen were over forty feet tall. Even sitting, they were imposing. Their stone thrones were bigger than most houses I'd lived in. The hall was... colossal, what was bigger than that? Gargantuan maybe? Whatever word meant "biggest of the bigs" that's what this hall was. I felt like a mouse.

And Bayn, he couldn't meet his parents while miniaturized, which meant he towered over me. I came up to just below that bulging muscle at the back of his calf. Being stepped on and smushed was a genuine concern.

Titan fashion trended toward ancient-Greek-chic, simple drapes of cloth and not much more. It made sense. In a land where showing off how big and strong you were mattered, then exposing all your muscled flesh was logical.

Bayn wore a simple white wrap around his waist. I had to keep reminding myself not to look up, or I might see a dick which was taller and thicker than I was. His mother and father wore the same, only their wraps were in deepest red. Apparently going topless as a titan woman was common. Not a practice I'd be taking up.

"The Disappointment has returned," Bayn's father, king Tagnaruk Dava, said with sneering contempt. "And he brings the enemy to our most sacred place!"

"Shut up, Father," Bayn boomed, the hall resonating with his deep voice. "Your words are meaningless. Let us prove ourselves with action. I challenge you for the throne."

Bayn and I had discussed this while we'd travelled. If he only challenged his father, his mother, Queen Duvonora

Dava would simply challenge him right after, and she was as strong as — if not stronger than — his father. So...

"And I challenge Queen Duvonora!" I shouted, using a voice enhancement technique Koar had taught me.

"We'll face you together," Bayn added, "As husband and wife."

"Accepted!" both the king and queen bellowed.

This was the first time a guy had ever taken me to see his parents... and we'd be fighting them to the death.

This was my life, now.

KOARTHANDRIS

Izzy and Bayn were given an hour to prepare themselves. Izzy took strength from me, to recover from the long day travelling. Then I let Bayn do the same, since he'd expended a lot of energy using his land-step to get us all here. It left me drained... but I'd done what I could to help them.

Yet again, Izzy would face death, and I'd not be able to protect her.

It rankled and stung, putting me in a foul mood.

"You okay?" Izzy asked as she limbered up, stretching a little. "What's wrong?"

"I can't protect you out there," I snarled, mad at myself, not her. Yet, the truth was far more insidious than that. I'd been thinking a lot since the assassination attempt on her, quietly working out if I could have done anything differently. And the sad truth was, I'd done everything possible to protect her... and she'd still nearly died. If Safir hadn't been there to take that last attack...

And that realization had been slowly crushing my soul.

When I said, *I can't protect you out there*, I hadn't meant,

I'm angry because I can't fight, but instead, *even if I was out there with you, I don't know if I'd make a difference.*

"I'll be okay," Izzy said, trying to soothe me. "With my strength, Bayn doesn't think I'll have any trouble beating his mother."

And that was another part of this multifaceted problem: in many ways Izzy didn't *need* me to protect her. And all this doubt was dragging up my old issues around my failure to protect Talmarion and his family.

I'd hoped that simply remaining close to Izzy would be enough. I'd thought that maybe Mynrial had died because I'd left her side to try to help her parents. But I'd been at Izzy's side when the assassins had struck, and it hadn't made a difference. And if I'd been allowed to fight in this death-match, would it change anything? As loath as I was to admit it, titans were stronger than dragons. One on one, I'd have little chance of success. It took roughly two dragons to fight one titan effectively. Titans were the descendants of elves, after all. Hence, this fight was among equals. A titan and an elf against two titans was a mostly level playing field. I would be a hindrance at worst or a mere bit of a help at best.

So... where did that leave me?

If it wasn't proximity that would help or save the woman I cared so deeply for... then what? If she was swarmed by elves, I'd be little help. And if she proved herself tonight, beat a titan queen, then did that mean she didn't need me by her side at all?

If I couldn't protect her, wasn't strong enough to make a difference, then what remained of my duty to the royal family?

I put on a fake smile to reassure Izzy that I'd be okay. She smiled in return and went back to her calisthenics.

Shifting my gaze, I looked over at Bayn. Could he protect her better than I could?

There was doubt in his brown eyes. Yet, I didn't believe it was doubt that he'd win this fight. No, I had a feeling it went far deeper than that.

I felt bad for Bayn. I still hated titans with a vengeance, that hadn't changed. I'd fought the big bastards too many times — lost too many friends to their savagery — for that to go away easily. But I saw Bayn as a titan less and less. He was just a man. And after our time together with Izzy, I couldn't help but notice how lost he seemed. He was a man out of place. A titan, but not accepted, shunned. Yet, as a titan he couldn't truly fit in anywhere else. All he had were a few friends, his sister, and Izzy. I'd seen how he'd looked at her during our bathroom escapades. There had been lust and passion, but also a certain desperation. He wanted — no needed — her to accept him, all of him, even his rather aggressive control issues. And so far, she had.

But I think he still feared Izzy, doubted her intentions, doubted all of us who surrounded her. My guess was, he dreaded losing control of the titans. The only reason Izzy was fighting with him was to make a show of force, to overwhelm and intimidate the titans so there would be no more challenges. And if she succeeded in that... would the titans only follow her... not him? What would become of him, then? That was my suspicion for the apprehension behind his eyes.

If so... he didn't know Izzy.

She'd happily hand control of the titans over to him. She didn't want to command anyone, really. But would her handing over control be a blow to his ego?

Perhaps.

Just as it had been a blow to mine to realize she didn't need me to protect her most of the time.

Hence, I felt a rather curious connection to the titan. Something I'd never thought possible.

"You ready?" Bayn boomed to Izzy. "Nearly time."

In fact, even as he said this, the massive door to our "little" training room opened and a titan told us it was time.

"As I'll ever be," Izzy said with a confident grin.

I rose and kissed her softly before she left.

"Crush her," I said almost as if it were a term of endearment.

"I will," she whispered with a wink, then kissed me back and turned to go.

Now, I had to trust fate.

No, not fate, I had to trust Izzy. Maybe that was all I needed? I hoped so.

IZZY

The arena was massive, like everything else in the titan lands. I wished I could say I was getting used to it, but being the size of a squirrel compared to everyone else really was off-putting. And this arena...

The throne room had been gargantuan, but now I needed a word for something that was many times the size of that room. Just like Cliffside Arena was a huge stadium, many times larger than any of the "large" lecture halls on campus, this arena was the same. My mind boggled at the scale. Carved from a natural cave, deep in a mountainside where the titans lived, I couldn't begin to comprehend how many "normal" people could fit in here. Millions? Tens of millions? It didn't really matter; I should be focusing on the two titans entering the far side of the arena onto the sandy floor.

I am not a squirrel, I am a strong elven woman, a badass. I repeated this to myself as part of my psych-up process.

On our day-long journey, Bayn and I had talked at length about strategies and preparation. He'd been rather surprised to learn I'd only learned earth magic and body enhancement a few days ago. So, he'd taken up my instruction where Lhorine had left off, giving me some advanced lessons. He'd seemed to like the fact that he knew far more than I did.

He'd walked me through a few high-level earth-wielding techniques as well as some advanced body enhancement methods. I'd soaked it all in and was using it now. It was still strange to think that I might be physically stronger than the towering woman stomping toward me across the arena, but I probably was. It wasn't muscle mass that made someone strong in this world, though that helped, and it was part of why the titans had made themselves into giants. No, it was your magic potential that made you strong.

So, I had a few tricks up my sleeve, though there was one that even Bayn didn't know about, something I'd been pondering ever since Bayn had shrunken himself a little more than usual in the bath. I'd talked to Grandma Oli about it before I'd left and she'd said it was theoretically possible, but she hadn't been certain if any nymph had ever tried it. Today would be a test run. We'd see if it worked.

Bayn and I stopped near the center of the arena. I'd been sprinting to keep up with his casual stride. His parents stopped about a titan's height away from us, both looked extremely imposing, glowering, ready for a fight.

"Most glorious titans!" some announcer's voice boomed through the arena. "Bayn The Deceiver has challenged his parents, the honorable and righteous King Tagnaruk Dava, and the beauteous and noble Queen Duvonora Dava to a deathmatch!"

Well, at least they're not being biased, I thought sarcastically.

"Bayn's second is a filthy elf whose name I shall not dignify."

Yup, definitely not biased.

"May the strongest win and rule over us with honor for millenniums to come!"

Yeah, I really didn't think this was going to go the way they wanted it to go. I could see now the overwhelming opposition Bayn had been struggling against to convince the titans to join us.

"Fight!" the announcer shouted, and at the same time a great gong sounded.

Bayn and his father charged each other.

The queen didn't even move, but her power surged. The ground between us rose up in a tidal way to crush me... and fell limp when it got within a dozen feet of me.

I smiled.

While we'd waited, I'd put a binding on the earth around me, making it immutable, so no one could use it against me... unless they were stronger than me and could override the binding. It seemed Queen Duvonora was not stronger than me.

She snarled and charged me, exactly as I'd been hoping.

She didn't deign to come down to my level, but instead simply tried to step on me.

I let her.

As the shadow of her massive bare foot covered me, I quickly made a hole and dropped down, before her foot landed. I then shifted laterally through the earth. I could sense where Duvonora stood, using my earth sense, and positioned myself roughly between her legs before shooting myself back to the surface.

She didn't even notice me, still pressing her foot down in a squashing motion shifting it back and forth.

Okay... time for my big surprise.

Surging my nymph shape-change abilities and empowering it with my elven body magic, I made myself as massive as she was, growing exponentially for half a second while bringing my fist up in a punch to her chin, which landed as I reached full height.

I probably should have foreseen the consequences of this change... namely... all my clothes being ripped to shreds leaving me naked.

Oh well. She'd been next to naked in only a skirt anyway, so... yeah. *Hello, titans!*

My fist connected solidly and sent the queen flying off her feet, arching through the air and landing fifty feet away on her back.

With two strides, I reached her and knelt, bringing my fist down so hard it pulverized her chest, punching right through her body.

Yikes!

Talk about not knowing my own strength!

I took my fist out and shook off the blood and gore. Disgusting. Then I touched her again, using my body-sense to feel for any life. Nope. The queen was dead.

Two hits had been all it took.

The crowd was deathly silent as I looked over to see how Bayn was doing.

He was having a bit more trouble defeating his father.

BAYN

I FELT MORE THAN SAW IZZY'S TRANSFORMATION. THEN MY mother went flying backward, which distracted me enough for my father to land a heavy blow to my chest, knocking me back and winding me.

I'd never tested myself against my father before. I'd always assumed we were close in strength, with myself being slightly stronger. That assumption was tested now. My father had gone absolutely berserk when the fight had started and I'd been on the defensive from the get-go. Yet, I'd matched him, blow for blow, able to deflect or evade his strikes and even get in a couple of my own, though they didn't land either. We'd been fairly evenly matched... until now.

After my lapse in attention and my father's stunning strike he pounced on that opportunity and swept my legs out from under me before I could move. I fell, hard, the wind knocked out of me again. And that gave my father another second's advantage, dropping hard with both knees onto my chest and crushing the air out of me once more.

I raised my arms to block my face as his fists rained down. My forearms took the brunt of his beating, until he switched to pummeling my upper chest.

I panicked.

I couldn't lose this fight.

Losing was death.

I'd lost so much already. I'd lost my home, my people, and so much of who I was. I'd been under someone else's thumb so long I'd forgotten my pride and heritage. I couldn't lose now.

I bucked hard, even though I couldn't breathe, even with my father's weight on me, even bruised and broken as I was, I put everything I had into the move.

My father slipped to one side and with a wild punch — which landed, surprising me — I knocked him off me, then I rolled away. I needed a second to recover, regain control, but my father was still raving mad and launched himself at me.

And hit Izzy.

She caught him in his wild charge and easily deflected him, throwing him with enough force to hurl him hundreds of feet into the wall of the arena, where he left a dent in the stone before he fell.

"You need a sec?" she asked, standing over me.

I did.

Even if I didn't want to admit it. It felt like weakness... and yet...

I nodded.

I couldn't deny the truth. Izzy had saved me. She'd *protected* me. No one had ever done that for me. As much as it felt like weakness, I was also overcome with gratitude. Did I want to fight my own fights? Sure. But I'd been on the back foot and needed time to recover.

I got up slowly as my breath returned, my strength finally rebounding.

When I looked over at Izzy, I finally noticed... she was stark naked. Of course she was. Her clothes wouldn't have survived this growth.

"You look good kicking ass," I breathed.

"Hell, yeah I do," she retorted.

I laughed.

"If you want to finish your father yourself...?" She let that question hang.

I smiled. I did. I really did. But something was starting to dawn on me. Life could be easier when you had help. Maybe, just maybe, it wasn't a weakness to ask for help, but a strength.

"Let's do it together," I said.

She smiled.

I had to admit, she looked damn good as a titan. I tore my eyes off her and back to my father, who'd recovered and was charging back at us.

And in that instant, I saw him for what he was. The man was unhinged. He'd always been a pretentious blowhard. A lot of that came with being a titan and literally the strongest of the strong. He'd bested all challengers over his long life. Yet his arrogance blinded him, unbalanced him. He wasn't the stalwart king I'd thought him to be as a boy. He was a scared little man, afraid that one day someone stronger would come along. Despite all his power, he still feared everyone around him...

...just like Valnea.

Maybe that's why the two of them had hit it off.

It didn't matter anymore. Here and now, I'd end him, *we'd* end him, Izzy and me. It was time for the titans to return to logic and rational behavior. Time to end the tyranny.

My father summoned earth to launch himself at me.

"Jump forward!" Izzy shouted and I did. At the same time a massive rock wall shunted up in front of my father mid-leap. He crashed into it, shattering the stone, slowing his advance. And I hit him a second later, driving him back, down to the ground, landing on him.

He grunted but was already trying to roll over and throw me off.

I blocked his elbow strike with a kick of my own, even as stone surged up over him trapping his legs in place while half rolled over.

My father shouted as his earth magic surged.

The stone didn't budge.

Izzy strode into view. Proud and strong and sexy as fuck.

"He's all yours," she said.

"Elven whore!" my father shouted. "You've befouled my son! All of titan kind-shall—"

My foot landed so hard on his neck, his spine snapped and his head rolled away, still looking startled.

"—revere me as their queen?" Izzy finished. "Yeah, that's what I thought you'd say."

She held out a hand to me and I took it, raising our joined hands above our head as Izzy — surprisingly — surged the stone beneath us and raised us up a few hundred feet for everyone to see.

"You remember you're naked, right?" I whispered out of the side of my mouth.

"Let them see their new queen in all her glory," she whispered back.

Fuck yeah. Right answer.

The crowd didn't seem to know what to do.

"Trust me?" I whispered.

"Not entirely, but right now, sure."

I used her hand in mine to pull her close then bent her back in a vicious dip of a kiss, one hand reaching up to crush her breast as I did so.

The crowd went nuts.

Izzy laughed against my lips. And when I pulled back enough for her to speak, she whispered. "Smart. Show them who's boss? Claim your queen. I get it."

She did.

She really did.

I'd needed to show these titans that I — a titan — was the one in charge. That I could dominate this woman who'd proven herself to be a force to be reckoned with.

Meanwhile, Izzy knew it was just a show.

Izzy had bested my mother — whom many said had been stronger than my father — in a matter of seconds, crushing her chest. Then she'd thrown my father across the ring. There was no denying her strength and power.

We left the arena, hand in hand, triumphant, making our way back to where we'd left Koar. And as we walked, I tried to sort through the surge of new emotions welling within me.

I felt... stronger with Izzy. Was that strange?

How could another person, who was clearly more powerful than me, make me feel stronger? The answer was clear, if unexpected. Because Izzy wasn't like others in this world. She didn't use her strength to push others down, but to lift them up. She made everyone around her better, stronger.

And with this strength and the knowledge of Izzy's

power, I felt... safe. Not entirely, not fully, but there was a hint of this new emotion: security. I'd never felt anything like this my entire life, always fighting, always proving myself, always scrambling for every inch of power, because I had to, to keep myself unharmed. I'd never been truly safe. But I was safe with Izzy, even if I didn't allow myself to give into this sensation quite yet.

Because I still didn't fully trust her.

I was starting to, and that was a huge leap for me. I'd never trusted anyone except my sister and a few close friends. Though if I was being honest, even my friends I'd always wondered about. Would they betray me? Everyone else had. I hadn't even fully trusted those closest to me.

But Izzy.

I could trust her. Even if I didn't let myself admit it yet.

I trusted her because she was damn strong. She *could* control me — her binding *still did* control me — but she'd never once used her power or the binding to harm me. She didn't lord it over me. She'd been trying to get rid of it, and I honestly believed she wanted it gone.

She didn't make me feel small, controlled. She lifted me up and made me stronger.

Which shattered all my assumptions about power.

I'd thought power was control. I'd felt powerless for so long because I couldn't control people the way I wished. But I'd been shown a different sort of power. One that wasn't about posturing and manipulation and control, but was instead uplifting, giving and generous.

Maybe all my assumptions had been wrong.

Maybe I knew nothing of real power.

But now... I desperately wanted to learn.

And I had the perfect mentor to instruct me, the proud and stunning woman who would be my wife. And looking at her, another new and strange emotion crept into my heart, something... soft and giving and caring.

It felt so wrong.

But also very right.

Whatever it was... it was going to take some getting used to.

IZZY

My show of force in the fight with the king and queen hadn't quite been enough. There had been one other challenger to my and Bayn's authority: the general of the titan armies. He'd not bent a knee the next day when we were presented as the new king and queen.

I'd maintained my enlarged form, it was just easier, since everyone around me was giant. I'd also been brave and adopted the titan style of dress, which meant a simple wrap skirt... and nothing else.

I'd seen the calculating look in the general's eyes. He'd been about to challenge Bayn, but not so he could defeat him then fight me and take control of the titans... but because he wanted to *have* me, be my king. Yeah, I'd not let that happen, so before he'd challenged Bayn, I'd challenged him.

Since we were short on time, I'd insisted we fight here and now, so the two of us stood in the throne room, in a circle made of watching titans. Bayn didn't look worried, in fact, he gave the general a pitying look.

The general swung. I used my self-defense training to capture his arm, spin, then shoulder throw him onto his back. I knelt on his chest with my hand around his neck, pinning him down, but I didn't follow through and crush his throat. Instead, I put the same binding on him I had on Saldrea. Any harm he wished on others would befall him.

I spoke loud enough for everyone to hear. "I do not wish to kill you. Too many titans have died already. We'll need all of you to fight the elves in the war to come. But I will not let you betray me either. The choice is yours." I didn't tell him of my binding. I stood and turned my back on him. I heard him rise, then a sickening sound and the crash of his body hitting the ground again.

I turned to see his head turned the wrong way around.

Yikes.

I should explain that to all the astonished on-lookers. "I put a binding on him," I shouted. "Any harm he thought to do to me, would happen to him. He killed himself with his arrogance. Let this be the last death of a titan at the hands of another titan. Let us fight the elves together, then live in peace with all races once we'd trounced those arrogant bastards once and for all!"

That got a hearty cheer.

I returned to my throne next to Bayn. "I hope I didn't steel your thunder," I whispered to him.

"I have a feeling you'll always be stealing my thunder, wife," he said with a smirk.

He was probably right.

That day was spent mobilizing the titans, most of whom were willing to follow me and Bayn. Some few slunk off in the night to join Valnea. Luckily, Bayn had thought of a way to use that to our advantage.

Now, finally, we had a chance to win this war.

By the time we'd returned to Veilblood Academy with the titans, we had four days till Valnea's assault. In some ways it seemed like an eternity, and yet, there weren't enough hours in the day for all the preparations still to be done. Every day our forces worked to build more defenses, high earthworks, a diversion of the river, winding paths of high stone walls to divert the enemy, dead zones where the salmaeri would lay down walls of fire.

Everyone worked, including me, and as much as I might have wanted to savor the time in the evenings with my guys, we weren't all there at the same time, too much to do. And nobody had energy for anything more than flopping into bed. Though the guys did find ways to help me relax and rest. Vyns gave the best foot rubs, Koar had hidden talents for deep tissue massage, one of Rook's underused talents was a voice like silk, which he used to lull me to sleep. Myel just needed to lay beside me and all my cares floated away. Bayn wasn't all that skilled with anything to help me relax, but he'd done something else, taking a figurative weight off my shoulders by organizing all our forces. He'd wanted to be our general and I trusted him enough now to let him take the lead. And it saved me so much stress and anxiety.

And all of this demonstrated even more how much I needed the guys, how much they meant to me. So, two nights before the battle, I took each aside to have a private word. We'd received intel that Valnea might move early, at night, potentially tomorrow night, hence why we did this now.

I simply held Myel close and let him feed on me. And when he'd finished, we stayed close. We didn't need words now. The bond was so strong, our emotions laid bare, that there wasn't anything left to say. We were scared, but there was hope. We loved each other dearly and deeply and knew we'd fight to our last breaths to protect each other. I'd meet up with Myel again, once I'd met with the other guys, so his soothing presence could help me sleep. We kissed softly and parted.

As I waited for Koar, I couldn't help the secret smile which spread on my lips. I'd lost track of days, but it had been less than a month since I'd come to this world and before that... I'd never have expected to have such a deep relationship with anyone. I'd been scared stiff of long-term, committed relationships. I'd always lost those closest to me, they died, or left, or I left before we could get too close. And here I was, with five guys, all of them deeply committed, and I might lose all of them in a matter of days. I couldn't fathom the loss, and yet... I wouldn't give up what we had for anything.

I hadn't really gotten over my fear of loss, but I'd certainly circumvented it somehow to let each of these men get so close.

Koar slipped up behind me, enfolding me in strong arms, pressing my back to his hard chest.

"I love you, Perfection," he whispered.

I loved his pet name for me. I didn't feel perfect, but I loved that he saw me as perfect... for him.

I hadn't said *the words* to Koar, or anyone other than Myel yet. And if I was going to break that seal, now would be the time. Still, I hesitated. It felt so *big*. Did I really love all these guys? Could I love them all?

Then I recalled what Koar had told me about love, his definition. It had been something about being best friends and wanting what's best for each other, giving and taking, and also finding each other attractive and wanting some form of physical relationship.

That fit what I had with my guys.

I gave a breathy little laugh.

"I love you too, big man," I said. I wished I had a better pet name for him but given how he seemed to soften a little and hold me closer, perhaps it wasn't needed.

"No one's ever said that to me before," he breathed.

I found that hard to believe. Wasn't he *stupidly* old?

Then he explained. "Dragons don't require love to mate. We find appropriate matches and have children. We don't even raise them, we let our elders do that, those too old to fight."

Sounded cold to me. And I'd thought dragons were all hot fire and passion.

"I will cherish what we have my entire life," he whispered, then chuckled. "And that's a long time."

"Don't say things like that," I whispered. "It makes it sound like... we won't have each other after this. I have to hope you'll all survive. I need you all."

He kissed the top of my head. "I know. Still, I don't regret saying it."

"You... okay?" I asked. I felt... something from him, some hesitancy I couldn't place or name.

He sighed heavily, his chest heaving behind me.

"I recently realized I can't protect you, not in the way I want to, that I *need* to. I still don't know exactly what to do with that."

I had no idea what to say, to reassure him. So, in lieu of words, I turned in his arms and reached up to pull his face down to mine for a long, deep, tender kiss. After, he rested his forehead on mine.

"Perfection," he breathed.

"If you want to protect my heart, you'll come back to me, alive, after all this," I whispered, not knowing where those words had come from.

"As long as you do too," he said.

"Deal."

I rested my head on his chest, and he crushed me close one last time, then we parted and Vyns joined me.

"What do you need, Angel?" he asked. He'd only just started with that nickname and it always made me smile. *He* was the angel. "Your spirit is... cloudy."

I felt into the strange connection I had with Vyns, a thing of curious sensations. It wasn't exactly emotions, like what I shared with Myel, but more... vague, though still powerful. Vyns always felt... warm. Though when he was in pain it felt like some out-of-body headache or stomachache. And when he was aroused it felt like sweltering summer rain, those humid days, when the rain brings no relief, only more sultry heat. He said my spirit shone like a sun or star, so me being "cloudy" was probably my anxiety over this coming battle.

"It's hard to be sunny with so much... uncertainty," I said as he enfolded me in his arms. Then he flashed out his wings and wrapped them around me too. I loved his wings, white and gold and soft and fluffy and warm.

"Of one thing I am certain," he whispered. "I love you more than anything. You are my sun and moon. You light my days and my nights."

I tried to think of some way to express how he felt to me, through my spirit.

"You are my eternal summer's day," I whispered, liking that analogy. Then I ruined it, "You make me... hot."

We both laughed.

That bit of levity made it easier for me to say, "I love you too." And I hugged him tighter.

And as we stood there in each other's arms, his spirit flowed into mine, bolstering and strong, unwavering.

"Thank you," I said with a sigh. "You always give so much."

"You give too, though I don't think you see it. It's often in little ways, but you do it for so many it adds up to a lot. It's one of the things I love about you."

He was right, I didn't see it, but I trusted him. If he said I did stuff like that... then maybe I did and I had no clue about it.

"Right now, you're giving thousands of people hope for a better future," he breathed.

Huh... I supposed that was true.

I smiled and felt a sense of ease settle over me.

"There we go, that's better," Vyns said with a sigh of his own.

Apparently, the master of foot rubs was also really good at spirit rubs. I didn't know if that was a thing, but that's what I was calling it.

He kissed my forehead. I tilted my head back and we shared a deep kiss before he stepped away, gazing at me like I was his entire world. He smiled and left.

Rook sauntered over.

"If you're expecting sappy stuff, I don't do that," he said, nonchalant.

"Keep telling yourself that, Inky, and maybe it'll be true one day, but I know you better. I've heard your innermost thoughts, remember?"

Rook blinked at me. "Inky?" His face scrunched up.

"What!" I blurted. "You all have fun pet names for me. I can't have one for you? I'm trying it out. Incubus… Inky…"

"Oh… Izzy… no, just don't. Now *Kink*, that would be a fun pet name for me."

I sighed. Maybe it would be, but since I hadn't come up with it, it lost its appeal. "Anyway, I know you have a soft side in addition to your…" I wiggled my brows and quirked my lips, "…*hard* side."

"Innuendo you can do, stick with that," he said as he drew close enough to pull me into a hug, his "hard side" crushed against me.

"You've felt a little… distant lately, since you came back from Urval," I said pulling him close in a squeezing embrace of my own. My words were a little muffled talking into his shoulder. "Your body is with me and your mind is with me, but your heart…"

He sighed heavily. "It's with you… and that's the problem."

I held him close and waited for him to elaborate.

"My mother," he began, and it was the last thing I expected. I supposed sex demons did have mothers, like everyone else, but still, talking about his parents seemed odd for some reason. "She's anti-love in a big way. We… argued… sort of. She loved my father more than she should have, and when he died…"

Ah.

"And you're afraid I'm going to die?"

He didn't say anything, but his tangled thoughts revealed the truth to me. It wasn't so much me specifically dying, but death in general. If he died, I'd be sad and he didn't want that for me. And if I died… well he'd seen what that had done to his mother.

"I'll do my best to stay alive, if you promise to do the same. That's... the best we can do." I hugged him tighter. He grunted in pain. I remembered my elven strength and eased off a bit. I even drew back enough to look him in the eyes.

"I have one strong reason to stay alive, and it's your orgasms. They're second to none. What reason do you have?"

He quirked a half smile. "Another threesome with you and Myel. That was positively sinful."

I smiled. "There, see? Keep that in mind, something to fight for. When the chips are down and things look bleak, think of me and Myel and fight to have another moment with us."

"How is it you know exactly what to say to make me feel okay?" he whispered.

"Because I'm a kick-ass, intelligent, goddess of a woman, of course."

"Yes... you are, aren't you?" There was no hint of sarcasm or hyperbole in his voice, like there had been in mine.

"See?" I breathed. "There you go being sappy." And I kissed him before he could argue or make some flippant comment.

I still maintain that kissing an incubus solved all of life's problems. In the same way Myel's presence comforted me, Rook's devastatingly sinful kisses melted the world away until all that remained were lips and tongues in a delicious communion of the senses.

Rook pulled back and my lips followed his. I didn't want it to end.

"If I didn't stop us, we'd stay here kissing forever," he breathed.

"Yeah..." I sighed the word. Would that really be so bad?

But... we had a war to fight.

Still that thought didn't dim my spirits. "Another thing to live for," I whispered.

"Hell, yeah," he said softly, gave me a quick peck, one last squeeze of a hug, then he left.

I grabbed his hand and pulled him back.

"I love you," I said holding him close once again.

He smiled then blew out a nervous breath and whispered, "I love you too, My Flame." The first time he'd said the words aloud. "I'll live for you, if you live for me."

"I'll live for you, if you live for me," I repeated the words back to him, it seemed like some vow.

Then we kissed again, which was a mistake. I don't know how long later Rook broke off with a chuckle, kissed my forehead, then left.

Bayn came over.

We didn't hug.

"You are lucky to have such dedicated and loving partners," he said with a glance back at the others, staying innocuous on the other side of my large bedroom.

"You have them too," I said, taking up one of his massive hands in both of mine. "They've become like brothers to each other, and I know they'll welcome you into their special little fraternity."

Bayn's round cheeks rose as he smiled. "I'd like that, even if... I may not be ready for it yet."

"You've gone through a lot in a short time. It's okay if this takes a while. There's no hurry. Just make sure you survive this fight and that we win, then you'll have all the time in the world."

"You make that sound easy," he rumbled softly.

"Isn't that what you've been doing your whole life? Fighting?"

He cocked his head. "True."

"Then this war should be the easy part. Learning how to live peacefully afterward, that... may take some work."

He blinked at me as if that was some devastating revelation.

"Huh... you're right." Then he smiled again. "And here I was worried about the war." It seemed like a weight lifted off him. He even chuckled softly. "But it's just one more battle — if a large one — in the war I've been fighting my entire life."

His gaze refocused on me. "Then... after...? You're right, I don't know how to love, not really. Or how to live peacefully with others. I... may need your help with that."

"Love is caring for someone like they're your best friend and wanting to fuck them at the same time, to paraphrase a wise dragon I know. You've got the fucking part down, so the rest shouldn't be too hard."

"Do you..." His brow furrowed, his face contorting. He looked away. He couldn't say it.

"Love you?" I finished.

He nodded.

With Bayn, I wouldn't mince words. "I wouldn't say you're at best friend level yet... but I'm starting to trust you, and that's not easy for me. I'm no longer scared of you, which is something. I feel... *strongly* for you, though what exactly those feelings are, I have yet to work out. So, yeah... I'm not quite there yet either. But... I've seen your heart. You care for your sister and your people. You didn't want them following a tyrant like Valnea, and you saved them from themselves. There's a lot to admire in that. I don't think love is too far off for us."

Bayn nodded. "You're certainly the best fuck I've ever had," he said, blunt. I had to smile, because he'd said it completely straight, entirely serious, not a hint of machismo or carnality. I got the feeling he wanted to say more, be... open, share some emotion, but he didn't.

Yeah, we weren't there yet.

"So, let's fight," I said softly. "Fight for a future where we don't have to fight anymore. And once we've won, we can get married, you can be king, and we can utterly ruin our marriage bed. Then we'll work on love and all the rest, how's that sound?"

His smile softened, a secret thing just for me. "Honestly, I'm not sure I wish to be king anymore."

"Oh, you're gonna be king," I insisted. "I don't want to rule alone. Even with the council we're setting up, I'd rather you be on it than me. Don't back out on me, now. And I'm making the others my king-consorts as well. I know that's not a thing, but if I'm queen I can make it a thing."

He chuckled. "Deal."

We stood in awkward silence before he asked, "Are you... able to remove the binding on me?"

Oh right! That.

"I don't know. I certainly feel differently now than I did then," I said. "Let me try."

Through our joined hands I reached into him and felt for my binding. I didn't so much try to break it as I did study it. My knowledge of bindings was progressing quickly, mostly through my own trial and error. When I poked at this one, it still felt... unresolved. There was something keeping me from breaking it.

I took an extra bit of time to see if I could examine the binding to figure out what was needed. The best I could determine was that it required an advanced level of trust. Having fought beside Bayn, I trusted him with my life, but perhaps I still didn't fully trust him with my heart. That was what this felt like.

I withdrew and opened my eyes to look at Bayn.

"No, not yet. Soon."

He grimaced.

I needed to give him something. "Until then, let me say this." I stood a bit taller, my gaze intent on his, my tone not quite demanding, but firm. "Bayn, you are free to act as you wish, to fight for what you need to fight for, to protect what you wish to protect, to be who you need to be. Let these words supersede anything else I might say to you, any command I might give you whether inadvertently or otherwise." I drew a long breath. "How's that sound?"

He nodded.

"Thank you, I know you didn't want this." He chuckled. "I've *almost* gotten used to it." He grew serious again. "But I don't think I can trust you all the way till you release me from it."

"Makes sense," I said. "But you trust me enough to follow me into battle?"

That secret smile returned as he nodded. "Battle is easy, the rest is hard, remember?"

I smiled too. "Right. Now come down here so I can kiss you."

He cocked his head. "Huh... it worked," he murmured. I'd commanded him and the binding hadn't enforced it.

Good.

He knelt and I took that soft-cheeked face in both hands and kissed him.

When we separated, he raised his brow. "Ruin our marriage bed, huh?"

"Yup."

"I'm looking forward to it." He rose, and I followed him back to the others.

This time, Bayn did join us on the bed as we all

collapsed into sleep. He laid across the foot of the bed, and it said something about how huge the bed was, that he fit without falling off the end, and that none of our feet were anywhere near him.

I hugged Myel close, let his soothing comfort relax me, and tried not to dream of death and destruction.

IZZY

BAYN HAD BEEN SMART. WHEN SOME OF THE TITANS HAD FLED to Valnea, he'd send a small group with them who were loyal to us. They had one job... let us know the instant the attack was to commence.

As we'd suspected she would, Valnea came early, just after midnight. In the wee hours of the morning her force began to flood over Veilblood campus.

And we were ready for them, or at least as ready as we could be. With the titans on our side, we outnumbered them, but they still had more battle-hardened warriors than we did. Far too many of our number had been servants or administrators not that long ago.

Still, we put up one hell of a fight.

Reports came in from all over campus to our secret underground bunker, a new one, not the one Lhorine had created off campus.

That's where I waited with my guys. A troop of elite warriors waited nearby as well. We needed to know where Valnea herself appeared and that's where I'd strike. Finally, one of the pixie runners sprinted in, out of breath, gasping that Valnea — along with a significant entourage to protect her — was at the north end of campus.

"Do what you must," Lhorine said to me, by way of farewell.

"Slay that bitch!" were Grandma Oli's parting words, as my guys and I ran to join our little force, then we fast-marched up to meet Valnea.

She was waiting for us.

Just like we'd been spying on her, it was no surprise to me that she'd known I was coming. With the massive number of people coming and going on campus, there had to have been spies for her as well. We hoped they didn't know *all* our secrets.

Valnea had created an opening for us. Her forces arrayed in a semi-circle behind her. There were dragons, some in dragon form, others in human form with wings out. Elves stood perfectly arrayed in rows, all in fancy-looking armor, which was far stronger than it appeared. She easily had five thousand in her force. We had barely five hundred.

Being outnumbered ten to one meant I needed to defeat the false queen as fast as possible and hope her forces capitulated once she'd been dealt with.

Valnea herself, in ornate golden armor, strode forward, alone and confident.

Something was up. I hadn't expected her to actually challenge me one on one. She had to know how easily I'd defeated her daughter. She was strong, but by all reports, I was stronger.

I waved a hand to keep the bulk of my forces back. My guys wouldn't let me do anything alone, so I didn't even try to leave them behind.

"Just... stay back a little," I asked them. So it wouldn't look like all of us were advancing to fight Valnea.

I got a good look at the false queen as we drew close. She was the spitting image of Saldrea, her daughter, or rather, Saldrea was the spitting image of her. Golden blond hair, falling in perfect waves around a heart-shaped face. Tall and slender, a model's figure with perfect, pale skin and eyes like sapphires. Objectively... she was attractive, but any man who fell for her charms had to hate himself, because there was cruelty behind those blue eyes. What was worse was the depth of sadistic experience in those eyes. She wasn't untested in her cruelty. She'd lived a long life, and I guessed she'd employed all manner of ways to make others suffer. There was also madness there, a raving surety of her superiority.

"Surrender," I offered. "Save the lives of your people."

Her face twisted. "What do I care for their lives?"

I should have expected that.

"Then surrender to save your own life," I said, voice low and lethal.

She laughed. Oh yeah, she definitely had something up her sleeve.

"Why would I do that? I'm in no danger. Did you think I'd come to this battle unprepared?"

No, I didn't. I just didn't know exactly what she had planned.

She sneered as she continued. "I did my homework on you and your pathetic force. You're weak in air magic. So, tell me, you little royal slut, who's going to protect your minds?"

And that seemed to be the signal for her forces. They began to move, but more importantly, a host of sylphim appeared out of nowhere. From my — admittedly limited — studies, I'd known some sylphim could use a form of invisibility, where they masked themselves from perception, an intricate mental trick, which was not supposed to be common. I now suspected those lessons had been false and the commonality was much higher but kept secret, given the thousand or so sylphim which appeared all around us, surrounding my force. They even cut me off from my guys.

Fuck!

I charged Valnea, but even as I did, mental claws raked my mind. Horrible images, illusions, played before my eyes. They weren't real, but that didn't stop them from distracting me. It was hard not to be distracted with my worst fears displayed in terrifying high definition. My attention was yanked away and tossed about like a ball of yarn in the paws of a cat. I stumbled, faltering.

And that's when Valnea attacked.

Whatever else she might be, the false queen was a vicious warrior. I may have been stronger than her in raw power, but her years of experience were evident in how she swiftly bound my feet in earth to keep me in place, then immediately followed up with her sword, combined with an attack of razor-sharp stone shards.

With my mind besieged, my stone wall defense was too late, she'd already carved into me, a nasty slash across my abdomen from below my left breast to my right hip. The stone shards dug into my skin, a rain of pain slicing deep. My wall didn't even get all the way up before Valnea stamped it back down. All I could think to do was heal myself while surging my endurance, my toughness and fortitude. That pushed some of the stone shards out and mended most of the gash on my stomach, but Valnea didn't let up, and it didn't matter how strong I was. If I stayed on the defensive, I'd lose this fight.

I couldn't afford to lose, nor could I afford to wait. The

longer I waited to defeat Valnea, the more of my forces would suffer and die.

But with my mind under attack, I could barely think. I hardly knew which way was up. Attacking would be impossible. I needed some relief, an out, an edge, and I couldn't find one. When I risked a glance to see if my guys would be coming to my aid, what I saw horrified me more than the visions playing around me.

The sylphim must have been inside their minds as well. They all stood stunned or fought invisible foes.

Fuck!

Why hadn't we accounted for this overwhelming attack on our minds?

That oversight might cost us everything.

BAYN

THIS WAS WRONG, ALL WRONG. I SHOULDN'T BE HERE, IN BED, not with *her*. I should be... somewhere else, but I couldn't remember where. Everything was fuzzy, but I had this sense of urgency burning through me. Though perhaps that urgency was to escape the clutches of Osserime.

We'd used chains in bed before. I personally preferred chaining her down, seeing her spread and wet, ready for my pleasure. But she insisted on chaining me at times and I let her, because we were equal, and I'd thought we had something special.

Had...

This wasn't right.

I wasn't with Osserime anymore, was I?

Why couldn't I think straight?

And it wasn't the chains which infuriated me... it was the binding. The damned woman had put a binding on me to get me to submit to her. I'd never agreed to that, but Osserime came from a line of strong earth-magic wielders and she was nearly a match for me in power. That means I should be able to break this bond, but she'd infused the binding with something else, which seemed to sap my strength and cloud my mind.

I struggled against the chains, but it was no good. Even if I could break the thick metal links, her binding would keep me here.

"That's a good little boy," she purred, taking out her phone and snapping a couple pictures. "The titans are going to love this. Prince Baynaruk, weak as a slug."

"Let me go!" I howled, but she just laughed.

"Nope, you're not going to see light for a long time. Your parents convinced me this was the right course of action. They even lent me some strength for that binding to ensure it held."

So that was it. My parents had turned against me. I'd been outspoken about siding with Valnea, but I hadn't thought my parents were so far gone into that elf's clutches as to do something like this to silence me.

"They're going to stick you in a dark hole for a while, but first... I'm going to have some fun with you, show all our people what their prince is really like!"

My fury boiled over, but it was an impotent rage. I could do nothing. I struggled in vain as she teased out an unwanted arousal from my body and used me, seeming to delight far more in my struggle than the actual sex. She flogged me while she had her way, getting off on my pain. I'd never known she had such a cruel side.

How could I have ever loved this woman? We were betrothed, but she'd betrayed me in such a visceral and humiliating way.

My mind twitched. I wasn't struggling in bed, but laying on a battlefield, with men and women fighting all around me. I writhed, struggling against...

...something...

And while I flailed in that instant of lucidity, I saw Izzy taking a beating from Valnea.

Izzy.

Yes!

I shouldn't be lost in some memory of Osserime, I should be with Izzy helping her...

...do something.

But what?

My mind clouded again and I was back in bed, but this time, it was Izzy riding me, glorifying in my struggle and binding.

"I said I'd set you free, remove the binding, but you never really believed me, did you?" She laughed, and the maniacal giggle sounded so wrong coming from her. "You're mine, Bayn, all mine, and I've got you right where I want you!" She whipped me, flogged me, humiliated me, like Osserime had.

And for some reason, this betrayal felt even worse than Osserime's.

I may not have fully trusted Izzy, may not have let down all my guards with her, but I'd started to feel... something, which I'd never felt for Osserime. Osserime had been a good match for me, strong and driven, a dedicated titan from a powerful family. Our union had been mostly a political thing. I'd never sought any emotion from her. We had similar tastes in bed, and that worked, as did our pride in titan culture and strength. We'd only differed on... Valnea and the elves. She'd agreed with my parents, and I'd been against the whole thing.

But Izzy...

...somehow the half-elf had stolen part of my heart. She was everything I wanted and she wanted me in return.

Or so I'd thought.

This sadistic woman reveling in my pain wasn't Izzy at all... and yet it was. *I... I need to fight... her?* I needed to fight someone...

My head was so damned heavy and mixed up I couldn't tell which way was up. And Izzy's betrayal, binding me, keeping me bound, going back on her word, that... that hurt far more than Osserime's betrayal ever had.

I struggled harder and harder, but nothing worked. The woman wouldn't relent. She laughed at my efforts, whipping me harder, getting off on my pain like Osserime had. It was everything I'd dreaded for the last hundred years. I couldn't believe Izzy would do this, but the proof was right before my eyes.

I think...

Why was everything so confusing and foggy?

It was Izzy's fault.

She'd done something to me.

That had to be it.

I thrashed and writhed, but she wouldn't let me go, laughing more and more.

How could she?

My spirit waned, flagging, giving in. I couldn't fight her; she was too strong. This would be my existence, trapped as her slave.

Her betrayal crushed me.

KOARTHANDRIS

I HAD ENOUGH AIR MAGIC TO RESIST THE MENTAL ATTACKS OF the sylphim all around me. Yet, I could see how it had twisted the minds of the others. Even Izzy wasn't immune. I needed to get to her, help her. Valnea was ripping her apart and all Izzy could do was raise a mild defense and heal. She needed me now more than ever!

But I had my own fight.

Valnea must have suspected I'd resist the mental attack, so she'd sent a whole squad of experienced dragons against me, six on one. Even so, I was so enraged, so desperate to help Izzy, that I fought those six to a standstill, a draw. But that was all I could do, overpowering them wouldn't be possible. They all had magic similar to mine, so my destruction and fire did little to them.

I fought in dragon form. Initially, I'd shifted to my natural form so my size would help to push away the sylphim, but those nasty little air-wielders had quickly recovered, keeping up their attack on me and my friends from a distance as elves moved in to attack. I'd tried to get to Izzy, but this flight of dragons had intercepted me, and our fight had spiraled up into the skies, farther and farther from the woman I'd sworn to protect at all costs.

No!

I fought with tooth and claw, magic and destruction, everything I had. I focused on one of my opponents, leaving myself open to the others, feeling their magic and physical attacks tear into me. But it worked. My rage-fueled attacks took down the dragon I'd targeted and I resumed my defenses against the others.

Maybe I could get out of this.

But then I realized how hurt I was, how much healing I had to do, and knew I'd been fooling myself. Leaving myself open like that again might work, but after that, I'd be too weak to fight any of them.

Fucking hell!

I needed a little help. Just a minor distraction and I could defeat these bastards and get to Izzy. But no help came. My comrades were all overwhelmed, just like I was.

It was an impossible fight.

And the only way we'd win would be through Izzy, if she somehow managed to regain herself and defeat Valnea.

But when I risked another glance at my beloved, her strength waned, flagging under the unrelenting assault from the false queen.

Izzy needed help more than I did.

And I should be the one to help her.

This was everything I'd feared.

The only way for us to win...

...would be a miracle.

VYNSIEL

It felt like a dream. Though, if it was, it was one of those far-too-real and terrifying dreams, a nightmare. Izzy fought with everything she had, but it wasn't enough. Valnea shouldn't have been able to overpower her, but she was.

I ran, a dead sprint, to the woman I loved, but something held me, slowed me. It was like running through molasses, the air thick around me. Must be those damned sylphim.

The more I ran, the farther away Izzy seemed to get, that was the truly horrifying part, and what seemed most like a dream. And yet everything else around me was far too real. Our forces fighting and dying, the campus grounds soaked in blood. We'd expected to be overwhelmed and outnumbered, but... the reality of it was daunting, spirit-breaking.

But I wouldn't give up, wouldn't let my spirit falter.

Then Valnea punched into Izzy's chest and pulled out her still beating heart.

My heart stopped for an instant in horrified dismay.

"No!" I shouted, but I couldn't reach them, couldn't help, couldn't do anything!

Izzy collapsed, far too still, and I waited for the echo of her death to billow into my spirit and crush me truly.

But it didn't happen.

Something was wrong.

I couldn't deny what my eyes were seeing, but my spirit didn't flag, didn't waver, wasn't filled with loss and pain... which meant somehow, Izzy was still alive.

It made no sense.

And that disjunction broke the hold on my mind. I saw the battlefield as it truly was, Izzy still alive and fighting, though beaten all to hell and not looking good by any means. My friends struggled, minds overwhelmed and defenseless as they were attacked by elves. I couldn't see Koar, had he escaped?

"This one's mind is strong!" a sylph hissed nearby.

"No, his spirit is strong, his mind is still weak, focus!" another said.

And even as I tried to reach them...

The dream returned.

Yet, as much as I knew it was a dream, I couldn't escape it, couldn't stop it. Again and again, I watched Izzy die, and every time my spirit rejected that reality, knowing she was still alive. But the dream would only start again, stretching out, me running so slow and unable to reach Izzy as she fought then inevitably died.

It was the most hideous thing, ripping apart my mind.

I had to keep striving, keep fighting, resist. It was the only way to break this cycle of vicious visions. My spirit strained, pushing hard to keep me going, keep me sane... but eventually even it would falter.

And I had no clue how to break from this dreadful nightmare before that happened.

AMARHUK (ROOK)

I KNEW WHAT WAS HAPPENING, BUT I COULDN'T STOP IT.

The limited mental powers I'd gleaned from Hana only worked against her. She couldn't break my mind... but other sylphim could, especially a whole host of them working together. I sensed it, felt the vision take me, even as I tried to shake it off and fight... but I couldn't.

Or... had I?

Fuck.

I couldn't tell what was real anymore. I was still on a battlefield, still fighting for my life against elves and sylphim and more, but... was this the true fight? Why would the sylphim make me see something so close to reality?

This had to be real... right?

Maybe?

Fuck, my head hurt like hell. But was that just from resisting the mind-altering effects of the angels or were they actually inside my head, making me see this... even if it seemed like little had changed.

"Rook! Please!" Izzy's cry drew my attention. I found her amongst the chaos around me and saw how she struggled against Valnea. The sylphim must be hindering her mind too, limiting her ability to fight. She should have overwhelmed the false queen long ago. But with her mind being attacked at the same time, it looked like she could barely defend herself.

I ran, sprinting to her, but even as I reached her, Valnea punched through that perfect chest of Izzy's and pulled out her heart. Izzy fell, dead, eyes wide and vacant, into my arms as I arrived too late.

"Noooooo!" I screamed with raw agony, my heart torn out and shredded at the sight of Izzy, bloody and broken before me. Is this what my mother had felt? It was so much worse than anything I'd imagined. My mother, at least, hadn't been on the battlefield, hadn't seen the exact moment, the horror of it. I had.

Valnea laughed as she stomped on Izzy's heart and I collapsed to my knees, clutching Izzy's lifeless body close.

"You fools. You thought you could defeat me?" Valnea cackled.

And the cold, dark emptiness inside my chest constricted even more, sucking in everything I was, an implosion of my being. It left behind an empty shell.

A shell, that had nothing left to lose.

"You've made a mistake," I hissed as I let the body of the woman I'd so deeply loved fall away. I rose, drawing my sword, summoning my magic. "I have no reason to live, but before I die, I'll take as many of you with me as I can!"

Valnea's shocked expression made me smile, a grim grin.

She fell back as I surged toward her, but I couldn't reach her. Other elves blocked my path. And they were strong, too strong, I'd never defeat all of them, but I didn't have to. I just had to cut down as many as I could before they killed me.

I fought with cold dispassion, hacking at the elves like so

much wheat. And yes, they cut me, broke me, made me bleed. But what did I care for blood, since my heart was already gone. The pain didn't matter, all that mattered was soon I'd find the cold comfort of death, but before that, I'd make so many others feel it too.

MYELAS

I KNELT, IZZY'S DEAD BODY IN MY ARMS AS THE OTHER MEN crowded close, hurling curses at me for my failure to protect her.

"She trusted you!"

"Look what you did!"

"How could you ever think you were worthy of her, of being one of us!"

And yet... I didn't believe a word of it.

This wasn't right at all.

If Izzy was dead... my soul would be crushed, the bond a void, pulling me toward madness or my own death. Yet, that wasn't happening. The bond held strong. I felt Izzy's pain and strain clear as the beating of my own heart.

Izzy was alive.

I focused... and the body in my hand faded away.

As I'd thought.

I pushed harder against this false reality and the men — my brothers — vanished. I stood slowly, flashing out my steel wings. The sting of pain wasn't as bad as the first time, I was getting used to it, and it served to clear my head even more.

The fog faded, and the true battlefield came into view.

"No!" hissed a sylph nearby. "How...?"

I turned to the angel, and what he saw in my eyes made him flinch.

"You're just a pathetic shifter... how...?"

I stalked toward him. "A shifter, yes, one with a mate bond to the woman you forced me to watch die. But *I know* she lives, and you've made a rather grave error."

"Still, I'm an angel. You can't..."

"Do you know what happens when a shifter watches their mate die? They either kill themselves or go mad." A vicious grin split my face. "Welcome to my madness, motherfucker!" And with a slash of my wing the angel lost his head.

The enemy had only sent one of the vile air-wielders after me. They'd dismissed me as easy to overcome, weak. I would show them the error of their ways.

A quick scan of the battlefield showed me where I was most needed. Yes, Vyns and Rook and Bayn all seemed lost in their own minds, but they also still fought as best they could. They flailed wildly and though it did little to the elves and sylphim attacking them — and they looked increasingly rough — they were all tough. They'd survive a little longer. Koar looked worse, and would need help sooner, but Izzy needed me the most.

With these steel wings, I couldn't fly, at least not well, but my shadow-step carried me quickly across the field, to Valnea's own shadow.

Her earth sense must have alerted her the instant I touched the ground, because she spun and met my wing attack on her sword.

Her eyes went wide.

"A shifter?"

I used her confused shock, attacking relentlessly with a savage roar. She defended well, even being on her back foot. But my goal wasn't to kill her. Well, that wasn't true. I burned with a fierce desire to kill her, but what I wanted more... was for Izzy to recover. And every second I kept the false queen occupied was another for Izzy to heal and regain her strength. She wouldn't need long.

A manic laugh escaped my lips as I landed a blow on the befuddled false queen, a deep gash, slicing through her fancy armor to draw blood on her shoulder. Then another cut to her abdomen.

"What are you!" Valnea hissed, eyes wild.

"I'm everything you didn't expect," I quipped. "I was there, in your room when you plotted against all the races. Everyone knows of your treachery. I see you in the dark when you least expect it. I am shadows and death!" And since our little fight had moved us around a bit, I used my shadow-step to get behind her again and this time she didn't spin fast enough and I slashed her leg out from under her.

She fell, but instantly earth pushed her back to her feet, her wounds healing. She was tough, but... I'd done what I'd came for.

"I'm also one hell of a distraction, aren't I?" I bantered. "Isn't there someone else you should be fighting?"

The realization hit Valnea as Izzy reached her, fully recovered. Izzy grabbed the woman's shoulder, spun her and clocked her hard in the jaw.

Valnea stumbled, reeling.

"Thanks!" Izzy said to me with a radiant smile. "I just needed a moment. I've got this now!"

I nodded and let her resume her fight with Valnea.

I took out the sylphim nearby so they'd not bother her, then I went to join Koar in his areal battle. I couldn't fly, not quite, but my shadow-step could get me *very close* behind some of those dragons, into their own shadows. I shifted to my hybrid form and blinked myself up there, sinking my clawed feet into a dragon's tough hide and slashing with my wings at the same time.

Another wild laugh escaped me as that dragon faltered and Koar realized why.

I kept stabbing that dragon with my wings as he fell, then I let my wings out and glided away as the dragon hit the ground, dead.

I'd just killed a dragon one-on-one.

And that's when it hit me.

I'd saved Izzy.

Me.

Not any of the other guys.

I'd resisted the sylph mind control.

I'd fought Valnea toe-to-toe and held my own.

I'd killed a dragon.

Holy fuck!

How could I say I was unworthy of anything after that? I couldn't. No one could. Well, they could say the words, but I'd no longer believe them.

A different sort of laugh, proud and savage, escaped me as I flashed into the sky again to bring down another dragon. With yet another gone, Koar had the upper hand.

Thanks! Koar sent to me telepathically. Then he roared and redoubled his vicious fight against the dragons around him, who suddenly didn't know how to handle what should have been an easy fight.

And as I dragged this second dragon to the ground, I caught Izzy's fight with Valnea, which was far different now than it had been before. Izzy had been hurt and probably used a lot of her power to resist the attacks till now, but it didn't matter. She was a beast and Valnea had no chance.

I swooped low. I'd help free the other guys first, then I'd return to Izzy, if she needed me.

IZZY

I WAS VAGUELY AWARE OF MYEL'S TRIUMPHANT BADASSERY, mostly through our bond, and the righteous might which surged through it into me.

I owed the man my life. I owed him everything. I'd been on the verge of giving up. Valnea's relentless attacks with earth and sword had me straining my healing and losing, bloody and broken, on the verge of blacking out. Then suddenly, Valnea's attacks had stopped.

I'd surged my healing taking advantage of the lapse, even though I didn't know why she might have ceased when she was on the verge of defeating me. I'd been so wounded, so befuddled, I couldn't even see straight. But once healed, I'd used my earth sense to figure out the truth of what was going on around me. I'd sensed Valnea fighting someone and known instantly, by his footwork and our bond, that it was Myel. I'd sensed others nearby, barely touching the ground, a mistake. Sylphim could fly but liked to show off by dancing so very lightly over the earth. Two claps of earth later and I'd killed two of those trying to break my mind. That had been enough to clear my head and go after Valnea.

Then Myel had finished off the other sylphim nearby, ensuring I could focus on the false queen.

And now, with no mental attacks hindering me and using all my strength, I found out just how strong Valnea was. The woman was a true elven warrior, strong in earth and body, but even with me digging into my reserves, she was no match for me.

"Wait!" she called as she stumbled back, her earth magic failing her, her sword flying from her hand.

I wouldn't wait, I'd end her now... but she did the last thing I expected.

"Your men!" She pointed.

Fuck!

And that's when all the sensations in the back of my mind and spirit caught up with me.

I kicked Valnea in the head to keep her down as I quickly checked on my guys. The situation was dire. Myel was on his way to help them, but I didn't know if he'd make it in time. Vyns was lost to delusions and being torn apart by elven warriors as sylphim laughed around him. His spirit wavered, giving in, and once that was gone, he'd have nothing left to keep him going. Bayn was doing better, but only by virtue of his natural toughness and endurance. He too was starting to falter. Rook fought but seemed only half-aware. And there was something wild in his attacks. I sensed his thoughts.

You killed her! I'll tear you apart. I'll take you with me. I'll take as many of you as I can with me when I die!

Yikes!

I needed to help them now!

And I knew exactly how.

Like Vyns had done so many times for me, I bolstered his spirit through our link. I gave him the strength to carry on, to keep fighting, and hopefully enough of a boost to shake off his visions and see the real threat before him.

I shouted into Rook's mind; it seemed the only way to overcome the delusions from which he suffered. *I'm here, I'm alive. Look to your left. See me. By all means keep being a badass and slaying those around you, but please don't die!*

Izzy?

He seemed so lost and desperate. He thought I was dead. How could I convince him it was me and not some vision...

I'm here... Inky!

Izzy!

Rook hesitated, blinking.

Hopefully that was enough.

Bayn wouldn't have had any connection to me... *if* I'd managed to remove my binding on him before now. I shouted at him as loud as I could and at the same time, tried to connect with him through my binding, similar to how I could connect with Myel. It wasn't the same, but there was *something* there. I pushed at it as hard as I could as I hoped my words reached him.

"I command you to ignore those fucking Sylphim!"

Bayn too stumbled and blinked.

All three started to come around.

Great.

I turned back to Valnea, but my lapse in attention had given her time to reclaim her sword and stand. She ran her blade through my stomach, all the way to the hilt.

A sneer of superiority twisted her face as she laughed.

"I win! Pitiful half-breed, I win!"

AMARHUK(ROOK)

Inky?

Only Izzy knew that name, and her voice had cut through my thoughts like a razor. She wasn't dead.

She wasn't dead!

I blinked away the last of the fog in my mind, my mental defenses strengthening. I looked to the left as she'd instructed… in time to see Valnea run Izzy through with her blade.

Fuck!

No!

She was alive, but for how much longer?

I went wild, and now that I could truly see those around me and wasn't fighting shadows, I threw myself at them with everything I had. Fire blazed out from me in a wave. Elves and sylphim screamed.

I pushed through the flames, trying to reach Izzy. I lost sight of her and my heart lurched again. I didn't even know why. She'd been in peril before, but somehow not seeing her made it even worse.

A burning elf lunged at me and I batted his sword to one

side with mine, then removed his head. The fire must have weakened him, or my fury strengthened me, I shouldn't have been able to do that to an elf.

I strode through the last of my flames and Izzy was still there, not much had changed. She seemed to be struggling with Valnea over the sword which was thrust through her body.

Just the sight of it made my entire soul cringe and my emotions run wild. I couldn't watch Izzy die, not again.

I killed a burning sylph and tried to run toward my love, but more enemies piled up in front of me, trying to keep any help from getting to Izzy. I hacked at them with my sword, screaming in emotional agony.

My conversation with my mother kept echoing in my mind.

...end it now...

...before fate takes her...

I don't' know what I'd do if I lost her... it's going to hurt like hell.

And I'd been wrong. I'd lived in Urval, essentially hell, for most of my life and life there was harsh and painful, but nothing compared to watching my love suffer.

And as I struck down another elf — it must be my fury empowering me, I hadn't been this strong before — I realized something: losing Izzy would always hurt.

Seeing her in pain was pure agony. There was nothing I could do about it, other than help her, save her... which I was trying to do, if these damned soldiers would get out of my fucking way! Because I needed more time with her. We needed more tender kisses and sinful kisses and times to just hold hands and enjoy each other's company. I needed to have dinner with her, and not fancy dinner out, but normal dinners, every night. It didn't matter what we ate, as long as we were together. I wanted to have kids with her, little elf-nymph-salmaeri-concubi running around and messing up our lives. I wanted to grow old with her, tend to her when she was sick, hold her when she hurt, celebrate with her when she rejoiced. I wanted it all. Because love hurt beyond any pain imaginable when it was taken away, but it was the abso-fuckin-lutely best thing in the world when you had it. And we needed more time to enjoy this miracle.

Huh... Maybe it wasn't my rage fueling me. Maybe it was my love creating this indomitable drive to save Izzy. In the face of that, what could any elf do?

A grim smile spread on my lips.

Previously, I'd fought in fury because I'd thought I'd lost her, but now, I fought with a burning desire to live with her, for her. That made all the difference. Flames leaped to life on my skin and lit my sword.

This is new. This fire burning through me and around me was my love, a searing need to cherish every moment with My Flame.

I'm coming Izzy, hold on!

VYNSIEL

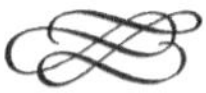

My spirit exploded with light and love and power.

It could only be one thing, one person. *Izzy*. The one whose spirit was inexorably connected to mine, my mate, my shining star! Her strength surged through me, and it instantly snapped me out of my cycle of nightmares, losing her over and over again.

I roared with righteous indignation at the sylphim around me, furious that they'd trapped me in such a horrific vision for who knew how long. I blasted light, probably harder than I should have at everyone around me, sylphim and elf alike. That cleared a wide swathe and gave me a moment to recover, but it also drained me, for I hadn't realized how beaten up I was. The elves had done a good job carving me up. I used what little remained of my strength to heal myself, then summoned a sword and shield of light. Elsewhere on the battlefield, Rook had become living fire. I guessed he'd suffered as I had and Izzy had snapped him out of it, because that's how I felt, so full of righteous fury that it leaked out of me physically.

Bayn also shook off the effects of the sylphim, just as Izzy was... stabbed through the stomach with Valnea glorifying in victory.

"No!" I cried out and my wings flashed to life, only... they weren't wings of white and gold feathers, but of white and gold light.

This was new!

I didn't know if they'd carry me, but when I flapped them, I rose as if they were solid. And when a sylph tried to get in my way and I flew straight past him, my wing of light cut the sucker in half.

I could get used to this.

Myel swooped down next to me, gliding on wings of steel. Okay, that was pretty damned badass... though wings of light were better.

"Izzy!" he called, pointing. Like I didn't already know.

But then Myel laughed, a curious sound. "Actually, she's got this," he said and peeled away to slice through a horde of sylphim and elves to help Bayn, who was being swamped.

Through my spirit... where I might have felt pain and confusion and fear, I felt only a swelling of light and life and power.

Oh...

Maybe Izzy did have this?

If anyone could come back from a sword through her body, it was Izzy. She'd been beaten to shit by Saldrea then gone all boss-bitch on the false princess. Still, I wanted to keep close to her, so I did similar to what Myel had done, only to those around Izzy, slicing through the foes to keep them back, make sure they didn't interfere with whatever my Angel had planned.

You've got this, I whispered to her in my own mind. *And*

I've got your back. She wouldn't be able to hear me, but my spirit would transmit my confidence and pride and what little power I had to her.

Time to end this fight.

BAYN

"I COMMAND YOU TO IGNORE THOSE FUCKING SYLPHIM!"

The words sliced through this all-wrong, fucked-up vision of Izzy dominating me. It vanished in an instant as her binding on me pulsed with power, her command sinking in.

Had she just saved me?

Again.

First, against my father, now this.

How could I ever have imagined Izzy hurting me? But I hadn't imagined it at all, had I? It was those damned sylphim. I roared, unleashing my earth magic. Spikes of stone eviscerated anything withing twenty feet of me, reaching high enough to spear those damned flying angels too. But it seemed the enemy thought I was a significant threat, as even more of Valnea's forces rushed me.

More sylphim tried to penetrate my mind, but Izzy's command forbade it, keeping them out.

And for the first time, I saw her binding on me not as a curse or something to be feared or removed, but a blessing. Not once had she ever made me do anything I hadn't wanted to. And now she was somehow boosting my own mental defenses, her binding more powerful than the sylphim's mind powers.

In the half-a-heartbeat before I was swamped again, I took in the field around me. The other guys were fighting hard. Had they always been freed? Had the sylphim not affected them? No… there were wounds on them.

And even as I watched, Myel, on wings of steel, sliced through a group nearby. That little shifter was… something else. I'd never seen any shifter take out elves like that.

Now it was my turn.

Though I hesitated as my sweeping gaze fell to Izzy and the sword puncturing her gut.

She needed me.

She'd freed me, and I needed to return the favor. With another roar, I blasted earth all around me. Though the elves were prepared this time and most defended themselves, stopping my earthen attack.

Fuck!

Myel landed next to me. "Don't worry about Izzy," he said with a massive manic grin as he spun, wings out, cutting down more of the foe. "She'll be fine. She's got Valnea right where she wants her."

Truly?

Myel was bound to Izzy in a far deeper way than I was and he didn't seem worried at all. I should trust him.

Ha!

Trust.

I hadn't trusted anyone for ages, but…

I did trust this little kick-ass shifter… and Izzy. I trusted her to have my back, to free me from my chains, and to be the indomitable warrior that she was.

So, I joined Myel in this fight. Slowly, we pushed toward Izzy, where Vyns was keeping a space around her.

Then a dragon landed nearby, Koar. And a flaming demon burned through more of the foe, Rook. With their aid, the four of us pushed through to where Vyns kept the others at bay and watched our woman be the badass she was.

IZZY

"How could you think you could ever win against me!" Valnea shouted in victory.

"Oh?" I said with a vicious grin, blood bubbling up out of my mouth and down over my chin. I grabbed her hands on the hilt of the sword, keeping them in place, so she couldn't do more damage by twisting the blade, or moving it, or even withdrawing it. I wanted to keep that blade right where it was.

The exultation and triumph in Valnea's eyes faltered.

With a thought, I healed the massive internal bleeding. It would hurt like hell when this sword came out and I'd have to heal myself again, but for now, I was stable. And with my hands clamped around Valnea's she could do little but spit at me.

Because I'd also woven a binding on the earth around us, like I'd done in the titan arena, cancelling any other earth magic which wasn't stronger than mine. And in the next instant, Valnea must have tried something because her eyes went even more wild.

"What did you do?" she hissed.

"I've beaten you," I whispered, then headbutted her for lack of anything better to do, since my hands were occupied.

Valnea staggered but couldn't fall back with her hands still trapped by mine. She swayed on her feet, and before she could recover, I bound her.

"Call off your forces, you've lost," I said, stronger.

"Never!" she spat, because I hadn't bound her to obey me. I'd put the same binding on her as I had on Saldrea. Every violent thought she had against me would happen to her instead.

Later, I would wish I'd done something else, because the binding showed me just how cruel and disgusting the false queen was. It all happened so fast, she didn't have time to stop it, to realize what she was doing and save herself.

Cuts sliced her skin, flaying her, as long claw marks tore off the skin of her face. Her eyes were yanked out, as was her tongue, then her teeth. Her arms and legs were crushed, bones broken to nothing, then the limbs were ripped right off. A massive slice from neck to navel opened her up and her ribs were broken wide open, her organs pulled out, as what remained of her seemed to be boiled alive.

She didn't even scream as she disintegrated before me in a horrifying display.

What.

The.

Fuck?

I was too stunned to be sick, which was good, because retching with this sword still through me wouldn't have been pleasant.

The battlefield went deathly still and silent.

A lot of people had seen that.

And the enemy would have no clue I'd put a binding on

Valnea, it would look like *I'd* done that to Valnea. Which... I supposed I had, in an indirect way.

And I used their hesitation, their horror, as much as I didn't want to.

"Cease this fighting now!" I bellowed, using magic to project my voice for hundreds of feet. "And send word to all your forces to surrender!"

Weapons clattered to the ground, men knelt in submission, orders were shouted and relayed.

It was done.

Five men came to me. They all looked rough themselves, but they fussed over me like mother hens.

"Are you okay?"

"Did you do that to Valnea?"

"I'd thought I'd lost you."

"Let me heal you."

"No, *I'll* heal her, you heal yourself, you wound-magnet."

"Shut up, I'm fine. It's not my blood... well, maybe fifty-fifty. Oh... wait, I'm still bleeding, never mind. I should heal myself."

They crowded close, a barrier against the world, shutting out the horrors of war and surrounding me in love.

Huh... Love.

I recalled thinking — however long ago — that life altering sex was worth winning this war for. But I'd been wrong. I wanted the sex, sure, but this love — this attention and adoration and dedication, this unity between all of us — was truly worth fighting for and winning for.

And after fighting so hard for it... I no longer feared it. I wanted it more than anything else in the world.

Well, second most to one other rather urgent need.

"Ah... I don't think I can do this myself, so could someone... pull this sword out of me?" I asked awkwardly.

Four stunned faces stared back at me. I could see it. They couldn't imagine hurting me. But one face gave a solemn nod, a sad smile. Myel came to me, he put one hand on my cheek and closed his eyes. Our bond surged even as he yanked the sword out...

And I felt nothing.

He cried out in pain, taking my agony from me. He doubled over, dropping the sword as I quickly healed myself again. Then I knelt and soothed him. He didn't need healing, but the pain still lingered in his soul.

And since this seemed like a teachable moment, I looked up at the other four. "Sometimes love is doing something you know will hurt you and your partner, but it has to be done." I didn't know where that came from, but it seemed legit.

"Also," I said, helping Myel sit up. "Can we all stop and appreciate what a fucking badass Myel was today? If not for him, we might all have died."

"I saw it all," Koar said, shaking his head. "He was the only one who shook off the Sylphim attack. Then he fought Valnea to give Izzy time to recover before slaying two dragons like it was nothing."

Koar knelt next to Myel. "You have my undying respect and honor," he said bowing his head to the man.

"Size isn't everything," Bayn said, and coming from that massive man, that meant something. "Heart is what really matters. And you've got the biggest heart I've ever seen."

"You mean balls," Rook corrected.

"That too," Bayn conceded.

Myel smiled at all of them then turned to me. "The terrified little shifter boy is gone," he said, voice regaining strength. "I know my worth."

"And so does everyone else," I said, kissing his dirt-smeared forehead.

I helped him up and pushed through the wall of lovers. "Now let's make sure this fight is over and our friends are safe."

"Yes, my queen," Koar said stoically.

Huh... I guessed there was no denying it now. I was queen. I'd definitely earned it.

Time to change this world for the better.

AMARHUK(ROOK)

Lhorine and Zora found us limping along, checking in on various battle sites to ensure the fighting had stopped.

They confirmed the enemy had fully surrendered and escorted us back to the command center. Zora gave us a report on how the other forces had done. The addition of the titans had helped immensely. Their earth magic, along with all the fortifications prepared ahead of time, had helped save thousands of lives. Still, the news wasn't what any of us would call "good." Tens of thousands had died on both sides. This had been the most devastating conflict since the last titan war.

Izzy beat herself up, of course, despite our victory. She kept mumbling about how if we'd planned for the sylphim mental attacks we might have won sooner, that *she* might have defeated Valnea and stopped the war sooner. In many ways, that was the day Izzy truly became queen, bearing the burden of leadership and the care of all her people with the solemnity that such an obligation deserved.

Luckily, Izzy was so drained that Lhorine and Olinara

and Zora didn't have to work too hard to convince her to rest and recover before she helped them rebuild a nation.

And so, we six returned to Izzy's residence, showered just enough to clean off the dirt and blood, then fell into bed.

Our recovery took time. We all had new wounds, both physical and mental to heal. I woke first the next day, other than Myel who seemed to have been up for a while. But he wasn't the only one in the room...

...My mother was puttering around Izzy's quarters.

"Mother? What are you doing here?" I asked in shock, drawing her aside.

Her smile held a note of mischief.

"I have accepted the position of head lady in waiting for our new queen," she said. I knew instantly she hadn't been offered this position. She'd probably found Lhorine and the others and demanded it. Not that she'd be bad in that role, but...

"Why? I thought you were happy with your life." Despite her youthful appearance, she was nearly ninety and had been retired from active service for years. And yes, in Urval, "active service" for a succubus meant exactly what you might think.

"I was, but now I want more." She beamed at me, before her smile faltered and faded. "And maybe... I want to be closer to my son. Since we are free to live wherever we like now, Seial seemed *safer*." That was true enough. "And I might have been a bit curious to see the woman who'd stolen your heart."

She peeked back over my shoulder to the bed. I turned and followed her gaze. Izzy was naked, having had no energy to put anything on after her shower. She'd fallen into bed as she was. She was also half-covered by other men, who were also naked. It looked like the aftermath of a small orgy.

"She's quite something," my mother breathed in awe.

I knew that tone. Turning back to her I gave her my best *don't-you-dare* look.

"I don't think she's into women, and even if she was, I'm *not* sharing her with *my mother*!" The practice wasn't entirely uncommon in Urval, the sharing of partners with adult children, but it wasn't for me. I may have fucked pretty much anything before I met Izzy, but I still liked to think I had some standards and boundaries.

She shrugged. "I don't think you get to make decisions for her. Why don't we let her decide?"

I sighed and facepalmed, then shook my head. "Can we talk about something else."

When my mother spoke again, her voice was far less coquettish and far more serious. "I also came... to say I'm sorry."

I looked up at her. Her gaze was distant and I knew instantly who she was thinking of and why she wanted to apologize.

"I loved him more than anything," she whispered. "It surprised me. At first, it didn't feel right at all. I felt... ashamed. I shouldn't favor anyone. All are welcome in my bed. But over time, I came to accept it, even... desire it. I lived for his next visit and made sure I had no other appointments when he was with me. I savored every moment with him. I thought for a while, it might be because he gave me the most spectacular orgasms, but eventually I realized it was far deeper." She pursed her lips, a tear tracing her cheek.

"And when he died..." her voice was so choked up she couldn't speak. I went to her, held her, like I'd done as a boy when she'd gotten like this. Back then, I'd not known why she wept. "I felt even more ashamed that I'd fallen for him." She still couldn't say the "L" word it seemed. "It hurt so bad and..." she sniffled, "...I didn't want you to ever feel that pain."

"I know," I whispered.

"But I only ever told you about the pain and never about the joy, and I'm sorry for that. You... you should know more of your father. And you should enjoy every second you have with Izzy."

I smiled. "I know," I said, my emotions settling. Izzy hadn't died. We'd both lived and now I no longer felt the anticipation of pain I'd felt before. I'd been living in the future, a future which didn't exist and wouldn't, at least not for a long time. And I'd probably go before she did, damned long-lived elves.

When I released my mother, she dried her tears and smiled at me. "We'll talk, soon," she whispered.

"I look forward to it. Until then, can you not lurk in our bedchambers? If you're a lady in waiting, could you... whip us up some breakfast?"

Her smile grew. "I suppose I could do that." She slowly turned to go, glancing back over her shoulder.

"Amar...?" she said as she paused looking back at the bed. "That big one, the titan, is he... entirely devoted to her, or...?"

"He is, now get!" I said, exasperated as she winked at me, then sauntered out.

I showered and by the time I dried and was dressing, the others were starting to rise. Bayn staggered in for a shower, and Vyns said he wanted to soak in the tub. Koar stayed close to Izzy as she slowly woke.

"Can I borrow her?" I asked the dragon. He nodded and wandered over to the far side of the massive room.

"Morning orgasms?" Izzy asked, then groaned as she shifted. "Maybe not, I'm sore… everywhere."

"Orgasms can help with that," I said sliding next to her on the bed and smoothing back her sleep-rumpled hair. I kissed her forehead, and she hummed a contented sound. "But can we talk first?"

"Serious talk?" she asked.

"Yeah."

"It's too early."

"You just have to listen, is that okay?"

"And orgasms after?" she said, still dopey with sleep.

"Orgasms after, I promise."

She slid up so she could lean her head on my chest, one hand straying up to undo the buttons on the shirt I'd just put on. Horny, was she? I'd talk fast.

"I know we joked, before the battle, about our reasons to live, but I need you to know… it isn't a threesome with you and Myel that gave me hope and made me fight yesterday." She gave a soft sound of acknowledgement. I sensed her mood shifting, turning dark. Her thoughts were clear to me, she didn't want to think about yesterday, about the pain and death.

I hurried on, "What gave me hope was… you," I whispered. "Just you. Just being with you and doing normal things with you, having soft and tender moments like this with you."

She snuggled in closer at that.

"Even though I'd said I love you, I was still keeping a part of me back. I was living in some theoretical future of pain, holding out on all the things I really wanted, afraid that having them would make that future even more painful. But I'm not doing that anymore. I want to… hold your hand and take a walk. I want to make you dinner. Hell, I want to have kids with you. Our kids would be adorable! They'd break so many hearts. I want to care for you, tend to you, hold you—" I wrapped my arm around her and pressed her close to my side, "—comfort you when you're in pain. I want to show you how much I love you for the rest of our lives."

She sighed and softened in my arms, her darker thoughts fading.

"I need you to know how big a deal this is, Izzy. An incubus, saying these things… it's…"

"A mental disorder?" she prompted.

"Yeah, exactly. I'm all wrong in the head, but all right in the heart and it's weird, but I don't want anything to change."

"Me neither, I love you too Rook, and I want all those things with you." She shifted, moving up and languidly rolling her body onto mine before rising to straddle me. Blazing Inferno, she was damned gorgeous and fucking sexy, even first thing in the morning. All that tousled hair made me think of post-sex-satisfied Izzy and my cock was suddenly on high alert.

She ground against my lap and smiled as her hands came up to cup my face.

"You, more than any other man… are the most like me," she said, voice soft. "I was afraid for so long, afraid of losing those I loved, so I didn't love. Thank you for saying it was scary. I was scared too, but I'm not afraid anymore. I want to squeeze all the sweet and sticky juices out of every second with you and the others." She rocked against me, her wetness pressing through my pants. "Yes," she breathed. "That was meant to sound dirty, but also… true. I know how close we all came to…" she swallowed hard. "And I want to live life to the fullest now, and love to the fullest too."

She leaned down and kissed me, soft and tender at first, then growing more and more needy until we were deep in each other's mouths.

"Are you done with the serious talk?" she breathed in the scant space between our faces as she pulled back a touch.

"Yup," I whispered back.

"Then show me your love, fill me to the fullest and give me those orgasms you promised."

I did, softly and gently, giving her everything she needed to ease away the ache of her body and the pain of her memories. I had a feeling she'd need many more tender moments like this in the next little while, as she recovered.

And I'd be so very happy to give them to her.

MYELAS

Izzy showered after her time with Rook, and as she was dressing, getting ready to face the world, Olinara arrived.

"If you think you're going out today, you're sorely mistaken, granddaughter," the nymph stated in no uncertain terms. "You're not queen yet, and frankly no one is ready for a coronation and won't be for a while, so sit down and relax. You've definitely earned it. You're on forced R&R until further notice."

Behind Olinara, the succubus who'd introduced herself as Izzy's head lady in waiting, wheeled in a trolley laden with food. It smelled great. My stomach rumbled, as did several others in the room.

"This is Malineth," Olinara introduced the woman. "She's your new head lady in waiting. She'll take care of all your needs."

Olinara put her hands on her ample hips and stared Izzy down. "If I hear you've done anything more strenuous than a casual walk around your residence, you'll be in big trouble. That goes for all of you. Take care of each other. That's an order."

"Alright, alright," Izzy said hands up in front of her. "You win. I'll rest."

"Good," Olinara said, then made sure to stare each of us down until we also acquiesced. Before she left, she came to me. "You're the healthiest of them, and the sanest. Keep an eye on them, will you?"

"Always," I promised.

She smiled, then left.

I joined the others at the large table next to the bank of windows in the far corner from the bed in Izzy's bedroom. Malineth had laid out trays of food then left, but not before adding, "If there is anything you need, just ask, mistress."

"Why do I get the feeling she means *anything*," Vyns asked as the woman left.

"She does, and please ignore her," Rook informed us.

That got five curious looks, and the incubus finally relented. "She's my mother. I don't know how she got this position, but I feel like I'm going to regret it for the rest of my life."

"She seems... nice," Izzy commented.

"She's great, but she will probably try to sleep with all of you. Please... tell her no and move on," Rook said.

"Not my type, too soft," Bayn grunted, mouth half full of eggs and sausage.

"Not my type, too... demony," Vyns said with a wink at Rook.

"Not my type," Izzy began and knowing Izzy — and her crude sense of humor — I fully expected her to say *not enough dick*. But instead, she went with, "Too mother-in-lawy."

That made everyone laugh.

"Oh Blazes... she will be your mother-in-law, won't she?

So... are you going to, like, officially marry all of us?" Rook asked.

"I've considered it." She looked around at us all. "Is that okay?"

Everyone smiled, some nodded, most of us made soft sounds of agreement.

"Usually the queen has a harem, her inamorati, but they're not actually spouses. You really are going to shake things up," Koar said.

"That's the plan," Izzy said with a grin, but it quickly faded. I could see — and feel through our bond — the burden of her impending rulership weighing on her.

"We'll all be there to help you," I whispered, reaching over to clasp her hand tightly.

She gave a bit of a smile at that, but her mood didn't lift much.

We didn't talk a lot after that, focusing on the food. We were all recovering and famished. We polished off everything Malineth had brought, then asked for more. Izzy excused herself while some of the others were still eating.

I got up with her and asked if we could talk.

She nodded and mumbled, "I just... need some air." So, I escorted her outside, where we meandered over the lawns around Izzy's residence.

I gave her some time to her thoughts before I spoke, but she seemed to only grow gloomier. I squeezed her hand, held in mine as we walked.

"I have a proposal," I said, hoping to jar her out of her dark thoughts.

She quirked one brow. "Like a down-on-one-knee proposal?"

I laughed. "I think *that's* a given. No, something else." I drew in a breath and plastered on a smile. "I want you to break the bond between us."

Izzy's mouth fell open. I sensed her confusion and distress, so I hurried to explain.

"I've been thinking about it a lot this morning." I'd been up first and had taken a walk earlier myself, pondering this and how to tell Izzy. I still hadn't come up with any good way to say it, hence the reason I'd blurted it out.

"I learned a lot about myself yesterday," I said. "I no longer feel unworthy. I *know* I'm enough. I may not be the strongest or the fastest, but I'm no slouch and I kicked ass in that battle. I'm... good now. I don't *need* the bond to prove that you love me. I know you do, and I love me too. I know you'll be there for me and I'll always be there for you. Nothing will ever change that. So... I'm good."

That made her smile, but she still looked a bit worried.

I pushed on. "And the bond, well, as much as I like feeling everything you feel, the whole imperative to mate can be a bit awkward at times. I don't know what the future holds, but I'm guessing it won't always be possible to stay close, and we both know how rough it feels to be apart. Don't get me wrong, I want to be close to you all the time, but I also want to be more than a husband."

This was the part I'd been thinking a lot about earlier.

"I want a role in your government. I want to help, somehow, though I don't know exactly how yet. I want to help the people of the three realms as much as you do. And if I do, I might be away from you for a while. I don't want to be, but it may be a part of whatever role I take on."

She nodded solemnly, lips pursed.

"Anything else," she asked.

"No, that's pretty much it."

She nodded and gave a tight smile. "Request denied."

I raised my brows.

She squeezed my hand.

"I get that you're feeling better about yourself and that you don't *need* the bond to feel whole. That's great, I'm proud of you. But my answer is no. Just because we don't need the bond doesn't mean we don't like it. I, at least, really like it. I love the soothing warmth I get when we're close. I don't want to lose that. It may be selfish, but this bond is a two-way street, and I would like to keep it."

Oh.

I had to smile. "Thanks," I whispered. Then, after a deep breath. "So... what do we do about being apart?" I asked.

She cocked her head to the side.

"What if we *adjusted* the bond? Shaped it into something we both want, something that doesn't hinder us?"

"Is that possible?" I asked. I'd never heard of a mate bond being "adjustable."

"Let's find out." Izzy squeezed my hand again, then we found a spot to sit, facing each other, my hands in hers. She closed her eyes, and moved through our bond, stretching and prodding.

She spoke softly as she explored this connection between us.

"Lhorine was right, it really isn't like other bindings, but... it *is* still a binding. I can work with this." She opened her eyes and looked at me, searching.

"So... what do we want it to be?" she asked me.

I shrugged. "I'd love to keep the deep connection we have, feeling each other. It pains me at times to sense your distress, but I'd still like to have all of that."

"And I don't mind the intimacy it brings. The soothing presence, the way it *enhances* our times together."

I laughed. "You mean the orgasms?"

"I do." She shivered, eyes rolling up a little as passion swept through her. I guessed she was recalling some of our times together. "They're amazing! Rook's orgasms are sinful, but yours are... deep and meaningful."

I smiled wider at that compliment, but also at how I didn't even care anymore that she'd compared me to another man. I was enough, for me and for her, and it didn't matter what any other man did.

"Okay," I said, "so we keep the orgasms. Anything else?"

"I think..." She was slowly coming back down to earth after reliving those steamy memories. "It's a matter of the imperative. We can keep everything except the part that makes us *have* to be together, the demand for sex, the need to be close."

"Yeah," I said with a smile. "Sounds perfect."

She returned the smile. "Let me give it a try." She closed her eyes and reached back into our bond.

I didn't know how difficult this might be, but Izzy was a fast learner and could conquer pretty much anything when she put her mind to it.

"Yeah," she mumbled. "There it is..."

Something shifted, and suddenly everything inside me... eased off.

"Oh... wow!" I breathed.

"I know, right?" Izzy said with a laugh as she opened her eyes. "It feels so much... lighter, freer."

"But still so close and... perfect." I was running out of words to describe this rather stunning sensation inside me. The bond was there, Izzy was there, deep in my soul, but as a known and comforting entity. There was no demand to be close to her, no forced anything. It was all joy and ease and liberty.

"Thank you," I whispered reverently.

We both leaned in and kissed softly. It wasn't an imperative, just what we *wanted* to do.

Oh, yes... I was definitely going to enjoy this!

And for the first time, possibly in my entire life, I felt completely unrestrained and truly happy.

"Oh wow... what was that?" Izzy breathed as we parted. "Your soul just... lit up!"

I laughed. It bubbled up out of me so freely. "I feel great! For the first time... I'm living for myself. I don't serve anyone, don't have to worry about anyone else's demands or expectations. I'm bound by nothing except love, and I feel so... alive and joyful and free!"

Izzy laughed with me.

But then her mirth died off.

My words had hit a chord. All of my shackles had fallen away, but Izzy was about to put on some of her own, willingly accepting a huge responsibility.

"Remember," I whispered to her. "We're going to do this *together*. This was what you wanted. And you won't be alone. We'll form a government of the people, a ruling council. Not everything will be on you."

Her mood lightened a little, but the responsibility of being queen hadn't been all that had been bothering her. She still felt so deeply for all the lives that had been lost to pave the way for freedom.

"Remember too," I said, squeezing her hands. "You didn't want this war. You fought only to save people, to free them. And you won. We did the best we could and saved thousands of lives by ending the war when we did. *Valnea* is responsible for the war, the death."

Izzy gave a soft smile, but it was forced. My words had helped, but my tender-hearted mate still claimed some responsibility for those who'd died.

I tried one last approach.

"Your compassion makes you stronger, better, a far more capable ruler than any elf that ever lived. Use what you're feeling now to drive you to make this world better, as you'd hoped. So that no one else has to die in a conflict like this."

She nodded. "You're right, thank you, Myel. I love you. I need you so damned much." She kissed me again, then whispered. "Whatever role you want in the new government, just don't rush into it, okay? I may need you around reminding me of everything you just said... for a while."

"Deal," I said. "I want you to be happy, and luckily, even if I'm not there, you've got others who want the same thing." And that made me happy. I didn't worry about the other guys anymore. I didn't compare myself to them, didn't fear I might lose something because of them. I felt only gratitude that they loved this wonderful woman too and would help her and take care of her like I would, if I wasn't there.

"Thank you, you're right... again," she said.

Then we cuddled close, laying in the grass, listening to the sound of the surf below us, calm and even. Izzy let my presence sooth her until her fears and concerns faded away. Only then, did we head back inside.

VYNSIEL

I HADN'T EXPECTED TO BE BACK IN ELYSIAL SO SOON. IT HAD been a week since the battle with Valnea's forces and I'd recovered well. During that time, some of the sylphim who'd surrendered had revealed an alarming and disturbing plot among their kind. Though sylphim were strong in mind, direct mind control was expressly forbidden. Valnea had obviously gotten them to overlook that, but as it turned out... they'd been inside Valnea's head first.

Some time ago, perhaps a couple hundred years, a group of sylphim high nobles, the elite of Elysial, had hatched a plan. They'd find a gullible high elf and start whispering in her ear, slowly gaining her trust. They'd be her spies and build up her power until she trusted them as her inner circle, then they'd begin the long process of corrupting her mind. Their target had been Valnea. They'd twisted her thoughts till she'd betrayed her own kind, inviting the titans in to assassinate the royal family. By that point, these sylphim had spies lurking in the titan realm, using their powers to remain unseen, while bending the minds of the titan king and queen, till they saw the world as Valnea did.

Valnea's insanity, her plot to destroy all the prime races, it had all been the doing of the sylphim.

Everyone had been dumbstruck to learn this. Luckily the bulk of the sylphim forces hadn't been involved in this plot. They went along because they had no choice; their leaders had dictated a course and whether they liked it or not the other sylphim followed.

Now, the lesser sylphim were repentant and remorseful, confessing this horrific plan. They even helped us track their leaders back to Elysial to be brought to justice. They crafted items to protect the minds of the seraphim and dragons who went with them, and we'd tracked the rogue sylphim to a castle of cloud, where they were now cornered.

We expected heavy resistance... but there was none at all, an ominous sign. Creeping through eerily quiet corridors, we kept on guard, but we needn't have bothered, for when we found the group in the large main hall, they were all dead, but for one.

High Lord Andulus Eyrial was known to be the strongest of the sylphim, their leader. He'd spent most of his life in the elven court serving the elves. His mental prowess was unparalleled as witnessed by the dozens of dead sylphim around him, all bleeding from the ears and nose and eyes, their minds... crushed.

He waited with a dagger in hand, sitting on the lord's throne at the far end of the hall. When he saw us, he said, "We simply wished to free ourselves. How were we to know the tyranny of the elves would one day end?" Then he slid the long dagger into his chest and ended himself.

I shook my head.

Such a waste.

The sylphim had been elevated in status by the elves, yet they'd craved even more power. They'd resented their elven masters. Perhaps they'd thought they were using their powers for good, to overthrow the elves, but given the grand scale of genocide Valnea had planned, somewhere along the line, their idealism had been corrupted.

I almost felt bad for those sylphim who remained. It was going to be a long time before anyone trusted them again.

Our force returned to Seial, a somber lot.

Izzy met me outside as I approached her residence.

"What's wrong? Did you not find them?" she asked, concerned. She must have misread the dismay and discomfiture in my spirit. She ran to me and embraced me tightly. My arms went around her reflexively, but I was still a little lost.

"No, we found them, but they'll never see justice. They were all dead," I said, shaking my head. "I just… can't understand how they could do all of this, cause so much destruction and death and claim it was in the name of freedom or a better world."

Izzy hugged me tighter. "I'm sorry," she whispered. "What do you need?"

I had to laugh.

"You're the one being coronated in three weeks, swamped with work trying to set up a new government for a bunch of well-meaning but unruly races. And here you are asking what *I* need?"

She pulled back so she could look me in the eye. "I've recently realized something. *This* is how things change, not with big sweeping governmental laws, but by one person helping another."

The profundity of that statement stunned me to silence for a while. Then I slowly shook my head. "You continue to amaze me, Angel, my guiding light." I pulled her close again.

"I am amazing, it's true," she said playfully.

"Thank you, again," I whispered, holding her tight. "I was lost, and you found me. You shone a bright light into my dark life and forced me to change my ways. You saved me from Saldrea, and from myself. You allowed me to forgive myself and start over, learn to grow again, be the man I want to be."

"I'm pretty sure you did most of that on your own."

"I did, yes, but I wouldn't have done any of it if you hadn't come into my life. And you did save my life, at least once."

"True," she whispered, hugging me back with her fierce elven strength.

"My heart and spirit are free now," I whispered. "They're both yours, now and forever."

"And you have my heart and spirit too," she whispered back. "Now and forever." Then she pulled back again, a quizzical look on her face. "That sounded a lot like vows, are we unofficially married now?" She smiled as if that was exactly what she wanted.

"Any marriage at this point would be a formality," I said, dipping down to kiss her softly. "Words are all well and good, but it's what we feel that counts."

She shifted, sliding her arm behind me as she came to my side. We continued the short walk to her residence.

Her voice was a little dreamy with remembrance when she said, "You once had issues with me being with just one other guy, are you okay with the small horde I've picked up?"

"I am," I said solemnly. "Their hearts are true. Together, you and I and them, we're unstoppable."

"Right answer," she said squeezing me from the side.

It was amazing how a few minutes with Izzy could lift

my spirits from the depths of gloom to the heights of joy. It's why I called her "Angel" and "guiding light" because she rescued me from myself every day, in so many little ways.

I squeezed her back as we made our way inside.

Izzy was going to make a great queen. She'd irrevocably change the realms of fae, even if she had to do it one life at a time.

BAYN

I KNELT BEFORE IZZY AS SHE — WITH HANDS CUPPING MY FACE — removed the binding from me.

It was the day before her coronation, nearly a month after the battle and so much had happened that we hadn't found the right time to do this until now. And I hadn't minded in the least. Izzy's command to me, before the battle, to act as I wished and be who I needed to be, had given me all the freedom I'd needed. I'd barely noticed the binding most days, another reason we'd waited this long to do anything about it.

"You're a free man," Izzy said with a playful grin as she released me. I stayed kneeling, it felt appropriate for what I had to say.

"I've been a free man ever since you helped me defeat my parents," I said. "I knew then, you'd never try to control me. It just took me a little longer to accept it." I hung my head. "I'm sorry, Izzy."

"You're sorry? I was the one who put the binding on you."

"I'm sorry I was such a royal asshat—" one of her words, which I'd grown to like, "—to you and everyone."

I shifted to face the other guys, who all stood nearby. "I'm sorry I asked so much of you when we first met. I was selfish."

"Your sister was wrongly imprisoned in a hellhole, you'd earned a bit of righteousness in wanting her freed," Rook said.

"Which isn't actually that selfish," Vyns finished.

"Still, I… could have helped you sooner. I'm sorry."

"Just get up, you big lug," Myel quipped.

I stood, but I wasn't done. I took everyone in with a sweeping glance, then continued.

"All my life I've scraped and clawed to get anything. I thought the only way to be in control was to dominate others, push them down. That's what everyone around me did. Well, everyone except for my sister." I probably should have listened to her more.

"But Izzy—" I smiled at her, "—and all of you, showed me another way. A self-control that doesn't require violence or demands on others. Control which comes from knowing yourself and accepting yourself. Power that comes from *freeing* others and lifting them up. Thank you all."

Everyone crowded around me with handshakes and back slaps and bro-hugs. Izzy shifted her form to grow, so she could give me a peck on the cheek and a proud smile over the tops of the heads of everyone else.

All of this felt… strange.

Having a loving family was not something I was used to. These men, who I would have considered my enemy not that long ago, were now my brothers, and Izzy would soon be my wife.

Wensuria had loved me, but I'd thought it a weakness

for so long and hadn't acknowledged it. Now I had her, and a whole new family. As great as it felt, it was still going to take some getting used to.

Malineth knocked then entered. "The tailors are here," she said. Rook's mother now had a team of women working with her as Izzy's ladies in waiting. One of whom was Izzy's friend Tala. They escorted in a small army of tailors and seamstresses. Izzy and I had already been measured for our outfits for the wedding, which was scheduled for a week after the coronation. So, the two of us slipped out and I was grateful for the time alone with her.

We sat in the large sitting room at the front of the residence, overlooking the lawns and the ocean beyond.

"You ready for tomorrow?" I asked. "How's your speech coming?"

Izzy grimaced. "Public speaking was never my thing. It's done, and Lhorine says it sounds great, but it still feels awkward to me." She sighed. "Though maybe it's being queen which feels awkward."

I nodded, thinking it more likely the latter option. I may have been born a prince and raised to rule, but Izzy wasn't used to this sort of thing.

"How's *your* speech coming?" she asked.

"Short and sweet, modest but rousing, perfectly eloquent," I said with a grin. "At least, that's how it is in my head. I haven't written a word yet."

"Plan on winging it?" she asked.

I shrugged. "I might. In truth it matters little what I have to say. Yours is the important one." The only reason I had a speech at all was because I was being recognized as the Lord General of the armies of Seial as part of the coronation. The powers that be had decided the titans rejoining society was a rather momentous occasion and had wanted to commemorate it. My new position was part of that effort.

"Yeah," Izzy groaned. "No pressure."

I slipped off my chair and knelt before hers, taking both of her hands in mine. I always found it miraculous that hands so small — at least compared to mine — were so damn strong.

"Don't try to be a queen, just be yourself. You have so much to give this world, so much to change. Be the woman I've heard so many stories about from the other guys. The one who got here on day one and fought the power, wanting to end oppression and bring justice and equality. You're doing that now, be proud of it, maybe even enjoy it."

She cocked her head in thought. "I guess I am doing that, aren't I?" She gave a little laugh, which still held a note of tension and anxiety. "There's just a big difference between talking about doing something and actually doing it."

"Always remember, you're doing what this world needs, and you'll never be alone. So many of us are here to help you."

She sighed. "You're right. Still, the theatrics of the coronation are a bit much for me."

I smiled. "The theatrics are for those who need theatrics. But your speech is to show everyone who you really are. Be yourself, however untheatrical that may be."

She laughed. "That might make Lhorine's and my grandmother's heads explode."

"I'll be sad to see them go," I said with mock sadness.

She laughed, a light and pure sound, before pulling one of her hands out from mine to slap my shoulder.

"I can't figure out whether you're a bad influence or a good one," she said, still laughing.

"The best... and the worst," I said as a very naughty idea

came to me. We were alone, and it might be the last time in a while.

I looked around, but all was quiet. A lady in waiting could wander by any time, or those tailors might finish their work and leave soon, but I didn't care.

I leaned forward to press my lips to hers and as I did, I released her hands so mine could go exploring. One roamed up over her blouse to cup a breast, the other slid up under her long skirt to push open her legs. I ran my thumb over her panties, feeling her core, so pliable and soft beneath. She whispered a moan into my mouth and I drank it down, thirsty for more.

But it wasn't until I hooked a finger around her panties to draw them down that she gasped and drew back.

"Not here!" she hissed.

"Yes, here," I breathed.

"What if someone comes?" she whispered.

"You'll *definitely* come," I replied. "Anyone else will ignore us. Royalty does all sorts of crazy horny things, people learn to not see what's going on."

I had her panties down to her knees by then. I reached back up to stroke her folds again with my thumb, loving how deliciously wet she was, and how she tensed and shivered when I found her clit.

Her eyes darted around... but she didn't stop me as I stroked her seam and massaged her clit.

"You're so fucking naughty," she breathed, sliding down, relaxing into the chair, opening her legs more for my large hand. My other hand deftly popped open a couple buttons on her blouse and slid inside to capture her soft flesh. I rolled her nipple, till it was diamond hard. All the while, watching her intently, loving how she slowly came apart as I worked.

She stifled a cry when I slid a thick finger inside her, eyes going wide. She was close, her pussy pulsing around my finger. And when I flicked her clit with my thumb, while massaging her G-spot, she bucked hard and bit her lip, trying not to alert everyone in the building of her orgasm.

"Fuck, you're so sexy when you come," I whispered, then leaned forward to breathe hot words into her ear. "My dick is so hard right now. If you say the word, I'll stop, but otherwise, I'm about to pick you up and fuck you against a wall, my sexy queen."

"Bayn, don't..." she whispered, breath catching. My heart fell a little. I'd respect her wishes. "Don't stop!" she finished and I nearly wept with joy at this naughty opportunity.

I picked her up, a limp and satisfied mess in my hands. She threw her arms around my neck and pulled herself closer, to press savage kisses to my lips and neck, raking her teeth over my jaw.

I pinned her to a wall with one hand around her tiny waist and pulled back. I needed to see her face for this next bit.

"You ready for me?" I asked, my free hand working to liberate my cock from my pants.

Her eyes rolled around and she bit her lips as she concentrated through her still singing bliss to alter herself. Then she nodded.

I moved in, her legs wrapped around my waist, pushing her skirt up and out of the way as I tested her core with my aching erection. She was damned wet and so very receptive as I slid into her.

I groaned. Izzy had adjusted her body to fit me in perfectly, still squeezing the fuck out of me. With everything we'd had going on, we'd not had a lot of time for sex these last few weeks and my dick was aching as I sheathed myself fully inside her.

"Fuck, yes!" she hissed. "Do it, like in the cave!"

So, she wanted it fast and rough? I guessed that made sense if she didn't want anyone to see us. I didn't mind at all.

I drove myself into her, watching what it did to her as I pounded her pussy hard. Her eyes crossed, her head went back, hitting the wall — not too hard — as her mouth opened in a silent scream.

And when her tightness clamped around me even harder, pulsing and wet, her eyes going even wider, her body stiff and shuddering, I knew she'd come again.

Bloody Bones! She was too damned sexy; I could understand why Koar called her Perfection. I couldn't help myself and I grunted as my cock pulsed with my release. I bent to press my lips to hers and drink down her panting bliss as we came together.

I carried her to the small bathroom off the sitting room before I drew out, knowing we'd make a massive mess. We cleaned ourselves up as best we could in that small — now very cramped — powder room, emerging a bit disheveled... right as the tailors were heading out. None of them looked in our direction, but they had to know what we'd done. The entire sitting room smell like sex.

Then Myel came stalking out to confront us.

"Do you know how embarrassing it is to nearly come while being fitted for a new suit?" He glared up at me, then pinned Izzy with a glare. "Twice!"

"He looked like he was going to explode," Rook said, covering a laugh.

"I was!" Myel blurted. "Then he grabbed Izzy's arm and dragged her back into the powder room. "If you'll excuse us, I have something Izzy needs to take care of."

Izzy giggled as she closed the door behind them.

The other three guys looked at me. Koar sniffed the air.

"You did it out here, in the open?" he asked.

I grinned.

"Very good," Rook said, coming to link his arm in mine. "Just a little more work and we'll make Izzy into a proper exhibitionist."

Vyns groaned.

Koar rolled his eyes.

But there was no judgement here, no jealousy. And that's why I was coming to love these guys, because they didn't care about that little tryst. We all wanted the same thing, for Izzy to be ridiculously happy.

And right now, she was.

Hence, so were we.

KOARTHANDRIS

It seemed only right to have Izzy's coronation at Veilblood Academy. This place was all she'd known of the fae realm, her home for the last couple months.

I had to smile. Izzy had been here for *two months* and she'd overthrown a false queen, started and ended a war, and learned a little magic in the meantime. Oh, and also permanently affected the lives of five men, of which I was one.

Luckily, the academy had two large forums suitable for an event such as the coronation, and we planned to use both. The coronation would happen twice, so more people could witness it. The first ceremony had finished at Anadendyra Hall, the massive great hall on campus, named for Izzy's royal family. Now Izzy led a parade through the campus — a long and winding and indirect path — to Cliffside Arena, where she'd be crowned all over again for a different crowd.

The parade in between was for the thousands of people who'd shown up and not been able to fit into either the great hall or the arena. Izzy waved as she walked past, smiling and proud. She looked radiant in a golden dress, modest and stylish, though she'd insisted on no train, which had broken the hearts of the palace tailors. For the parade, she wore no crown. She'd wanted to meet the people as one of them, even though she'd already been crowned once and would be again in a little while.

She even stopped to shake hands or talk to people, probably more than she should have. Luckily, we'd made sure there was lots of time for her to make it to the second venue. She truly wanted to meet all the peoples of the fae realms. It may have been a bit of a slight to those in the two larger venues, most of whom were from what had been the higher classes. She hadn't talked to anyone there, but here, where so many of "the rabble" had gathered, she lingered and talked and laughed with them.

I hoped she didn't make any more enemies.

Already, there had been a divide among the elves. Only about a third had fully accepted Izzy. Roughly another third were skeptical, taking a wait-and-see approach, and the last third had already vacated the capital, heading for the wastes where the titans had once dwelled, furious at the changes Izzy wished to make.

No one was really worried. All the other races had united around Izzy, all of them would be "elevated" at least a little if made equal to the elves.

We had other enemies, but none of great concern. The nephilim of Elysial and the pyrkai of Urval were still vying for control of those realms, but, to a certain extent, no one cared. Most of the other races had come to live here in Seial, The seraphim and the repentant sylphim would make new homes in the high mountains. The vast plains would suit the salmaeri and concubi just fine, a step up from their previous home of fire and darkness.

Izzy had plans to talk to both the nephilim and the pyrkai at some point, to see if she could set up trade and diffuse the tensions between us and them, which had lasted for thousands of years. Few thought it possible, but they didn't know Izzy like I did. If anyone could do it, she could.

I cleared my throat as Izzy spoke to a pixie at length about ways to enhance and simplify the bureaucracy of the realm.

She looked over at me.

I made a pointed look toward Cliffside Arena. We were close, on the last leg, and our time was drawing short.

Izzy sighed, got the name of the pixie and told her to find us "after all this nonsense," then was back on the path.

"I was learning a lot!" she said to me as we walked side by side.

"There will be time for that later, we wouldn't want to be late."

Izzy sighed as the arena loomed closer. "I don't have many fond memories of this place," she murmured to me.

Myel had been imprisoned here, then faced a death-match. And Izzy had fought for her life on the same arena floor where she was about to be coronated.

I grunted my agreement.

"Still," I said.

"One must face many unpleasant things once one is queen," Izzy said a bit stiff. She was quoting her grandmother verbatim. Olinara was a massive resource for royal life, having been the last true queen's inamora, the highest of the inamorati. But not all of what she had to impart to Izzy were easy things to hear.

"It'll be over soon," I said.

"The coronation, yes, but then I'll be queen in truth and I'll have so much more on my plate."

"You wanted this."

"I wanted to change the world, not be queen."

"Those go hand in hand."

She slipped her hand into mine and squeezed. I squeezed hers back. It had become a common thing for Izzy and one or more of us guys, this small gesture of support when she couldn't show her uncertainty and overwhelm.

I couldn't help myself; I leaned closer and whispered, "be a good girl and you'll get a reward later." I'd been experimenting with being... playful, a little less uptight about... everything.

Izzy eyed me with a half-grin before her gaze returned to the crowd and her lips to the wide smile she wore for everyone else.

"Oh?" she whispered back. "What kind?"

"The kind that'll make you scream and make a certain shifter very uncomfortable unless he joins us."

Izzy's giggle was very un-queen-like.

We arrived at the arena and were whisked away through corridors to a staging room where we waited to go out. Here, it was just Izzy and us guys and Olinara, who was our master of ceremonies for these events.

"How long do I have?" Izzy asked while sipping some water.

"A few minutes, Lhorine will give her speech, then you're on," Olinara answered.

"Enough time to put a flush on my cheeks?"

Olinara seemed confused at the question before Izzy tilted her head towards us men with a significant look."

"Oh," Olinara sighed. "Really? Now?"

"Weren't you the one who said something about how I'll have to find intimacy in the rare moments when I can find it?"

"I regret that wording now." Izzy's grandmother shook her head, then sighed again. "Fine, but only one of them, and a hand-job only, no penises, you horny slut."

"Takes one to know one," Izzy said over her shoulder to her grandmother, who nodded at the veracity of that statement. Then Izzy turned to me, looping her arms around my neck and pulling me down for a kiss.

"Reward time," she whispered.

When I hiked up her dress, I found a distinct lack of underwear.

"Did you plan this?" I asked, my hand cupping her core.

"Hmmm, harder, and no, this dress is heavy and it's warm and I wanted my lady bits to breathe. Anything else is a happy accident." She ground herself against my palm. I slid a finger along her slit and it came away wet.

"Fucking hell," Myel hissed. "Not this again."

"Let me help with that," Rook said, kneeling before the shifter and opening his fly to swallow down his hard erection.

"Fuck, that's sexy," Izzy purred, watching them while I worked her with my hand. "Hmm, fuck, yes!"

Olinara turned her back, checking outside. But I'd caught a smile on the nymph's face before she did. It made me wonder how horny the previous true queen had been.

With Izzy and Myel both feeling each other's bliss, it didn't take long before she was coming on my hand and he was emptying himself into Rook's mouth.

"And... time," Olinara called. "You ready?"

Izzy gave a giggle as she pushed her skirt down. She definitely had a heady blush on her cheeks now.

"Yup!" she said, popping the "p." Olinara quickly checked her over and adjusted a few minor things, then ushered us out.

"Maybe," Izzy said as we made our way toward the podium at the center of the arena, "I could get used to the perks of being queen."

"Now *I'll* need a reward later," I said, hoping the massive crowd wasn't focused on the bulge in my pants.

"I'll make it my first official act as queen," Izzy said, a rejuvenated lightness in her voice. When she took the podium and went — yet again — through the long ritual of being crowned and all that entailed, she faced it with a brilliant smile on her face. And I was glad I'd been able to "sooth away" her anxiety and help her focus on what lay ahead.

I'd be there for whatever she needed, whether that was protection or pleasure or just a friend. My role in her life was far more than just her guard. In a week's time I'd pledge my life to hers as her husband, becoming a prince of the realm. And I also knew... we'd not be alone. I'd failed the previous royal family because I'd tried to do everything myself. I wouldn't need to worry about that anymore. Whatever Izzy and I faced, we'd face it with four others to help us and so many others who'd dedicated their lives to Izzy.

She brought out the best in everyone, and she'd finally allowed me to forgive myself for my past and look with anticipation toward the future.

IZZY

"Do you, Steelwing Myel, take Anadendyra Isolde, as part of this loving bond and union, to be your queen and wife?"

Myel beamed as his full name was spoken.

Because... he *had* a full name now. Up until yesterday, shifters had never had surnames. But I'd made an announcement that shifters could now choose their own surnames and take their places with all races as equals in this world. And I'd done it by formally acknowledging Myel's name. Steelwing wasn't a name Myel had chosen for himself, but one that so many others had given him and he'd decided to accept it.

Now, all over Seial, shifters were literally making a name for themselves. Surnames still came first, which sounded weird to me, but that was something I'd have to get used to. What I *had* done, was get rid of all the class signifiers before names: "el" and "di" and "sa" and so on. There were no more classes, everyone could be or do anything they wanted and would be judged on the merit of their actions, not their race or class. It hadn't fully sunk in yet, but that had been one of my first edicts as queen and it was slowly taking effect.

"Yes," Myel said with gusto. "I do."

Turns out weddings here were pretty similar to the human realm, though there was a lot less ingrained "women as chattel" in this ceremony, since women had historically been the ones in charge here. Our particular ceremony had also been adjusted to account for five husbands.

I'd essentially had a mini ceremony with each of them, Myel being the last.

"And do you Anadendyra Isolde, take Steelwing Myel, as part of this loving bond and union, to be your faithful husband" I didn't like using my true name, but it was growing on me. It always made me think of Safir, the infuriating — and loyal — shifter who'd first revealed it to me. We'd had a memorial for him — a mostly private affair — a few weeks ago. Without him, I wouldn't have had the web of allies which had helped us win the war.

"I do," I said with a wide grin.

Unlike some girls, I hadn't dreamed of my wedding day. I'd assumed I'd be a bachelorette for life. Men had been a nuisance to be tolerated, occasional pleasure providers, nothing more. I'd been so against any long-term relationships that marriage hadn't been on my radar.

Now, here I was, married to five men.

Five men who adored me and worshiped me and whom I adored equally as much.

So much had changed so quickly that I felt like I was playing catch up half the time. From commitment-phobe to five husbands. From nearly broke bartender to queen. From pushing people away to accepting tens of thousands under my care. From wishing and wondering how I could help people, to actually making a difference in the lives of so many.

Yeah, a lot had changed, but most of it had been for the better.

If you didn't count the war and death part. That still weighed on me. I expected so many to blame me for the deaths of their loved ones... but they didn't. Everyone I talked to, spoke only of how much they appreciated the changes I was making, and how those who'd died had given their lives for something meaningful. More and more people told stories of how proud their friends had been to fight for me, and the vision of a world where all were equal.

"May all who join in this union gather before me," Zora, our officiant, said, motioning to the other four men to join Myel and I once more.

I'd insisted on Zora, despite objections to a non-elf presiding over the marriage of the queen. For so long, the high priestess of Titania had married royalty, but she'd fled with the other traitor elves to the distant wilds. And choosing Zora hadn't been meant to distance myself from those who worshiped Titania — that was just a happy side effect — but more to show Seial that I practiced what I preached and everyone really was equal. Zora was a non-denominational officiant, but there were many who were starting new religions in this realm. For so long, the elder elves — Titania and her daughters, Anadendyra, Dryada, Nymphyla, and Undira — had been the only gods. Now there was a small cult that worshiped me, which I actively discouraged, and a larger group who'd started a sort of universalism, who saw the divine in everyone and sought to elevate and aid all. I could get behind that.

The six of us formed a semi-circle before Zora. Bayn and

I in the middle, Koar to my other side and Myel beside him, Rook and Vyns on the other side of Bayn.

"Do you all, as joint rulers, take this nation and this realm as yours to care for, tend to, and serve, providing justice and equality for all?"

I mouthed the words along with Zora. I'd put that part in, liking the idea of marrying us to the realm as servitors, not tyrants.

"We do," we all said as one.

"And will you care for each other, in sickness and health, for as long as you all shall live?"

"We do."

"Then I now pronounce you wife and husbands and caretakers of Seial."

The crowd in the massive great hall of Anadendyra palace went wild. We six turned and acknowledge them, then I went down the line and kissed each of my guys. The whole "you may kiss your spouse" thing wasn't a part of the ceremony in Seial, but I'd wanted it anyway.

The crowd cheered louder.

Then the recessional played and the five of us marched down the very long aisle.

The reception was a blur of speeches and meals and meeting people and smiling till my cheeks hurt. Honestly, I would have been happy with a private party, but my grandmother had insisted on this.

I left early, not needing to feign fatigue after a very long day and knowing tomorrow I'd be right back into my queenly duties. I very much wanted to rest... but I also very much wanted to enjoy my wedding night before I rested, which may have been another reason I left early.

And when five hot bodies closed in around me in the massive royal bedchamber — I had chosen new rooms for my suite, in a completely different wing of the palace from where Valnea had lived — a shiver of anticipation thrilled through me.

"We've talked," Rook said, voice husky, sending even more electrifying delight through me. "Since we knew this would be an *important* night." Someone began undoing the many buttons down the back of my pristine dress. "We each wanted time with you, alone, then we'll pleasure you in groups of two or three, then all together. We promise ten orgasms or your money back."

I laughed at that, a breathy and excited thing, gasping near the end as the guys pressed closer, taking turns slowly undressing me.

Oh... wow.

My five prince-consorts were going to make me very happy tonight... and for a long time to come. This would be a wedding night to remember, and a fantastic start to my new life as queen.

EPILOGUE

The guys all pressed close as my dress was slowly removed. By the time it slid off I was covered in a sheen of sweat with my folds leaking like a dam about to burst.

I'd expected, given Rook's sinful description of the night, that one of them would then whisk me away to the massive bed... or better yet, pin me to a wall and have their way with me, but nope... more waiting, more anticipation as they all began to kiss every steamy inch of my skin.

"Who do you want first?" Rook asked, breath hot on my ear as one of his hands seized a breast which was very much in need of erotic massage.

"Anyone," I moaned as Myel's tongue licked up the inside of my thigh and over my seam. "Please!" I begged.

Bayn's massive hand slapped my ass so hard my soul vibrated, and the sting of pain launched my building pleasure through the roof. Myel moaned against my core as I gushed for him. Then his tongue flicked my clit and I nearly came just standing there.

"Seems only fair to share her in the order we met her,"

Rook said. "Which would mean I'd go first, but she didn't really know who I was then, so Myel... all yours."

And as four hot bodies moved away, I felt a sudden chill. It didn't last long though as Myel deftly lifted each of my legs to his shoulders, face buried deep in my core, then lifted me and found a wall, pinning me there as he gorged himself on my wetness.

My first orgasm was a surprising peak, when two fingers slid inside me as Myel's mouth worked wonders. Those long digits softly stroked my G-spot as his tongue swirled around my clit and I tensed, then came apart.

But my Goth hero didn't stop. He drank down my release with a moan and I discovered that thrilling peak was just a foothill on my way to a much higher destination.

Myel shrugged my thighs off his shoulder, his hands pinning my legs to the wall, spread wide as he slowly cleaned up my folds, savoring every last drop of my wetness. When he looked up at me the sheer passion in his eyes nearly made me come again. He was more than ready. Our bond pounded with his desire, especially since he experienced what I felt and had to be aching for a release of his own.

He slid me down the wall till his face was level with my chest, sucking one taut nipple into his mouth, moaning yet again. I joined him, so damned sensitive, I couldn't concentrate on anything other than what he was doing to that achingly hard nub.

"Myel, yes, Please!" I begged him, my voice catching, breath already coming hard.

He popped his lips off my breast and I cried out with the loss.

"Say it," he purred. "Tell me what you want, what to do, how to please you."

I could barely talk, but I found the words, dirty little Izzy coming out to play.

"Impale me on that perfect dick of yours," I panted. "Then fuck me till I explode and fill me with all your hot cum."

"Fuck." The word came from elsewhere in the room.

Keep talking like that and you'll make me lose it before I have my turn, Rook whispered into my mind.

Sounds like a goal to me, I replied with a sinfully playful tone.

His only reply was a mental chuckle.

Myel lowered me slowly, till the tip of his steel-hard cock brushed my folds.

"Yes," I breathed, "Fill me, fuck me, break me!" I cried out.

Myel's eyes went a little wide and wild at that, and he dropped me the remaining few inches slamming hard into me, my clit smashing against him so hard, I had a mini-orgasm on my way to my next peak.

I made sure to scream out exactly how good that made me feel.

Then I wrapped my arms and legs around Myel as he thrusted in earnest. With my mouth next to his ear, I panted, "Yes, oh God yes! Your dick feels so good! Fuck my pussy! Fill me with all your hot jizz!" And all the while I stared at Rook.

The incubus was naked, watching, grabbing the base of his ever-so-hard cock and squeezing.

He loved my potty mouth, and that combined with the intense lust Myel and I had to be giving off, would hopefully push him toward the brink.

I grinned.

Rook swore.

"Fuck, yes! Myel, God, Yes!" I screamed, no longer an act. Myel's aggressive thrusting, bouncing me on his cock, and the residual grinding of my clit on his base when I came down hard on him was deliciously driving me toward my next release.

"God, I'm so close. You're going to make me come. Your thick dick is making me come! Yes!"

The orgasm hit so hard, I couldn't speak, letting out squeaks of joy as I squeezed Myel's cock so hard, he groaned.

"Fucking hell!" Rook hissed, falling to his knees and doubling over.

Mission accomplished.

Also, *damn* Myel, that was one hell of an orgasm!

And when my sexy shifter gave one last thrust and exploded inside me, I let out a sound as close to a purr as I'd ever come, raking my nails over his skin, thrilled to bits at this perfect union. Our souls crashed tidal waves into each other, bliss washing back and forth and keeping us locked together for what seemed like a very pleasant eternity.

Myel staggered to the bed, slowly laid me down on it, then withdrew, before staggering to a wall to hold himself up, deliriously drained.

"Top that," he mumbled to whoever was listening.

"I probably won't, but that doesn't mean this won't be damn good for both of us," Vyns said as he sauntered over to me.

Oh God!

That had only been round one of so very many and I'd already had three orgasms, one tiny, one medium, and one extra-large. My mind couldn't quite comprehend the amount of pleasure I was going to experience tonight. It was a good thing I was an elf and could heal myself, or I had a feeling I'd be walking funny on my way to hold court tomorrow.

Thankfully, Vyns was soft and soothing, taking it easy on me, which I needed, because every part of me was searingly sensitive. Somehow, with soft touches, the brush of his lips as kisses, and gentle words, he brought me to a very soothing orgasm, helping me heal and relax and nearly putting me to sleep. His cock never got anywhere near me, but he didn't seem to mind, chuckling as I lay in the blissed-out euphoria of a soft release.

"All yours, Inky," Vyns said with a laugh.

Rook hated that name but was coming to accept that somehow it had become his nickname among the rest of the guys. I didn't even use it anymore, but one of them had picked it up and it had stuck.

Through bleary eyes I watched Rook come to the side of the bed. He grabbed my legs and unceremoniously flipped me over. Then he climbed on top of me, his flaming hot body pressed to mine, his mouth near my ear.

"You did it," he whispered. "You made me lose control... almost. I came, but I held my release... just so I could give it to you... now. Payback's a sexy romp with an incubus, My Flame."

Then he got off me and opened my legs, pulling me back till I was bent over the bed and his lips and fingers could kiss and play among my folds.

He moaned softly as his tongue dipped inside me.

Oh yes, I do love tasting that shifter's salty cum leaking out of your well fucked pussy, Rook whispered into my mind. Something about that sentence was so very wrong, but so very right. I had to bow to the master of filthy talk. He was an incubus after all. And those dirty words alone roused me from the dreamy state Vyns had left me in and got me all hot and bothered once more. That, and a little bit of Rook's lust magic, was all it took to make me desperate for him.

He stood and slid his cock inside me, his hands gripping my ass.

Since you made me lose control earlier, I thought I'd give you a little... something extra, he whispered into my mind.

I didn't much care, given how wonderful he was making me feel. That perfect dick of his slowly filled me, and the way it pressed on my deepest places, was deliciously sinful. There was a whole other world of orgasms with an incubus and Rook loved to take me to those worlds and show me around.

Then, one of his hands, which had been resting on my ass, shifted a little and his thumb pressed on my rear entrance. And there it was, another level of erotic bliss. The incubus' lustful touch made me open for him and his thumb slid slowly into me.

I let out a rough groan as I hit my peak, hard... but the other thing Rook could do was keep me from releasing, hold me at my peak, as he'd done for himself earlier. That compressed ecstasy wrecked my mind as he pushed his thumb deep into my ass, then began a slow rhythmic thrusting of his cock into my pussy. My body shook hard, convulsing with pleasure, which built like a tidal wave inside me, desperate for any outlet, but finding none.

This... this is what I felt earlier, My Flame. My gift to you.

I couldn't respond, my brain breaking at this potent pressure pulsing through every muscle in my body.

I wept hot tears of raw bliss, the silken sheets beneath me might as well have been sandpaper, given how they felt with every jerk of my body against them. My breasts felt raw and exposed and somehow that only added to my rapture.

"She's at her limit!" Myel gasped from somewhere.

Thank you, my beloved, for saying what I couldn't. Any more of this pent-up pleasure and I'd explode.

"Oh... I know," Rook purred.

Then he let it hit me, let me release, and by all the gods, and angels and demons, it was the most divine orgasm I'd ever had. That release felt so damned good, so needed, I wept again with tears of blissful relief. My body didn't stop shaking, if anything it shook harder as I came. I also sort of contorted around, my back arching like a cat, hands and arms tense, my head the only thing on the mattress as I throbbed with that epic orgasm.

"Fucking hell, that's too much!" Rook hissed, and his thrusts became fast and erratic, his hands slid to my hips, fingers digging in as he slammed me back against him again and again, until he was pulsing as hard as I was, spilling his release into me.

I was wrecked by the time we finished.

Rook pulled out and flopped onto the bed beside me as I tried and failed to roll over, too weak. Strong hands helped me move, rolling me over till I was looking up at Koar.

I gave him a look which I hoped said, *give me a minute*, because I still couldn't speak.

"She needs a bit," Rook said.

At the same time Myel whispered, "Give her some time."

Thank you both!

Koar lay next to me, taking one of my hands and laying it on his chest.

"My body to yours, my essence I give freely. Take what you need of me."

Oh! Yes, that. I needed that. I didn't need to say the words anymore, he'd given me energy so much I could do it with barely a second thought.

I siphoned off a little of his life energy.

Okay... maybe more than a little.

"Oh wow, I see," he grunted as my hand slid off him. "Better now?"

I nodded. "Thank you, yes, also... water?"

Myel was there the instant I said it, anticipating my needs. I sat up on the bed and drank the glass down in almost one gulp. Myel took it, refilled it, and gave it back. After the fourth cup, I was feeling stronger and well hydrated, ready for more.

"I don't know if it's a good thing or bad, that sex with you all is more draining than an ultramarathon in a desert."

"A good thing," Rook mumbled, a silly grin on his face.

Of course the sex demon would say that.

He was right, though. Of all the activities that made you feel utterly exhausted, one that also made you feel sinfully sensual and loved and magnificently sublime ... was probably the best.

I gazed at Koar, lying on the bed next to me, casually stroking his thick erection. "So, what do you have planned? Going to break me with bliss?"

He grinned. "No, I'll take Vyns' approach... sort of..."

I raised a brow.

The dragon smiled and shrugged. "You'll see. Lie down on your front."

I shrugged, trusting him, and laid down, hands crossed under my head. "Do your worst!" I said in my best mock rebellious-victim voice.

He straddled my legs. Then incredibly strong hands began massaging my back, working out every knot and tightness I'd gathered during Rook's epic, tension-building session.

"Oh... yes... this is good," I purred.

"It gets better," Koar whispered. He leaned over and he

kissed my shoulders and back around where he massaged, adding a pleasant, warm sensuality to his relaxing ministrations. "Rook, if you would?" the dragon said, and I tried to crane my head around to look but couldn't see what he was talking about.

Then I *felt* it.

Rook's lust-touch on my ass made me open wide, throbbing, aching for something to fill me there.

And Koar obliged.

And if Rook's thumb had felt huge, Koar's rather exceptional cock was massive, gigantic, gargantuan...

"Ugh, yes!"

He filled me slowly as he kept up his massage and kisses. I could see now why this was only "sort of" Vyns' approach. Vyns had focused on a relaxing soft orgasm. Koar was relaxing me, while also testing my limits in the most delicious way. A contradiction which had me moaning and sighing and groaning and straining, then relaxing again. It was unlike anything I'd ever felt before.

Koar was careful and slow with this thrusts, gently stretching my ass to the extreme as his hands turned my back and shoulders to putty.

My orgasm came in waves, first sharp and hard, slamming into me, then slowly soothing and washing away all my aches and worries, then back to gripping me in its sensuous clutches.

I gasped over and over at this strange mix, my body tingling, my mind floating serenely on a river of ecstasy, which was sometimes smooth and other times rough rapids.

Koar tensed, then began to pull out.

"No! I want to feel..." I gasped.

I couldn't say more, but he got the point. This had been

for me only and he'd been saving himself, but I wanted to feel him come.

"As you wish," he grunted, voice strained. He gave two hard thrusts into my ass, then erupted with his release.

Oh yeah...

Feeling him lose himself only added to my rollercoaster of an orgasm. He leaned down over me, resting his heavy body on mine, knowing I could take it, and kissed my neck and hair.

"Thank you, Perfection," he whispered.

I sighed as the orgasm evened out to a pleasant wash of bliss with only minor little blips of tense excitement whenever Koar's cock twitched in the throes of his release.

We lay there for some time, cooling, before Koar shifted and moved. Then, we both headed to the bathroom to clean up, Vyns carrying me. I could use my elven powers to strengthen myself and walk... but this was better.

And when I returned, Bayn lay on the bed, on his back, that ridiculously huge dick like a thick tower as he stroked it slowly.

"You've had a lot of others controlling you tonight. With me, you can take control," he said. And his position now made sense. We were going full cowgirl. God! Riding that massive dick would be... well... I'd soon find out.

I climbed up onto the bed, then straddled Bayn's wide and thick body. I kept his cock before me, grabbing it and pressing it to my belly. I stroked him softly as I met his gaze with mock seriousness.

"See this," I said. "See how high it goes, well past my bellybutton? Remember this when you're inside me, how much *accommodating* I have to do to make you fit. All sorts of rearranging of things."

He shrugged. "You could make yourself bigger, I don't mind."

"You could make yourself smaller too, but please don't. And I'm not getting bigger either." I made a pouty face. "Maybe I like feeling you so deep it's truly impossible."

He grinned, putting his hand behind his head. "Thought so."

"You could put those hands to good use," I said, shifting my own hands off his dick to slide up my body and cup my breasts suggestively.

"No. I like this show. You're in control remember, you do whatever you need to, to get off."

Oh, so it was like that? Well, I'd show him. I'd give him the sexiest show he'd ever seen.

I shifted forward, lifted myself... then had to pull my legs up and squat to lift myself even higher, before I was poised over him.

"Ready, massive man?"

"Yup." He popped the "p" and grinned wider.

I adjusted myself, then slowly... lowered... myself... *ugh, yes wow*... onto... *fuck he was big*... him. As usual, the feel of that massive dick pressed so fully inside me made my eyes cross and my entire body tremble. I also may have drooled a little. I didn't care, let him see what he did to me.

Then I slowly rocked forward — feeling him move inside me — and let out a series of grunts as I did.

"Oh yeah, that's right," he purred.

"You... going to... do... anything?" I grunted as I slowly moved that monolith inside me, rocking gently.

Bayn grinned. "You seem to be having a good time all on your own. One buck from me and I might break you. Well, not your body, you're strong like that, but definitely your mind."

He wasn't wrong there.

I slowly lowered my torso till I lay on him, shifting a little to move my breasts over his upper abbs, making sure he felt my rigid nipples digging into him. Yet when I looked up to see if I'd affected him, he was only mildly moved, biting his lip as he grinned down at me.

Fine.

I pushed myself up till I leaned over him on straight arms, my hands gripping his hard flesh. Then, as jarring as it was, I bounced on that mega-dick. I even used my nymph powers to enlarge my breasts so they swayed and jiggled above him.

That got a response, a heated smile, a twitch of his arm. He wanted to grab me, squeeze me, but he took a long shuddering breath and kept his hands where they were, behind his head.

God, what would it take to break this man? I was nearly at my limits, my body shaking, my mind barely functioning as I bounced on that huge shaft and drove myself mad with bliss.

One last thing to try.

I leaned back, grabbing my ample chest and giving myself everything I wanted, moaning as my own touch added to the thrill of his rigidness inside me. I gave only little jerks and bucks of my hips, ramping up my pleasure until I was so... damn... close! Then I slid one hand down and savagely rubbed my clit, making sure my fingers massaged his base at the same time.

That did it.

He grunted, and his dick twitched so hard it levered me forward as my own orgasm hit heavily. I dragged my wet hand back up to squeeze my breasts again as I shook and shuddered on his dick, coming hard, clenched around him.

Finally, he broke, his smugness shattered as he grunted and tensed and came with me. The pulse of his cock felt divine, and I moaned unabashed, throwing my head back to focus on feeling this incredible moment.

"You're too much!" Bayn hissed.

Yeah, I was.

And it felt amazing!

I collapsed on Bayn when we'd both finished, worn out.

The guys had promised me at least ten orgasms and I had to be most of the way there, I'd lost count. There'd been at least five, one with each of them, but a few had given me multiples and... well... let's just say I was one damned lucky woman to have these sinfully hot guys willing to give me all the aching orgasms I wanted.

I rested, with Bayn curled around me, and the others joined us. I was so damned relaxed by this point, I dozed a little. Someone kissed my leg. Someone else stroked my side. Someone pressed their lips into my hair. It was delightful, all these soft and soothing sensations.

"Did we wear you out?" Rook asked.

I mumbled something in response, but it didn't come out as words.

"That's a yes," Bayn said with a chuckle.

No. Want more. Give more orgasms please! I relayed to Rook mentally. This might be the last time all five of us were together like this for a while. I wanted to take advantage of it. I could sleep some other night.

Rook laughed. "I've heard from our beloved wife, and she requests even more orgasms."

"She can't even talk!" Vyns said.

"And?" Rook replied.

"And... I guess... we'll give her what she wants," Vyns said. "You sure, Angel?" he asked.

Yup!

"She is, yes."

"We only have your word for that," Vyns said to the incubus.

"No, she wants more," Myel said. I can feel it.

I used a bit of my elven strength to bolster myself enough to whisper. "Yes please!"

Vyns chuckled. "Alright Angel."

And so we went *all night*. I'd thought myself sexually experienced, but I learned things that night. Positions I hadn't thought possible, combinations of men in or around me which baffled me in the best possible way, and sensations from the pinnacle of bliss to wondrously soothing serenity. It was... perfect.

Needless to say, we made a mess.

I'd tell the ladies in waiting to burn the mattress and the sheets in the morning, let them wonder what we'd done. Well, most would wonder. Malineth, who was never far away, would have felt all of it.

And because the bed was toast, the six of us huddled together in a nest of pillows and cushions from around my bedchamber to catch what little sleep we could before the sun rose.

And all I could think as I drifted off was, I've come a hell of a long way from the bartender in Providence, who was terrified of commitment and thought herself mostly average. I knew now...

Love was the best damn thing in the world.

Also, I was a beast, with incredible magic over water and earth, body and shape, strength and bindings.

And I had five men who adored me and wanted nothing but the best for me.

What else could a girl want?

Ice cream?

Oooh, I'd have to see if they had that in this world!

OTHER BOOKS BY CLARA WILS

Fantasy Reverse Harem

THE MISTS OF ELISTA TRILOGY

Bonds and Blood, book 1

Shape and Shadows, book 2

Form and Fury, book 3

THE SISTER SPIRITS SERIES

Double Discover, book 1

Double Danger, book 2

Double Disaster, book 3

Double Doom, book 4

Double Destiny, book 5

THE LADY BLADE TRILOGY

Mistress Guard, book 1

Sword Skirt, book 2

Mystic Knight, book 3

THE VEILBLOOD ACADEMY TRILOGY

Blood of the Veil, book 1

Test of Tyrants, book 2

Clash of Queens, book 3

Portal Fantasy Reverse Harem

THE GRECIAN GODDESS TRILOGY

Kiss of the Goddess, book 1

Power of the Goddess, book 2

Bonds of the Goddess, book 3

Paranormal Reverse Harem

THE SECRETS GODS KEEP TRILOGY

Craving Demons, book 1

Chaos Demons, book 2

Claiming Demons, book 3

HER BAD BOY WOLVE TRILOGY

Pack To The Wall, book 1

Want You Pack, book 2

Pack In Business, book 3

www.ingramcontent.com/pod-product-compliance
Lightning Source LLC
LaVergne TN
LVHW050923080826
845145LV00001B/195

* 9 7 8 1 9 9 0 5 8 7 7 5 7 *